WHAT IF . . .

*Albert Einstein had decided to give up physics—
and became a violin teacher instead . . .*

*Lenin had been assassinated in 1917 and Joseph
Stalin had taken his place as the spearhead of the
Russian Revolution . . .*

*Abe Lincoln traveled into the future—and discovered
that the South had won the Civil War . . .*

*In the ninth century a confidential letter from the pope
had fallen into the wrong hands and accidentally
converted the English—to paganism . . .*

*Two guys in a stolen 1950 Cadillac had stopped
the invention of the hydrogen bomb—with one
fiery crash . . .*

**The world looks very different in the universe
next door!**

What Might Have Been?

VOLUME 2: ALTERNATE HEROES

Edited by Gregory Benford and Martin H. Greenberg

BANTAM BOOKS

NEW YORK · TORONTO · LONDON · SYDNEY · AUCKLAND

ALTERNATE HEROES

A Bantam Spectra Book / January 1990

PRINTING HISTORY

Contents

Introduction

Poignant questions resound through history, beginning with that wistful phrase, *if only*. . . .

If only Kennedy had lived. If only Hitler had died in World War I. If only the Muslims had conquered Europe. If only a minor commander had not ordered the library at Alexandria burned, cutting us off from thousands of great works of antiquity. . . .

So many questions turn upon the presence of a particular figure at a crucial moment. Or do they?

Do individuals matter? Did Napoleon truly shape the failing French Revolution into a dynamic, military phase by the strength of his personality? Or would some similar minor officer of the artillery have sufficed? Later revolutions seem to show a similar pattern, leading inevitably to a man on a white horse who resorts to military control while damping the political ardor which started it all; think of Stalin, Mao, Castro. Were they essentially replaceable?

Nobody knows, of course, for history performs no repeatable experiments. But such riddles frame our own deep suspicions that perhaps even the currently high-and-mighty are but flotsam carried on the river of time, revealing the current's passing but unable to deflect the stream of events in the slightest.

This is the second volume exploring the fragility of history. The first, subtitled *Alternate Empires*, considered the importance of great events. This volume ponders the role of the Great Man (or Woman). Both are collections of original, commissioned fiction devoted to refashioning history in a logical manner, to exploring what could or might have been.

The theme has a considerable history itself. The question of Napoleon's role goes back to Louis-Napoleon Geoffroy-Chateau's *Napoleon and the Conquest of the World, 1812–1823*.

This nationalist vision, published in 1836, told how a crucial decision to not tarry in Moscow as winter drew on saved the French forces. Napoleon then had the entire planet on the run and established a lasting world empire. In a sense the book argues that a slightly different Napoleon would have made all the difference. It does not call into question whether Great Men really matter.

Historians give no clear answer to this question. The appeal of the notion lies in our suspicion that some crucial figures have great leverage, yet seeming inconsequentialities can be the fulcrum.

Given the theme of what might have been, and all the vivid figures of history, our authors could write whatever they liked. Interestingly, two of the three women authors take military figures as critical. The third, Sheila Finch, considers the quieter and probably more profound changes wrought by an ex-employee of the Swiss Patent Office. As we might have expected, the American Civil War remains a vexing matter, yielding three tales with very different approaches.

In the end, there will always be a plausible argument for the impersonality of great historical movements. It probably did not matter whether Columbus or some other southern European sailed westward at the historically ripe moment. But were the extraordinary victories of Cortez inevitable? Sometimes, people really do matter. Our pains and pleasures carry weight.

Or so we would like to think. We hope you will find this range of imaginative experiments thought-provoking and perhaps even unsettling.

GREGORY BENFORD

What Might Have Been

A Sleep and a Forgetting

ROBERT SILVERBERG

"Channeling?" I said. "For Christ's sake, Joe! You brought me all the way down here for dumb bullshit like that?"

"This isn't channeling," Joe said.

"The kid who drove me from the airport said you've got a machine that can talk with dead people."

A slow, angry flush spread across Joe's face. He's a small, compact man with very glossy skin and very sharp features, and when he's annoyed he inflates like a puff-adder.

"He shouldn't have said that."

"Is that what you're doing here?" I asked. "Some sort of channeling experiments?"

"Forget that shithead word, will you, Mike?" Joe sounded impatient and irritable. But there was an odd fluttery look in his eye, conveying—what? Uncertainty? Vulnerability? Those were traits I hadn't ever associated with Joe Hedley, not in the thirty years we'd known each other. "We aren't sure what the fuck we're doing here," he said. "We thought maybe you could tell us."

"Me?"

"You, yes. Here, put the helmet on. Come on, put it on, Mike. Put it on. Please."

I stared. Nothing ever changes. Ever since we were kids Joe's been using me for one cockeyed thing or another, because he knows he can count on me to give him a sober-minded commonsense opinion. Always bouncing this bizarre scheme or that off me, so he can measure the caroms.

The helmet was a golden strip of wire mesh studded with a row of microwave pickups the size of a dime and flanked by a pair of suction electrodes that fit over the temples. It looked like some vagrant piece of death-house equipment.

I ran my fingers over it. "How much curent is this thing capable of sending through my head?"

He looked even angrier. "Oh, fuck you, you hypercautious bastard! Would I ever ask you to do anything that could harm you?"

With a patient little sigh I said, "Okay. How do I do this?"

"Ear to ear, over the top of your head. I'll adjust the electrodes for you."

"You won't tell me what any of this is all about?"

"I want an uncontaminated response. That's science talk, Mike. I'm a scientist. You know that, don't you?"

"So that's what you are. I wondered."

Joe bustled about above me, moving the helmet around, pressing the electrodes against my skull.

"How does it fit?"

"Like a glove."

"You always wear your gloves on your head?" he asked.

"You must be goddamn nervous if you think that's funny."

"I am," he said. "You must be too, if you take a line like that seriously. But I tell you that you won't get hurt. I promise you that, Mike."

"All right."

"Just sit down here. We need to check the impedances, and then we can get going."

"I wish I understood at least a little bit about—"

"Please," he said. He gestured through a glass partition at a technician in the adjoining room, and she began to do things with dials and switches. This was turning into a movie, a very silly one, full of mad doctors in white jackets and sputtering electrical gadgets. The tinkering went on and on, and I felt myself passing beyond apprehension and annoyance into a kind of gray realm of Zen serenity, the way I sometimes do while sitting in the dentist's chair waiting for the scraping and poking to begin.

On the hillside visible from the laboratory window, yellow hibiscus was blooming against a background of billowing scarlet bougainvillea in brilliant California sunshine. It had been cold and raining, this February morning, when I drove to Sea-Tac Airport thirteen hundred miles to the north. Hedley's lab is just outside La Jolla, on a sandy bluff high up over the blue Pacific. When Joe and I were kids growing up in Santa Monica we took this kind of luminous winter day for granted, but I had lived in the Northwest for twenty years now, and I couldn't help thinking I'd gone on a day trip to Eden. I studied the colors on the hillside until my eyes began to get blurry.

"Here we go, now," Joe said, from a point somewhere far away behind my left shoulder.

It was like stepping into a big cage full of parakeets and mynahs and crazed macaws. I heard scratchy screeching sounds, and a harsh loony almost-laughter that soared through three or four octaves, and a low ominous burbling noise, as if some hydraulic device was about to blow a gasket. I heard weird wire-edged shrieks that went tumbling away as though the sound was falling through an infinite abyss. I heard queeblings. I heard hissings.

Then came a sudden burst of clearly enunciated syllables, floating in isolation above the noise:

—*Onoodor*—

That startled me.

A nonsense word? No, no, a real one, one that had meaning for me, a word in an obscure language that I just happen to understand.

"Today," that's what it means. In Khalkha. My specialty. But it was crazy that this machine would be speaking Khalkha to me. This had to be some sort of coincidence. What I'd heard was a random clumping of sounds that I must automatically have arranged into a meaningful pattern. I was kidding myself. Or else Joe was playing an elaborate practical joke. Only he seemed very serious.

I strained to hear more. But everything was babble again.

Then, out of the chaos:

—*Usan deer*—

Khalkha, again: "On the water." It couldn't be a coincidence. More noise. Skwkaark skreek yubble gobble.

—*Aawa namaig yawuulawa*—

"Father sent me."

Skwkaark. Yabble. Eeeeesh.

"Go on," I said. I felt sweat rolling down my back. "Your father sent you where? Where? *Khaana*. Tell me where."

—*Usan deer*—

"On the water, yes."

Yarkhh. Skreek. Tshhhhhhh.

—*Akhanartan*—

"To his elder brother. Yes."

I closed my eyes and let my mind rove out into the darkness. It drifted on a sea of scratchy noise. Now and again I caught an actual syllable, half a syllable, a slice of a word, a clipped fragment of meaning. The voice was brusque, forceful, a drill-sergeant voice, carrying an undertone of barely suppressed rage.

Somebody very angry was speaking to me across a great distance, over a channel clotted with interference, in a language that hardly anyone in the United States knew anything about: Khalkha. Spoken a little oddly, with an unfamiliar intonation, but plainly recognizable.

I said, speaking very slowly and carefully and trying to match the odd intonation of the voice at the other end, "I can hear you and I can understand you. But there's a lot of interference. Say everything three times and I'll try to follow."

I waited. But now there was only a roaring silence in my ears. Not even the shrieking, not even the babble.

I looked up at Hedley like someone coming out of a trance.

"It's gone dead."

"You sure?"

"I don't hear anything, Joe."

He snatched the helmet from me and put it on, fiddling with the electrodes in that edgy, compulsively precise way of his. He listened for a moment, scowled, nodded. "The relay satellite must have passed around the far side of the sun. We won't get anything more for hours if it has."

"The relay satellite? Where the hell was that broadcast coming from?"

"In a minute," he said. He reached around and took the helmet off. His eyes had a brassy gleam and his mouth was twisted off to the corner of his face, almost as if he'd had a stroke. "You were actually able to understand what he was saying, weren't you?"

I nodded.

"I knew you would. And was he speaking Mongolian?"

"Khalkha, yes. The main Mongolian dialect."

The tension left his face. He gave me a warm, loving grin. "I was sure you'd know. We had a man in from the university here, the comparative linguistics department—you probably know him, Malmstrom's his name—and he said it sounded to him like an Altaic language, maybe Turkic—is that right, Turkic?—but more likely one of the Mongolian languages, and the moment he said Mongolian I thought, that's it, get Mike down here right away—" He paused. "So it's the language that they speak in Mongolia right this very day, would you say?"

"Not quite. His accent was a little strange. Something stiff about it, almost archaic."

"Archaic."

"It had that feel, yes. I can't tell you why. There's just something formal and old-fashioned about it, something, well—"

"Archaic," Hedley said again. Suddenly there were tears in his eyes. I couldn't remember ever having seen him cry before.

What they have, the kid who picked me up at the airport had said, *is a machine that lets them talk with the dead.*

"Joe?" I said. "Joe, what in God's name is this all about?"

We had dinner that night in a sleek restaurant on a sleek, quiet La Jolla street of elegant shops and glossy-leaved trees, just the two of us, the first time in a long while that we'd gone out alone like that. Lately we tended to see each other once or twice a year at most, and Joe, who is almost always between marriages, would usually bring along his latest squeeze, the one who was finally going to bring order and stability and other such things to his tempestuous private life. And since he always needs to show the new one what a remarkable human being he is, he's forever putting on a performance, for the woman, for me, for the waiters, for the people at the nearby tables. Generally the fun's at my expense, for compared with Hedley I'm very staid and proper and I'm eighteen years into my one and only marriage so far, and Joe often seems to enjoy making me feel that there's something wrong with that. I never see him with the same woman twice, except when he happens to marry one of them. But tonight it was all different. He was alone, and the conversation was subdued and gentle and rueful, mostly about the years we'd had put in knowing each other, the fun we'd had, the regret Joe felt during the occasional long periods when we didn't see much of each other. He did most of the talking. There was nothing new about that. But mostly it was just chatter. We were three quarters of the way down the bottle of silky cabernet before Joe brought himself around to the topic of the experiment. I hadn't wanted to push.

"It was pure serendipity," he said. "You know, the art of finding what you're not looking for. We were trying to clean up some problems in radio transmission from the Icarus relay station—that's the one that the Japs and the French hung around the sun inside the orbit of Mercury—and we were fiddling with this and fiddling with that, sending out an assortment of test signals at a lot of different frequencies, when out of nowhere we got a voice coming back at us. A man's voice. Speaking a strange language. Which turned out to be Chaucerian English."

"Some kind of academic prank?" I suggested.

He looked annoyed. "I don't think so. But let me tell it, Mike, okay? Okay?" He cracked his knuckles and rearranged the knot of his tie. "We listened to this guy and gradually we figured out a little of what he was saying and we called in a grad student from U.C.S.D. who confirmed it—thirteenth-century English—and it absolutely knocked us on our asses." He tugged at his earlobes and rearranged his tie again. A sort of manic sheen was coming into his eyes. "Before we could even begin to comprehend what we were dealing with, the Englishman was gone and we were picking up some woman making a speech in medieval French. Like we were getting a broadcast from Joan of Arc, do you see? Not that I'm arguing that that's who she was. We had her for half an hour, a minute here and a minute there with a shitload of interference, and then came a solar flare that disrupted communications, and when we had things tuned again we got a quick burst of what turned out to be Arabic, and then someone else talking in Middle English, and then, last week, this absolutely incomprehensible stuff, which Malmstrom guessed was Mongolian and you have now confirmed. The Mongol has stayed on the line longer than all the others put together."

"Give me some more wine," I said.

"I don't blame you. It's made us all crazy too. The best we can explain it to ourselves, it's that our beam passes through the sun, which as I think you know, even though your specialty happens to be Chinese history and not physics, is a place where the extreme concentration of mass creates some unusual stresses on the fabric of the continuum, and some kind of relativistic force warps the hell out of it, so that the solar field sends our signal kinking off into God knows where, and the effect is to give us a telephone line to the Middle Ages. If that sounds like gibberish to you, imagine how it sounds to us." Hedley spoke without raising his head, while moving his silverware around busily from one side of his plate to the other. "You see now about channeling? It's no fucking joke. Shit, we *are* channeling, only looks like it might actually be real, doesn't it?"

"I see," I said. "So at some point you're going to have to call up the secretary of defense and say, Guess what, we've been getting telephone calls on the Icarus beam from Joan of Arc. And then they'll shut down your lab here and send you off to get your heads replumbed."

He stared at me. His nostrils flickered contemptuously.

"Wrong. Completely wrong. You never had any notion of flair, did you? The sensational gesture that knocks everybody out? No. Of course not. Not *you*. Look, Mike, if I can go in there and say, We can talk to the dead, and we can *prove* it, they'll kiss our asses for us. Don't you see how fucking sensational it would be, something coming out of these government labs that ordinary people can actually understand and cheer and yell about? Telephone line to the past! George Washington himself, talking to Mr. and Mrs. America! Abe Lincoln! Something straight out of the *National Enquirer*, right, only *real*? We'd all be heroes. But it's got to be real, that's the kicker. We don't need a rational explanation for it, at least not right away. All it has to do is work. Christ, ninety-nine percent of the people don't even know why electric lights light up when you flip the switch. We have to find out what we really have and get to understand it at least a little and be two hundred percent sure of ourselves. And then we present it to Washington and we say, Here, this is what we did and this is what happens, and don't blame us if it seems crazy. But we have to keep it absolutely to ourselves until we understand enough of what we've stumbled on to be able to explain it to them with confidence. If we do it right we're goddamned kings of the world. A Nobel would be just the beginning. You understand now?"

"Maybe we should get another bottle of wine," I said.

*   *   *

We were back in the lab by midnight. I followed Hedley through a maze of darkened rooms, ominous with mysterious equipment glowing in the night.

A dozen or so staffers were on duty. They smiled wanly at Hedley as if there was nothing unusual about his coming back to work at this hour.

"Doesn't anyone sleep around here?" I asked.

"It's a twenty-four-hour information world," Joe said. "We'll be recapturing the Icarus beam in forty-three minutes. You want to hear some of the earlier tapes?"

He touched a switch and from an unseen speaker came crackles and bleebles and then a young woman's voice, strong and a little harsh, uttering brief blurts of something that sounded like strange singsong French, to me not at all understandable.

"Her accent's terrible," I said. "What's she saying?"

"It's too fragmentary to add up to anything much. She's praying, mostly. May the king live, may God strengthen his arm, something like that. For all we know it *is* Joan of Arc. We haven't gotten more than a few minutes total coherent verbal output out of any of them, usually a lot less. Except for the Mongol. He goes on and on. It's like he doesn't want to let go of the phone."

"And it really is a phone?" I asked. "What we say here, they can hear there?"

"We don't know that, because we haven't been able to make much sense out of what they say, and by the time we get it deciphered we've lost contact. But it's got to be a two-way contact. They must be getting *something* from us, because we're able to get their attention somehow and they talk back to us."

"They receive your signal without a helmet?"

"The helmet's just for your benefit. The actual Icarus signal comes in digitally. The helmet's the interface between our computer and your ears."

"Medieval people don't have digital computers either, Joe."

A muscle started popping in one of his cheeks. "No, they don't," he said. "It must come like a voice out of the sky. Or right inside their heads. But they hear us."

"How?"

"Do I know? You want this to make sense, Mike? *Nothing* about this makes sense. Let me give you an example. You were talking with that Mongol, weren't you? You asked him something and he answered you?"

"Yes. But—"

"Let me finish. What did you ask him?"

"He said his father sent him somewhere. I asked him where, and he said, On the water. To visit his elder brother."

"He answered you right away?"

"Yes," I said.

"Well, that's actually impossible. The Icarus is ninety-three million miles from here. There has to be something like an eight-minute time lag in radio transmission. You follow? You ask him something and it's eight minutes before the beam reaches Icarus, and eight minutes more for his answer to come back. He sure as hell can't hold a real-time conversation with you. But you say he was."

"It may only have seemed that way. It could just have been coincidence that what I asked and what he happened to say next fit together like question and response."

"Maybe. Or maybe whatever kink in time we're operating across eats up the lag for us, too. I tell you, nothing makes sense about this. But one way or another the beam is reaching them and it carries coherent information. I don't know why that is. It just is. Once you start dealing in impossible stuff, anything might be true. So why can't our voices come out of thin air to them?" Hedley laughed nervously. Or perhaps it was a cough, I thought. "The thing is," he went on, "this Mongol is staying on line longer than any of the others, so with you here we have a chance to have some real communication with him. You speak his language. You can validate this whole goddamn grotesque event for us, do you see? You can have an honest-to-God chat with some guy who lived six hundred years ago, and find out where he really is and what he thinks is going on, and tell us all about it."

I stole a glance at the wall clock. Half past twelve. I couldn't remember the last time I'd been up this late. I lead a nice quiet tenured life, full professor thirteen years now, University of Washington Department of Sinological Studies.

"We're about ready to acquire signal again," Hedley said. "Put the helmet on."

I slipped it into place. I thought about that little communications satellite chugging around the sun, swimming through inconceivable heat and unthinkable waves of hard radiation and somehow surviving, coming around the far side now, beaming electromagnetic improbabilities out of the distant past at my head.

The squawking and screeching began.

Then, emerging from the noise and murk and sonic darkness, came the Mongol's voice, clear and steady:

"Where are you, you voice, you? Speak to me."

"Here," I said. "Can you hear me?"

Aark. Yaaarp. Tshhhhhhh.

The Mongol said, "Voice, what are you? Are you mortal or are you a prince of the Master?"

I wrestled with the puzzling words. I'm fluent enough in Khalkha, though I don't get many opportunities for speaking it. But there was a problem of context here.

"Which master?" I asked finally. "What prince?"

"There is only one Master," said the Mongol. He said this with tremendous force and assurance, putting terrific spin on every syllable, and the capital letter was apparent in his tone. "I am His servant. The *angeloi* are his princes. Are you an *angelos*, voice?"

Angeloi? That was Greek. A Mongol, asking me if I was an angel of God?

"Not an angel, no," I said.

"Then how can you speak to me this way?"

"It's a kind of—" I paused. I couldn't come up with the Khalka for "miracle." After a moment I said, "It's by the grace of heaven on high. I'm speaking to you from far away."

"How far?"

"Tell me where you are."

Skrawwwwk. Tshhhhhh.

"Again. Where are you?"

"Nova Roma. Constantinopolis."

I blinked. "Byzantium?"

"Byzantium, yes."

"I am very far from there."

"*How* far?" the Mongol said fiercely.

"Many, many days' ride. Many many." I hesitated. "Tell me what year it is, where you are."

Vzsqkk. Blzzp. Yiiiiik.

"What's he saying to you?" Hedley asked. I waved at him furiously to be quiet.

"The year," I said again. "Tell me what year it is."

The Mongol said scornfully, "Everyone knows the year, voice."

"Tell me."

"It is the year 1187 of our Savior."

I began to shiver. Our Savior? Weirder and weirder, I thought. A Christian Mongol? Living in Byzantium? Talking to me on the space telephone out of the twelfth century? The room around me took on a smoky, insubstantial look. My elbows were aching, and something was throbbing just above my left cheekbone. This had been a long day for me. I was very tired. I was heading into that sort of weariness where walls melted and bones turned soft. Joe was dancing around in front of me like someone with tertiary Saint Vitus'.

"And your name?" I said.

"I am Petros Alexios."

"Why do you speak Khalkha if you are Greek?"

A long silence, unbroken even by the hellish static.

"I am not Greek," came the reply finally. "I am by birth Khalkha Mongol, but raised Christian among the Christians from age eleven, when my father sent me on the water and I was taken. My name was Temujin. Now I am twenty and I know the Savior."

I gasped and put my hand to my throat as though it had been skewered out of the darkness by a spear.

"Temujin," I said, barely getting the word out.

"My father was Yesugei the chieftain."

"Temujin," I said again. "Son of Yesugei." I shook my head.

Aaark. Blzzzp. Tshhhhhh.

Then no static, no voice, only the hushed hiss of silence.

"Are you okay?" Hedley asked.

"We've lost contact, I think."

"Right. It just broke. You look like your brain has shorted out."

I slipped the helmet off. My hands were shaking.

"You know," I said, "maybe that French woman really was Joan of Arc."

"What?"

I shrugged. "She really might have been," I said wearily. "Anything's possible, isn't it?"

"What the hell are you trying to tell me, Mike?"

"Why shouldn't she have been Joan of Arc?" I asked. "Listen, Joe. This is making me just as nutty as you are. You know what I've just been doing? I've been talking to Genghis Kahn on this fucking telephone of yours."

I managed to get a few hours of sleep by simply refusing to tell Hedley anything else until I'd had a chance to rest. The way I said it, I left him no options, and he seemed to grasp that right away. At the hotel, I sank from consciousness like a leaden whale, hoping I wouldn't surface again before noon, but old habit seized me and pushed me up out of the tepid depths at seven, irreversibly awake and not a bit less depleted. I put in a quick call to Seattle to tell Elaine that I was going to stay down in La Jolla a little longer than expected. She seemed worried—not that I might be up to any funny business, not me, but only that I sounded so groggy. "You know Joe," I said. "For him it's a twenty-four-hour information world." I told her nothing else. When I stepped out on the breakfast patio half an hour later, I could see the lab's blue van already waiting in the hotel lot to pick me up.

Hedley seemed to have slept at the lab. He was rumpled and red-eyed but somehow he was at normal functioning level, scurrying around the place like a yappy little dog. "Here's a printout of last night's contact," he said, the moment I came in. "I'm sorry if the transcript looks cockeyed. The computer doesn't know how to spell in Mongolian." He shoved it into my hands. "Take a squint at it and see if you really heard all the things you thought you heard."

I peered at the single long sheet. It seemed to be full of jabberwocky, but once I figured out the computer's system of phonetic equivalents I could read it readily enough. I looked up after a moment, feeling very badly shaken.

"I was hoping I dreamed all this. I didn't."

"You want to explain it to me?"

"I can't."

Joe scowled. "I'm not asking for fundamental existential analysis. Just give me a goddamned translation, all right?"

"Sure," I said.

He listened with a kind of taut, explosive attention that seemed to me to be masking a mixture of uneasiness and bubbling excitement. When I was done he said, "Okay. What's this Genghis Khan stuff?"

"Temujin was Genghis Khan's real name. He was born around 1167 and his father Yesugei was a minor chief somewhere in northeastern Mongolia. When Temujin was still a boy, his father was poisoned by enemies, and he became a fugitive, but by the time he was fifteen he started putting together a confederacy of Mongol tribes, hundreds of them, and eventually he conquered everything in sight. Genghis Khan means 'Ruler of the Universe.' "

"So? Our Mongol lives in Constantinople, you say. He's a Christian and he uses a Greek name."

"He's Temujin, Son of Yesugei. He's twenty years old in the year when Genghis Khan was twenty years old."

Hedley looked belligerent. "Some other Temujin. Some other Yesugei."

"Listen to the way he speaks. He's scary. Even if you can't understand a word of what he's saying, can't you feel the power in him? The coiled-up anger? That's the voice of somebody capable of conquering whole continents."

"Genghis Khan wasn't a Christian. Genghis Khan wasn't kidnapped by strangers and taken to live in Constantinople."

"I know," I said. To my own amazement I added, "But maybe this one was."

"Jesus God Almighty. What's that supposed to mean?"

"I'm not certain."

Hedley's eyes took on a glaze. "I hoped you were going to be part of the solution, Mike. Not part of the problem."

"Just let me think this through," I said, waving my hands above his face as if trying to conjure some patience into him. Joe was peering at me in a stunned, astounded way. My eyeballs throbbed. Things were jangling up and down along my spinal column. Lack of sleep had coated my brain with a hard crust of adrenaline. Bewilderingly strange ideas were rising like sewer gases in my mind and making weird bubbles. "All right, try this," I said at last. "Say that there are all sorts of possible worlds. A world in which you're the king of England, a world in which I played third base for the Yankees, a world in which the dinosaurs never died out and Los Angeles gets invaded every summer by hungry tyrannosaurs.

And one world where Yesugei's son Temujin wound up in twelfth-century Byzantium as a Christian instead of founding the Mongol Empire. And that's the Temujin I've been talking to. This cockeyed beam of yours not only crosses time lines, somehow it crosses probability lines too, and we've fished up some alternate reality that—"

"I don't believe this," Hedley said.

"Neither do I, really. Not seriously. I'm just putting forth one possible hypothesis that might explain—"

"I don't mean your fucking hypothesis. I mean I find it hard to believe that you of all people, my old pal Mike Michaelson, can be standing here running off at the mouth this way, working hard at turning a mystifying event into a goddamned nonsensical one—you, good old sensible steady Mike, telling me some shit about tyrannosaurs amok in Los Angeles—"

"It was only an example of—"

"Oh, fuck your example," Hedley said. His face darkened with exasperation bordering on fury. He looked ready to cry. "Your example is absolute crap. Your example is garbage. You know, man, if I wanted someone to feed me a lot of New Age crap I didn't have to go all the way to Seattle to find one. Alternate realities! Third base for the Yankees!"

A girl in a lab coat appeared out of nowhere and said, "We have signal acquisition, Dr. Hedley."

I said, "I'll catch the next plane north, okay?"

Joe's face was red and starting to do its puff-adder trick and his Adam's apple bobbed as if trying to find the way out.

"I wasn't trying to mess up your head," I said. "I'm sorry if I did. Forget everything I was just saying. I hope I was at least of some help, anyway."

Something softened in Joe's eyes.

"I'm so goddamned tired, Mike."

"I know."

"I didn't mean to yell at you like that."

"No offense taken, Joe."

"But I have trouble with this alternate-reality thing of yours. You think it was easy for me to believe that what we were doing here was talking to people in the past? But I brought myself around to it, weird though it was. Now you give it an even weirder twist, and it's too much. It's too fucking much. It violates my sense of what's right and proper and fitting. You know what Occam's razor is, Mike? The old medieval axiom, *Never multiply hypotheses needlessly*? Take the simplest one. Here even the simplest one is crazy. You push it too far."

"Listen," I said, "if you'll just have someone drive me over to the hotel—"

"No."

"No?"

"Let me think a minute," he said. "Just because it doesn't make sense doesn't mean that it's impossible, right? And if we get one impossible thing, we can have two, or six, or sixteen. Right? Right?" His eyes were like two black holes with cold stars blazing at their bottoms. "Hell, we aren't at the point where we need to worry about explanations. We have to find out the basic stuff first. Mike, I don't want you to leave. I want you to stay here."

"What?"

"Don't go. Please. I still need somebody to talk to the Mongol for me. Don't go. Please, Mike? Please?"

The times, Temujin said, were very bad. The infidels under Saladin had smashed the Crusader forces in the Holy Land, and Jerusalem itself had fallen to the Moslems. Christians everywhere mourn the loss, said Temujin. In Byzantium— where Temujin was captain of the guards in the private army of a prince named Theodore Lascaris—God's grace seemed also to have been withdrawn. The great empire was in heavy weather. Insurrections had brought down two emperors in the past four years and the current man was weak and timid. The provinces of Hungary, Cyprus, Serbia, and Bulgaria were all in revolt. The Normans of Sicily were chopping up Byzantine Greece and on the other side of the empire the Seljuk Turks were chewing their way through Asia Minor. "It is the time of the wolf," said Temujin. "But the sword of the Lord will prevail."

The sheer force of him was astounding. It lay not so much in what he said, although that was sharp and fierce, as in the way he said it. I could feel the strength of the man in the velocity and impact of each syllable. Temujin hurled his words as if from a catapult. They arrived carrying a crackling electrical charge. Talking with him was like holding live cables in my hands.

Hedley, jigging and fidgeting around the lab, paused now and then to stare at me with what looked like awe and wonder in his eyes, as if to say, *You really can make sense of this stuff?* I smiled at him. I felt bizarrely cool and unflustered. Sitting there with some electronic thing on my head, letting that terrific force go hurtling through my brain. Discussing twelfth-century politics with an invisible Byzantine Mongol. Making small talk with Genghis Khan. All right. I could handle it.

I beckoned for notepaper. *Need printout of world historical background late twelfth century,* I scrawled, without interrupting my conversation with Temujin. *Esp. Byzantine history, Crusades, etc.*

The kings of England and France, said Temujin, were talking about launching a new Crusade. But at the moment they happened to be at war with each other, which made cooperation difficult. The powerful Emperor Frederick Barbarossa of Germany was also supposed to be getting up a Crusade, but that, he said, might mean more trouble for Byzantium than for the Saracens, because Frederick was the friend of Byzantium's enemies in the rebellious provinces, and he'd have to march through those provinces on the way to the Holy Land.

"It is a perilous time," I agreed.

Then suddenly I was feeling the strain. Temujin's rapid-fire delivery was exhausting to follow, he spoke Mongolian with what I took to be a Byzantine accent, and he sprinkled his statements with the names of emperors, princes, and even nations that meant nothing to me. Also there was that powerful force of him to contend with—it hit you like an avalanche—and beyond that his anger: the whip-crack inflection that seemed the thinnest of bulwarks against some unstated inner rage, fury, frustration. It's hard to feel at ease with anyone who seethes that way. Suddenly I just wanted to go somewhere and lie down.

But someone put printout sheets in front of me, closely packed columns of stuff from the *Britannica*. Names swam before my eyes: Henry II, Barbarossa, Stephan Nemanya, Isaac II (Angelos), Guy of Jerusalem, Richard the Lion-Hearted.

Antioch, Tripoli, Thessaloniki, Venice. I nodded my thanks and pushed the sheets aside.

Cautiously I asked Temujin about Mongolia. It turned out that he knew almost nothing about Mongolia. He'd had no contact at all with his native land since his abduction at the age of eleven by Byzantine traders who carried him off to Constantinople. His country, his father, his brothers, the girl to whom he had been betrothed when he was still a child—they were all just phantoms to him now, far away, forgotten. But in the privacy of his own soul he still spoke Khalkha. That was all that was left.

By 1187, I knew, the Temujin who would become Genghis Khan had already made himself the ruler of half of Mongolia. His fame would surely have spread to cosmopolitan Byzantium. How could this Temujin be unaware of him? Well, I saw one way. But Joe had already shot it down. And it sounded pretty nutty even to me.

"Do you want a drink?" Hedley asked. "Tranks? Aspirin?"

I shook my head. "I'm okay," I murmured.

To Temujin I said, "Do you have a wife? Children?"

"I have vowed not to marry until Jesus rules again in His own land."

"So you're going to go on the next Crusade?" I asked.

Whatever answer Temujin made was smothered by static. Awkkk. Skrrkkk. Tssssshhhhhhh.

Then silence, lengthening into endlessness.

"Signal's gone," someone said.

"I could use that drink now," I said. "Scotch."

The lab clock said it was ten in the morning. To me it felt like the middle of the night.

An hour had passed. The signal hadn't returned.

Hedley said. "You really think he's Genghis Khan?"

"I really think he *could* have been."

"In some other probability world."

Carefully I said, "I don't want to get you all upset again, Joe."

"You won't. Why the hell *not* believe we're tuned into an alternate reality? It's no more goofy than any of the rest of this. But tell me this: is what he says consistent with being Genghis Khan?"

"His name's the same. His age. His childhood, up to the point when he wandered into some Byzantine trading caravan and they took him away to Constantinople with them. I can imagine the sort of fight he put up, too. But his life-line must have diverged completely from that point on. A whole new world-line split off from ours. And in that world, instead of turning into Genghis Khan, ruler of all Mongolia, he grew up to be Petros Alexios of Prince Theodore Lascaris's private guards."

"And he has no idea of who he could have been?" Joe asked.

"How could he? It isn't even a dream to him. He was born into another world that wasn't ever destined to have a Genghis Khan. You know the poem:

> *"Our birth is but a sleep and a forgetting:*
> *The soul that rises with us, our life's star,*
> *Hath had elsewhere its setting,*
> *And cometh from afar."*

"Very pretty. Is that Yeats?" Hedley said.

"Wordsworth," I said. "When's the signal coming back?"

"An hour, two, three. It's hard to say. You want to take a nap, and we'll wake you when we have acquisition?"

"I'm not sleepy."

"You look pretty ragged," Joe said.

I wouldn't give him the satisfaction.

"I'm okay. I'll sleep for a week, later on. What if you can't raise him again?"

"There's always that chance, I suppose. We've already had him on the line five times as long as all the rest put together."

"He's a very determined man," I said.

"He ought to be. He's Genghis fucking Khan."

"Get him back," I said. "I don't want you to lose him. I want to talk to him some more."

Morning ticked on into afternoon. I phoned Elaine twice while we waited, and I stood for a long time at the window watching the shadows of the oncoming winter evening fall across the hibiscus and the bougainvillea, and I hunched my shoulders up and tried to pull in the signal by sheer body english. Contemplating the possibility that they might never pick up Temujin again left me feeling weirdly forlorn. I was beginning to feel that I had a real relationship with that eerie disembodied angry voice coming out of the crackling night. Toward midafternoon I thought I was starting to understand what was making Temujin so angry, and I had some things I wanted to say to him about that.

Maybe you ought to get some sleep, I told myself.

At half past four someone came to me and said the Mongol was on the line again.

The static was very bad. But then came the full force of Temujin soaring over it. I heard him saying, "The Holy Land must be redeemed. I cannot sleep so long as the infidels possess it."

I took a deep breath.

In wonder, I watched myself set out to do something unlike anything I had ever done before.

"Then you must redeem it yourself," I said firmly.

"I?"

"Listen to me, Temujin. Think of another world far from yours. There is a Temujin in that world too, son of Yesugei, husband to Bortei who is daughter of Dai the Wise."

"Another world? What are you saying?"

"Listen. Listen. He is a great warrior, that other Temujin. No one can withstand him. His own brothers bow before him. All Mongols everywhere bow before him. His sons are like wolves, and they ride into every land and no one can withstand them. This Temujin is master of all Mongolia. He is the Great Khan, the Genghis Khan, the ruler of the universe."

There was silence. Then Temujin said, "What is this to me?"

"He is you, Temujin. You are the Genghis Khan."

Silence again, longer, broken by hideous shrieks of interplanetary noise.

"I have no sons and I have not seen Mongolia in years, or even thought of it. What are you saying?"

"That you can be as great in your world as this other Temujin is in his."

"I am Byzantine. I am Christian. Mongolia is nothing to me. Why would I want to be master in that savage place?"

"I'm not talking about Mongolia. You are Byzantine, yes. You are Christian. But you were born to lead and fight and conquer," I said. "What are you doing as a captain of another man's palace guards? You waste your life that way, and you know it, and it maddens you. You should have armies of your own. You should carry the Cross into Jerusalem."

"The leaders of the new Crusade are quarrelsome fools. It will end in disaster."

"Perhaps not. Frederick Barbarossa's Crusade will be unstoppable."

"Barbarossa will attack Byzantium instead of the Moslems. Everyone knows that."

"No," I said. That inner force of Temujin was rising and rising in intensity, like a gale climbing toward being a hurricane. I was awash in sweat, now, and I was dimly aware of the others staring at me as though I had lost my senses. A strange exhilaration gripped me. I went plunging joyously ahead. "Emperor Isaac Angelos will come to terms with Barbarossa. The Germans will march through Byzantium and go on toward the Holy Land. But there Barbarossa will die and his army will scatter—unless you are there, at his right hand, taking command in his place when he falls, leading them onward to Jerusalem. You, the invincible, the Genghis Khan."

There was silence once more, this time so prolonged that I was afraid the contact had been broken for good.

Then Temujin returned. "Will you send soldiers to fight by my side?" he asked.

"That I cannot do."

"You have the power to send them, I know," said Temujin. "You speak to me out of the air. I know you are an angel, or else you are a demon. If you are a demon, I invoke the name of Christos Pantokrator upon you, and begone. But if you are an angel, you can send me help. Send it, then, and I will lead your troops to victory. I will take the Holy Land from the infidel. I will create the Empire of Jesus in the world and bring all things to fulfillment. Help me. Help me."

"I've done all I can," I said. "The rest is for you to achieve."

There was another spell of silence.

"Yes," Temujin said finally. "I understand. Yes. Yes. The rest is for me."

*   *   *

"Christ, you look peculiar," Joe Hedley said, staring at me almost fearfully. "I've never seen you looking like this before. You look like a wild man."

"Do I?" I said.

"You must be dead tired, Mike. You must be asleep on your feet. Listen, go over to the hotel and get some rest. We'll have a late dinner, okay? You can fill me in then on whatever you've just been jabbering about. We'll have a late dinner, okay? But relax now. The Mongol's gone and we may not get him back until tomorrow."

"You won't get him back at all," I said.

"You think?" He peered close. "Hey, are you okay? Your eyes—your face—" Something quivered in his cheek. "If I didn't know better I'd say you were stoned."

"I've been changing the world. It's hard work."

"Changing the world?"

"Not this world. The other one. Look," I said hoarsely, "they never had a Genghis Khan, so they never had a Mongol Empire, and the whole history of China and Russia and the Near East and a lot of other places was very different. But I've got this Temujin all fired up now to be a Christian Genghis Khan. He got so Christian in Byzantium that he forgot what was really inside him, but I've reminded him, I've told him how he can still do the thing that he was designed to do, and he understands. He's found his true self again. He'll go out to fight in the name of Jesus and he'll build an empire that'll eat the Moslem powers for breakfast and then blow away Byzantium and Venice and go on from there to do God knows what. He'll probably conquer all of Europe before he's finished. And I did it. I set it all in motion. He was sending me all this energy, this Genghis Khan zap that he has inside him, and I figured the least I could do for him was turn some of it around and send it back to him, and say, Here, go, be what you were supposed to be."

"Mike—"

I stood close against him, looming over him. He gave me a bewildered look.

"You really didn't think I had it in me, did you?" I said. "You son of a bitch. You've always thought I'm as timid as a turtle. Your good old sober stick-in-the-mud pal Mike. What do you know? What the hell do you know?" Then I laughed. He looked so stunned that I had to soften it for him a little. Gently I touched his shoulder. "I need a shower and a drink. And then let's think about dinner."

Joe gawked at me. "What if it wasn't some other world you changed, though? Suppose it was this one."

"Suppose it was," I said. "Let's worry about that later. I still need that shower."

The Old Man and C

SHEILA FINCH

Light sprang to the wall when his wife opened the casement window to let in a little breeze from the lake. It shattered, sparkling over bookshelves and wallpaper, as his young student's bow scraped across the E string and the fingers of her left hand searched for high C.

She still could not seem to get it right. The note must sing, not screech! He had shown Rosa over and over, patiently correcting her fingering, the pressure of the bow across the string, explaining to her how the sound was produced in the hope that if she understood perhaps she could improve. She was so brilliant in every other respect.

"*Kaffee*, Papa?" his wife whispered in his ear.

He shook his head.

"Don't lost sight of the time. Eddie comes this afternoon. And Lisl will want to go with her *Opa* on the boat!"

Rosa had progressed to the Arabesque, a passage she played excellently, her fingers flying like the scintillating reflection of water on the wall.

His wife left him to his pupil and the music lesson, closing the music room door quietly behind her. He gazed at Rosa. Eyes closed, she bit her lower lip in concentration. Wisps of fair hair escaped from braids trailing over her shoulders. She was a good girl, the best student he had ever had. If she mastered this one note, she should easily take the gold medal—perhaps the last he would see a pupil take. She had more natural talent than any of his previous medalists.

But the other students in the competition, children who came from the wealthy suburbs of Zurich where they had *Waschmaschinen* and *Fernsehapparaten,* they could afford to spend all day practising, whereas Rosa got up at first light and helped her father milk the cows. Time for the violin had to be sandwiched between farm chores and schoolwork. Now she was approaching sixteen; her father had begun to think of the day she would marry a solid farm lad and give him one less mouth to feed. This was her last chance, too. He had worked hard with Rosa, giving long lessons and extra lessons that her family had paid for with cream and eggs. Who could say if it would be enough?

Rosa finished the piece with a flourish, the notes sparkling almost visibly in the air between them.

"So, Herr Professor, are you pleased?" Triumph shining on her round face showed what answer she expected.

"I'm very pleased," he agreed.

"We're going to win the medal," she promised.

It was important to him that this little farm girl take the very last gold medal. Yet he knew he should not allow his own sense of self-worth to become bound to a pupil's performance in a competition. How had it happened? When one is young, he thought, how many choices lie at one's fingertips? How many roads beckon the eager traveler? Time spreads out before the young man like a map of a marvelous sunlit country. He knows he can write symphonies, build castles, discover the secrets of the universe—which will it be? He does not know (for God is merciful) that the choice of one road shuts out the possibility of another. Who can guarantee which is right to take?

His mother had always wanted him to play the violin. And he had been an indifferent scholar in school.

"Herr Einstein?" Rosa said, her young face creased in a frown. "Aren't you well?"

He discovered that he was sweating and took out a linen handkerchief to mop his brow. "I'm well, Rosa. It's hot today, that's all. What else should we expect of July?"

"If I get my chores done early enough, my mother says I can take my little brothers swimming." She looked up at him, blue eyes innocent as infinity. "Do you wish me to play something else, Herr Professor?"

He patted her hand. "Enough for today, *Liebchen.* Enjoy the lake!"

And the light, he thought, the vast potential of the realms of light.

Rosa put the violin away in its case, gathered up her music, dropped him a hasty curtsy, and scurried from the room. The dancing light, fragmented by her departure, gathered itself together again, settling back on the walls and the Turkish rug and the dark wood of the grand piano.

The day's post lay on the floor by the armchair under the open window where he had left it at the beginning of Rosa's lesson. Sunshine fell on the fat pile, a correspondence he carried on with old friends, poets, pacifists and Zionists, people he had met all over Europe when he had still been touring with the orchestra. They sent letters full of music and philosophy and grand theory, wonderful talk. It was like a rich, festive meal that today he did not feel like eating. He set most of the letters aside, unopened. There had been a time when he had shared his friends' sense of holding the universe in the palm of his hand, a gift of a benign God who revealed His existence in the harmony of His creation.

He shook his head mutely. It was a young man's belief. The world had fought two terrible wars since then. Now it was enough to sit quietly and look at what had become of the promises.

He was so tired today.

One letter was from his widowed cousin Elsa, full of news about her daughters, no doubt; he had always liked Elsa. He tore the stamps off the envelope carefully, saving them for his granddaughter, Lisl.

"Papa?" His wife appeared in the doorway, her hands still floury from making *Dampfnudeln*. "Are you coming to lunch?"

"Ah, Millie," he said. "I'm getting old."

"Seventy-five isn't old!"

"And what have I accomplished?"

Millie spread her arms wide. "This house, two fine sons, your sailboat down there on the lake, your pupils—perhaps Rosa gets the gold this year. How many will that make for you? And you ask what you've accomplished?"

He was silent, looking at the shimmering light from the lake that shot its arrows into his soul.

"Besides," his wife said, "Lisl adores you. That must be worth something?"

But the sense there might have been more gnawed at him.

Later, with his son and granddaughter, he took the sailboat far out on Lake Zurich, tilting gently in a mild breeze and grand weather, sailing under the lee of slopes covered with ripening vineyards, presided over by the hump of the Albishorn.

Millie was right, he thought. All the tiny joys had to add up to something.

"I picked up a translation of a new thing that came out last year from this American writer, Hemingway," Eddie said, as Lisl trailed fingers in the cold, clear water, shattering the drowned light in its depths into diamond fragments. "It's about an old man fishing, and sharks."

"I don't like to fish."

"You'd like this story!"

He gazed at his younger son, a banker, already thickening into comfortable middle age. "I don't have as much time to read as you, apparently."

"Nonsense! You read the wrong things—about wars and terrible things like that. You should read fiction."

"So many wars. Where will it all end?"

"Pfft!" Eddie made a derisive sound. "These Asians are all alike. The Koreans will run out of steam just as the Japanese did in 1947. You'll see. The Americans hate to do anything violent. They'll make another treaty."

"Opa," Lisl interrupted, hanging over the low side of the boat, brown hair trailing through sun-spangled water. "Are there sharks in this lake? May I go swimming?"

"Careful!" Eddie warned. "You'll fall in fully clothed, and then your grandmother will scold!"

The sun's slanting radiance scattered from the child's flowing hair. He stared at it, fascinated. The play of light had always obsessed him.

"Opa?" Lisl urged.

"A man should leave a mark," he said, watching the flash and dazzle in the lake. "It's not enough just to have lived."

"Exactly the point of the Hemingway story I referred to!" his son said with obvious satisfaction. "I took the liberty of putting my copy on your desk, Papa."

The child began to cry.

Venus, the evening star, was already burning in the western sky.

They heeled over and brought the sailboat swooping back to the dock.

*   *   *

The map does not indicate which is the best road, only that more than one possibility exists.

One afternoon many years ago (perhaps early May, for he remembered the cuckoo's melancholy call outside the open window) he had been at his desk in the patent office in Bern. Splinters of sunlight fell through green branches onto the papers he was reading. The work was sterile, soul-killing. He lived for the evenings when the street lamps were lit; then he walked under pale yellow flowers of the linden trees to the back room of a small *Gasthaus*. There, he joined a string quartet, explorers working their way across Beethoven's stark territory, the rich jungles of Brahms, the tidy gardens of Johann Sebastian Bach. He had just recently graduated from the Polytechnic Academy, where he'd studied math. But music had proved to be his Lorelei.

This particular day, he remembered, he had trouble chaining his mind to the endless march of dull papers across his desk, while outside the marvelous vernal light called to him. Instead, he played with numbers (the abstract language of music, he had always thought) that combined and recombined in mysterious ways, numbers like the swarming stars that dazzled overhead in the clear Alpine night.

"Ho, Jew boy!" The supervisor, a spindly little man with a receding hairline who had taken an instant dislike to the new employee, stopped by his desk.

He hastily slid a pile of half-finished forms over the mathematical doodlings. The supervisor leered over the desk, hoping to catch him in blatant error so there would be cause to fire him.

"Is the report ready, young genius? Or have you been too busy to bother?"

"I'll have it done on time."

"You certainly will—or you'll look elsewhere for employment!"

He was not born to work behind a desk, filling out forms, following someone else's orders. But he also was not capable of ignoring a challenge. For two hours he worked without stopping till the report was done, far more thoroughly than even the thin supervisor had a right to expect.

That evening at music practice, a warm spring breeze

blowing, full of starshine and promises, he received his first request to give tuition on the violin to the child of the Gasthaus keeper.

The next morning he gave notice at the patent office.

Rosa worked the bow smoothly across her instrument, moving through the difficult passage that led inexorably up the scale to high C, her nemesis. He leaned back in the armchair, eyes closed, evaluating, trying to hear the Rachmaninoff the way the judges would. Rain spattered the closed window, and Millie had lit the lamps in the middle of the afternoon. One week to go, he thought. One week to make a mark, to change the path of the stars that told man's fate, to mold the universe to one old man's will.

He was tired all the time now. The earth under his feet tugged at him, bending him out of shape.

Then she faltered once again on the high note and he leaped up from his chair, forgetful of stiff joints.

"No! No! No!" He seized the instrument from her hands. "What have I told you? You aren't milking cows here! You must glide up the notes like a fish swimming in a river! Like this."

He ran the bow smoothly up and down the scale, arthritic fingers for once remembering how they had moved in their youth when he had been the soloist with the orchestra in Paris and Vienna and at the Albert Hall.

Rosa lowered blond lashes over her ruddy cheeks, and he caught the gleam of tears in the glow of the lamps.

He relented. "All right now. We've worked hard enough for one lesson. Perhaps it'll go better tomorrow, or the next day."

"I'm sorry, Herr Professor. I don't wish to let you down."

But perhaps he had let himself down? Perhaps if he had stayed longer in the patent office, used the time to think about numbers?

"Let me try it again," she pleaded. "I *will* get it right!"

He gave her back the violin, thinking about possibilities and life that had a habit of squeezing them down.

His Uncle Jakob had urged something else, but Mama had her heart set on music. And music had been good to him, he could not deny that. He had moved back to Zurich,

married his university sweetheart, and raised two young sons
in relative comfort. In his orchestra days, he had seen something of the world. He had books and music, and friends
around the globe who wrote to him and came to visit. He had
had good students—more silvers and bronzes than any other
teacher in the canton, and a respectable number of golds.
One had even gone on to world-class competition—he remembered a brief, breathtaking visit to New York.

And now he was at home with the lake and the boat and
the crisp Alpine light sculpting the mountains.

If he had been someone like Van Gogh, he would have
painted that light. Sometimes he thought about the incandes-
cent heart of distant galaxies, spewing brightness through the
universe to break at last under its own weight on the shores
of Lake Zurich. It made his heart ache to think of it.

Rosa tried the passage again. This time he did not have
to wince as she reached high C.

That evening, drinking his coffee with whipped cream
and chocolate, sitting beside Millie, hand in hand on the
balcony, watching the moon come and go in the scudding
clouds over the lake, he thought about the mystery of roads
where one made decisions in darkness.

"Do you never wonder, Millie, if your life might have
been different?"

"How so, different?" she asked suspiciously.

"Do you never entertain the idea that perhaps you might
have done something else with your time, something you
might have been *better* at?"

"No," Millie said.

He sighed. "We could have traveled. We could have
seen more of America."

"We could have had problems and divorced!" she said
sourly.

He patted her hand. "Never."

The ache persisted, nevertheless.

The next morning, Hans Albert telephoned from Berlin
where he was a professor of physics.

"Have you read the newspaper, Papa?"

Behind the telephone in the hall, the wallpaper—Millie's
favorite pattern, clumps of creamy roses festooned with little

pink ribbons—glowed in warm sunshine. He stared, imagining the artist making the very first drawing from a real vase of roses, the blooms illuminated by a ray of sunlight falling like a benediction on the studio. In some sense, it was all happening now: the painter, the roses blooming in the garden before somebody cut them, the old violin teacher gazing at wallpaper. The past, like the future, was only a stubborn linguistic illusion.

"Papa?"

"Ah. What should I have read?"

"The war, of course! Don't you always read about the war in Korea?"

Yes, the war. The strangeness of the place names, *Seoul, Pyongyang, Pusan*. And the stupidity of young boys killing other young boys in jungles and rice paddies where light slanted through palm trees and bamboo thickets, light that had crossed the darkness of space from a distant star to illuminate a scene for painters.

"They're still fighting?"

"Papa!" Then another idea seemed to occur to his son. "Are you feeling well?"

"You're going to tell me that the American airplanes dropped a most peculiar bomb on a Korean town with a name as singular as roses. Isn't this so?"

"Yes—but roses? Anyway, let me tell you about this weapon, Papa! A great advance—the future beckoning! You see what they've proved? A particle of matter can be converted into enormous outbursts of energy. This is something we've been working on here at the university, splitting uranium atoms."

"Light," he said. "It travels so fast! No time at all, really, from our point of view."

Hans Albert was silent. After a while he said casually, "Is Mama there? Let me speak to her."

The afternoon was quite warm, but Millie insisted he wear his hat anyway. He had the impression if he had argued she would have dragged out muffler and gloves too. "Stop at the barber's on your way," she had ordered. "Your hair is all over the place again!"

He descended the narrow street that took him from his house, built during Zwingli's Protestant Reformation in the sixteenth century, to the violin maker's shop on Bahnhofstrasse in the center of the modern tourist district. Strange, the road that unwound in time from one to the other, he thought, and he too trudging down it. A Mercedes-Benz with German license plates blared at him as he stepped off a curb without looking. A donkey cart clopped by in the opposite direction, its driver wearing a peasant smock that Zwingli might have recognized. There was no such thing as past or future, he saw. It all happened at once in the wonderful, brimming light. He felt the weight of it, soft as petals on his face and hands.

The shop was cool and dim inside until his eyes adjusted. Sawdust muffled his footsteps. His nose filled with the scent of pine and ebony, maple and resin. Unstrung instruments hung on the wall like dreaming angels, waiting to wake and sing. He would not—could not—deny he loved music. He ran his fingers over wood like satin and velvet.

"Stradivari's design remains the standard of excellence, even today."

He glanced up at the speaker, a pale, stooped young man who carried on his father's and grandfather's business of making some of the best violins in Europe.

"That's my latest copy you're holding."

The young man took the instrument from his hands, tightened pegs, plucked strings, then took a bow and drew from the instrument a cascade of sound so rich it was like listening to a river of radiance pour down from the sky.

"High C," he said. "Let me hear it."

The young man demonstrated a pure, singing note.

He nodded. "Ah. And it lies easily under the fingers?"

"Very much so," the young man agreed. "But why does that concern you, my friend, expert musician that you are?"

"I have a student with a great deal of talent and a small hand."

The instrument maker glanced quizzically at him. They were, after all, speaking of violins, not pianos.

"And a present might give her the confidence she needs to take the gold."

"I see." The young man laid the violin in its case and closed the lid. "On your account?"

"On my account, thank you."

And if it had not been music, he thought as he was

leaving the shop, his gift in his hand, what then? What grand enterprise would have filled his life?

Whatever might have been, surely it would have been sufficient. God was subtle, but he was not malicious.

One time, when he had been perhaps eleven or twelve, there had been a conversation around the kitchen table in his parents' home in Munich. An early snow sifted down outside, and his mother had pulled heavy velvet curtains across the windows. In his memory, the kitchen was hazy with blue-gray smoke from his uncle's pipe, like a stage scene painted on gauze.

"Another poor report!" his father said, his hand over his eyes as if the mellow amber glow of the table lamp was too much for him. "I don't see why you don't just leave school now and come and join your uncle and me in the factory, instead of wasting your time and my money in the classroom."

"It was just low marks in history and geography, Hermann!" his mother pointed out. She stood with his father's *bierkrug* in her hand, on the way to the cellar to refill it. "It said nothing about other subjects."

"Ah, leave the boy alone," Uncle Jakob counseled. "He's a slow learner, but he's capable of good things."

"You say so?" his father asked. "Well, I don't see it."

A small fire chuckled to itself behind the glass doors of the potbellied stove; it was not yet cold enough in the room to open the doors.

"Sometimes . . ." he began hesitantly, not because he was afraid of his father but because he was not sure himself what he wanted to say. "Sometimes I think there's some great work for me to do."

His father forked up a slice of cold meat and added it to a hunk of dark bread and cheese he had been preparing before the subject of young Albert's bad marks came up. "Electrical engineering is great work, lad! It's the future."

"He's good at mathematics, a natural," Uncle Jakob said thoughtfully. "Too good to be just an engineer, like you and me, Hermann."

"Music is like mathematics, isn't it?" his mother asked, coming back into the room with a full *krug*. Foam leaked out from under the pewter lid.

"Then let him be a civil servant!" his father said. "But this schooling is a waste."

"There's something I have to do," he insisted. "I think there's a plan to my life. A riddle I have to solve—"

"So good at words, and yet he can't pass his composition test!" his father mocked.

His mother smoothed his hair—even as a young boy it had been unruly. "There's always more than one way, *Liebchen*."

"I think—"

"Life's a great game of chance," Uncle Jakob said. He leaned back from the table and relit his pipe. "An uncertain ride on a merry-go-round at the Oktoberfest!"

"But Uncle, that's like saying God is a gambler, throwing the dice for our lives—"

"The dice tell me you are no good in school!" his father roared. "I don't need God to advise me not to spend more money on a poor scholar!"

His mother pulled him to her, pressing his face against her starched apron. "Don't worry, *Liebchen*. I have money for music lessons. My money. Neither God nor your father shall have any say in how I spend it. I'll buy you a new violin."

"Come, Papa. You haven't even tasted your champagne!" Millie linked her arm through his and drew him through the crowded living room, past the neighbors, the friends from their musical circle, the rabbi and the priest of the local Catholic church deep in a discussion of the world soccer cup, past his sons who were arguing over the Korean bomb.

"This atom they've split has unleashed a terrible demon in our world!" Eddie said.

Hans Albert had made the trip unexpectedly from Berlin on the *Schnellzug*. "You don't understand. When the governments of the world are aware of the power of the atom, they'll finally make peace!"

He was not fooled. One more gold medal was hardly cause enough for his oldest son's visit. They worried about his health. Strange, for he did not worry about it himself.

Rosa, flushed and shining in a new dress, stood by the refreshment table that Mille and the housekeeper had worked all afternoon to set up with Millie's heirloom silver and best china. The gold medal flamed like a sun on Rosa's chest. Her parents stood with her, thick-bodied, slow-thinking. They were good people from the farm, not quite sure they understood why all these elegant folk in silk and velvet and glittering rings had come in taxis to kiss their little Rosa on both cheeks and shake her father's hand. The future unfolded before them like a rose petal uncurling, and they did not have the wit to know it.

"Herr Einstein," Rosa called. "Thank you!"

She blew him a kiss with her fingertips that had so flawlessly reached high C. Then she turned to the young man beside her—a cousin, he knew, a farm lad—and tucked the hand with the gifted fingers in his.

Millie herded him to an armchair from which he could see everybody in the room. He sank into it, feeling for a moment like the apple whose falling to earth had demonstrated gravity. Lisl promptly climbed on his lap, spilling champagne over the new gray trousers Millie had made him wear. His daughter-in-law retrieved the child and took her away to bed; her own cheeks were as rosy from champagne as the child's were from the summer sun. Across the room, he caught sight of his oldest grandchild, a serious boy, much too old now to sit on a grandparent's knee. He showed signs of following his uncle into the sciences.

Hans Albert, still glowering from the argument with his brother, came to sit in the chair beside him.

"Grand theories are in the air now," Hans Albert said. "Wonderful ideas about extending the Poincaré theory of dynamics to include gravitation. But some fools oppose the work."

"Ah. Who invents this?"

"Papa, physicists don't *invent*. They're not engineers. They propose theories and test them. Anyway, the ideas come from some Americans, Dyson and Feynman. And from our Heisenberg too, of course."

"Light," he said, gazing at the warm play of candlelight on silver.

Hans Albert nodded impatiently. "Of course! The role of light, following an innate curve made by matter, that's in the theory. And space and time too, threaded together and warped by matter. The equations describing this reduce to Newton's familiar prescriptions in the limit of essentially flat geometries. That's what's so exciting. I wish I could make you understand! You see— "

"How heavy it is."

"What is?" His son frowned at the interruption.

"Each ray as subtle as a rose petal," he said dreamily, "bending down to the earth."

"Something like that," the younger man said carefully.

"And everywhere it bends. If we go far enough away, does the light streaming out from the stars seem to curve?"

"Well, I don't—"

"Even to the end of things? Mustn't light bend then, at least?"

Hans Albert stared at him. "No disrespect, Papa, but you're certainly not a physicist!"

When Millie's back was turned, he slipped out of the crowded room.

The balcony was dark and empty, and the air rising off the lake was fresh. Overhead, a huge tapestry of stars blazed, a panoply of light streaking outward to the far horizons of the universe. It was a time to see not just backwards but forwards too. Someday, he thought, man would follow the elusive light of the stars, sailing out into the far reaches of space. Hans Albert could have told him how this would be done, but he already knew the truth of it in his heart.

He had the sense again tonight of endings, of a wave that had travelled so far finally curving on a distant shore. So be it. He was ready for it; there were few things to regret. All in all, it had been a good life.

Rosa had reached her C.

And yet—and yet.

The book Eddie had left for him was wrong in one respect. The sharks who snatched away the victory were not external. They swam in the dark waters of the soul. The trick was not to let them.

He gazed up into the sky at the great gorgeous light.

The Last Article

HARRY TURTLEDOVE

Nonviolence is the first article of my faith. It is also the last article of my creed.

—MOHANDAS GANDHI

The one means that wins the easiest victory over reason: terror and force.

—ADOLF HITLER,
Mein Kampf

The tank rumbled down the Rajpath, past the ruins of the Memorial Arch, toward the India Gate. The gateway arch was still standing, although it had taken a couple of shell hits in the fighting before New Delhi fell. The Union Jack fluttered above it.

British troops lined both sides of the Rajpath, watching silently as the tank rolled past them. Their khaki uniforms were filthy and torn; many wore bandages. They had the weary, past-caring stares of beaten men, though the Army of India had fought until flesh and munitions gave out.

The India Gate drew near. A military band, smartened up for the occasion, began to play as the tank went past. The bagpipes sounded thin and lost in the hot, humid air.

A single man stood waiting in the shadow of the Gate. Field Marshal Walther Model leaned down into the cupola of the Panzer IV. "No one can match the British at ceremonies of this sort," he said to his aide.

Major Dieter Lasch laughed, a bit unkindly. "They've had enough practice, sir," he answered, raising his voice to be heard over the flatulent roar of the tank's engine.

"What is that tune?" the field marshal asked. "Does it have a meaning?"

"It's called 'The World Turned Upside Down,'" said Lasch, who had been involved with his British opposite number in planning the formal surrender. "Lord Cornwallis's army musicians played it when he yielded to the Americans at Yorktown."

"Ah, the Americans." Model was for a moment so lost in his own thoughts that his monocle threatened to slip from his right eye. He screwed it back in. The single lens was the only thing he shared with the clichéd image of a high German officer. He was no lean, hawk-faced Prussian. But his rounded features were unyielding, and his stocky body sustained the energy of his will better than the thin, dyspeptic frames of so many aristocrats. "The Americans," he repeated. "Well, that will be the next step, won't it? But enough. One thing at a time."

The panzer stopped. The driver switched off the engine. The sudden quiet was startling. Model leaped nimbly down. He had been leaping down from tanks for eight years now, since his days as a staff officer for the IV Corps in the Polish campaign.

The man in the shadows stepped forward, saluted. Flash-bulbs lit his long, tired face as German photographers recorded the moment for history. The Englishman ignored cameras and cameramen alike. "Field Marshal Model," he said politely. He might have been about to discuss the weather.

Model admired his sangfroid. "Field Marshal Auchinleck," he replied, returning the salute and giving Auchinleck a last few seconds to remain his equal. Then he came back to the matter at hand. "Field Marshal, have you signed the instrument of surrender of the British Army of India to the forces of the Reich?"

"I have," Auchinleck replied. He reached into the left blouse pocket of his battledress, removed a folded sheet of paper. Before handing it to Model, though, he said, "I should like to request your permission to make a brief statement at this time."

"Of course, sir. You may say what you like, at whatever length you like." In victory, Model could afford to be magnanimous. He had even granted Marshal Zhukov leave to speak in the Soviet capitulation at Kuibyshev, before the marshal was taken out and shot.

"I thank you." Auchinleck stiffly dipped his head. "I will say, then, that I find the terms I have been forced to accept to be cruelly hard on the brave men who have served under my command."

"That is your privilege, sir." But Model's round face was no longer kindly, and his voice had iron in it as he replied, "I must remind you, however, that my treating with you at all under the rules of war is an act of mercy for which Berlin may yet reprimand me. When Britain surrendered in 1941, all Imperial forces were also ordered to lay down their arms. I daresay you did not expect us to come so far, but I would be within my rights in reckoning you no more than so many bandits."

A slow flush darkened Auchinleck's cheeks. "We gave you a bloody good run, for bandits."

"So you did." Model remained polite. He did not say he would ten times rather fight straight-up battles than deal with the partisans who to this day harassed the Germans and their allies in occupied Russia. "Have you anything further to add?"

"No, sir, I do not." Auchinleck gave the German the signed surrender, handed him his sidearm. Model put the pistol in the empty holster he wore for the occasion. It did not fit well; the holster was made for a Walther P38, not this man-killing brute of a Webley and Scott. That mattered little, though—the ceremony was almost over.

Auchinleck and Model exchanged salutes for the last time. The British field marshal stepped away. A German lieutenant came up to lead him into captivity.

Major Lasch waved his left hand. The Union Jack came down from the flagpole on the India Gate. The swastika rose to replace it.

Lasch tapped discreetly on the door, stuck his head into the field marshal's office. "That Indian politician is here for his appointment with you, sir."

"Oh, yes. Very well, Dieter, send him in." Model had been dealing with Indian politicians even before the British surrender, and with hordes of them now that resistance was over. He had no more liking for the breed than for Russian politicians, or even German ones. No matter what pious principles they spouted, his experience was that they were all out for their own good first.

The small, frail brown man the aide showed in made him wonder. The Indian's emaciated frame and the plain white cotton loincloth that was his only garment contrasted starkly with the Victorian splendor of the Viceregal Palace from which Model was administering the Reich's new conquest. "Sit down, *Herr* Gandhi," the field marshal urged.

"I thank you very much, sir." As he took his seat, Gandhi seemed a child in an adult's chair: it was much too wide for him, and its soft, overstuffed cushions hardly sagged under his meager weight. But his eyes, Model saw, were not a child's eyes. They peered with disconcerting keenness through his wire-framed spectacles as he said, "I have come to enquire when we may expect German troops to depart from our country."

Model leaned forward, frowning. For a moment he thought he had misunderstood Gandhi's Gujarati-flavored English. When he was sure he had not, he said, "Do you think perhaps we have come all this way as tourists?"

"Indeed I do not." Gandhi's voice was sharp with disapproval. "Tourists do not leave so many dead behind them."

Model's temper kindled. "No, tourists do not pay such a high price for the journey. Having come regardless of that cost, I assure you we shall stay."

"I am very sorry, sir; I cannot permit it."

"*You* cannot?" Again, Model had to concentrate to keep his monocle from falling out. He had heard arrogance from politicians before, but this scrawny old devil surpassed belief. "Do you forget I can call my aide and have you shot behind this building? You would not be the first, I assure you."

"Yes, I know that," Gandhi said sadly. "If you have that fate in mind for me, I am an old man. I will not run."

Combat had taught Model a hard indifference to the prospect of injury or death. He saw the older man possessed something of the same sort, however he had acquired it. A moment later, he realized his threat had not only failed to frighten Gandhi, but had actually amused him. Disconcerted, the field marshal said, "Have you any serious issues to address?"

"Only the one I named just now. We are a nation of more than three hundred million; it is no more just for Germany to rule us than for the British."

Model shrugged. "If we are able to, we will. We have the strength to hold what we have conquered, I assure you."

"Where there is no right, there can be no strength," Gandhi said. "We will not permit you to hold us in bondage."

"Do you think to threaten me?" Model growled. In fact, though, the Indian's audacity surprised him. Most of the locals had fallen over themselves fawning on their new masters. Here, at least, was a man out of the ordinary.

Gandhi was still shaking his head, although Model saw he had still not frightened him (a man out of the ordinary indeed, thought the field marshal, who respected courage when he found it). "I make no threats, sir, but I will do what I believe to be right."

"Most noble," Model said, but to his annoyance the words came out sincere rather than with the sardonic edge he had intended. He had heard such canting phrases before, from Englishmen, from Russians, yes, and from Germans as well. Somehow, though, this Gandhi struck him as one who always meant exactly what he said. He rubbed his chin, considering how to handle such an intransigent.

A large green fly came buzzing into the office. Model's air of detachment vanished the moment he heard that malignant whine. He sprang from his seat, swatted at the fly. He missed. The insect flew around a while longer, then settled on the arm of Gandhi's chair. "Kill it," Model told him. "Last week one of those accursed things bit me on the neck, and I still have the lump to prove it."

Gandhi brought his hand down, but several inches from the fly. Frightened, it took off. Gandhi rose. He was surprisingly nimble for a man nearing eighty. He chivvied the fly out of the office, ignoring Model, who watched his performance in open-mouthed wonder.

"I hope it will not trouble you again," Gandhi said, returning as calmly as if he had done nothing out of the ordinary. "I am one of those who practice *ahimsa:* I will do no injury to any living thing."

Model remembered the fall of Moscow, and the smell of burning bodies filling the chilly autumn air. He remembered machine guns knocking down Cossack cavalry before they could close, and the screams of the wounded horses, more heartrending then any woman's. He knew of other things, too, things he had not seen for himself and of which he had no desire to learn more.

"*Herr* Gandhi," he said, "how do you propose to bend to your will someone who opposes you, if you will not use force for the purpose?"

"I have never said I will not use force, sir." Gandhi's smile invited the field marshal to enjoy with him the distinction he was making. "I will not use violence. If my people refuse to cooperate in any way with yours, how can you compel them? What choice will you have but to grant us leave to do as we will?"

Without the intelligence estimates he had read, Model

would have dismissed the Indian as a madman. No madman, though, could have caused the British so much trouble. But perhaps the decadent raj simply had not made him afraid. Model tried again. "You understand that what you have said is treason against the Reich," he said harshly.

Gandhi bowed in his seat. "You may, of course, do what you will with me. My spirit will in any case survive among my people."

Model felt his face heat. Few men were immune to fear. Just his luck, he thought sourly, to have run into one of them. "I warn you, *Herr* Gandhi, to obey the authority of the officials of the Reich, or it will be the worse for you."

"I will do what I believe to be right, and nothing else. If you Germans exert yourselves toward the freeing of India, joyfully will I work with you. If not, then I regret we must be foes."

The field marshal gave him one last chance to see reason. "Were it you and I alone, there might be some doubt as to what would happen." Not much, he thought, not when Gandhi was twenty-odd years older and thin enough to break like a stick. He fought down the irrelevance, went on, "But where, *Herr* Gandhi, is your *Wehrmacht*?"

Of all things, he had least expected to amuse the Indian again. Yet Gandhi's eyes unmistakably twinkled behind the lenses of his spectacles. "Field Marshal, I have an army too."

Model's patience, never of the most enduring sort, wore thin all at once. "Get out!" he snapped.

Gandhi stood, bowed, and departed. Major Lasch stuck his head into the office. The field marshal's glare drove him out again in a hurry.

"Well?" Jawaharlal Nehru paced back and forth. Tall, slim, and saturnine, he towered over Gandhi without dominating him. "Dare we use the same policies against the Germans that we employed against the English?"

"If we wish our land free, dare we do otherwise?" Gandhi replied. "They will not grant our wish of their own volition. Model struck me as a man not much different from various British leaders whom we have succeeded in vexing in the past." He smiled at the memory of what passive resistance had done to officials charged with combating it.

"Very well, *satyagraha* it is." But Nehru was not smiling. He had less humor than his older colleague.

Gandhi teased him gently: "Do you fear another spell in prison, then?" Both men had spent time behind bars during the war, until the British released them in a last, vain effort to rally the support of the Indian people to the raj.

"You know better." Nehru refused to be drawn, and persisted, "The rumors that come out of Europe frighten me."

"Do you tell me you take them seriously?" Gandhi shook his head in surprise and a little reproof. "Each side in any war will always paint its opponents as blackly as it can."

"I hope you are right, and that that is all. Still, I confess I would feel more at ease with what we plan to do if you found me one Jew, officer or other rank, in the army now occupying us."

"You would be hard-pressed to find any among the forces they defeated. The British have little love for Jews either."

"Yes, but I daresay it could be done. With the Germans, they are banned by law. The English would never make such a rule. And while the laws are vile enough, I think of the tales that man Wiesenthal told, the one who came here the gods know how across Russia and Persia from Poland."

"Those I do not believe," Gandhi said firmly. "No nation could act in that way and hope to survive. Where could men be found to carry out such horrors?"

"*Azad Hind,*" Nehru said, quoting the "Free India" motto of the locals who had fought on the German side.

But Gandhi shook his head. "They are only soldiers, doing as soldiers have always done. Wiesenthal's claims are for an entirely different order of bestiality, one which could not exist without destroying the fabric of the state that gave it birth."

"I hope very much you are right," Nehru said.

Walther Model slammed the door behind him hard enough to make his aide, whose desk faced away from the field marshal's office, jump in alarm. "Enough of this twaddle for one day," Model said. "I need schnapps, to get the taste of these Indians out of my mouth. Come along if you care to, Dieter."

"Thank you, sir." Major Lasch threw down his pen, eagerly got to his feet. "I sometimes think conquering India was easier than ruling it will be."

Model rolled his eyes. "I *know* it was. I would ten times rather be planning a new campaign than sitting here bogged down in pettifogging details. The sooner Berlin sends me people trained in colonial administration, the happier I will be."

The bar might have been taken from an English pub. It was dark, quiet, and paneled in walnut; a dart board still hung on the wall. But a German sergeant in field gray stood behind the bar, and despite the lazily turning ceiling fan, the temperature was close to thirty-five Celsius. The one might have been possible in occupied London, the other not.

Model knocked back his first shot at a gulp. He sipped his second more slowly, savoring it. Warmth spread through him, warmth that had nothing to do with the heat of the evening. He leaned back in his chair, steepled his fingers. "A long day," he said.

"Yes, sir," Lasch agreed. "After the effrontery of that Gandhi, any day would seem a long one. I've rarely seen you so angry." Considering Model's temper, that was no small statement.

"Ah, yes, Gandhi." Model's tone was reflective rather than irate; Lasch looked at him curiously. The field marshal said, "For my money, he's worth a dozen of the ordinary sort."

"Sir?" The aide no longer tried to hide his surprise.

"He is an honest man. He tells me what he thinks, and he will stick by that. I may kill him—I may have to kill him—but he and I will both know why, and I will not change his mind." Model took another sip of schnapps. He hesitated, as if unsure whether to go on. At last he did. "Do you know, Dieter, after he left I had a vision."

"Sir?" Now Lasch sounded alarmed.

The field marshal might have read his aide's thoughts. He chuckled wryly. "No, no, I am not about to swear off eating beefsteak and wear sandals instead of my boots, that I promise. But I saw myself as a Roman procurator, listening to the rantings of some early Christian priest."

Lasch raised an eyebrow. Such musings were unlike Model, who was usually direct to the point of bluntness and altogether materialistic—assets in the makeup of a general officer. The major cautiously sounded these unexpected depths: "How do you suppose the Roman felt, facing that kind of man?"

"Bloody confused, I suspect," Model said, which sounded more like him. "And because he and his comrades did not know how to handle such fanatics, you and I are Christians today, Dieter."

"So we are." The major rubbed his chin. "Is that a bad thing?"

Model laughed and finished his drink. "From your point of view or mine, no, but I doubt that old Roman would agree with us, any more than Gandhi agrees with me over what will happen next here. But then, I have two advantages over the dead procurator." He raised his finger; the sergeant hurried over to fill his glass.

At Lasch's nod, the young man also poured more schnapps for him. The major drank, then said, "I should hope so. We are more civilized, more sophisticated, than the Romans ever dreamed of being."

But Model was still in that fey mood. "Are we? My procurator was such a sophisticate that he tolerated anything, and never saw the danger in a foe who would not do the same. Our Christian God, though, is a jealous god, who puts up with no rivals. And one who is a National Socialist serves also the *Volk*, to whom he owes sole loyalty. I am immune to Gandhi's virus in a way the Roman was not to the Christian's."

"Yes, that makes sense," Lasch agreed after a moment. "I had not thought of it in that way, but I see it is so. And what is our other advantage over the Roman procurator?"

Suddenly the field marshal looked hard and cold, much the way he had looked leading the tanks of Third Panzer against the Kremlin compound. "The machine gun," he said.

The rising sun's rays made the sandstone of the Red Fort seem even more the color of blood. Gandhi frowned and turned his back on the fortress, not caring for that thought. Even at dawn, the air was warm and muggy.

"I wish you were not here," Nehru told him. The younger man lifted his trademark fore-and-aft cap, scratched his graying hair, and glanced at the crowd growing around them. "The Germans' orders forbid assemblies, and they will hold you responsible for this gathering."

"I am, am I not?" Gandhi replied. "Would you have me send my followers into a danger I do not care to face myself? How would I presume to lead them afterwards?"

"A general does not fight in the front ranks," Nehru came back. "If you are lost to our cause, will we be able to go on?"

"If not, then surely the cause is not worthy, yes? Now let us be going."

Nehru threw his hands in the air. Gandhi nodded, satisfied, and worked his way toward the head of the crowd. Men and women stepped aside to let him through. Still shaking his head, Nehru followed.

The crowd slowly began to march east up Chandni Chauk, the Street of Silversmiths. Some of the fancy shops had been wrecked in the fighting, more looted afterwards. But others were opening up, their owners as happy to take German money as they had been to serve the British before.

One of the proprietors, a man who had managed to stay plump even through the past year of hardship, came rushing out of his shop when he saw the procession go by. He ran to the head of the march and spotted Nehru, whose height and elegant dress singled him out.

"Are you out of your mind?" the silversmith shouted. "The Germans have banned assemblies. If they see you, something dreadful will happen."

"Is it not dreadful that they take away the liberty which properly belongs to us?" Gandhi asked. The silversmith spun round. His eyes grew wide when he recognized the man who was speaking to him. Gandhi went on, "Not only is it dreadful, it is wrong. And so we do not recognize the Germans' right to ban anything we may choose to do. Join us, will you?"

"Great-souled one, I—I—" the silversmith spluttered. Then his glance slid past Gandhi. "The Germans!" he squeaked. He turned and ran.

Gandhi led the procession toward the approaching squad. The Germans stamped down Chandni Chauk as if they expected the people in front of them to melt from their path. Their gear, Gandhi thought, was not that much different from what British soldiers wore: ankle boots, shorts, and open-necked tunics. But their coal-scuttle helmets gave them a look of sullen, beetle-browed ferocity the British tin hat did not convey. Even for a man of Gandhi's equanimity it was daunting, as no doubt it was intended to be.

"Hello, my friends," he said. "Do any of you speak English?"

"I speak it, a little," one of them replied. His shoulder straps had the twin pips of a sergeant-major; he was the squad-leader, then. He hefted his rifle, not menacingly, Gandhi thought, but to emphasize what he was saying. "Go to your homes back. This coming together is *verboten*."

"I am sorry, but I must refuse to obey your order," Gandhi said. "We are walking peacefully on our own street in our own city. We will harm no one, no matter what; this I promise you. But walk we will, as we wish." He repeated himself until he was sure the sergeant-major understood.

The German spoke to his comrades in his own language. One of the soldiers raised his gun and with a nasty smile pointed it at Gandhi. He nodded politely. The German blinked to see him unafraid. The sergeant-major slapped the rifle down. One of his men had a field telephone on his back. The sergeant-major cranked it, waited for a reply, spoke urgently into it.

Nehru caught Gandhi's eye. His dark, tired gaze was full of worry. Somehow that nettled Gandhi more than the Germans' arrogance in ordering about his people. He began to walk forward again. The marchers followed him, flowing around the German squad like water round a boulder.

The soldier who had pointed his rifle at Gandhi shouted in alarm. He brought up the weapon again. The sergeant-major barked at him. Reluctantly, he lowered it.

"A sensible man," Gandhi said to Nehru. "He sees we do no injury to him or his, and so does none to us."

"Sadly, though, not everyone is so sensible," the younger man replied, "as witness his lance-corporal there. And even a sensible man may not be well-inclined to us. You notice he is still on the telephone."

The phone on Field Marshal Model's desk jangled. He jumped and swore; he had left orders he was to be disturbed only for an emergency. He had to find time to work. He picked up the phone. "This had better be good," he growled without preamble.

He listened, swore again, slammed the receiver down. "Lasch!" he shouted.

It was his aide's turn to jump. "Sir?"

"Don't just sit there on your fat arse," the field marshal said unfairly. "Call out my car and driver, and quickly. Then belt on your sidearm and come along. The Indians are doing something stupid. Oh, yes, order out a platoon and have them come after us. Up on Chandni Chauk, the trouble is."

Lasch called for the car and the troops, then hurried after Model. "A riot?" he asked as he caught up.

"No, no." Model moved his stumpy frame along so fast that the taller Lasch had to trot beside him. "Some of Gandhi's tricks, damn him."

The field marshal's Mercedes was waiting when he and his aide hurried out of the viceregal palace. "Chandni Chauk," Model snapped as the driver held the door open for him. After that he sat in furious silence as the powerful car roared up Irwin Road, round a third of Connaught Circle, and north on Chelmsford Road past the bombed-out railway station until, for no reason Model could see, the street's name changed to Qutb Road.

A little later, the driver said, "Some kind of disturbance up ahead, sir."

"Disturbance?" Lasch echoed, leaning forward to peer through the windscreen. "It's a whole damned regiment's worth of Indians coming at us. Don't they know better than that? And what the devil," he added, his voice rising, "are so many of our men doing ambling along beside them? Don't they know they're supposed to break up this sort of thing?" In his indignation, he did not notice he was repeating himself.

"I suspect they don't," Model said dryly. "Gandhi, I gather, can have that effect on people who aren't ready for his peculiar brand of stubbornness. That, however, does not include me." He tapped the driver on the shoulder. "Pull up about two hundred meters in front of the first rank of them, Joachim."

"Yes, sir."

Even before the car had stopped moving, Model jumped out of it. Lasch, hand on his pistol, was close behind, protesting, "What if one of those fanatics has a gun?"

"Then Colonel-General Weidling assumes command, and a lot of Indians end up dead."

Model strode toward Gandhi. As it had at the surrender ceremony, India's damp heat smote him. Even while he was sitting quietly in the car, his tunic had stuck to him. Sweat started streaming down his face the moment he started to move. Each breath felt as if he were taking in warm soup; the air even had a faint smell of soup, soup that had gone slightly off.

In its own way, he thought, surprised at himself, this beastly weather was worse than a Russian winter. Either was plenty to lay a man low by itself, but countless exotic diseases flourished in the moisture, warmth, and filth here. The snows at least were clean.

The field marshal ignored the German troops who were drawing themselves to stiff, horrified attention at the sight of his uniform. He would deal with them later. For the moment, Gandhi was more important.

He had stopped—which meant the rest of the marchers did too—and was waiting politely for Model to approach. The German commandant was not impressed. He thought Gandhi sincere, and could not doubt his courage, but none of that mattered at all. He said harshly, "You were warned against this sort of behavior."

Gandhi looked him in the eye. They were very much of a height. "And I told you, I do not recognize your right to give such orders. This is our country, not yours, and if some of us choose to walk on our streets, we will do so."

From behind Gandhi, Nehru's glance flicked worriedly from one of the antagonists to the other. Model noticed him only peripherally; if he was already afraid, he could be handled whenever necessary. Gandhi was a tougher nut. The field marshal waved at the crowd behind the old man. "You are responsible for all these people. If harm comes to them, you will be to blame."

"Why should harm come to them? They are not soldiers. They do not attack your men. I told that to one of your sergeants, and he understood it, and refrained from hindering us. Surely you, sir, an educated, cultured man, can see that what I say is self-evident truth."

Model turned his head to speak to his aide in German: "If we did not have Goebbels, this would be the one for his job." He shuddered to think of the propaganda victory Gandhi would win if he got away with flouting German ordinances. The whole countryside would be boiling with partisans in a week. And he had already managed to hoodwink some Germans into letting him do it!

Then Gandhi surprised him again. "*Ich danke Ihnen, Herr Generalfeldmarschall, aber das glaube ich kein Kompliment zu sein,*" he said in slow but clear German: "I thank you, field marshal, but I believe that to be no compliment."

Having to hold his monocle in place helped Model keep his face straight. "Take it however you like," he said. "Get these people off the street, or they and you will face the consequences. We will do what you force us to."

"I force you to nothing. As for these people who follow, each does so of his or her own free will. We are free, and will show it, not by violence, but through firmness in truth."

Now Model listened with only half an ear. He had kept Gandhi talking long enough for the platoon he had ordered out to arrive. Half a dozen SdKfz 251 armored personnel carriers came clanking up. The men piled out of them. "Give me a firing line, three ranks deep," Model shouted. As the troopers scrambled to obey, he waved the halftracks into position behind them, all but blocking Qutb Road. The halftracks' commanders swiveled the machine guns at the front of the vehicles' troop compartments so they bore on the Indians.

Gandhi watched these preparations as calmly as if they had nothing to do with him. Again Model had to admire his calm. His followers were less able to keep fear from their faces. Very few, though, used the pause to slip away. Gandhi's discipline was a long way from the military sort, but effective all the same.

"Tell them to disperse now, and we can still get away without bloodshed," the field marshal said.

"We will shed no one's blood, sir. But we will continue on our pleasant journey. Moving carefully, we will, I think, be able to get between your large lorries there." Gandhi turned to wave his people forward once more.

"You insolent—" Rage choked Model, which was as well, for it kept him from cursing Gandhi like a fishwife. To give him time to master his temper, he plucked his monocle from his eye and began polishing the lens with a silk handkerchief.

He replaced the monocle, started to jam the handkerchief back into his trouser pocket, then suddenly had a better idea.

"Come, Lasch," he said, and started toward the waiting German troops. About halfway to them, he dropped the handkerchief on the ground. He spoke in loud, simple German so his men and Gandhi could both follow: "If any Indians come past this spot, I wash my hands of them."

He might have known Gandhi would have a comeback ready. "That is what Pilate said also, you will recall, sir."

"Pilate washed his hands to evade responsibility," the field marshal answered steadily; he was in control of himself again. "I accept it: I am responsible to my Führer and to the *Oberkommando-Wehrmacht* for maintaining Reichs control over India, and will do what I see fit to carry out that obligation."

For the first time since they had come to know each other, Gandhi looked sad. "I too, sir, have my responsibilities." He bowed slightly to Model.

Lasch chose that moment to whisper in his commander's ear: "Sir, what of our men over there? Had you planned to leave them in the line of fire?"

The field marshal frowned. He had planned to do just that; the wretches deserved no better, for being taken in by Gandhi. But Lasch had a point. The platoon might balk at shooting countrymen, if it came to that. "You men," Model said sourly, jabbing his marshal's baton at them, "fall in behind the armored personnel carriers, at once."

The Germans' boots pounded on the macadam as they dashed to obey. They were still all right, then, with a clear order in front of them. Something, Model thought, but not much.

He had also worried that the Indians would take advantage of the moment of confusion to press forward, but they did not. Gandhi and Nehru and a couple of other men were arguing among themselves. Model nodded once. Some of them knew he was in earnest, then. And Gandhi's followers' discipline, as the field marshal had thought a few minutes ago, was not of the military sort. He could not simply issue an order and know his will would be done.

"I issue no orders," Gandhi said. "Let each man follow his conscience as he will—what else is freedom?"

"They will follow *you* if you go forward, great-souled one," Nehru replied, "and that German, I fear, means to carry out his threat. Will you throw your life away, and those of your countrymen?"

"I will not throw my life away," Gandhi said, but before the men around him could relax he went on, "I will gladly give it, if freedom requires that. I am but one man. If I fall, others will surely carry on; perhaps the memory of me will serve to make them more steadfast."

He stepped forward.

"Oh, damnation," Nehru said softly, and followed.

For all his vigor, Gandhi was far from young. Nehru did not need to nod to the marchers close by him; of their own accord, they hurried ahead of the man who had led them for so long, forming with their bodies a barrier between him and the German guns.

He tried to go faster. "Stop! Leave me my place! What are you doing?" he cried, though in his heart he understood only too well.

"This once, they will not listen to you," Nehru said.

"But they must!" Gandhi peered through eyes dimmed now by tears as well as age. "Where is that stupid handkerchief? We must be almost to it!"

"For the last time, I warn you to halt!" Model shouted. The Indians still came on. The sound of their feet, sandal-clad or bare, was like a growing murmur on the pavement, very different from the clatter of German boots. "Fools!" the field marshal muttered under his breath. He turned to his men. "Take your aim!"

The advance slowed when the rifles came up; of that Model was certain. For a moment he thought that ultimate threat would be enough to bring the marchers to their senses. But then they advanced again. The Polish cavalry had shown that same reckless bravery, charging with lances and sabers and carbines against the German tanks. Model wondered whether the inhabitants of the *Reichsgeneralgouvernement* of Poland thought the gallantry worthwhile.

A man stepped on the field marshal's handkerchief. "Fire!" Model said.

A second passed, two. Nothing happened. Model scowled

at his men. Gandhi's deviltry had got into them; sneaky as a Jew, he was turning the appearance of weakness into a strange kind of strength. But then trained discipline paid its dividend. One finger tightened on a Mauser trigger. A single shot rang out. As if it were a signal that recalled the other men to their duty, they too began to fire. From the armored personnel carriers, the machine guns started their deadly chatter. Model heard screams above the gunfire.

The volley smashed into the front ranks of marchers at close range. Men fell. Others ran, or tried to, only to be held by the power of the stream still advancing behind them. Once begun, the Germans methodically poured fire into the column of Indians. The march dissolved into a panic-stricken mob.

Gandhi still tried to press forward. A fleeing wounded man smashed into him, splashing him with blood and knocking him to the ground. Nehru and another man immediately lay down on top of him.

"Let me up! Let me up!" he shouted.

"No," Nehru screamed in his ear. "With shooting like this, you are in the safest spot you can be. We need you, and need you alive. Now we have martyrs around whom to rally our cause."

"Now we have dead husbands and wives, fathers and mothers. Who will tend to their loved ones?"

Gandhi had no time for more protest. Nehru and the other man hauled him to his feet and dragged him away. Soon they were among their people, all running now from the German guns. A bullet struck the back of the unknown man who was helping Gandhi escape. Gandhi heard the slap of the impact, felt the man jerk. Then the strong grip on him loosened as the man fell.

He tried to tear free from Nehru. Before he could, another Indian laid hold of him. Even at that horrid moment, he felt the irony of his predicament. All his life he had championed individual liberty, and here his own followers were robbing him of his. In other circumstances, it might have been funny.

"In here!" Nehru shouted. Several people had already

broken down the door to a shop and, Gandhi saw a moment later, the rear exit as well. Then he was hustled into the alley behind the shop, and through a maze of lanes which reminded him that old Delhi, unlike its British-designed sister city, was an Indian town through and through.

At last the nameless man with Gandhi and Nehru knocked on the back door of a tearoom. The woman who opened it gasped to recognize her unexpected guests, then pressed her hands together in front of her and stepped aside to let them in. "You will be safe here," the man said, "at least for a while. Now I must see to my own family."

"From the bottom of our hearts, we thank you," Nehru replied as the fellow hurried away. Gandhi said nothing. He was winded, battered, and filled with anguish at the failure of the march and at the suffering it had brought to so many marchers and to their kinsfolk.

The woman sat the two fugitive leaders at a small table in the kitchen, served them tea and cakes. "I will leave you now, best ones," she said quietly, "lest those out front wonder why I neglect them for so long."

Gandhi left the cake on his plate. He sipped the tea. Its warmth began to restore him physically, but the wound in his spirit would never heal. "The Amritsar massacre pales beside this," he said, setting down the empty cup. "There the British panicked and opened fire. This had nothing of panic about it. Model told me what he would do, and he did it." He shook his head, still hardly believing what he had just been through.

"So he did." Nehru had gobbled his cake like a starving wolf, and ate his companion's when he saw Gandhi did not want it. His once-immaculate white jacket and pants were torn, filthy, and blood-spattered; his cap sat awry on his head. But his eyes, usually so somber, were lit with a fierce glow. "And by his brutality, he has delivered himself into our hands. No one now can imagine the Germans have anything but their own interests at heart. We will gain followers all over the country. After this, not a wheel will turn in India."

"Yes, I will declare the *satyagraha* campaign," Gandhi said. "Noncooperation will show how we reject foreign rule, and will cost the Germans dear because they will not be able to exploit us. The combination of nonviolence and determined spirit will surely shame them into granting us our liberty."

"There—you see." Encouraged by his mentor's rally, Nehru rose and came round the table to embrace the older man. "We will triumph yet."

"So we will," Gandhi said, and sighed heavily. He had pursued India's freedom for half his long life, and this change of masters was a setback he had not truly planned for, even after England and Russia fell. The British were finally beginning to listen to him when the Germans swept them aside. Now he had to begin anew. He sighed again. "It will cost our poor people dear, though."

"Cease firing," Model said. Few good targets were left on Qutb Road; almost all the Indians in the procession were down or had run from the guns.

Even after the bullets stopped, the street was far from silent. Most of the people the German platoon had shot were alive and shrieking. As if he needed more proof—the Russian campaign had taught the field marshal how hard human beings were to kill outright.

Still, the din distressed him, and evidently Lasch as well. "We ought to put them out of their misery," the major said.

"So we should." Model had a happy inspiration. "And I know just how. Come with me."

The two men turned their backs on the carnage and walked around the row of armored personnel carriers. As they passed the lieutenant commanding the platoon, Model nodded to him and said, "Well done."

The lieutenant saluted. "Thank you, sir." The soldiers in earshot nodded at one another. Nothing bucked up the odds of getting promoted like performing under the commander's eye.

The Germans behind the armored vehicles were not so proud of themselves. They were the ones who had let the march get this big and come this far in the first place. Model slapped his boot with his field marshal's baton. "You all deserve courts-martial," he said coldly, glaring at them. "You know the orders concerning native assemblies, yet there you were tagging along, more like sheepdogs than soldiers." He spat in disgust.

"But, sir—" began one of them, a sergeant-major, Model

saw. He subsided in a hurry when Model's gaze swung his way.

"Speak," the field marshal urged. "Enlighten me—tell me what possessed you to act in the disgraceful way you did. Was it some evil spirit, perhaps? This country abounds with them, if you listen to the natives—as you all too obviously have been."

The sergeant-major flushed under Model's sarcasm, but finally burst out, "Sir, it didn't look to me as if they were up to any harm, that's all. The old man heading them up swore they were peaceful, and he looked too feeble to be anything but, if you take my meaning."

Model's smile had all the warmth of a Moscow December night. "And so in your wisdom you set aside the commands you had received. The results of that wisdom you hear now." The field marshal briefly let himself listen to the cries of the wounded, a sound the war had taught him to screen out. "Now then, come with me—yes you, Sergeant-major, and the rest of your shirkers too, or those of you who wish to avoid a court."

As he had known they would, they all trooped after him. "There is your handiwork," he said, pointing to the shambles in the street. His voice hardened. "You are responsible for those people lying there—had you acted as you should, you would have broken up that march long before it ever got so far or so large. Now the least you can do is give those people their release." He set hands on hips, waited.

No one moved. "Sir?" the sergeant-major said faintly. He seemed to have become the group's spokesman.

Model made an impatient gesture. "Go on, finish them. A bullet in the back of the head will quiet them once and for all."

"In cold blood, sir?" The sergeant-major had not wanted to understand him before. Now he had no choice.

The field marshal was inexorable. "They—and you— disobeyed Reich commands. They made themselves liable to capital punishment the moment they gathered. You at least have the chance to atone, by carrying out this just sentence."

"I don't think I can," the sergeant-major muttered.

He was probably just talking to himself, but Model gave him no chance to change his mind. He turned to the lieutenant of the platoon that had broken the march. "Place this man under arrest." After the sergeant-major had been seized,

Model turned his chill, monocled stare on the rest of the reluctant soldiers. "Any others?"

Two more men let themselves be arrested rather than draw their weapons. The field marshal nodded to the others. "Carry out your orders." He had an afterthought. "If you find Gandhi or Nehru out there, bring them to me alive."

The Germans moved out hesitantly. They were no *Einsatzkommandos*, and not used to this kind of work. Some looked away as they administered the first coup de grace; one missed as a result, and had his bullet ricochet off the pavement and almost hit a comrade. But as the soldiers worked their way up Qutb Road they became quicker, more confident, and more competent. War was like that, Model thought. So soon one became used to what had been unimaginable.

After a while the flat cracks died away, but from lack of targets rather than reluctance. A few at a time, the soldiers returned to Model. "No sign of the two leaders?" he asked. They all shook their heads.

"Very well—dismissed. And obey your orders like good Germans henceforward."

"No further reprisals?" Lasch asked as the relieved troopers hurried away.

"No, let them go. They carried out their part of the bargain, and I will meet mine. I am a fair man, after all, Dieter."

"Very well, sir."

Gandhi listened with undisguised dismay as the shopkeeper babbled out his tale of horror. "This is madness!" he cried.

"I doubt Field Marshal Model, for his part, understands the principle of *ahimsa*," Nehru put in. Neither Gandhi nor he knew exactly where they were: a safe house somewhere not far from the center of Delhi was the best guess he could make. The men who brought the shopkeeper were masked. What one did not know, one could not tell the Germans if captured.

"Neither do you," the older man replied, which was true; Nehru had a more pragmatic nature than Gandhi. Gandhi went on, "Rather more to the point, neither do the British. And Model, to speak to, seemed no different from any high-ranking British military man. His specialty has made him harsh and rigid, but he is not stupid and does not appear unusually cruel."

"Just a simple soldier, doing his job." Nehru's irony was palpable.

"He must have gone insane," Gandhi said; it was the only explanation that made even the slightest sense of the massacre of the wounded. "Undoubtedly he will be censured when news of this atrocity reaches Berlin, as General Dyer was by the British after Amritsar."

"Such is to be hoped." But again Nehru did not sound hopeful.

"How could it be otherwise, after such an appalling action? What government, what leaders could fail to be filled with humiliation and remorse at it?"

Model strode into the mess. The officers stood and raised their glasses in salute. "Sit, sit," the field marshal growled, using gruffness to hide his pleasure.

An Indian servant brought him a fair imitation of roast beef and Yorkshire pudding: better than they were eating in London these days, he thought. The servant was silent and unsmiling, but Model would only have noticed more about him had he been otherwise. Servants were supposed to assume a cloak of invisibility.

When the meal was done, Model took out his cigar case. The *Waffen-SS* officer on his left produced a lighter. Model leaned forward, puffed a cigar into life. "My thanks, *Brigadeführer*," the field marshal said. He had little use for SS titles of rank, but brigade commander was at least recognizably close to brigadier.

"Sir, it is my great pleasure," Jürgen Stroop declared. "You could not have handled things better. A lesson for the Indians—less than they deserve, too" (he also took no notice of the servant) "and a good one for your men as well. We train ours harshly too."

Model nodded. He knew about SS training methods. No one denied the daring of the *Waffen-SS* divisions. No one (except the SS) denied that the *Wehrmacht* had better officers.

Stroop drank. "A lesson," he repeated in a pedantic tone that went oddly with the SS's reputation for aggressiveness.

"Force is the only thing the racially inferior can understand. Why, when I was in Warsaw—"

That had been four or five years ago, Model suddenly recalled. Stroop had been a *Brigadeführer* then too, if memory served; no wonder he was still one now, even after all the hard fighting since. He was lucky not to be a buck private. Imagine letting a pack of desperate, starving Jews chew up the finest troops in the world.

And imagine, afterwards, submitting a seventy-five-page operations report bound in leather and grandiosely called *The Warsaw Ghetto Is No More*. And imagine, with all that, having the crust to boast about it afterwards. No wonder the man sounded like a pompous ass. He *was* a pompous ass, and an inept butcher to boot. Model had done enough butchery before today's work—anyone who fought in Russia learned all about butchery—but he had never botched it.

He did not revel in it, either. He wished Stroop would shut up. He thought about telling the *Brigadeführer* he would sooner have been listening to Gandhi. The look on the fellow's face, he thought, would be worth it. But no. One could never be sure who was listening. Better safe.

The shortwave set crackled to life. It was in a secret cellar, a tiny dark hot room lit only by the glow of its dial and by the red end of the cigarette in its owner's mouth. The Germans had made not turning in a radio a capital crime. Of course, Gandhi thought, harboring him was also a capital crime. That weighed on his conscience. But the man knew the risk he was taking.

The fellow (Gandhi knew him only as Lal) fiddled with the controls. "Usually we listen to the Americans," he said. "There is some hope of truth from them. But tonight you want to hear Berlin."

"Yes," Gandhi said. "I must learn what action is to be taken against Model."

"If any," Nehru added. He was once again impeccably attired in white, which made him the most easily visible object in the cellar.

"We have argued this before," Gandhi said tiredly. "No government can uphold the author of a cold-blooded slaughter of wounded men and women. The world would cry out in abhorrence."

Lal said, "That government controls too much of the world already." He adjusted the tuning knob again. After a burst of static, the strains of a Strauss waltz filled the little room. Lal grunted in satisfaction. "We are a little early yet."

After a few minutes, the incongruously sweet music died away. "This is Radio Berlin's English-language channel," an announcer declared. "In a moment, the news programme." Another German tune rang out: the Horst Wessel Song. Gandhi's nostrils flared with distaste.

A new voice came over the air. "Good day. This is William Joyce." The nasal Oxonian accent was that of the archetypical British aristocrat, now vanished from India as well as England. It was the accent that flavored Gandhi's own English, and Nehru's as well. In fact, Gandhi had heard, Joyce was a New York-born rabble-rouser of Irish blood who also happened to be a passionately sincere Nazi. The combination struck the Indian as distressing.

"What did the English used to call him?" Nehru murmured. "Lord Haw-Haw?"

Gandhi waved his friend to silence. Joyce was reading the news, or what the Propaganda Ministry in Berlin wanted to present to English-speakers as the news.

Most of it was on the dull side: a trade agreement between Manchukuo, Japanese-dominated China, and Japanese-dominated Siberia; advances by German-supported French troops against American-supported French troops in a war by proxy in the African jungles. Slightly more interesting was the German warning about American interference in the East Asia Co-Prosperity Sphere.

One day soon, Gandhi thought sadly, the two mighty powers of the Old World would turn on the one great nation that stood between them. He feared the outcome. Thinking herself secure behind ocean barriers, the United States had stayed out of the European war. Now the war was bigger than Europe, and the oceans barriers no longer, but highways for her foes.

Lord Haw-Haw droned on and on. He gloated over the fate of rebels hunted down in Scotland: they were publicly hanged. Nehru leaned forward. "Now," he guessed. Gandhi nodded.

But the commentator passed on to unlikely-sounding boasts about the prosperity of Europe under the New Order. Against his will, Gandhi felt anger rise in him. Were Indians too insignificant to the Reich even to be mentioned?

More music came from the radio: the first bars of the other German anthem, *Deutschland über alles*. William Joyce said solemnly, "And now, a special announcement from the Ministry for Administration of Acquired Territories. *Reichsminister* Reinhard Heydrich commends Field Marshal Walther Model's heroic suppression of insurrection in India, and warns that his leniency will not be repeated."

"Leniency!" Nehru and Gandhi burst out together, the latter making it into as much of a curse as he allowed himself.

As if explaining to them, the voice on the radio went on, "Henceforward, hostages will be taken at the slightest sound of disorder, and will be executed forthwith if it continues. Field Marshal Model has also placed a reward of fifty thousand rupees on the capture of the criminal revolutionary Gandhi, and twenty-five thousand on the capture of his henchman Nehru."

Deutschland über alles rang out again, to signal the end of the announcement. Joyce went on to the next piece of news. "Turn that off," Nehru said after a moment. Lal obeyed, plunging the cellar into complete darkness. Nehru surprised Gandhi by laughing. "I have never before been the henchman of a criminal revolutionary."

The older man might as well not have heard him. "They commended him," he said. "Commended!" Disbelief put the full tally of his years in his voice, which usually sounded much stronger and younger.

"What will you do?" Lal asked quietly. A match flared, dazzling in the dark, as he lit another cigarette.

"They shall not govern India in this fashion," Gandhi snapped. "Not a soul will cooperate with them from now on. We outnumber them a thousand to one; what can they accomplish without us? We shall use that to full advantage."

"I hope the price is not more than the people can pay," Nehru said.

"The British shot us down too, and we were on our way toward prevailing," Gandhi said stoutly. As he would not have a few days before, though, he added, "So do I."

* * *

Field Marshal Model scowled and yawned at the same time. The pot of tea that should have been on his desk was nowhere to be found. His stomach growled. A plate of rolls should have been beside the teapot.

"How am I supposed to get anything done without breakfast?" he asked rhetorically (no one was in the office to hear him complain). Rhetorical complaint was not enough to satisfy him. "Lasch!" he shouted.

"Sir?" The aide came rushing in.

Model jerked his chin at the empty space on his desk where the silver tray full of good things should have been. "What's become of what's-his-name? Naoroji, that's it. If he's home with a hangover, he could have had the courtesy to let us know."

"I will enquire with the liaison officer for native personnel, sir, and also have the kitchen staff send you up something to eat." Lasch picked up a telephone, spoke into it. The longer he talked, the less happy he looked. When he turned back to the field marshal, his expression was a good match for the stony one Model often wore. He said, "None of the locals has shown up for work today, sir."

"What? None?" Model's frown made his monocle dig into his cheek. He hesitated. "I will feel better if you tell me some new hideous malady has broken out among them."

Lasch spoke with the liaison officer again. He shook his head. "Nothing like that, sir, or at least," he corrected himself with the caution that made him a good aide, "nothing Captain Wechsler knows about."

Model's phone rang again. It startled him; he jumped. "*Bitte?*" he growled into the mouthpiece, embarrassed at starting even though only Lasch had seen. He listened. Then he growled again, in good earnest this time. He slammed the phone down. "That was our railway officer. Hardly any natives are coming in to the station."

The phone rang again. "*Bitte?*" This time it was a swear word. Model snarled, cutting off whatever the man on the other end was saying, and hung up. "The damned clerks are staying out too," he shouted at Lasch, as if it were the major's fault. "I know what's wrong with the blasted locals, by God—an overdose of Gandhi, that's what."

"We should have shot him down in that riot he led," Lasch said angrily.

"Not for lack of effort that we didn't," Model said. Now that he saw where his trouble was coming from, he began thinking like a General Staff-trained officer again. That discipline went deep in him. His voice was cool and musing as he corrected his aide: "It was no riot, Dieter. That man is a skilled agitator. Armed with no more than words, he gave the British fits. Remember that the Führer started out as an agitator too."

"Ah, but the Führer wasn't above breaking heads to back up what he said." Lasch smiled reminiscently, and raised a fist. He was a Munich man, and wore on his sleeve the hashmark that showed Party membership before 1933.

But the field marshal said, "You think Gandhi doesn't? His way is to break them from the inside out, to make his foes doubt themselves. Those soldiers who took courts rather than obey their commanding officer had their heads broken, wouldn't you say? Think of him as a Russian tank commander, say, rather than as a political agitator. He is fighting us every bit as much as much as the Russians did."

Lasch thought about it. Plainly, he did not like it. "A coward's way of fighting."

"The weak cannot use the weapons of the strong," Model shrugged. "He does what he can, and skillfully. But I can make his backers doubt themselves, too. See if I don't."

"Sir?"

"We'll start with the railway workers. They are the most essential to have back on the job, yes? Get a list of names. Cross off every twentieth one. Send a squad to each of those homes, haul the slackers out, and shoot them in the street. If the survivors don't report tomorrow, do it again. Keep at it every day until they go back to work or no workers are left."

"Yes, sir." Lasch hesitated. At last he asked, "Are you sure, sir?"

"Have you a better idea, Dieter? We have a dozen divisions here; Gandhi has the whole subcontinent. I have to convince them in a hurry that obeying me is a better idea than obeying him. Obeying is what counts. I don't care a *pfennig* as to whether they love me. *Oderint, dum metuant.*"

"Sir?" The major had no Latin.

" 'Let them hate, so long as they fear.' "

"Ah," Lasch said. "Yes, I like that." He fingered his chin as he thought. "In aid of which, the Muslims hereabouts like the Hindus none too well. I daresay we could use them to help hunt Gandhi down."

"Now that *I* like," Model said. "Most of our Indian Legion lads are Muslims. They will know people, or know people who know people. And"—the field marshal chuckled cynically—"the reward will do no harm, either. Now get those orders out, and ring up Legion-Colonel Sadar. We'll get those feelers in motion—and if they pay off, you'll probably have earned yourself a new pip on your shoulderboards."

"Thank you very much, sir!"

"My pleasure. As I say, you'll have earned it. So long as things go as they should, I am a very easy man to get along with. Even Gandhi could, if he wanted to. He will end up having caused a lot of people to be killed because he does not."

"Yes, sir," Lasch agreed. "If only he would see that, since we have won India from the British, we will not turn around and tamely yield it to those who could not claim it for themselves."

"You're turning into a political philosopher now, Dieter?"

"Ha! Not likely." But the major looked pleased as he picked up the phone.

"My dear friend, my ally, my teacher, we are losing," Nehru said as the messenger scuttled away from this latest in a series of what were hopefully called safe houses. "Day by day, more people return to their jobs."

Gandhi shook his head, slowly, as if the motion caused him physical pain. "But they must not. Each one who cooperates with the Germans sets back the day of his own freedom."

"Each one who fails to ends up dead," Nehru said dryly. "Most men lack your courage, great-souled one. To them, that carries more weight than the other. Some are willing to resist, but would rather take up arms than the restraint of *satyagraha.*"

"If they take up arms, they will be defeated. The British could not beat the Germans with guns and tanks and planes; how shall we? Besides, if we shoot a German here and there, we give them the excuse they need to strike at us. When one of their lieutenants was waylaid last month, their bombers leveled a village in reprisal. Against those who fight through nonviolence, they have no such justification."

THE LAST ARTICLE

"They do not seem to need one, either," Nehru pointed out.

Before Gandhi could reply to that, a man burst into the hovel where they were hiding. "You must flee!" he cried. "The Germans have found this place! They are coming. Out with me, quick! I have a cart waiting."

Nehru snatched up the canvas bag in which he carried his few belongings. For a man used to being something of a dandy, the haggard life of a fugitive came hard. Gandhi had never wanted much. Now that he had nothing, that did not disturb him. He rose calmly, followed the man who had come to warn them.

"Hurry!" the fellow shouted as they scrambled into his oxcart while the humpbacked cattle watched indifferently with their liquid brown eyes. When Gandhi and Nehru were lying in the cart, the man piled blankets and straw mats over them. He scrambled up to take the reins, saying, *"Inshallah,* we shall be safely away from here before the platoon arrives." He flicked a switch over the backs of the cattle. They lowed indignantly. The cart rattled away.

Lying in the sweltering semidarkness under the conceal- ment the man had draped on him, Gandhi peered through chinks, trying to figure out where in Delhi he was going next. He had played the game more than once these last few weeks, though he knew doctrine said he should not. The less he knew, the less he could reveal. Unlike most men, though, he was confident he could not be made to talk against his will.

"We are using the technique the American Poe called 'the purloined letter,' I see," he remarked to Nehru. "We will be close by the German barracks. They will not think to look for us there."

The younger man frowned. "I did not know we had safe houses there," he said. Then he relaxed, as well as he could when folded into too small a space. "Of course, I do not pretend to know everything there is to know about such matters. It would be dangerous if I did."

"I was thinking much the same myself, though with me as subject of the sentence." Gandhi laughed quietly. "Try as we will, we always have ourselves at the center of things, don't we?"

He had to raise his voice to finish. An armored personnel

carrier came rumbling and rattling toward them, getting louder as it approached. The silence when the driver suddenly killed the engine was a startling contrast to the previous racket. Then there was noise again, as soldiers shouted in German.

"What are they saying?" Nehru asked.

"Hush," Gandhi said absently, not from ill manners, but out of the concentration he needed to follow German at all. After a moment he resumed, "They are swearing at a black-bearded man, asking why he flagged them down."

"Why would anyone flag down German sol—" Nehru began, then stopped in abrupt dismay. The fellow who had burst into their hiding-place wore a bushy black beard. "We had better get out of—" Again Nehru broke off in midsentence, this time because the oxcart driver was throwing off the coverings that concealed his two passengers.

Nehru started to get to his feet so he could try to scramble out and run. Too late—a rifle barrel that looked wide as a tunnel was shoved in his face as a German came dashing up to the cart. The big curved magazine said the gun was one of the automatic assault rifles that had wreaked such havoc among the British infantry. A burst would turn a man into bloody hash. Nehru sank back in despair.

Gandhi, less spry than his friend, had only sat up in the bottom of the cart. "Good day, gentlemen," he said to the Germans peering down at him. His tone took no notice of their weapons.

"Down." The word was in such gutturally accented Hindi that Gandhi hardly understood it, but the accompanying gesture with a rifle was unmistakable.

Face a mask of misery, Nehru got out of the cart. A German helped Gandhi descend. "*Danke*," he said. The soldier nodded gruffly. He pointed the barrel of his rifle—toward the armored personnel carrier.

"My rupees!" the black-bearded man shouted.

Nehru turned on him, so quickly he almost got shot for it. "Your thirty pieces of silver, you mean," he cried.

"Ah, a British education," Gandhi murmured. No one was listening to him.

"My rupees," the man repeated. He did not understand Nehru; so often, Gandhi thought sadly, that was at the root of everything.

"You'll get them," promised the sergeant leading the

German squad. Gandhi wondered if he was telling the truth. Probably so, he decided. The British had had centuries to build a network of Indian clients. Here but a matter of months, the Germans would need all they could find.

"In." The soldier with a few words of Hindi nodded to the back of the armored personnel carrier. Up close, the vehicle took on a war-battered individuality its kind had lacked when they were just big, intimidating shapes rumbling down the highway. It was bullet-scarred and patched in a couple of places, with sheets of steel crudely welded on.

Inside, the jagged lips of the bullet holes had been hammered down so they did not gouge a man's back. The carrier smelled of leather, sweat, tobacco, smokeless powder, and exhaust fumes. It was crowded, all the more so with the two Indians added to its usual contingent. The motor's roar when it started up challenged even Gandhi's equanimity.

Not, he thought with uncharacteristic bitterness, that that equanimity had done him much good.

"They are here, sir," Lasch told Model, then, at the field marshal's blank look amplified: "Gandhi and Nehru."

Model's eyebrow came down toward his monocle. "I won't bother with Nehru. Now that we have him, take him out and give him a noodle"—army slang for a bullet in the back of the neck—"but don't waste my time over him. Gandhi, now, is interesting. Fetch him in."

"Yes, sir," the major sighed. Model smiled. Lasch did not find Gandhi interesting. Lasch would never carry a field marshal's baton, not if he lived to be ninety.

Model waved away the soldiers who escorted Gandhi into his office. Either of them could have broken the little Indian like a stick. "Have a care," Gandhi said. "If I am the desperate criminal bandit you have styled me, I may overpower you and escape."

"If you do, you will have earned it," Model retorted. "Sit, if you care to."

"Thank you." Gandhi sat. "They took Jawaharlal away. Why have you summoned me instead?"

"To talk for a while, before you join him." Model saw that Gandhi knew what he meant, and that the old man remained unafraid. Not that that would change anything,

Model thought, although he respected his opponent's courage the more for his keeping it in the last extremity.

"I will talk, in the hope of persuading you to have mercy on my people. For myself I ask nothing."

Model shrugged. "I was as merciful as the circumstances of war allowed, until you began your campaign against us. Since then, I have done what I needed to restore order. When it returns, I may be milder again."

"You seem a decent man," Gandhi said, puzzlement in his voice. "How can you so callously massacre people who have done you no harm?"

"I never would have, had you not urged them to folly."

"Seeking freedom is not folly."

"It is when you cannot gain it—and you cannot. Already your people are losing their stomach for—what do you call it? Passive resistance? A silly notion. A passive resister simply ends up dead, with no chance to hit back at his foe."

That hit a nerve, Model thought. Gandhi's voice was less detached as he answered, "*Satyagraha* strikes the oppressor's soul, not his body. You must be without honor or conscience, to fail to feel your victims' anguish."

Nettled in turn, the field marshal snapped, "I have honor. I follow the oath of obedience I swore with the army to the Führer and through him to the Reich. I need consider nothing past that."

Now Gandhi's calm was gone. "But he is a madman! What has he done to the Jews of Europe?"

"Removed them," Model said matter-of-factly; *Einsatzgruppe* B had followed Army Group Central to Moscow and beyond. "They were capitalists or Bolsheviks, and either way enemies of the Reich. When an enemy falls into a man's hands, what else is there to do but destroy him, lest he revive to turn the tables one day?"

Gandhi had buried his face in his hands. Without looking at Model, he said, "Make him a friend."

"Even the British knew better than that, or they would not have held India as long as they did," the field marshal snorted. "They must have begun to forget, though, or your movement would have got what it deserves long ago. You first made the mistake of confusing us with them long ago, by the way." He touched a fat dossier on his desk.

"When was that?" Gandhi asked indifferently. The man

was beaten now, Model thought with a touch of pride: he had succeeded where a generation of degenerate, decadent Englishmen had failed. Of course, the field marshal told himself, he had beaten the British too.

He opened the dossier, riffled through it. "Here we are," he said, nodding in satisfaction. "It was after *Kristallnacht*, eh, in 1938, when you urged the German Jews to play at the same game of passive resistance you were using here. Had they been fools enough to try it, we would have thanked you, you know: it would have let us bag the enemies of the Reich all the more easily."

"Yes, I made a mistake," Gandhi said. Now he was looking at the field marshal, looking at him with such fierceness that for a moment Model thought he would attack him despite advanced age and effete philosophy. But Gandhi only continued sorrowfully, "I made the mistake of thinking I faced a regime ruled by conscience, one that could at the very least be shamed into doing that which is right."

Model refused to be baited. "We do what is right for our *Volk*, for our Reich. We are meant to rule, and rule we do—as you see." The field marshal tapped the dossier again. "You could be sentenced to death for this earlier meddling in the affairs of the fatherland, you know, even without these later acts of insane defiance you have caused."

"History will judge us," Gandhi warned as the field marshal rose to have him taken away.

Model smiled then. "Winners write history." He watched the two strapping German guards lead the old man off. "A very good morning's work," the field marshal told Lasch when Gandhi was gone. "What's on the menu for lunch?"

"Blood sausage and sauerkraut, I believe."

"Ah, good. Something to look forward to." Model sat down. He went back to work.

Mules in Horses' Harness

MICHAEL CASSUTT

I

In the humid depths of August downtown Atlanta looked like a tomb and smelled like a charnel house, or so Gene imagined. There was less traffic than one would find on a Secession Day weekend and in all the streets between the Peachtree Tunnel and Butler House Gene counted no more than a dozen men in suits. The fragrance of nearby darktown settled on the scene like a noxious cloud. Yet each corner had its cluster of the usual painted and preening entrepreneurs of both sexes. Gene noted that the prostitutes outnumbered their potential customers, making him wonder, again, just how accurate those frightening stories out of New Orleans were.

He left the car with the contract valet at the hotel and took his time getting to the Atrium. Shelby would be late, of course; the only question for Gene was how late. So he was quite surprised to find her already seated and drinking iced tea.

"Have you called Daddy lately?" she said as soon as they'd kissed.

"Is this what passes for 'hello' at Bradley these days?" Gene said. Brother and sister were both fair and slight, though Shelby's Confederate princess camouflage made her dishwater blond hair look positively golden and reddened her lips so that most men (though not Gene) would have described them as lucious. Only when she rolled her eyes, as she did now, did Shelby truly resemble Gene, becoming, if only for a moment, a twelve-year-old—the proper age for a younger sister, in Gene's opinion. In December she would be twenty-one. "As a matter of fact, I haven't. Don't tell me you have."

"Gene . . ." This was an argument that, in one form or another, had been going on since the divorce ten years ago. "He's our *father*."

"Only chemically," Gene said. "In every other way he separated himself from our life in 1978. He's got a new wife who is exactly your age—" He was exaggerating for effect. Their step-mother was closer to twenty-three. "—and the perfect new heir. Dylan James Tyler. Christ, how pretentious can you get? I'm only surprised that he hasn't filed suit to get me to change my name." Dad was Gene, Sr. "If he gets disgusted enough, maybe he'll change *his*." Gene smiled.

Shelby sighed. "Never *mind*. I was only asking."

"Fair enough. You didn't invite me to the Atrium to ask me about Daddy, though."

"No." Shelby was suddenly distant, in a way that was uniquely hers. Confederate princesses—at least those few whose company Gene had tolerated, however briefly—were trained to pay, in any encounter between the sexes, supreme and total attention to the man.

The waiter arrived to take up one of the four places at the table. Gene ordered a whiskey, which caused Shelby to frown. "I only did it to get your attention," he said.

"I don't believe you."

"And how is school?"

"Boring."

"That's a great thing to say about the finest school for women in eleven states including Cuba." He was kidding her, but the answer disturbed him. Without parental support— there was some money from Mom, but not enough to cover more than a fraction of the tuition and costs—Shelby had worked hard to earn a scholarship. To Gene's pleasure and pride, she had chosen to study medicine, one of the few fields in which a woman could find a career these days.

"Oh, you know what I mean. It's summer. It's hot and there's no one around—"

"There's no one around Bradley in the *winter*, darling."

"Then you can imagine what it's like in summer." She was playing with her iced tea, drawing figures in the condensation. "Maybe I miss being . . . young."

"Oh, you miss being dragged all over the Confederacy by Daddy so you could wait in a hotel room while he did his 'bidness'? Or is it the custody battle you're thinking of? Now *that* was a lot of fun—"

"Gene, stop it. You know *exactly* what I mean."

Yes, he did. She was thinking of summers on the lake

and in the fields behind the big house in Marietta. Their land bordered a state park dedicated to the battle of Stone Mountain, and so, aside from park rangers and the occasional Northern tourists, they had the run of acres of woodland. And before the divorce Gene, Sr., had kept horses. "Sorry. This time of year gets to me, too."

"Why don't you go someplace? God knows you've got vacation coming to you."

"Why, *sister* dear, the project would fall ap*art* without me." He laid on a thick accent, the kind they'd heard from the contractees at the Marietta house. It never failed to make her laugh. "Differential computation is the best hope of the Confederacy. Taking a vacation would be—unpatriotic."

"I thought you were under the lash of some sissy professors at Emory."

"Soci*ology* professors at Emory," he corrected, his eyes narrowing. "I'll have you know there *are* no sissies in the Confederacy."

Gene knew this was dangerous ground, even between loving brother and sister, but battle was postponed. Shelby was on her feet, a beauty-queen smile on her face, waving. "Over here!"

Before Gene could turn around, a handsome young man in a gray suit was at the table, kissing Shelby in a manner generally reserved, in public at least, for family members. Then he offered his hand to Gene. "I'm Charlie Holder," he said.

"My fiancé," Shelby said.

Gene tried hard not to despise Holder on sight, a task made unusually difficult by the speed with which this prospective brother-in-law made himself at home, and by the deference shown him by the waiter. He didn't even *ask* for Mr. Holder's order. In the space of seconds, without any proper signs at all, Gene found himself no longer host, but guest. Holder had even interposed his tanned, well-exercised frame between Gene and Shelby.

"I perceive that you've been here *before*, Mr. Holder," Gene said, smiling so pleasantly his lips ached.

Shelby, who recognized the coming fury, reached out for Gene's hand. "Charlie works for Sumner and Horn," she said, naming with what Gene took to be excessive enthusiasm the biggest law firm in the state. "Their offices are right across the street."

"I'm just an associate, of course," Holder said. "On what they pay me I'm lucky if I can eat here twice a month."

"Does that mean supporting my dear sister will be especially . . . challenging?" Gene said this while looking at Shelby, who had given up anger and was now attempting to soothe him by looking hurt. He said, "Now don't you worry, sister. I'm not *seriously* questioning Mr. Holder's abilities—"

"Please call me Charlie."

"Charlie it is." He made it sound like a disease. "But I *am* the senior male in the family. I have certain responsibilities regarding my sister's welfare." He turned to Shelby. "Charlie understands that."

Holder smiled right back. "Perfectly."

"Then," Shelby said, "dear brother, you'll be pleased to know that Charlie has been nominated for a partnership. He'll have it *long* before the wedding."

With those words Shelby let him know that she had gone over to the other side. Gene felt like Longstreet at the Last Redoubt: out of ammunition, Sherman's blue hordes swarming up the parapet. The war was over; lunch was only beginning.

Current popular wisdom suggested that a diet of greens was one way to ward off the summer vapors. Like Shelby and Holder, Gene found himself staring at a Cantonese salad for which he now had even less enthusiasm than ever. He signaled the waiter and got a second drink. Shelby was so busy tittering at Holder that she didn't even notice.

Exactly on cue, two bites into the salad, Holder looked up. "Shelby tells me you work in differentials. That must be an exciting field."

"Well, I'm sure it can't compare to contract law," Gene said.

"Come on." Holder was determined not to let Gene insult him. "It's the cutting edge of Confederate technology. Without your—what do they call them?—bugs and counters we'd be nothing but a warmer Canada." He stabbed at the salad, and dabbed at his mouth. "We handle all D.C.D.'s work, you know."

Differential Calculating Devices was the Atlanta conglomerate that dominated the global market. There wasn't a government that functioned without the machines, not even the government of the United States of America, which would sooner buy from Satan than from the Confederacy. The company had the further bonus of being Gene's ostensible employer. "If you're involved in D.C.D., then you know more about our 'importance' than I do. I'm just a soldier."

"A soldier who's fighting a particularly interesting war, I hear. Project Deconstruction, isn't it?"

Gene's glance shifted from Holder, who was impassive in his command of the situation, to Shelby, who allowed herself a wiggle of triumph at the obvious perfection of her catch. "That's not a name I'm used to hearing at city lunches," Gene said finally, hoping that a bit of dignified reproach might be sufficient to raise him back to equal standing with this person.

"Certainly not," Holder said. "It's privileged. Family stuff. But, then, we're all family here, aren't we, Shel?" Not only did Holder suddenly use what had heretofore been Gene's private name for Shelby, but he caused her to blush, confirming to Gene that she had, indeed, spilled to Holder all of the many "privileged" details she knew about Deconstruction.

Gene examined the bottom of his drink and wished for a sudden outbreak of war—or death—anything to deliver him from this lunch. But fate declined to oblige.

Shelby was saying, "You know, I've heard bits and pieces of this, but never quite the whole story. I'm dying to know. That is, if it's all right."

"I have no objection . . . if your brother doesn't," Holder said, neatly positioning Gene to label his own sister as untrustworthy.

"If we can't take such a fine example of Southern womanhood into our confidence, what kind of men are we?" Gene said, slipping into his little-used country club locutions. "Shelby, darling, Project Deconstruction is a device by which we unravel the past so that we might actually tell the future."

"I *do* know that much."

"One of the professors at Emory—a tsarist refugee named Asimoff—theorized some years ago that one could predict future events mathematically. But nobody had any idea how to translate events into symbols, nor the ability to perform calculations involving millions or billions of symbols.

"Over the years people have made attempts to break down historical events, social movements, people, personality traits, even the weather, into irreducible units which somebody started calling 'memes.' They'd wind up with these vast systems and complex formulae that would just go up the chimney the moment you applied them to some known historical situation, like the Secession. The world-model bore no relationship to the real world." He smiled. "Unfortunately, it's taken us years to realize this. We keep adjusting the numbers and redoing the formulas, but we still haven't managed to come up with a system that tells you that if Abraham Lincoln is assassinated on July 4, 1863, by a Copperhead named Nathan Shaw, the Confederacy will be occupied by Federal troops for forty years." He spread his hands. "At the moment, I guess you could say we're stuck."

Holder, who had, Gene thought, been waiting for an opportunity, chose this moment to say, "Until now."

"I beg your pardon?"

"You're the first person on Deconstruction who's had the courage to admit that it's stuck. I've thought so for some time."

"Imagine how pleased we'll all be to know how our attorneys judge our work."

"Please don't be angry," Charlie said, aflush with enthusiasm. "A lot of valuable data has come out of the project so far. I'm not aware of *any* unhappiness at the higher levels of the company—"

"Thank God." Gene tried not to be sarcastic.

"But the problem, as you surely know, with companies as large as D.C.D., is the flow of information. Acting, as we do, as counsel to the whole organization, we tend to have a better view of what's going on than most of the gentlemen on the thirty-fourth floor." He leaned forward and lowered his voice. Shelby had effectively ceased to exist. "The pharmaceutical division has a project of its own that may provide you with your missing link."

"What would drugs have to do with Deconstruction?"

"I'm not talking about drugs."

Ordinarily Gene wouldn't have deigned to play a guessing game. He was stopped in this case by Shelby's getting up from her chair. "Excuse me," she said, "I don't want to inhibit you two—"

Holder couldn't get to his feet fast enough. "I'm sorry, Shel, that was rude of me." He looked to Gene for help.

"Charlie," Gene said, forcing out the words, "why don't you and I get together some other time? I'd really like to hear about this missing link."

"I'll call tonight at six," Holder said, extending his hand. To Shelby he said, "I have to get back."

Before Shelby could protest, Gene said, "Walk him out, Shel," giving the name a little spin. He picked up the check. "This is my treat." Arm in arm, the couple left.

Shelby's initial assault had driven Gene back from his lines . . . but he had not broken. It was time for a counterattack.

"Are you going to see him?"

Two hours later, it was Shelby who came to call. Gene was sitting in his office at Emory watching some students playing a half-hearted game of rounders when she knocked. She asked the question before she even sat down.

"What choice do I have, Shel? I realize he's your fiancé, but he's also involved in my work. I'm sort of *bound* to listen to what he has to say."

"I suppose." There was silence while Shelby fumed. "I'm sorry I even introduced you two."

"Sooner or later you'd have had to, honey. Unless you were planning to elope to Havana." Gene was doing a bit of fuming, too. "Look, there's no sense in fighting. It never really occurred to me that you were ready for marriage—"

"Gene, I'm going to be twenty-one!"

"This is the twentieth century, Shel. You haven't even finished school. Are you going to just throw it all away?" He hauled out the secret weapon. "I thought you wanted to be better than Mom."

"That's a shitty thing to say."

"My, my, we've been learning some naughty words at school."

Shelby stood up and started to leave. At the door she paused long enough to say, "I can't vote and I can't own property and if I'm too old or ugly I'm doomed to be a nurse or a schoolteacher for the rest of my life. And here you are, a man, telling me I'm *supposed* to be self-reliant and independent, that we've got this brave new South here, but even you have to treat me like a little girl." Then she gently closed the door, a gesture which startled Gene because it was not the slam one expected from a child, or from a Confederate princess.

He was still wondering what he should do about Shelby when the contract girl out front asked permission to go home for the evening, adding that a Mr. Charleston Holder was here.

"I feel as though I'm here to sell you something," Holder said, removing a folder from his briefcase and passing it to Gene. Night had fallen; the quad outside the office window was dark and quiet, as was the rest of the building, save for the lone contract janitor swishing his mop in the hall.

"Is there a problem with that?"

Holder shrugged. "I was raised to believe that a gentleman didn't solicit business. It would come to him in the natural order of things." He smiled again, all charm. "Yet your father is a salesman, and a very successful one, too, from what Shelby says—"

"But he's no gentleman," Gene said, irritated again at Holder's immersion—there was no other word—in Tyler family matters. "We shouldn't pursue that subject or I'll have to call you out—whether I love my father or not."

"I meant no offense. I'm unused to working outside normal channels." Gene doubted that this was even remotely true, but chose not to argue the point. The best parts of his own life were outside normal channels. "What I've given you," Holder said, getting back to business, "is a report on what is, forgive me, D.C.D.'s most closely held and radical research: the creation of life itself."

For a man unused to the crass protocols of business, Holder knew just how obtrusive he could be and still allow Gene to understand what he was reading. The only words he honestly heard were "radical" and "creation." What he saw before him was a memorandum describing the design and construction of microscopic creatures called, in what must have been some lab technician's idea of a joke, "federals."

Federals were originally cousins to planaria and other relatively simple organisms whose genetic material had been altered to give them greater "intelligence" and, more interestingly, mobility, thus removing them from the kingdom of the protozoans, making them animals.

"This sounds like a fascinating discovery. I would have thought it would take millions of federal 'years' to accomplish that sort of evolution."

"I believe that it did," Holder said, reaching for the memo and flipping ahead several pages. "A generation of federals is born, grows up, and dies in only a few minutes. And though there's no indication in this document, the project has been going on since 1939."

Fifty years ago the United States had been involved in the disastrous World Wide War against the German States and their allies. Although the Confederacy had maintained a public neutrality, Southern sympathies were clearly with their Northern brothers, and many Confederate companies supplied arms and materials to U.S. armies. Gene knew that D.C.D.'s first differential calculators had been employed to that end. And the McCarran Pharmaceutical Company, later acquired by D.C.D. to become its bio division, was rumored to have been involved in the search for chemical weapons. "These things aren't dangerous, are they?"

"Well, they *have* been kept under wraps for a long time," Holder said, as if that were sufficient answer.

"This is fascinating information," Gene said, "but I'm afraid I don't know what I can do with it." He slid the memo back to Holder, who pinned it in place with his hand.

"Please correct me if I'm wrong, but didn't you say that the problem with the Deconstruction process is that it lacks a means of testing?"

"Yes." Gene was vaguely irritated now. For a moment he had been able to think of Holder as just another suit; now he was remembering that he would soon be his brother-in-law. Before the irritation could surface, however, another thought did: the missing link. Means of testing. "Oh," was all he could say.

Holder was smiling. "How big is this federal population?" Gene said, reaching for the memo with a bit more vigor.

"There are several discrete populations," Holder said,

"but I don't think you'd have any trouble putting together a single group numbering, say, a hundred million individuals."

"Which is a number far greater than the population of the United States and Confederacy in 1863 . . . dear God."

"I don't ordinarily approve of blasphemy," Holder said, "but in this case, it's highly appropriate, don't you agree?"

To be the Almighty Himself—ruling a microcosmic world! "Don't say another word."

Project Deconstruction was relatively small as D.C.D. enterprises went. At its peak no more than three dozen employees were charged to its budget. With the cutback in funding and other reductions due to staff vacations, there were only about fifteen people who would have the faintest interest in what Gene was doing. And of those fifteen, only three had authority over him.

Four of those who did not gathered in Gene's office the next morning as he explained what he wanted them to do. They were all graduate students in differential sciences and largely true to the stereotype: extraordinarily pale, uniformly bespectacled, deliberately ill-fed, and unusually intelligent. The only one who deviated was Stashower, a red-haired farmboy from Nashville whose utter and complete self-absorption was the only thing that kept Gene's more predatory instincts in check. That and his resolve never to fish off the company pier.

Stashower was the first to see the possibilities. "Jesus, Gene, we've been beating our heads against this how-do-we-simulate-organic-life-in-a-differential? shit for two years! If we can record the growth, death, and migration patterns of a hundred million federals, we'll increase the memes in our own model by a factor of ten thousand."

One of the others, a bearded boy from the red clay country, joined in. He was eager to get to work on the transition models. "We can start out just arbitrarily assigning certain values to federal activities, then keep crunching them over and over again until we match Real Life."

They were all out of their chairs now, sketching systems on the board. "Gentlemen, gentlemen!" Gene said. "I hate to interrupt, but permit me a boring management kind of query: When can it be ready and how much will it cost?"

"Two months," Stashower said, with his charming Yankee naïveté, "and you're going to spend twice as much in differential time charges." Gene nodded, mentally doubling the estimates again. He didn't need a Deconstruction program to tell him that Stashower tended to underestimate such matters.

The meeting broke up. Gene was proud of them, but his pride was tempered by annoyance at the speed with which they absorbed the new idea. Their new energy and their prior lack of protest made it clear that at the age of twenty-five he was already too old for creative work.

II

On the Fourth of July, 1863, President Abraham Lincoln made a surprise visit to Union veterans at a temporary hospital in Georgetown, near Washington. By all accounts it was an impulsive gesture, a search, perhaps, for distraction. The President was awaiting news of the seige of Vicksburg and, more importantly, of Lee's advances through nearby Gettysburg, Pennsylvania. But for the circumstances, it would not have been one of Lincoln's more memorable speeches. He was halfway through it when a man wearing the coat of a hospital orderly stepped out of the crowd and fired a pistol at Lincoln, who was hit twice in the chest.

In spite of the presence of several doctors, the first to reach him was a Captain Butler, his aide, who heard Lincoln's last words ("I'm sorry"). The President was carried to a room in the hospital, where he died within hours.

The assassin was later identified as a Nathan Shaw twenty-eight-year-old itinerant minister from Baltimore with a history of abolitionist activity and ties to Copperhead democrats unhappy with Lincoln's prosecution of the war. Shaw claimed that he was angered by Lincoln's call for a new draft—that it was unfair for a rich man to be able to pay a three-hundred-dollar bounty to avoid serving the Union—but it was later suspected, though never proved, that he had ties to Confederate agents and may, in fact, have been stalking Lincoln since March of 1861. In any case, Shaw went to the gallows in October, unrepentant and silent as to his accomplices.

Vice-president Hannibal Hamlin of Maine took the oath of office just as the news of the victories at Gettysburg and Vicksburg reached the capital. Lincoln's allies, greater in number after his death than prior to it, and his rivals joined in a call for the utter destruction of the Confederacy. It was hardly necessary. Word of Lincoln's death at the hands of an assassin had reached Meade's troops before either army had fully withdrawn from Gettysburg. In a frenzy, Union forces trapped Lee's battered men on the northern bank of the swollen Potomac near the misnamed Falling Waters, capturing their leader and effectively destroying the Army of Virginia.

In the west, Generals Grant and Sherman began a total war of attrition, moving through Mississippi, Alabama, Tennessee, and Georgia like the horsemen of doom, laying waste to Jackson, Montgomery, Memphis, and Atlanta, then wheeling north. Union forces under Meade met them below burned Richmond, which, like Carthage, had ceased to be a human abode, and pursued Longstreet, catching him at Lynchburg. It was now July 1864. Both political parties sought to name Grant as their candidate, and the Democrats won. Grant turned over leadership of the Union armies, and directorship of the "pacification" of the South, to Sherman, and handily defeated President Hamlin that November.

August gave way to an unusually warm September, but Gene's relationship with Shelby remained cool. They were not openly at war: Shelby indicated that she forgave him for "stealing" her fiancé once she learned that, but for the single meeting, Gene and Charlie never saw each other unless she was present. Nevertheless, they ceased to communicate with the old regularity. Gene assumed it was the pressure of her studies in addition to the logistical challenges of a wedding due a Confederate princess. (He kept up with these developments thirdhand, through Shelby's friends, since Gene, Sr., had elected to bestow his advice upon his only daughter.) But he eventually realized that he himself had drawn back from her.

Perhaps it was because of the nightmares.

He had been living with the events of the Lincoln assassination for so long it was no surprise. Every time the boys ran their federal-enhanced program, an event which occurred as many as ten times a day, it started all over again. And that night, as he churned in his bed in his dormitory rooms, Gene would see himself shot . . . see himself shooting . . . see the burning fields . . . find himself yoked, as in the title of the most famous of the postwar novels, like a mule in horse's harness.

Sometimes he would simply lie awake briefly, wondering again how his country could have recovered from such devastation to the point where all over the eleven states dark-skinned contract employees, the children of slaves, labored to make the tiny bugs of which differential machines were composed—the machines which no one in the world, not the United States, not the Yellow Empire, not Britain, could match. Comforted by these schoolbook images, he would sleep again.

Other times he would not. Then, as if testing his resolve to be better than he had been, he would dress and get in the car, driving all the way into the city, to stare at the contract boys under the lamp posts. Occasionally he would stop and meet the eyes of one of them . . . but the moment a step was made in his direction, he would be off, heart pounding, cursing his own weakness. So he would be "good" again for at least two days. The dreams would be calmer; then it would start again.

So it went all through August and September and into October, while Stashower and the others rewrote history, while Gene told the project manager what he needed to know in order to take full credit, until one day late in the month, a week before Redoubt Day, when Shelby came to visit.

"You've been avoiding me," she said, pouting.

"Don't be silly. Maybe I haven't called, but neither have you."

"Nevertheless, because I love you, because of what you mean to me, I'm going to forgive you."

Gene almost laughed. He knew that with a woman like Shelby—or more precisely, what Shelby, with repeated exposure to Dad and his new wife, was becoming—he must kill an assertion, not merely wound it.

"In that case, I apologize. May I plead overwork? The project of a lifetime? And how is school?"

"I'm dropping out," she said calmly. "That's why I came to see you—" She paused, eclipsed by his sudden fury.

"Are you out of your *mind*? You worked *years* to get where you are! You've only got two more *semesters* before you get a certificate!"

"A certificate I don't need," she said, eclipsing him in return.

"Of course. *Charlie* will take care of you. I can't believe this."

"Before either of us says more that we will regret, why don't we talk about the weather. Or your work. How *is* it going?" Just like that, her tone had changed. They might have been having tea at the Atrium . . . or lying in the field behind the house in Marietta, looking at the sky. Gene was willing to play along. He wasn't ready to give up his sister.

"To tell you the truth, Shel, it's amazing. Three months ago you'd never have convinced me that it would be possible to create a model—a simulation—of our world so detailed that it accurately 'predicts' what the price of wheat was in northeastern Kansas in 1888—"

" 'Predicts' what it *was?*"

"The language is sadly inadequate to the task, especially when we're talking about end results as opposed to processes. There were three things we needed to do to make Deconstruction work: We needed to convert human beings and all their traits and activities, from having children to voting for President, into numbers. Then we had to find a way to move those numbers—billions of them, actually—in a way that paralleled the growth or evolution of a society. That's where Charlie's federals came in. We'd always thought that the laws that controlled societies were similar to those that controlled biological processes, but we never had any biological process to play with until now.

"The real challenge, of course, was the interface between the numbers and the federals—the translation, we call it. That's what we've been running over and over again, adjusting, changing and rewriting, for months, until we finally got an overall program—all three elements working together—that allowed us not only to recapitulate American history from 1863 until now, but to learn things we didn't know ourselves."

"The price of wheat in Kansas." She seemed amused.

"The length of women's skirts in 1915. The number of people killed by the Yellow Flu in 1946. It's like walking into a library of books you've never been able to open . . . until now."

"And what good is it?"

"Well, once you've got a working model, you can go back and change certain key events—or change things that happen to certain key people. Ulysses Grant fires his cabinet in 1872 and doesn't get impeached. Jeremy King is only wounded in 1968, and the contract system is abolished. That sort of thing."

"I can't believe you can find one microscopic Abraham Lincoln."

"Oh, you can't. One lesson we're learning is that individuals are almost completely irrelevant to history—as individuals. I mean, yes, there *are* so-called 'Great Men,' but they appear in our translation program . . . not in the biological model. In fact, we've worked up a pretty good profile of the Key Individual, the Great Man, and found that at any given time, there are dozens if not hundreds of them around . . . waiting for the confluence of events that will allow them to fulfill their 'destiny.' Or whatever.

"I mean, in some of our models, poor old Abe Lincoln, who was really nothing more than a victim of circumstances, forced into war because of the Secession and killed just as it appeared he would win, lives long enough to emerge as a Great Man. In that same model, Longstreet serves as a general in a longer, more drawn-out war and never emerges as the President who rebuilt the Confederacy."

"Don't you find this sad?"

"Why should I?"

"To know that, at a certain level, nothing you do with your life really matters . . . that you're only responding to these biological imperatives. Taking advantage of—what did you call it?—the confluence of events." She shuddered. "Charlie will hate this." With some of the tension bled out of their conversation, Shelby apparently felt it was safe to mention Holder.

"Don't kid yourself, Shel. Your Charlie will *love* this. What businessman wouldn't want to know the future?"

"You don't know him at all, Gene. He wants to believe that he can *change* the future. In many ways, he's a lot like one of those Great Men. He has ideas, big ideas. He wants the South to be more than it is. He thinks we've become rigid and calcified— "

"He's right about that. But I never got the idea that *he* had just the solutions to everyone's problems. Great."

"It's one of the reasons I love him, Gene."

"Do you really? Or do you, dear sister, just love the idea that you've done what you were raised to do: caught yourself a great man?"

"I think I should leave." She stood up.

"I'm glad you came. By the way—" She was waiting at the door. There were tears in her eyes, of sadness or defiance he didn't know. He pulled a small package out of his desk. He'd bought it weeks earlier, not knowing when or if he would have the opportunity to deliver it. "It's a week late . . . Happy birthday."

Shelby took it, but she did not thank him.

The federal "world" was located at D.C.D.'s Decatur site in a little-used warehouse off-limits to all but a few personnel—"deep, dark government work" was the rumored reason. It worked so well that Gene grew to wonder just how much deep, dark government work the company had done in the past. Nevertheless, he controlled access . . . which was why, on his way into the building the next day, he was so surprised to find Holder coming out.

The man was shameless. He shouldn't have been within miles of the place, but all he had to say was, "Playing hooky from Emory, I see."

"Once a week, whether I need to or not," Gene said, as furious at himself for showing his anger as he was at Holder. "How the hell did you get in there?"

Holder smiled. "When I was going to law school I worked here one summer as a security guard. Relax, Gene, as far as anyone at D.C.D. is concerned I'm tied up with a libel action in Pine Mountain. No one is going to kick you out of your sandbox."

"Have you seen enough? Or would you like an official tour?" He flashed his badge at the guard, a man Holder's age whose name Gene didn't know, who would, if Gene had his way, be working somewhere else at this time tomorrow.

"Love to." As they breached the innermost door, Holder said quietly, "Don't be too hard on old Matthew—" The guard. "—I made it impossible for him to keep me out." One gentleman to another. Holder had just made it impossible for Gene to punish the guard.

The federals lived in what always struck Gene as the world's biggest ant colony—a glass-roofed chamber the size of a rounders court, over which Stashower and his colleagues hovered like angels on high, their cameras and telescopes trained on heaven's floor. "Incredible," Holder said. "It's just incredible."

Holder seemed genuinely impressed, which pleased and disgusted Gene. "Well, Charlie, there never would have been a link between Deconstruction and the federals if not for you."

To Gene's greater annoyance, Holder didn't deny it. "It was pure blind luck. Did I tell you? My first job at the firm was handling insurance forms for D.C.D. I amused myself by reading some of the résumés and personnel files. That's how I learned that you were the key man on Deconstruction." Oblivious to Gene's growing outrage, Holder went on to deliver the final blow: "In fact, that's how I learned that you had a sister at Bradley."

By now Gene was so used to creating scenarios that they came to him unbidden. He didn't like the one being created for him now . . . this Confederate hustler using his past connections and purloined material to uncover people's secrets . . . seeking Gene out in order to make him do his bidding . . . and worst of all, cultivating *his own sister* in order to forge a connection between them. What else did Holder know?

Holder nodded toward Stashower and the others. "Your boys seem to like looking through the scopes."

"They've convinced themselves the federals have 'cities' and 'fields.' I think they just enjoy playing microcosmic god." Gene had looked once and only found the action blurred to incomprehensibility. When he could look at all, that is. In the accelerated life of a federal, one "day" lasted two seconds, and the constant flickering of the "sun" gave Gene a head-ache. "But, then, they're not the only ones."

Holder laughed out loud. "Come on, Gene. I'm not *that* manipulative!"

When Gene offered no comment, Holder lowered his voice and said, "Look, you're gong to come out of this a happy man. When the boys on thirty-four see what you've got here, they'll be on you like a duck on a June bug."

"Assuming they don't already know."

"So far I've managed to refrain from enlightening them . . . much as I'd love to. This one belongs to Gene Tyler."

"How will I ever thank you?"

Holder couldn't miss the sarcasm; he hesitated just long enough to let Gene know he hadn't. "You'll find a way." Then, back in the country-club mode, he slapped Gene on the back. "Got to run." Over his shoulder, he called, "When am I going to see you at Shel's?"

"He's using you," he said.

Shelby blushed. "You know, Gene, a simple 'hello' would be nice. Do you like the couch?" They had just sat down in the tiny living room of Shelby's flat.

"Forget the couch, Shel. I'm telling you, you don't have any idea what kind of monster you're involved with."

"You're making this awfully difficult."

"Blame it on your Charlie. Your 'great man.' "

He was hurting her; he knew it. "Shel—" He reached for her, but she shied away.

"Don't touch me."

"I'm sorry. But I can't just let this happen. This man has . . . lied his way into our lives all because he wants what my project can give him. It's power he's after, Shel—"

"Oh, Gene, grow up!" She was facing him now. "You've been searching for months to drive a wedge between Charlie and me. You couldn't do it with sweet reason, so now it's because of your nasty little project." She was angrier now than Gene had ever seen. "Are you *sure* that's what the real problem is?"

"Whatever do you mean?"

Shelby stared at him. "I know more about you than you think I do. . . ."

Oh, Christ, he thought. *No.*

"Gene, I'm not going to judge you. I love you. I know you had a much more difficult time with Daddy than I did. Whom you love is your business—"

"Shelby, stop this. You sound like some radio mentalist."

"Well, you chose not to share this secret with me, so I'm probably going to say this all wrong." There was a surprising amount of sarcasm in her voice, and for a moment Gene realized that he had underestimated her will. "I don't know anything about a world in which men go with other men. I can't even *picture* it," she said, no doubt picturing it all too vividly, as Gene had often pictured Shelby with some man. Who was it who said you can't be intimidated by people once you see them naked and on their knees? "But what I see is that you're jealous."

"This is ridiculous." It was his turn to recoil from her. He got up from the couch and looked for his jacket.

"Is it? Then prove it to me. Because until you do, I have to assume that you're acting like this because you want Charlie for yourself."

Before she finished he was out the door.

He stayed late in his office that night preparing the document about Holder. It was easier than he thought it would be. His familiarity with the D.C.D. data system allowed him greater access to its personnel files—and those of its captive law firm—than any clerk could achieve. All of it, the résumé, the D.C.D. background search (quite secret; gentlemen did not check up on the claims of gentlemen), evaluations, ancillary materials from a financial institution with ties to D.C.D., all integrated with Gene's perceptions of Holder's personality traits, combined in one "character" who could be put through the Deconstruction model.

The program ran to completion in less than ten minutes and the translation only took another hour, but Gene couldn't bring himself to read it for much longer than that.

Just as he suspected. The marriage would go well for a year, until Shelby produced an heir. (If Shelby did not get pregnant, this phase was merely extended by a year or so.) Holder would be a partner by then. He would also have become, again, a patron of the more reputable houses of pleasure, having given them up upon announcement of the engagement. He would dote on the child, boy or girl, and would encourage Shelby's work in social causes, charities, whatnot, but she would be required to have at least a second child, while Holder would run for his first office—something in the state legislature. . . .

Within ten years Holder would be governor; within fifteen, senator or higher. He would campaign for contract rights, and, given reasonable assumptions concerning demographics and economic growth, and the lack of major wars, he would be successful—for the male underclass of the Confederacy.

But what of Shelby? She and women like her would receive none of this largesse. It was too ingrained in the Confederate culture, where archaic antebellum attitudes about women were hardened and set for all time by the forty-year Occupation. It was commonly thought that, for the Confederacy, Lincoln had died too late. Now Gene knew that for the Shelbys of the world—who never had the chance to become real people—Lincoln died too soon.

It was early the next morning when he found the nerve to call her. "You'll notice I'm saying 'hello' this time."

"Hello, Gene." He could hear the relief in her voice. He tried not to wonder if Holder was by her side. "I—"

"Don't say anything," he told her. "Just meet me at the Atrium at once."

He had the data folded and resting by his plate when Shelby came in. She seemed genuinely happy to see him. "I've felt so awful because I didn't thank you for the present!" she said, as if their last discussion had never happened.

"That's all right. I was being a beast."

They passed a quarter of an hour in small talk. News of Gene, Jr. Plans for the wedding. "I'm glad you mentioned the wedding," Gene said.

She grew quiet. "Charlie and me?"

"You said you wanted proof." He had his hand on the printout. Shelby stared at it.

"I suppose that's it. My future life?"

"One of your future lives."

She held out her hand. He passed the paper to her. She

looked at it without unfolding it. "How strange—to hold your life in your hand."

"Read it."

"I'd rather not."

"Shel—" He cleared his throat. "I guess I was just thinking about . . . what you could be."

She set the paper aside. "I'm sorry for what I said about you and Charlie."

"Frankly, my dear, he's not my type."

Shelby blushed in disbelief. Enjoying her embarrassment, Gene leaned back in his chair. His eyes roamed around the Atrium and found one of the busboys, a husky contractee. "I like men," he found himself saying, amazingly relieved, "from the lower classes. Much darker than Charlie."

Shelby glanced at the busboy, then looked at Gene. For a moment they were children again, sharing a secret they could keep from Daddy. "Do you ever want to change? To want women?"

"I used to. But, you know, Shel, I don't think I can." Suddenly she had won. Gene wanted to laugh. This Great Man business was fine for the history books, even those yet unwritten, but what could it possibly mean to someone with a wayward child? An old man dying of cancer? A woman in love? Tell them they can't change their futures? That they are nothing more than mules in horses' harness? You might as well kill them.

"I'm sorry, Shel. I really am. I've been a real shit about this. Maybe we can just start over. . . ."

Her face showed equal parts triumph and terror. She reached for his hand. "Yes." Then she sat back, crumpled the paper, and tore it in half. "I should go."

"I'll see you soon."

"At Daddy's next week?"

"Don't push your luck, Shel." Then, with a smile, she was gone.

"Would you like me to get rid of that for you?" the waiter said, nodding toward the crumpled printout.

"Yes," Gene said. "Throw it away."

The waiter scooped it up along with the plates and walked off. Gene remembered that there was a place on

Beecher Road where like-minded gentlemen could meet for a bit of excitement. He looked at his watch. The staff meeting wouldn't take place until four.

He had plenty of time.

Lenin in Odessa

GEORGE ZEBROWSKI

> *"Lenin is a rotten little incessant intriguer. . . . He just wants power. He ought to be killed by some moral sanitary authority."*
>
> —H. G. WELLS
> (Letter dated July 1918, sent to the *New York Weekly Review*)

1

In 1918, Sidney Reilly, who had worked as a British agent against the Germans and Japanese, returned to our newly formed Soviet Russia. He was again working for England and her allies, but this time he was also out for himself, intending to assassinate Vladimir Ilyich Lenin and bring himself to power at the head of the regime that he imagined his homeland deserved.

Jew though he was, Reilly saw himself as a Russian coming home to make good. It angered him that another expatriot, Lenin, had gotten there first—with German help, and with what Reilly considered suspect motives. Reilly was convinced that his own vision was the proper response to the problems of life in Russia, which, as Sigmund Rosenblum, a bastard born in Odessa, he had escaped in his youth. He believed that the right man could, with sufficient thought and preparation, make of history his own handiwork.

It was obvious to me that Reilly's thinking was a curious patchwork of ideas, daring and naive at the same time, but lacking the systematic approach of a genuine scientific philosophy. His distaste for the bourgeois society that had oppressed him in his childhood was real, but he had developed a taste for its pleasures.

Of course, Reilly knew that he was sent in as a tool of the British and their allies, who opposed Bolshevism from the outset, and he let them continue to think that they could count on him, for at least as long as his aims would not conflict with theirs. Lenin himself had been eased back into Russia by the Germans, who hoped that he would take Russia out of the war in Europe. No German agent could have done that job better. Reilly was determined to remove or kill Lenin, as the prelude to a new Russia. What that Russia would be was

103

not clear. The best that I could say about Reilly's intentions was that he was not a czarist.

There was an undeniable effectiveness in Reilly, of which he was keenly aware. He was not a mere power seeker, even though he took pride in his physical prowess and craft as a secret agent; to see him as out for personal gain would be to underestimate the danger that he posed to those of us who understand power more fully than he did.

Reilly compared himself to Lenin. They had both been exiles from their homeland, dreaming of return, but Vladimir Ilyich Ulyanov had gone home on German hopes and seized power. Russia would be remade according to a heretical Marxism, in Reilly's view. Lenin's combination of revisionist ideology and good fortune was intolerable to Reilly; it wounded his craftsman's ego, which saw chance as a minor player in history. He ignored the evidence of Lenin's organizational skills, by which a spontaneous revolution had been shaped into one with purpose.

Reilly viewed himself and his hopes for Russia with romantic agony and a sense of personal responsibility that were at odds with his practical intellect and shrewdness, both of which should have told him that he could not succeed. But Reilly's cleverness delighted in craft and planning. His actions against the Germans and Japanese were all but inconceivable to the common man. Even military strategists doubted that one man could have carried out Reilly's decisive schemes. His greatest joy was in doing what others believed to be impossible.

Another clue to Reilly's personality lay in his love of technology, especially naval aviation. He was an accomplished flyer who looked to the future of transport. He was fascinated, for example, by the Michelson-Morley experiment to detect the aether wind, which was predicted on the basis of the idea of the earth's motion through a stationary medium. When this detection failed, Reilly wrote a letter to a scientific journal (supplied to me by one of my intellectual operatives in London) insisting that the aether was too subtle a substance to register on current instruments. One day, he claimed, aether ships would move between the worlds.

Reilly's mind worried a problem until he found an imaginative solution; then his practical bent would find a way to accomplish the task. As a child he was able to remain invisible to his family simply by staying one step ahead of their house search for him. As a spy he once eluded his pursuers by joining them in the search for him. However rigorous and distasteful the means might be, Reilly would see what was possible and not flinch. With Lenin he understood that a single mind could change the world with thought and daring; but unlike Vladimir Ilyich, Reilly's mind lacked the direction of historical truth. He was capable of bringing into being new things, but they were only short-lived sports, chimeras of an exceptional but misguided will. His self-imposed exile from his homeland had left divisions as incongruous as his Irish pseudonym.

Sidney Reilly sought escape from the triviality of his life, in which his skills had been used to prop up imperialism. He had been paid in money and women. By the time he returned to Russia, I already sensed that he would be useful to me. It seemed possible, on the basis of his revolutionary leanings, that I might win him to our cause.

2

"Comrade Stalin," Vladimir Ilyich said to me one gloomy summer morning, "tell me who is plotting against us this week." He was sitting in the middle of a large red sofa, under a bare spot on the wall where a czarist portrait had hung. He seemed very small as he sank into the dusty cushions.

"Only the ones I told you about last week. Not one of them is practical enough to succeed."

He stared at me for a moment, as if disbelieving, but I knew he was only tired. In a moment he closed his eyes and was dozing. I wondered if his bourgeois conscience would balk at the measures we would soon have to take to keep power. It seemed to me that he had put me on the Bolshevik Central Committee to do the things for which he had no stomach. Too many opportunists were ready to step into our shoes if we stumbled. Telling foe from ally was impossible; given the chance, anyone might turn on us.

Reilly was already in Moscow. I learned later that he had come by the usual northern route, and had taken a cheap hotel room. On the following morning, he had abandoned that room, leaving behind an old suitcase with some work clothes in it. He had gone to a safe house, where he met a woman of middle years who knew how to use a handgun.

She was not an imposing figure—an impression she knew how to create; but there was no doubt in Reilly's mind that she would pull the trigger with no care for what happened to her afterwards.

Lenin's death was crucial to Reilly's plot, even though he knew that it might make Vladimir Ilyich a Bolshevik martyr. Reilly was also depending on our other weaknesses to work for him. While Trotsky was feverishly organizing the Red Army, we were dependent on small forces—our original Red Guard, made up of factory workers and sailors, a few thousand Chinese railway workers, and the Latvian regiments, who acted as our Praetorian Guard. The Red Guard was loyal but militarily incompetent. The Chinese served in return for food. The Latvians hated the Germans for overrunning their country, but had to be paid. Reilly knew that he could bribe the Latvians and Chinese to turn against us, making it possible for the czarist officers in hiding to unite and finish the job. With Lenin and myself either arrested or dead, he could then turn south and isolate Trotsky, who had taken Odessa back from the European allies and was busy shipping in supplies by sea. His position there would become impossible if the British brought in warships. If we failed in the north, we would be vulnerable from two sides.

Lenin's death would alter expectations in everyone. Reilly's cohorts would seize vital centers throughout Moscow. Our czarist officers would go over to Reilly, taking their men with them. The opportunists among us would desert. Reilly's leaflets had already planted doubts in them. Lenin's death would be their weather vane. Even the martyrdom of Vladimir Ilyich, I realized, might not be enough to help us.

As I gazed at Lenin's sleeping face, I imagined him already dead and forgotten. His wife Nadezhda came into the room and covered him with a blanket. She did not look at where I sat behind the large library desk as she left.

3

"Comrade Lenin has been shot!" the messenger cried as he burst into the conference room.

I looked up from the table, "Is he dead?"

The young cadet was flushed from the cold. His teeth chattered as he shook his head in denial. "No—the doctors have him."

"Where?" I asked.

He shook his head. "You're to come with me, Comrade Stalin, for your own safety."

"What else do you know?" I demanded.

"Several of our units, including Cheka, are not responding to orders."

"They've gone over," I said, glancing down at the lists of names I had been studying.

The cadet was silent as I got up and went to the window. The gray courtyard below was deserted. There was no sign of the Latvian guards, and the dead horse I had seen earlier was gone. I turned my head slightly, and saw the cadet in the window glass. He was fumbling with his pistol holster. I reached under my long coat and grasped the revolver in my shoulder harness, then turned and pointed it at him under my coat. He had not drawn his pistol.

"No, Comrade Stalin!" he cried, "I was only unsnapping the case. It sticks."

I looked into his eyes. He was only a boy, and his fear was convincing.

"We must leave here immediately, Comrade Stalin," he added quickly. "We may be arrested at any moment."

I slipped my gun back into its sheath. "Lead the way."

"We'll go out the back," he said, his voice shaking with relief.

"Did it happen at the factory?" I asked.

"Just as he finished his speech, a woman shot at him," he replied.

I tried to imagine what Reilly was doing at this very moment.

The cadet led me down the back stairs of the old office block. The iron railing was rusting, and the stairwell smelled of urine. On the first landing the cadet turned around and found his courage.

"You *are* under arrest, Comrade Stalin," he said with a nervous smile.

My boot caught him under the chin. I felt his neck break as he fired the pistol into the railing, scattering rust into my face. He fell backward onto the landing. I hurried down and wrenched the gun from his stiffening fingers, then went back up to the office.

There was a hiding place behind the toilet, but I would use it only if I had to. I came into the room and paused, listening, but there was only the sound of wind rattling the windows. Was it possible that they had sent only one person for me? Something had gone wrong, or the cadet had come for me on his own initiative, hoping to ingratiate himself with the other side. All of which meant I could expect another visit at any moment.

I hurried down the front stairs to the lobby, went out cautiously through the main doors, and spotted a motorcycle nearby—probably the cadet's. I rushed to it, got on, and started it on the first kick. I gripped the handlebars, gunned the engine into a roar, then turned the bike around with a screech and rolled into the street, expecting to see them coming for me.

But there was no one on the street. Something had gone wrong. The Latvians had been removed to leave me exposed, but the next step, my arrest and execution, had somehow been delayed. Only the cadet had showed up.

I tried to think. Where would they have taken Vladimir Ilyich? It had to be the old safe house outside of Moscow, just south of the city. That would be the only place now. I wondered if I had enough petrol to reach it.

4

Lenin was at the country house. He was not mortally wounded. His assassin was there also, having been taken prisoner by the Cheka guards who had gone with Lenin to the factory.

"Comrade Stalin!" Vladimir Ilyich exclaimed as I sat

down by his cot in the book-lined study. "You are safe, but our situation is desperate."

"What has happened?" I asked, still unsteady from the long motorcycle ride.

"Moscow has fallen. Our Latvian regiments have deserted, along with our Chinese workers. Most of the Red Guards have been imprisoned. The Social Revolutionaries have joined the counterrevolution. My assassin is one of them. I suspect that killing me was to have been their token of good faith. There's no word from Trotsky's southern volunteers. There doesn't seem to be much we can do. We might even have to flee the country."

"Never," I replied.

He raised his hand to his massive forehead. "Don't shout, I'm in terrible pain. The bullet was in my shoulder, but I have a headache that won't stop."

I looked around for Nadezhda, but she was not in the room. I saw several haggard, unfamiliar faces, and realized that no one of great importance had escaped with Lenin from Moscow. By now they were in Reilly's hands, dead, or about to be executed. He would not wait long. I had underestimated the Bastard of Odessa.

"What shall we do?" I asked.

Vladimir Ilyich sighed and closed his eyes. "I would like your suggestions."

"We must go where they won't find us easily," I replied. "I know several places in Georgia."

His eyes opened and fixed on me. "As long as you don't want to return to robbing banks."

His words irritated me, but I didn't show it.

"We needed the money," I said calmly, remembering that he had once described me as crude and vulgar. Living among émigré Russians in Europe had affected his practical sense.

"Of course, of course," he replied with a feeble wave of his hand. "You are a dedicated and useful man."

There was a muffled shot from outside. It seemed to relax Vladimir Ilyich. Dora Kaplan, his assassin, had been executed.

5

Just before leaving the safe house, we learned that Lenin's wife had been executed. Vladimir Ilyich began to rave as we led him out to the truck, insisting to me that Reilly could not have killed Nadezhda, and that the report had to be false. I said nothing; to me her death had been inevitable. As Lenin's lifelong partner, and a theoretician herself, she would have posed a threat in his absence. Reilly's swiftness in removing her impressed me. Lenin's reaction to her death was unworthy of a Bolshevik; suddenly his wife was only an unimportant woman. Nadezhda Krupskaya had not been an innocent.

We fled south, heading for a railway station that was still in our hands, just south of Moscow, where a special train was waiting to take us to Odessa. If the situation in that city turned out to be intractable, we would attempt to reach a hiding place in my native Georgia.

Three Chekas came with us in the truck—a young lieutenant and two privates, both of whom had abandoned the czar's forces for the revolution. I watched the boyish faces of the two privates from time to time, looking for signs of doubt. The lieutenant, who was also a mechanic, drove the old Ford, nursing the truck through the ten muddy kilometers to the station.

"He could have held her hostage," Vladimir Ilyich insisted to me as the truck sputtered and coughed along. "Don't you think so? Maybe he thought we were dead, and she would be of no use to him as a hostage?"

For the next hour he asked his own questions and gave his own impossible answers. It depressed me to hear how much of the bourgeois there was still in him. I felt the confusion in the minds of the two Chekas.

It began to rain as the sun went down. We couldn't see the road ahead. The lieutenant pulled over and waited. Water seeped in on us through the musty canvas. Vladimir Ilyich began to weep.

"She was a soldier in our cause," I said loudly, hating his sentimentality.

He stared out into the rainy twilight. Lightning flashed as he turned to look at me, and for a moment it seemed that his face had turned to marble. "You're right," he said, eyes wild with conviction, "I must remember that."

Of course, I had always disliked Nadezhda's hovering, familiar-like ways. She had been a bony raven at his shoulder, forever whispering asides, but I had always taken great care to be polite to her. Now more than ever I realized what a buttress she had been to Vladimir Ilyich.

The rain lessened. The lieutenant tried to start the Ford, but it was dead.

"There's not much time," I said. "How much farther?"

"Less than half a kilometer."

"We'll go on foot," I said. "There's no telling who may be behind us."

I helped Vladimir Ilyich down from the truck. He managed to stand alone, and refused my arm as we began to march on the muddy road. He moved steadily at my side, but his breathing was labored.

We were within sight of the station when he collapsed.

"Help!" I called out.

The lieutenant and one of the privates came back, lifted Vladimir Ilyich onto their shoulders, and hurried ahead with him. It was like a scene from the street rallies, but without the crowds.

"Is he very ill?" the other private asked me as I caught up.

I did not answer. Ahead, the train waited in a conflagration of storm lamps and steam.

6

Our train consisted of a dining car, a kitchen, one supply car, and the engine. A military evacuation train was being readied on the track next to ours, to carry away those who would be fleeing Moscow in the next day or two. I was surprised at this bit of organization. When I asked how it had been accomplished, a sergeant said one word to me: "Trotsky."

We sped off into the warm, misty night. Vladimir Ilyich recovered enough to have dinner with me and our three soldiers. The plush luxury of the czarist interior seemed to brighten his mood.

"I only hope that Trotsky is in Odessa when we arrive," he said, sipping his brandy, "and that he can raise a force we can work with. Our foreign vendors have been paid, fortunately, but we will have to keep our southern port open to be supplied."

He was looking into the large mirror at our right as he spoke. I nodded to his reflection.

"The troops behind us," the youthful lieutenant added, "will help insure that."

Vladimir Ilyich put down his glass and looked at me directly. "Do you think, Comrade Stalin, that we hoped for too much?" He sounded lost.

"No," I answered. "We have popular support. The people are waiting to hear from you. Reilly's pamphlets have struck a nerve of longing with promises of foreign help and bourgeois progress, but he is actually depending only on the uncertainty of our followers. His mercenaries won't count for much when the news that you are alive gets out. Most of his support can be taken from him with that alone, but we will have to follow our victory with a period of terror, to compel loyalty among the doubters."

He nodded to me, then looked into the darkness of the window. In that mirror we rode not only in a well-appointed, brightly lit dining room, but in the cave of all Russia.

"You must get some sleep," I said.

We found blankets and made ourselves comfortable on the leather couches. The lieutenant turned down the lights.

I tried to sleep, but my thoughts seemed to organize themselves to the clatter of the train wheels. Contempt for my own kind crept into me, especially for the idealists in our party. Too many utopian fools were setting themselves up against their own nature and what was possible. They did not grasp that progress was like the exponent in one of Einstein's fashionable equations—a small modifying quantity that has an effect only when the big term grew very large. They failed to see that only when the biggest letter of human history, material wealth, became sufficiently large, would there be a chance for social progress. Only then would we be able to afford to become humane. My role in this revolution was to remember this fact, and to act when it was neglected. . . .

7

Our mood was apprehensive as our train pulled into Odessa. We stepped out into bright sunlight, and a deserted station.

"We don't know what may have happened here," I said.

"There hasn't been time," Vladimir Ilyich replied. His voice was gruff after three days on the train, and he seemed ready to bark at me in his usual way. I felt reassured. This was the Lenin who had taken a spontaneous uprising and interpreted the yearning of the masses, so they would know what to do; the Lenin who would make ours a Communist revolution despite Marx. Like Reilly, Lenin was irreplaceable. Without him there would only be a struggle for power, with no vision justifying action.

Suddenly, a Ford Model T sedan pulled into the station and rattled toward us down the platform. I took Lenin's arm, ready to shove him out of harm's way; but the car slowed and stopped.

"Welcome!" the driver shouted as he threw open the door and got out. When he opened the back door for us, I saw that he was Trotsky's youngest son, Sergei. I greeted him and smiled, but his eyes worshiped only Lenin as we got into the back seat, as if I didn't exist.

Sergei drove quickly, but the ride was comfortable. With the windows closed, Odessa seemed distant. We climbed a hill and saw the sun glistening on the Black Sea. I remembered the smell of leather in my father's shoe shop. Warm days gave the shop a keener odor. I pictured myself in the small church library, which was open to sons who might one day be priests. The books had been dusty, the air full of waxy smells from the lamps and candles. I remembered the young girl I had seduced on a sunny afternoon, and for an instant the world's failings seemed far away. I began to wonder if we were driving into a betrayal.

A crowd surrounded us as we pulled into the center of the city. They peered inside, saw Lenin, and cheered.

Trotsky was waiting for us with a company of soldiers on the courthouse steps. We climbed out into a bright paradise of good feeling. Trotsky saluted us, then came down and embraced Vladimir Ilyich, who looked shabby in his brown waistcoat under that silk blue sky.

The crowd cheered them. As Lenin turned to address the throng, I felt Reilly plotting against us in Moscow, and I knew in that moment what it would take to stop him.

"Comrades!" Lenin cried, regaining his old self with one word. "A dangerous counterrevolution has seized Moscow! It is supported by the foreign allies, who are not content with defeating Germany. They also want our lands. But we will regroup here, and strike north. With Comrade Trotsky's Red Army, and your bravery, we shall prevail . . ."

As he spoke, I wondered if anyone in Moscow would believe that he was still alive, short of seeing him there. Open military actions would not defeat Reilly in any reasonable time. It would take years, while the revolution withered, especially if Reilly avoided decisive battles. Reilly had to be killed as quickly and as publicly as possible. Like Lenin he was a leader who needed his followers as much as they needed him. There was no arguing with this fact of human attachment. Without Reilly, the counterrevolution would collapse in a matter of days. His foreign supporters would not easily shift their faith to another figure.

He had to die in a week, two at the latest, and I knew how it would have to be done. There was no other way.

"Long live Comrade Lenin!" the crowd chanted—loudly enough, it seemed to me, for Reilly to hear it in his bed in Moscow.

8

From the reports I had read about Reilly's life and activities, I suspected that he was a man who liked to brood. It was a way of searching, of pointing himself toward his hopes. He prayed to himself, beseeching a hidden center, where the future sang of sweet possibilities.

As head of his government, he would have to act against both czarists and Bolsheviks. He could count on czarists joining his regime, but he would never trust a Bolshevik. Czarists would be fairly predictable in their military actions, but Bolsheviks, he knew, would spare no outrage to bring him down.

He was probably in what remained of the British Embassy in Moscow, sipping brandy in the master bedroom, perhaps playing with the idea that he might have joined us. I knew there had been efforts to recruit him for our intelligence service. He would have disappeared and reemerged as another man, as he did when he left Odessa for South America in his youth, to escape his adulterous family's bourgeois pesthole. It would have been simple justice for him to return in the same way, even as a Bolshevik.

But for the moment, Russia was his to mold. I could almost hear the Jew congratulating himself in that great bed of English oak.

Within the week there would be a knock on his bedroom door, and a messenger would bring him word that Lenin was in Odessa. Reilly would sit up and lean uncomfortably against the large wooden headboard, where once there had been luxurious pillows (a pity that the mobs had torn them to pieces). He would read the message with a rush of excitement, and realize that a British seaplane could get him to Odessa within a day. The entire mission would flash through his mind, as if he were remembering the future.

He would fly to the Black Sea, then swing north to Odessa, using the night for cover. What feelings would pass through him as he landed on the moonlit water? Here he was, returning to the city of his childhood in order to test himself against his greatest enemies. The years would run back in his mind as he sat in the open doorway of the amphibious aircraft, breathing in the night air and remembering the youth who had startled himself with his superiority to the people around him. He had blackmailed his mother's lover for the money to escape Odessa. The man had nearly choked when he'd called him father.

He would know that he was risking his counterrevolution by coming here alone. The Bolsheviks would be able to pull down any of his possible successors. But it was the very implausibility of his coming here alone that would protect him, he would tell himself. Tarnishing Lenin's name by revealing Germany's hand in his return was not enough. Lenin had to die before his followers could regroup, before reports of his death were proven false. Only then would the counterrevolution be able to rally the support of disenchanted czarists, moderate democrats, churchmen, and Mensheviks—all those who still hoped for a regime that would replace monarchy but avoid Bolshevism.

Reilly was a hopeless bourgeois, but more intelligent than most, hence more dangerous, despite his romantic imagination. He sincerely believed that Bolshevism would only gain Russia the world's animosity, and insure our country's cultural and economic poverty.

He would come into Odessa one morning, in a small boat, perhaps dressed as a fisherman. He would savor the irony of his return to the city of his youth, wearing old clothes, following the pattern of all his solo missions. It was a form of rebirth. He trusted it, and so would I.

9

The warmer climate of Odessa speeded Lenin's physical recovery. He would get up with the sun and walk along the street that led to the Great Steps (the site of the 1905 massacre of the townspeople by czarist Cossacks, which the expatriot homosexual director, Sergei Eisenstein, later filmed in Hollywood). I let the Cheka guards sleep late, and kept an eye on Vladimir Ilyich myself.

One morning, as I watched him through field glasses from the terrace of our hotel, he stopped and gazed out over city and sea, then sat down on the first step, something he had not done before. His shoulders slumped in defeat. He was probably reminiscing about his bourgeois European life with Krupskaya, and regretting their return to Russia. His euphoric recovery during the first week after our arrival had eroded, and he had slowly slipped back into a brooding silence.

As I watched, a man's head floated up from the steps below the seated Lenin. The figure of a fisherman came into view, stopped next to Vladimir Ilyich, and tipped his hat to him. I turned my glasses to the sea and searched. Yes! There was something on the horizon—a small boat, or the wings of a seaplane. The reports I had received of engine sounds in the early morning had been correct.

I whipped back to the two figures. They were conversing amiably. Vladimir Ilyich seemed pleased by the encounter, but then he had always shown a naive faith in simple folk, and sometimes spoke to them as if he were confessing. Krupskaya's death had made him unobservant, and Reilly was a superb actor.

Reilly was taking his time out of sheer vanity, it seemed to me. He would not kill his great rival without first talking to him.

I put down the field glasses, checked my revolver, then slipped it into my shoulder holster and hurried downstairs, wearing only my white shirt and trousers. I ran through the deserted streets, sweating in the warm morning air, expecting at any moment to hear a shot. I reached the row of houses just above the Great Steps, slipped into a doorway, then crept out.

The blood was pounding in my ears as I peered around the corner. Lenin and the fisherman were sitting on the top step with their back to me. Vladimir Ilyich was gesturing with his right hand. I could almost hear him. The words sounded familiar.

I waited, thinking that the man was a fisherman, and that I had expected too much of Reilly.

Then the stranger put his arm around Vladimir Ilyich's shoulders. What had they been saying to each other? Had they reached some kind of rapprochement? Perhaps Lenin was in fact a German agent, and these two had been working together all along. Could I have been so wrong? The sight of them sitting side by side like old friends unnerved me.

The fisherman gripped Lenin's head with both hands and twisted it. The neck snapped, and in that long moment it seemed to me that he would tear the head from the body. I drew my revolver and rushed forward.

"Did you think it would be that easy, Rosenblum?" I said as I came up behind him.

The fisherman turned and looked up at me, not with surprise, but with irritation, and let go of Lenin.

"Don't move," I said as the corpse slumped face down across the stairs.

The fisherman seemed to relax, but he was watching me carefully. "So you used him as bait," he said, gesturing at the body. "Why didn't you just kill him yourself?"

His question was meant to annoy me.

He looked out to sea. "Yes, an economical solution to

counterrevolution. You liquidate us both while preserving the appearance of innocence. You're certain that Moscow will fall without me."

I did not reply.

He squinted up at me. "Are you sure it's me you've captured? I may have sent someone else." He laughed.

I gestured with my revolver. "The seaplane—only Sidney Reilly would have come here in one. You had to come quickly."

He nodded to himself, as if admitting his sins.

"What did Vladimir Ilyich say to you?" I asked.

His mood changed, as if I had suddenly given him what he needed.

"Well?" I demanded.

"You're very curious about that," he said without looking at me. "I may not tell you."

"Suit yourself."

He considered for a moment. "I will tell you. He feared for Russia's future, and that moved me, Comrade Stalin. He was afraid because there are too many of the likes of you. I was surprised to hear it from him."

"The likes of me?"

"Yes, the cynics and doubters who won't be content until they've made the world as barren for everyone else as they've made it for themselves. His wife's death brought it all home to him, as nothing else could have. His words touched me."

"Did you tell him that you killed her?"

"I was too late to save her."

"And he believed you?"

"Yes. I told him who I was. His dreams were dead. He wanted to die."

My hand was sweaty on the revolver. "Bourgeois sentiments destroyed him. I hope you two enjoyed exchanging idealist bouquets. Did you tell him what you would have done if you had caught us in Moscow?"

He looked up and smiled at me. "I would have paraded all of you through the streets without your pants and underwear, shirttails flapping in the breeze!"

"And then killed us."

"No, I wouldn't have made martyrs. Prison would have served well enough after such ridicule."

"But you came here to kill him."

"Perhaps not," he said with a sigh. "I might have taken him back as my prisoner, but he wanted to die. I killed him as I would have an injured dog. In any case, Moscow believes that he died weeks ago."

"Well, you've botched it all now, haven't you?"

"At least I know that Lenin died a true Bolshevik."

"So now you claim to understand Bolshevism?"

"I always have. True Bolshevism contains enough constructive ideas to make possible a high social justice. It shares that with Christianity and the French Revolution, but it's the likes of you, Comrade Stalin, who will prevent a proper wedding of ideals and practical government." He smiled. "Well, perhaps the marriage will take place despite you. The little Soviets may hold fast to their democratic structures and bring you down in time. Who knows, they may one day lead the world to the highest ideal of statesmanship—internationalism."

"Fine words," I said, tightening my grip on the revolver, "but the reality is that you've done our Soviet cause a great service—by being a foreign agent, a counterrevolutionary, a Jewish bastard, and Lenin's assassin, all in one."

"I've only done *you* a service," he said bitterly, and I felt his hatred and frustration.

"You simply don't understand the realities of power, Rosenblum."

"Do tell," he said with derision.

"Only limited things are possible with humanity," I replied. "The mad dog within the great mass of people must be kept muzzled. Civil order is the best any society can hope to achieve."

The morning sun was hot on my face. As I reached up to wipe my forehead with my sleeve, Reilly leaped over Lenin's body and fled down the long stairs.

I aimed and fired, but my fingers had stiffened during our little dialogue. My bullet got off late and missed. I fired again as he jumped a dozen steps, but the bullet hit well behind him.

"Stop him!" I shouted to a group of people below him. They had just come out of the church at the foot of the stairs. "He's killed Comrade Lenin!"

Reilly saw that he couldn't get by them. He turned and started back toward me, drawing a knife as he went. He stopped and threw it, but it struck the steps to my right. I laughed, and he came for me with his bare hands. I aimed, knowing that he might reach me if I missed. It impressed me that he would gamble on my aim rather than risk the drop over the great railings.

I pulled the trigger. The hammer struck a defective cartridge. Reilly grunted as he sensed victory, and kept coming.

I fired again.

The bullet pierced his throat. He staggered up and fell bleeding at my feet, one hand clawing at my heavy boots. His desperation was both strange and unexpected. Nothing had ever failed for him in quite this way. Its simplicity affronted his intelligence.

"I also feel for dogs," I said, squeezing a round into the back of his head. He lay still, free of life's metaphysics.

I holstered my revolver and nudged his body forward. It sprawled next to Lenin, then rolled down to the next landing. The people from the church came up, paused around Vladimir Ilyich, then looked up to me.

"Vladimir Ilyich's assassin is dead!" I shouted. "The counterrevolution has failed." A breeze blew in from the sea and cooled my face. I breathed deeply and looked saddened.

Reilly was hung up by his neck in his hometown, but I was the only one who knew enough to appreciate the irony. Fishermen sailed out and towed his seaplane to shore.

Lenin's body was placed in a tent set up in the harbor area, where all Odessans could come to pay their last respects. Trotsky and I stood in line with everyone else. One of our warships fired its guns in a final salute.

10

We sent the news to Moscow in two carefully timed salvos.

First, that Reilly, a British agent, had been killed during an attempt on Lenin's life; then, that our beloved Vladimir Ilyich had succumbed to wounds received, after a valiant struggle.

We went north with our troops, carrying Lenin's coffin, recruiting all the way. Everywhere people met our train with shouts of allegiance. Trotsky appointed officers, gathered arms, and kept records. He also scribbled in his diary like a schoolgirl.

I knew now that I was Lenin's true heir, truer than he had been to himself in his last weeks. I would hold fast to that and to Russia, especially when Trotsky began to lecture me again about the urgent need for world revolution.

In the years that followed I searched for men like Reilly to direct our espionage and intelligence services. If he had been turned, our KGB would have been built on a firmer foundation of skills and techniques. He would have recruited English agents for us with ease, especially from their universities, where the British played at revolution and ideology, and sentimentalized justice. I could not rid myself of the feeling that in time Rosenblum would have turned back to his mother country; he had never been, after all, a czarist. I regretted having had to kill him on that sunny morning in Odessa, because in later years I found myself measuring so many men against him. I wondered if a defective cartridge or a jammed revolver could have changed the outcome. Probably not. I would have been forced to club him to death. Still, he might have disarmed me. . . .

But on that train in 1918, on the snowy track to Moscow, I could only wonder at Reilly's naive belief that he could have altered the course of Soviet inevitability, which now so clearly belonged to me.

Abe Lincoln in McDonald's

JAMES MORROW

He caught the last train out of 1863 and got off at the blustery December of 2009, not far from Christmas, where he walked well past the turn of the decade and, without looking back, settled down in the fifth of July for a good look around. To be a mere tourist in this place would not suffice. No, he must get it under his skin, work it into his bones, enfold it with his soul.

In his vest pocket, pressed against his heart's grim cadence, lay the final draft of the dreadful Seward Treaty. He needed but to add his name—Jefferson Davis had already signed it on behalf of the secessionist states—and a cleft nation would become whole. A signature, that was all, a simple "A. Lincoln."

Adjusting his string tie, he waded into the chaos grinding and snorting down Pennsylvania Avenue and began his quest for a savings bank.

"The news isn't good," came Norman Grant's terrible announcement, stabbing from the phone like a poisoned dagger. "Jimmy's test was positive."

Walter Sherman's flabby, pumpkinlike face whitened with dread. "Are you sure?" *Positive*, what a paradoxical term, so ironic in its clinical denotations: nullity, disease, doom.

"We ran two separate blood checks, followed by a fluorescent antibody analysis. Sorry. Poor Jim's got Blue Nile Fever."

Walter groaned. Thank God his daughter was over at the Sheridans'. Jimmy had been Tanya's main Christmas present of three years ago—he came with a special note from Santa—and her affection for the old slave ran deep. Second father, she called him. Walter never could figure out why Tanya had asked for a sexagenarian and not a whelp like most kids wanted, but who could know the mind of a preschooler?

If only one of their others had caught the lousy virus.

125

Jimmy wasn't the usual chore-boy. Indeed, when it came to cultivating a garden, washing a rug, or painting a house, he didn't know his nose from the nine of spades. Ah, but his bond with Tanya! Jimmy was her guardian, playmate, confidant, and, yes, her teacher. Walter never ceased marveling at the great discovery of the last century: if you chained a whelp to a computer at the right age (no younger than two, no older than six), he'd soak up vast tracts of knowledge and subsequently pass them on to your children. Through Jimmy and Jimmy alone, Tanya had learned a formidable amount of plane geometry, music theory, American history, and Greek before ever setting foot in kindergarten.

"Prognosis?"

The doctor sighed. "Blue Nile Fever follows a predictable course. In a year or so, Jimmy's T-cell defenses will collapse, leaving him prey to a hundred opportunistic infections. What worries me, of course, is Marge's pregnancy."

A dull dread crept through Walter's white flesh. "You mean—it could hurt the baby?"

"Well, there's this policy—the Centers for Disease Control urge permanent removal of Nile-positive chattel from all households containing pregnant women."

"Removed?" Walter echoed indignantly. "I thought it didn't cross the pigmentation barrier."

"That's probably true." Grant's voice descended several registers. "But *fetuses*, Walter, know what I'm saying? *Fetuses*, with their undeveloped immune systems. We don't want to ask for trouble, not with a retrovirus."

"God, this is depressing. You really think there's a risk?"

"I'll put it this way. If my wife were pregnant—"

"I know, I know."

"Bring Jimmy down here next week, and we'll take care of it. Quick. Painless. Is Tuesday at two-thirty good?"

Of course it was good. Walter had gone into orthodontics for the flexible hours, the dearth of authentic emergencies. That, and never having to pay for his own kids' braces. "See you then," he replied, laying a hand on his shattered heart.

The President strode out of Northeast Federal Savings and Loan and continued toward the derby-hatted Capitol. Such an exquisite building—at least some of the city remained intact; all was not glass-faced offices and dull boxy banks. "If we were still on the gold standard, this would be a more normal transaction," the assistant manager, a fool named Meade, had whined when Abe presented his coins for conversion. Not on the gold standard! A Democrat's doing, no doubt.

Luckily, Aaron Green, Abe's Chief Soothsayer and Time-Travel Advisor, had prepared him for the wondrous monstrosities and wrenching innovations that now assailed his senses. The self-propelled railway coaches roaring along causeways of black stone. The sky-high mechanical condors whisking travelers across the nation at hundreds of miles per hour. The dense medley of honks, bleeps, and technological growls.

So Washington was indeed living in its proper century— but what of the nation at large?

Stripped to the waist, two slave teams were busily transforming Pennsylvania Avenue, the first chopping into the asphalt with pick axes, the second filling the gorge with huge cylindrical pipes. Their sweat-speckled backs were free of gashes and scars—hardly a surprise, as the overseers carried no whips, merely queer one-chamber pistols and portable Gatling guns.

Among the clutter at the Constitution Avenue intersection— signs, trash receptacles, small landlocked lighthouses regulating the coaches' flow—a pair of green arrows commanded Abe's notice. CAPITOL BUILDING, announced the eastward-pointing arrow. LINCOLN MEMORIAL, said its opposite. His own memorial! So this particular tomorrow, the one fated by the awful Seward Treaty, would be kind to him.

The President hailed a cab. Removing his stovepipe hat, he wedged his six-foot-four frame into the passenger compartment—don't ride up front, Aaron Green had briefed him— and offered a cheery "Good morning."

The driver, a blowsy woman, slid back a section of the soft rubbery glass. "Lincoln, right?" she called through the opening like Pyramus talking to Thisbe. "You're supposed to be Abe Lincoln. Costume party?"

"Republican."

"Where to?"

"Boston." If any city had let itself get mired in the past, Abe figured, that city would be Boston.

"Boston, *Massachusetts*?"

"Correct."

"Hey, that's crazy, Mac. You're talking six hours at least, and that's if we push the speed limit all the way. I'd have to charge you my return trip."

The President lifted a sack of money from his greatcoat. Even if backed only by good intentions, twentieth century currency was aesthetically satisfying, that noble profile on the pennies, that handsome three-quarter view on the fives. As far as he could tell, he and Washington were the only ones to score twice. "How much altogether?"

"You serious? Probably four hundred dollars."

Abe peeled the driver's price from his wad and passed the bills through the window. "Take me to Boston."

"They're so *adorable!*" Tanya exclaimed as she and Walter strolled past Sonny's Super Slaver, a Chestnut Hill Mall emporium second in size only to the sporting goods store. "Ah, look at *that* one—those big ears!" Recently weaned babies jammed the glass cages, tumbling over themselves, clutching stuffed jackhammers and toy garden hoses. "Could we get one, Pappy?"

As Walter fixed on his daughter's face, its glow nearly made him squint. "Tanya, I've got some bad news. Jimmy's real sick."

"Sick? He looks fine."

"It's Blue Nile, honey. He could die."

"Die?" Tanya's angelic face crinkled with the effort of fighting tears. What a brave little tomato she was. "Soon?"

"Soon." Walter's throat swelled like a broken ankle. "Tell you what. Let's go pick out a whelp right now. We'll have them put it aside until . . ."

"Until Jimmy"—a wrenching gulp—"goes away?"

"Uh-huh."

"Poor Jimmy."

The sweet, bracing fragrance of newborn chattel wafted into Walter's nostrils as they approached the counter, behind which a wiry Asian man, tongue pinned against his upper lip, methodically arranged a display of Tarbaby Treats. "Now *here's* a girl who needs a friend," he sang out, flashing Tanya a fake smile.

"Our best slave has Blue Nile," Walter explained, "and we wanted to—"

"Say no more." The clerk lifted his palms as if stopping traffic. "We can hold one for you clear till August."

"I'm afraid it won't be that long."

The clerk led them to a cage containing a solitary whelp chewing on a small plastic lawn mower. MALE, the sign said. TEN MONTHS. $399.95. "This guy arrived only yesterday. You'll have him litter trained in two weeks—this we guarantee."

"Had his shots?"

"You bet. The polio booster's due next month."

"Oh, Daddy, I *love* him," Tanya gushed, jumping up and down. "I completely *love* him. Let's bring him home tonight!"

"No, tomato. Jimmy'd get jealous." Walter gave the clerk a wink and, simultaneously, a twenty. "See that he gets a couple of really good meals this weekend, right?"

"Sure thing."

"Pappy?"

"Yes, tomato?"

"When Jimmy dies, will he go to slave heaven? Will he get to see his old friends?"

"Certainly."

"Like Buzzy?"

"He'll definitely see Buzzy."

A smile of intense pride leaped spontaneously to Walter's face. Buzzy had died when Tanya was only four, yet she remembered, she actually remembered!

So hard-edged, the future, Abe thought, levering himself out of the taxi and unflexing his long cramped limbs. Boston had become a thing of brick and rock, tar and glass, iron and steel. "Wait here," he told the driver.

He entered the public gardens. A truly lovely spot, he decided, sauntering past a slave team planting flower beds—impetuous tulips, swirling gladiolus, purse-lipped daffodils. Not far beyond, a white family cruised across a duck pond in a swan-shaped boat peddled by a scowling adolescent with skin like obsidian.

Leaving the park, Abe started down Boylston Street. A hundred yards away, a burly Irish overseer stood beneath a gargantuan structure called the John Hancock Tower and began raising the scaffold, thus sending aloft a dozen slaves equipped with window-washing fluid. Dear Lord, what a job—the facade must contain a million square yards of mirrored glass.

Hard-edged, ungiving—and yet the city brought Abe peace.

In recent months, he had started to grasp the true cause of the war. The issue, he realized, was not slavery. As with all things political, the issue was power. The rebel states had seceded because they despaired of ever seizing the helm of state; as long as its fate was linked to a grimy, uncouth, industrialized north, Dixie could never fully flower. By endeavoring to expand slavery into the territories, those southerners who hated the institution and those who loved it were speaking with a single tongue, saying, "The Republic's true destiny is manifest: an agrarian Utopia, now and forever."

But here was Boston, full of slaves and steeped in progress. Clearly the Seward Treaty would not prove the recipe for feudalism and inertia Abe's advisors feared. Crude, yes; morally ambiguous, true; and yet slavery wasn't dragging the Republic into the past, wasn't retarding its bid for modernity and might.

"Sign the treaty," an inner voice instructed Abe. "End the war."

Sunday was the Fourth of July, which meant the annual backyard picnic with the Burnsides, boring Ralph and boorish Helen, a tedious afternoon of horseshoe tossing, conspicuous drinking, and stupefying poolside chat, the whole ordeal relieved only by Libby's barbecued spare ribs. Libby was one of those wonderful yard-sale items Marge had such a knack for finding, a healthy, well-mannered female who turned out to be a splendid cook, easily worth ten times her sticker price.

The Burnsides were an hour late—their rickshaw puller, Zippy, had broken his foot the day before, and so they were forced to use Bubbles, their unathletic gardener—a whole glorious hour of not hearing Ralph's thoughts on the Boston sports scene. When they did finally show, the first thing out of Ralph's mouth was, "Is it a law the Sox can't own a decent pitcher? I mean did they actually pass a *law*?" and Walter steeled himself. Luckily, Libby used a loose hand with the bourbon, and by three o'clock Walter was so anesthetized by mint juleps he could have floated happily through an amputation, not to mention Ralph's vapid views on the Sox, Celtics, Bruins, and Patriots.

With the sixth drink his numbness segued into a kind of contented courage, and he took unflinching stock of himself. Yes, his wife had probably bedded down with a couple of her teachers from the Wellesley Adult Education Center—that superfluously muscled pottery instructor, most likely, though the drama coach also seemed to have a roving dick—but it wasn't as if Walter didn't occasionally use his orthodontic chair as a motel bed, wasn't as if he didn't frolic with Katie Mulligan every Wednesday afternoon at the West Newton Hot Tubs. And look at his splendid house, with its Jacuzzi, bowling alley, tennis court, and twenty-five-meter pool. Look at his thriving practice. His portfolio. Porsche. Silver rickshaw. Graceful daughter flopping through sterile turquoise waters (damn that Happy, always using too much chlorine). And look at his sturdy, handsome Marge, back-floating, her pregnancy rising from the deep end like a volcanic island. Walter was sure the kid was his. Eighty-five percent sure.

He'd achieved something in this life.

At dusk, while Happy set off the fireworks, the talk got around to Blue Nile. "We had Jimmy tested last week," Walter revealed, exhaling a small tornado of despair. "Positive."

"God, and you let him stay in the house?" wailed Ralph, fingering the grip of his Luger Parabellum P08. A cardboard rocket screeched into the sky and became a dozen crimson starbursts, their reflections cruising across the pool like phosphorescent fish. "You should've told us. He might infect Bubbles."

"It's a pretty hard virus to contract," Walter retorted. A buzz bomb whistled overhead, annihilating itself in a glittery blue-and-red mandala. "There has to be an exchange of saliva or blood."

"Still, I can't believe you're keeping him, with Marge pregnant and everything."

Ten fiery spheres popped from a Roman candle and sailed into the night like clay pigeons. "Matter of fact, I've got an appointment with Grant on Monday."

"You know, Walter, if Jimmy were mine, I'd allow him a little dignity. I wouldn't take him to a lousy clinic."

The pièce de résistance blossomed over the yard—Abe Lincoln's portrait in sparks. "What would you do?"

"You know perfectly well what I'd do."

Walter grimaced. Dignity. Ralph was right, by damn. Jimmy had served the family with devotion and zest. They owed him an honorable exit.

The President chomped into a Big Mac, reveling in the soggy sauces and sultry juices as they bathed his tongue and rolled down his gullet. Were he not permanently lodged elsewhere—rail splitter, country lawyer, the whole captivating myth—he might well have wished to settle down here in 2010. Big Macs were a quality commodity. The entire menu, in fact, the large fries, vanilla shakes, Diet Cokes, and Chicken McNuggets, seemed to Abe a major improvement over nineteenth-century cuisine. And such a soothing environment, its every surface clean and sleek, as if carved from tepid ice.

An enormous clown named Ronald was emblazoned on the picture window. Outside, across the street, an elegant sign—Old English characters on whitewashed wood—heralded the Chestnut Hill Country Club. On the grassy slopes beyond, smooth and green like a billiard table, a curious event unfolded, men and women whacking balls into the air with sticks. When not employed, the sticks resided in cylindrical bags slung over the shoulders of sturdy male slaves.

"Excuse me, madame," Abe addressed the chubby woman in the next booth. "What are those people doing? Is it religious?"

"That's quite a convincing Lincoln you've got on." Hunched over a newspaper, the woman wielded a writing implement, using it to fill tiny squares with alphabet letters. "Are you serious? They're golfing."

"A game?"

"Uh-huh." The woman started on her second Quarter Pounder. "The game of golf."

"It's like croquet, isn't it?"

"It's like golf."

Dipping and swelling like a verdant sea, the golf field

put Abe in mind of Virginia's hilly provinces. Virginia, Lee's stronghold. A soft moan left the sixteenth President. Having thrown Hooker and Sedgwick back across the Rappahannock, Lee was ideally positioned to bring the war to the Union, either by attacking Washington directly or, more likely, by forming separate corps under Longstreet, Hill, and Ewell and invading Pennsylvania. Overrunning the border towns, he could probably cut the flow of reinforcements to Vicksburg while simultaneously equipping the Army of Northern Virginia for a push on the capital.

It was all too nightmarish to contemplate.

Sighing heavily, Abe took the Seward Treaty from his vest and asked to borrow his neighbor's pen.

Monday was a holiday. Right after breakfast, Walter changed into his golfing togs, hunted down his clubs, and told Jimmy they'd be spending the day on the links. He ended up playing the entire course, partly to improve his game, partly to postpone the inevitable.

His best shot of the day—a three-hundred-and-fifty-yard blast with his one-iron—carried straight down the eighteenth fairway and ran right up on the green. Sink the putt, and he'd finish the day one under par.

Sweating in the relentless fifth-of-July sun, Jimmy pulled out the putter. Such a fine fellow, with his trim body and huge eager eyes, zags of silver shooting through his steel-wool hair like the aftermath of an electrocution, his black biceps and white polo shirt meeting like adjacent squares on a chess board. He would be sorely missed.

"No, Jimmy, we won't be needing that. Just pass the bag over here. Thanks."

As Walter retrieved his .22 caliber army rifle from among the clubs, Jimmy's face hardened with bewilderment.

"May I ask why you require a firearm?" said the slave.

"You may."

"Why?"

"I'm going to shoot you."

"Huh?"

"Shoot you."

"*What?*"

"Results came Thursday, Jimmy. You have Blue Nile.

Sorry. I'd love to keep you around, but it's too dangerous, what with Marge's pregnancy and everything."

"Blue Nile?"

"Sorry."

Jimmy's teeth came together in a tight, dense grid. "In the name of reason, *sell* me. Surely that's a viable option."

"Let's be realistic. Nobody's going to take in a Nile-positive just to watch him wilt and die."

"Very well—then turn me loose." Sweat spouted from the slave's ebony face. "I'll pursue my remaining years on the road. I'll—"

"Loose? I can't go around undermining the economy like that, Jim. I'm sure you understand."

"There's something I've always wanted to tell you, Mr. Sherman."

"I'm listening."

"I believe you are the biggest asshole in the whole Commonwealth of Massachusetts."

"No need for that kind of talk, fellow. Just sit down on the green, and I'll—"

"No."

"Let's not make this difficult. Sit down, and you'll get a swift shot in the head—no pain, a dignified death. Run away, and you'll take it in the back. It's your choice."

"Of course I'm going to run, you degenerate moron."

"Sit!"

"No."

"Sit!"

Spinning around, Jimmy sprinted toward the rough. Walter jammed the stock against his shoulder and, like a biologist focusing his microscope on a protozoan, found the retreating chattel in his high-powered optical sight.

"Stop!"

Jimmy reached the western edge of the fairway just as Walter fired, a clean shot right through the slave's left calf. With a deep wolfish howl, he pitched forward and, to Walter's surprise, rose almost instantly, clutching a rusty discarded nine-iron that he evidently hoped to use as a crutch. But the slave got no farther. As he stood fully erect, his high wrinkled forehead neatly entered the gunsight, the cross hairs branding him with an X, and Walter had but to squeeze the trigger again.

Impacting, the bullet dug out a substantial portion of cranium—a glutinous divot of skin, bone, and cerebrum shooting away from Jimmy's temple like a missile launched from a brown planet. He spun around twice and fell into the rough, landing behind a clump of rose bushes spangled with white blossoms. So: an honorable exit after all.

Tears bubbled out of Walter as if from a medicine dropper. Oh, Jimmy, Jimmy . . . and the worst was yet to come, wasn't it? Of course, he wouldn't tell Tanya the facts. "Jimmy was in pain," he'd say. "Unbearable agony. The doctors put him to sleep. He's in slave heaven now." And they'd give him a classy send-off, oh, yes, with flowers and a moment of silence. Maybe Pastor McClellan would be willing to preside.

Walter staggered toward the rough. To do a funeral, you needed a body. Doubtless the morticians could patch up his head, mold a gentle smile, bend his arms across his chest in a posture suggesting serenity . . .

A tall, bearded man in an Abe Lincoln suit was on the eighteenth fairway, coming Walter's way. An eccentric, probably. Maybe a full-blown nut. Walter locked his gaze on the roses and marched straight ahead.

"I saw what you did," said the stranger, voice edged with indignation.

"Fellow had Blue Nile," Walter explained. The sun beat against his face like a hortator pounding a drum on a Roman galley. "It was an act of mercy. Hey, Abe, the Fourth of July was yesterday. Why the getup?"

"Yesterday is never too late," said the stranger cryptically, pulling a yellowed sheaf from his vest. "Never too late," he repeated as, swathed in the hot, buttery light, he neatly ripped the document in half.

For Walter Sherman, pummeled by the heat, grieving for his lost slave, wearied by the imperatives of mercy, the world now became a swamp, an all-enveloping mire blurring the stranger's methodical progress toward McDonald's. An odd evening was coming, Walter sensed, with odder days to follow, days in which all the earth's stable things would be wrenched from their moorings and unbolted from their bases. Here and now, standing on the crisp border between the fairway and the putting green, Walter apprehended this discomforting future.

He felt it more emphatically as, eyes swirling, heart shivering, brain drifting in a sea of insane light, he staggered toward the roses.

And he knew it with a knife-sharp certainty as, searching through the rough, he found not Jimmy's corpse but only the warm hulk of a humanoid machine, prostrate in the dusk, afloat in the slick oily fluid leaking from its broken brow.

Another Goddamned Showboat

BARRY N. MALZBERG

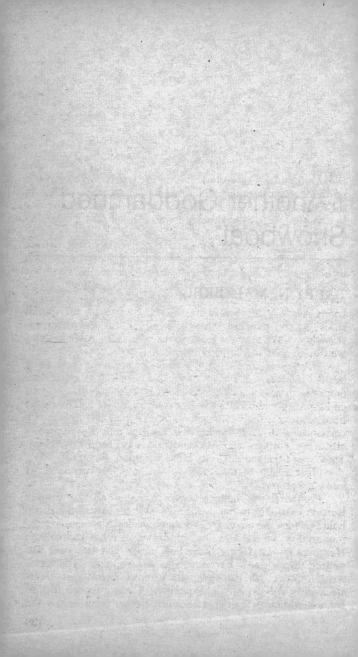

"**M**ontmartre," Hemingway said to Hadley. "We've got to go there, try something different. Barcelona, the running of the bulls, maybe. Got to get out of here; can't take it any more. Scott has really thrown a wrench. All of it a stink, an ooze—"

This was during the period when he was still writing science fiction, desperately trying to slip something by long distance past Campbell or at least Alden H. Norton, but nothing, *nothing* was connecting there and, despairingly, Hemingway was thinking of going back to westerns or maybe trying *Black Mask*. Stubborn old Cap Shaw with his special rules. At the moment it was geographic change which enticed him. "We'll take a peek south at Lisbon. After Lisbon, we can go back to Portugal."

"*Lisbon is* in Portugal," Hadley said. She had been beside him, old girl, for more than twenty years of this craperoo, had kept faith, kept things together with odd jobs and unmentionable duties but now, even as she still humored him, constraint seemed to radiate from her to say nothing of a certain lofty disdain. Hadley was running out of patience, of attitude. "Portugal and Spain are separate countries, Hem. They aren't the same. Pretty close together, though."

"Just a slip of the tongue," he said, embarrassed. "I know geography."

Campbell was bouncing everything, it all was coming back. A novelette in the post today, still reeking of the damp hold in which the envelope had spent weeks. Alternate worlds, immortality, far galaxies, extrapolations of robot technology: Hemingway was trying the whole range but the stuff was getting through only far enough to inspire mean little handwritten notes: *No constellations around Antares* or *Overstocked on robots.* All right, perhaps it was a foolish idea to try something as insular as science fiction from across the ocean but soon enough all the money would run out and that would be the end of this last desperate plan of his. Meanwhile, it helped to sit around the cafe and plan an itinerary. Science fiction or pseudo-science as they called it was probably the last shot before he packed in the whole thing, sailed home in disgrace, went crawling to some hot little country weekly, begging for a chance to run type.

"Pretty good, this new *Story*," Hadley said, showing him the magazine. It had come in on the boat with the rejections. "This Saroyan is a prospect."

"Don't tell me about Saroyan."

"*He* can do fantasy for Burnett. Maybe you're trying the wrong places; his stuff is really weird."

"It's not fantasy I'm trying. That's for *Unknown*. I'm writing science fiction." Hadley stared incomprehendingly. "They're different fields," Hemingway said. "Sort of. I don't want to talk about Saroyan or Burnett or even writing now. It's not the way to go, I told him that years ago." Indeed he had; the fiftieth rejection note (he had counted) had caused Hemingway to finally lose patience and he had written Burnett a letter which still made him blush. He looked at the manuscript on his lap, resisted the impulse to crumple it. "It's all an inside job for Burnett, people he meets at parties or sleeps with."

Hadley shrugged. They had been through this, of course. "Algren, Farrell, Fuchs, Saroyan, he can't be sleeping with them *all*, can he? You gave up too soon; you should have kept trying."

"For five years. Papers in and out, papers on the boat—"

"Joyce paid to publish *Finnegan's Wake*. *Ulysses* was banned—"

"Am I to answer that?" He clutched the manuscript, stood, looked at his still beautiful middle-aged wife through a haze which might have been recrimination or then again just the damned Parisian smog. Conditions here were really impossible; his sinuses were clogged all the time and the French had become evil to Americans. Pseudo-science, of all things. But the detective magazines had been full of fake-tough writing which no man could take seriously and after scuffling around with the Loyalists how could you take *Ranch Romances* seriously? He was in a hell of a box. *Ulysses*. Why did Hadley have to mention that? *Ulysses* was what had broken him, seeing what had happened to that crazy novel, the crazy Irishman. Seeing evidence that the failure and ban had driven Joyce crazy, Hemingway had said: *Get hold of yourself. There is a darkness out there that is not for me.* But the pulps. Maybe that had been a mistake. Maybe it had all been a mistake. So—

"Sit," Hadley said. "Come on, it's too early in the day. Have a glass of Côtes de Rhone, enjoy the mistral. Maybe we'll drift back to the *pensione* for a fuck. And maybe we'll go to Lisbon. Maybe we'll swim the channel. We're still expatriates, we're not supposed to have responsibilities." She signalled a waiter. "Get him a glass of vin ordinaire," she said. The waiter shrugged. "Go on," Hadley said. "It's not *that* early in the day."

"I shouldn't drink before noon."

"But you *do,* Hem. You drink before ten. Why don't you stop fighting the truth? Get him the wine," she said to the waiter. "He wants it." The waiter muttered and turned away. It occurred to Hemingway—with no surge of jealousy, just a dim, middle-aged man's curiosity—that Hadley could as easily be fucking the waiter as not. She could be fucking any number of people. How would she know? How would he know anything? It was hard to keep things sorted out: Scott's heart attack, the war, the trouble with the magazines, they were muddling his mind. Less and less was he here. Vin ordinaire.

He sat, put the manuscript under his chair, took out the latest issue of *Astounding* which Campbell, as either a gift or hint, had enclosed. September, 1941, and there was Asimov on the cover. He stared. "Isaac Asimov," he said. "Look who's on the cover. With 'Nightfall.'"

"Oh?"

"First time, I think. He's a kid, you know. Twenty-one, twenty-two years old, that's all. And he's got the cover."

"I guess that's good," Hadley said without interest. She had been against the pulp markets from the first, had fought with some intensity, felt that no real writer would waste his time with these. Hemingway had tried to explain, patiently, that he wasn't a real writer any more, the last real writer, maybe, had been James Joyce or maybe Geoffrey Chaucer, and look what had happened to *them.* Scott had thought he was a real writer but that was a fatal heart attack. Hadley leaned against his shoulder, stared at the magazine. " 'Night-fall,' " she said. "That's a Daniel Fuchs title. *Night Falls in Brooklyn*, maybe."

She didn't know Asimov from Heinlein, Nat Schachner from de Camp, but she was still trying to be supportive, still trying to be a writer's wife. Ridiculous, Hemingway thought, flushing. Forty-two years old this year, forty-two with a war on, still in cafes, feeling bitter about Saroyan, torn up by Scott's death, furious about *Ulysses* and now *Finnegan's Wake* and trying to cobble up alternate worlds scenarios. Almost two decades out of the country and still not a word in print while kids like Asimov or this new Caleb Saunders seemed to have the formula. Sit down and turn out this stuff and take it as true. Paris is going to fall soon, he thought. I'm going to sit here with pulp magazines and torment and *Der Führer* is going to march right up these streets and clap me away.

The waiter returned with two glasses. Hemingway hesitated, looked at Hadley, who scrambled through her handbag and put a couple of franc notes on the tray. The waiter looked at them one more time and then went away. People were going away a lot now, and not all of them were paid for the pleasure.

"Drink up," Hadley said, "it's not going to stay too good too long."

"Is that a report from the front?"

"*This* front. That's all I know."

He put the issue away. "Scott Fitzgerald had the right idea, that's what I think."

"Don't say that."

"He left with a little dignity. Kept his pride. He picked the right time to check out and there's a whole hell of a lot of stuff he never has to face now."

"I hate to hear you talk like that."

"Hollywood," Hemingway said. "I knew Scott would come to no good; I told him that in '29. I told him to dump that bitch and go out and live a little, didn't I? He wouldn't listen. I told him, 'Scott, that woman is out to kill you unless you kill her first in the only way she knows.' He wouldn't have any of it."

"He was a sick man."

"Not back then. Not that way. I thought I was smarter than him, just like I thought I was smarter than Jim Joyce. I mean, I wasn't banned in my own country or called a pornographer or made a fool of for something that I had written from the heart." He drained the wine, feeling a little sick now, working on the rage, feeling it build in the only way possible to stave off the nausea. The nausea could send him back to pillow and rack but no fuck then for her old man. "But you see," he said, "*they* didn't end writing about robots, trying to beat out kids for a spot on yellow paper at a cent a word. So who was really smart, who had the right viewpoint on things after all?"

"You got out of Paris, before."

"I wouldn't call Madrid a vacation. Or Toledo."

"Oh come on," Hadley said, "enough of this. I'm *not* going to sit around here and listen to you complain before noon. You don't like your life, Hem, change it; if I'm not a part of the change then boot me out or go your own way. But stop complaining." She disposed of her glass, her fine chin muscles working hard to make her not look like a drunk, put the glass on the table and stood.

"I'm going to wander down the Boulevard," she said. "I'll be back in a while. I want to do some thinking. No, don't reach toward me, don't apologize. Nothing to apologize for. I'm not mad and I'm not sulking. I'm just getting older and I want to think. Sometimes that happens when it closes in."

"Goodbye," he said.

She waved at him in that difficult gesture which had so entranced, had so ensnared him long ago when he and Scott and the others had been making big plans on this same Boulevard, and walked away. He watched her go, as fascinated but as detached as the waiter.

Soon enough, like the ambulance and the tanks and the big guns on the plains, she was gone.

Hemingway sighed, a great sigh, drained his own glass, picked up the *Astounding* yet again, leafing through it in a desultory way. Heinlein, de Camp, Caleb Saunders. The kid's novelette with the Emerson quote, his first cover. Must be a big time for the kid. I hope he's draft exempt, Hemingway thought. I hope they're *all* draft exempt over there; I hope they have other avenues because there are big plans for them.

Emerson and the stars and the City of God. Maybe there would be a clue there; maybe there would be something he could learn. Clutching the gearshift under fire, scuttling on those fields he had told himself that he would learn, thinking of *Ulysses* he had told himself he would learn, reeling with Scott and Zelda and Hadley through corridors of a different sort, he surely had told himself that he was busily storing experience, that it could turn out differently. Well, maybe he had, maybe he would. Was Hadley going to come back?

Yes, she would come back. Like him, she had absolutely nowhere to go. He began to read dutifully, then with intensity. He *would* learn, forty-two was not too late, he would learn what he could. Joyce was destroyed; his novels would not be known. Scott was dead in Hollywood and the darkness was coming. All of the other markets were closed to him; he could sell nothing. He would learn how to write this stuff. He would make of himself a science fiction writer. Caleb Saunders had broken in this month, there was always a new guy coming. The machinery of time would not otherwise wait.

The war was on. The war was coming. Bit by bit, one by one, the stars were coming out.

Loose Cannon

SUSAN SHWARTZ

*Men prayed me that I set our work, the inviolate
  house, as a memory of you.
But for fit monument I shattered it, unfinished . . .*

T.E. LAWRENCE,
Seven Pillars of Wisdom

The whining overhead crashed into a brief silence, and the ground shook from the bomb's impact. The low, heavy vaulting in St. Paul's crypt quivered in response. A thin trickle of dust fell past the bronze memorial statue that the man stood studying. Kennington had done his usual fine job on the portrait bust, which bore the watcher's face: high brow, thick, side-parted metal waves of hair, eyes fixed, Alexander-fashion, on some goal only he could see. Had he really been that young? The face on the statue: was it the face of someone who had not lost youth, integrity, and honor? Then, in the motorcycle crash that he had only now begun to recall—he had lost everything else.

"Except my life, except my life, except my life," he murmured. He would willingly have parted with that before he lost the other things. The man standing in even deeper shadows—his "alienist," the word was—muttered something. The watcher approved neither of the word nor of the idea that such a man was attending him, eager to discuss Shakespeare and Sophocles and the long-secret details of his family: that is, his mother, his father, and his brothers. He had no wife nor child of his own, nor ever would.

Another crash, jolting the heavy pavement. This time, the dust that hid the funeral bust fell in a thicker stream, smelling of mold. His hearing, never good since the blow on his head—*don't strike those bicycles . . . swerve . . . van coming up fast . . . too fast! . . . falling . . . the handlebars flashed beneath his horrified gaze, and he was flying over them . . . falling . . . panic and a horror of pain he could not master . . .*

Light behind his eyes, before them, exploding in redness . . .

. . . as the Turks thrust desperately toward Maan, he rode shouting toward Aba el Lissan, and his camel fell as if poleaxed . . . sailing grandly through the air to land with a

147

crash that drove power . . . no, it drove the pain into him . . .

. . . must not think of pain, not while the wheel whirred idly overhead, and shouts . . . "Macht schnell! Er ist tot!" *The van roared away.*

. . . Pain is only pain, punishment, atonement . . . don't scream . . . what was that damned silly poem?

> 'For Lord I was free of all Thy flowers, but I chose the world's sad roses,
>   And that is why my feet are torn and mine eyes are blind with sweat.'

. . . Not sweat but blood and burning . . .

The rest was silence until the bandages were unwrapped, the knives laid aside, and Dr. Jones' clever, accented voice—*terrifyingly like the voices crowing over his body*—forced him back to life.

Again, the cathedral shuddered at the City's agony. Rapid footsteps pounded behind them. Helmeted and booted for the air raid, the anxious verger approached, as appalled, probably, by the racket he made in church as he was by the blitz. The world might end, but propriety remained.

"Colonel . . ."

Behind him, the man he had learned to call Detective Thompson stirred uneasily.

He and Dr. Jones would want him to leave the cathedral and seek shelter. After all, it would hardly do to waste the hopes and labor of the doctors, alienists, and police who had scraped him out from beneath his ruined motorcycle, then reassembled the remains first in hospital after hospital, then later in the peace of Clouds Hill.

First, though, one more look at the shadowed, somber face, the heroic portrait that, they told him, had stood in the crypt for years. They had pronounced him dead, had praised him, mourned him, missed him. Just his rotten luck that the charade could not be made dead flesh: now they claimed they needed him.

"Play the man," he muttered at the bronze fraud. Turning his back, he walked rapidly, despite his limp from a twisted leg, past sand buckets and tombs, past scribbled placards and worn Latin inscriptions, unreadable in the darkness, up into the blacked-out nave. Light filtered through chinks in the boarded windows, and the building trembled once again.

"A bad one, that," Dr. Jones observed.

Detective Inspector Thompson grimaced, and moved to escort him outside.

He jerked away from the touch on his elbow. In hospital, he had had to submit to the ministrations and hurts of strange hands; he had always hated to be touched.

"Sorry, Colonel." The hand dropped away.

"Lead on, Inspector."

The policeman almost snapped to attention, and the Colonel, as he supposed he would have to be called again, grimaced at his success in shamming leadership.

They walked rapidly outside the cathedral. Sir Christopher Wren's great dome was half shrouded in cloud, half illuminated by red flares and flames, as London burned and shuddered in its fever. More bombs dropped; the ground convulsed; and guns and planes screamed defiance at each other over the crackle of flames and the crash of burning rubble.

Shouts rose to one side, mingling with more feeble wails of pain. He forced his limping body into a run, grabbed a spar, and wedged it, lever-fashion, into the rubble. . . .

"Lumme, 'e's just a littl' un."

"Help me, you men!" he gasped, and thrust his weight and the remnants of his strength against his lever. Thompson was at his side, lending him the advantages of his great height and bulk. The stone began to rock upward as two wardens pounced on the broken body beneath. It whined and moaned, too badly hurt to scream; but its eyes flickered open and fixed on Lawrence.

Had *he* looked like that when the stretcher bearers came for him? A wonder they could patch him up at all.

Pity, worse than a beating, twisted in him, and he laid a careful hand on the dusty, battered forehead. "Steady on there," he whispered, and slipped his fingers down over the man's eyes until they closed in a merciful swoon . . . at least he hoped it was only that.

The ground shuddered again and again, the sky lighting with white and red, slashing through the clouds of burning

London. The Great Fire had destroyed Old St. Paul's; would this one perish in flames, too?

"Sir . . ."

He wanted to wait until he knew for certain whether the man lived or died, but he could see by Thompson's face that the detective had granted him all the leeway that he dared.

" 'E looks familiar, don't 'e?" He read the words on a warden's chapped lips, rather than heard them in the din. A siren howled, first one note, then another, like the shrieks of Bedouin wives.

He rose and dusted his hands, waving away thanks and averting his head lest some man with a longer memory decide that he had seen the ghost of a soldier from the Great War, come back to aid his country in its time of need.

Breathing heavily—fifty-odd or not, he had gotten intolerably soft these past five years and more of convalescence—he trotted back to . . . "his staff."

"Lawrence, for God's sake . . ." Dr. Ernest Jones, his alienist, began. Jones was frightened. Interesting. Able to delve into the intolerable muck of a man's thoughts, but afraid of bombs. Well, Lawrence could understand it. He had set a few explosions himself, he and his friends; but the sheer magnitude of this bombardment appalled him.

Overriding the foreign doctor's fears, Detective Thompson leaned toward Lawrence, calmly asking, "Shall we head on over to Number 10, Colonel? The P.M. is waiting for you."

The area around Whitehall had been bombed repeatedly, and Number 10 Downing Street bore evidence of hasty reinforcement.

"They're going to move the offices over to St. James Park by Storey Gate soon," said Thompson. "There's a shelter downstairs, though. Go right ahead, sir."

As Lawrence approached the door of Number 10 Downing Street, it was flung wide, and he walked in ahead of the others. He frowned to himself. After so many years of being an aircraftsman, who saluted and opened doors for his betters, he found it all too easy to walk again through doors held for him, to note and acknowledge the recognition in the eyes of the tired but distinguished men who had been awaiting his convenience, to pretend to ignore the susurrus of whispers, "Lawrence, Lawrence, Lawrence . . ." that heralded him, just as he had ignored the cries of "Aurens! Aurens!" from his bodyguard. But it was all a lie. Those whispers were water in the desert to him.

Never learn your lessons, do you, my lad? You'll have to pay for that, you know, he told himself, and planned to keep that vow a secret from the alienist, who frowned on his habits of penance.

The whispers continued, and he stiffened at their tone. There was no need to pity him. *Was that pride too?* The schoolmen had called it the deadliest of the seven deadly sins. He had forgotten his Milton . . . what was it? *"If thou beest he . . ."* No, that wasn't it. Something about *"Why then, how changed?"* It bothered him that he could not remember. Would all that careful five years of healing come apart, now that he had been summoned?

No doubt of that. He *had* been summoned. The P.M. had plans for him again. Half a lifetime ago, he'd had to beg to get Churchill to release him from the Middle East Department of the Colonial Office.

"This way, sir."

Odd to be called sir again. God knows, he himself would have been glad enough to be one of the spruce messengers who kept Number 10's street floor spotless in uncomplicated humility.

"You'll want to wash up before you see the P.M., sir."

Not a suggestion. Lawrence let himself be steered past a comfortable-looking coal fire toward a cloakroom, a dazzling luxury of thick towels, ivory combs, and the unwelcome brightness of mirrors that showed the thick shock of hair much whitened, the blue eyes paler now, embedded in wrinkles etched by desert sun, sandstorms, and pain. It was too opulent. He washed his hands and waved them until they dried.

Churchill's private secretary, a Mr. John Colvin, waited for him. Harrow and Cambridge, Lawrence remembered; a fine young man with a fine future ahead of him, and probably a place in the Honours list if he behaved with more sense and circumspection than Lawrence had. Odd to see a young man out of uniform.

"Feeling quite fit, sir?" Colvin asked.

Lawrence nodded. "Well enough. How is the P.M.?"

Colvin grinned. "Shouting about the Lend/Lease program and how the bloody Yanks had better hurry up and get into the war before there's noth—" he broke off, shaking his head apologetically. "Begging your pardon, sir."

Lawrence waved his chagrin aside. He'd heard that word and far worse; used them, if the truth be known, in *The Mint*, so full of oaths that it had had to be printed with holes in the text, as if moths had gotten at a soldier's blouse.

"If Roosevelt doesn't listen to him, he may have more to worry about than the Jerries," he said. He had always valued the company of younger people and was good at getting them to unbend. "Remember, I've worked with Mr. Churchill before. He's a demanding master."

"So he is, sir. But this is my last month on the job. I'm joining the R.A.F. Pilot training."

"Good man!" Lawrence shook Colvin's hand enthusiastically. For once, he forgot to recoil from the contact. "He'd be the last man to hold you back from that." *But, if you had simply wanted to change your name to Ross, say, and join up as an aircraftsman, he'd have pitched a fit that would make the carnage outside look like a picnic.*

Colvin led him to the Private Office, through room after paneled room, past clusters of desks and suited male secretaries. The lady clerks had been sent down from London; Lawrence felt better for their absence.

He knocked at the thick, richly burnished door. Not the Cabinet Room, thank God. This would be private.

"Don't stand out in the cold, man. Come in, come in! I've been waiting for you!" Churchill's voice, with its lisp and deep intonations, leapt out of the room, capturing his respect as it always had, tempting him—*to what? to be Colonel T. E. Lawrence, instead of Aircraftsman Ross, or a nameless dead man? To have a future and deeds to do once again?*

Not even you, Mr. Prime Minister. Not this time.

Churchill rose to greet him, cigar pumping up and down in his mouth. Lawrence straightened to attention. Involuntarily, he grinned. If England were a nation of shopkeepers, here was the bulldog set to guard them, bow-tied, bull-necked, bald head stubbornly lowered even as he welcomed Lawrence. Hard to believe that the P.M. was around fifteen years older than he; Lawrence felt older than God, and the mirrors downstairs had done nothing to dispel that feeling.

"Come in and sit down, Lawrence. Have you eaten? Drink?" Churchill gestured invitingly at the tantalus. "Tea?"

"It doesn't matter."

"Nonsense." Churchill poured him out a whiskey, which Lawrence allowed to sit on the polished table beside him. "You're neither a young nor a well man. We'll have none of these endurance tests of yours, man. Not when I need you . . ."

There it was. The need. The hope that Lawrence could once again be the man of the hour—*or the mountebank*. The demand that he accept, do, achieve, when all he wanted, all he ever wanted, was simply to be left alone.

No, that wasn't true. Once, he had wanted to be knighted and a general by the time he was thirty. Once, he had wanted to lead a revolution that would restore self-respect to all the races of the East. He had dreamed of nothing less; but the kings and diplomats had put paid to that. He remembered them all, Balfour and Weizmann and Faisal and Churchill, struggling toward agreement, and failing, after all the blood, the sacrifices, his own loss of honor and faith. Now he wanted to be left alone. He felt his hands start to shake, and closed one around the whiskey glass to still it; he very well knew that the man sitting across from him would never let him be.

"Is that why . . . ?" Lawrence waved his other hand, encompassing the past five years of medical and psychiatric interventions, the support and the secrecy. "Is that why you had me saved?"

"Dammit, Lawrence!" *Ah, now the bullying would start.* "I had you watched, of course. But I wasn't, apparently, the only one. Mind you, *I* wouldn't have tried to run you down. It was the damned Germans did that. And it wasn't I that saved you, either."

Lawrence cocked his head as he stared up at the taller man.

"You can thank Aaron Aaronsohn and his people that you're alive. God knows, I'm grateful enough."

Lawrence's glass crashed down on the table, almost spilling the amber whiskey. "Hell! He's still alive? I'd have thought someone had put a bullet through his head by now."

"No such luck. At least, that's your good luck." Churchill

grinned at him through a cigar stub. "He'd been living at Zichron Ya'akov. In 'retirement,' he called it; but how much can any of that set retire? When the War broke out, he came back to England via the Orkneys again, to help Weizmann and the others make Balfour's life a misery."

"The others," as Lawrence perfectly well knew, being the Zionists with whom Churchill had such staunch, inexplicable sympathy.

"They say they're fighting two wars. One against Jerry, and the other, as this Ben-Gurion—name used to be Green, but he changed it—calls it, against our White Paper. Aaronsohn joined up. . . ."

It rankled to owe his life to Aaron Aaronsohn and his lunatic cabal. He'd met the man in Cairo; the dislike had been instant and mutual. "Thinks very highly of himself," he had heard Aaronsohn wrote of him. And when he'd spoken of the Jewish settlements in Palestine, Aaronsohn could only comment that he thought he was "attending a Prussian anti-Semitic lecture." Impossible to get through to the man! There were others in that group, though: best not to think of the dead.

But Churchill was watching him with that terrible shrewdness that Lawrence remembered.

"What does Aaronsohn want of me?"

"You? What he wants of everyone. A homeland for the Jews in Palestine. God knows, they need something. Weizmann's got proof that Hitler's rounding them up and exterminating them. Like the Armenians in the last war, but on a grander scale, damn the Nazis' efficiency. Goebbels is in on it."

Lawrence grimaced. "I speak German, but I'm no assassin. Aaronsohn saved my life for no purpose."

"Not what he thinks. Nor what I think. I've always thought that some overpowering need would draw you from the modest path you chose to tread and set you once again in full action at the center of memorable events."

Now, that sounded like one of Churchill's better speeches. Lawrence suppressed an urge to applaud that surely would have provoked one of the P.M.'s better rages.

"Begging your pardon, sir, but no. All I want is to be left in peace. Left alone."

"Lawrence, in plain talk, we need you. England needs you. While you were . . . convalescing out at Clouds Hill, men have been dying in North Africa. Hitler's got a general out there we don't seem able to get the better of. Rommel. They don't call him the Desert Fox for nothing."

Rommel. Papers and books had been full of the stories of the middle-aged Swabian general, no Prussian or Junker, but from a staunch middle-class family and loyal past death to his country. Rommel. Lawrence had found himself fascinated even by the name, which tolled like a bell, hailing him back from peace to the very plots and bustle that he feared.

"No one knows the desert better than you, Lawrence. Or the way a desert fighter's mind works. The Arabs have turned against us, by and large, but there's the Berbers. We want you to go out and—"

"And what?" Abruptly, Lawrence felt himself go pale with rage. "Be that clown in the pantos that they call 'Lawrence of Arabia,' all white robes, headcloth, and bathos? Lead the Berbers as if they're Arabs? Well, they're not. They're a different cat altogether out in Libya. It's not as if they're all wogs with funny-sounding names."

Churchill shook his head, grinning more openly, and with great satisfaction. "So you can still be baited, can you?

"Berbers," he went on, "or Ageyli, Harithi, or Howeitat, Lawrence; we need you. Talk to them. Lead them; back to us, if you can; away from the Eighth Army, if you can't. And we need to pit you against Rommel before he launches his final attack on Tobruk."

"You expect me to assassinate him for you?" Lawrence raised an eyebrow. "By your good offices, I've been raised from the dead, so now you want me to work you a miracle and kill—"

"I know. You're no assassin. And his skill in the desert is uncanny. But if anyone can match him at that, it's you. You'll know how to intercept him. Kill him if you can. Or, if you're feeling like a miracle, try to meet him." Churchill paused and drew reflectively on his cigar, and Lawrence suppressed a perverse desire to cough. "Talk to him. Dear God, if you could *turn* him—"

"Against Germany? That won't happen."

"Not against Germany. Against Hitler. Promise him what you must. We can worry about payment later."

"I've heard," Lawrence whispered, "they're trying to build a Reich that will last a thousand years."

"It's lasted too long already! Hell, *give* him Paree; what do I care, so long as he's stopped. But dead is safer. In fact—" He broke off. "You'll be briefed here and in Cairo."

Lawrence shook his head. "I haven't got it in me."

Churchill smiled and bit down on his cigar. "I knew you'd say that."

"How if I say 'no,' too, while I'm being so predictable? Sir."

"You can't, Lawrence," Churchill told him. For the first time in their conversation, he looked away. If such a thing were possible, Lawrence would have sworn he looked embarrassed and ashamed.

"Why not?" asked Lawrence. "After all, I'm supposed to be dead, aren't I? I've just come from seeing my own effigy in St. Paul's. You must have had to close down the City for that memorial service."

"Not quite," said Churchill. "Disinformation is an old game. Rommel wouldn't be surprised if you turned up; half the fortune-tellers in Soho think that you're not dead but 'in another place.' You know your *Morte d'Arthur* better than I do."

"It's not going to happen." Lawrence pressed his hand against the table. "I'm not going to appear melodramatically at the hour of Britain's greatest need—"

"Which this is."

"Let me join the service again. Let me repair engines. Anything but this."

"No."

"Then I cannot help you," Lawrence told the Prime Minister. Resisting him was harder than Lawrence had believed possible.

"I am sorry, Lawrence. You don't have a choice." Churchill reached for a folder among the heaps of folders, books, papers on his vast desk. "There. Read these. And you can't know how I regret having to use them."

The letters all had dates from between 1931 and 1934. "John Bruce," Lawrence muttered to himself. He felt himself flushing. For very shame, sweat poured down his sides . . . *five nights running while he wrote of Deraa, he had had nightmares in which the Bey coughed and the whip furrowed his back, to be shaken awake by his bunkmates* . . . he had persuaded the younger man to flog him, hoping to drive out, suppress the darkness within him, to expiate the disastrous loss of integrity he'd suffered that night.

He looked down, pretending to read the letters that, years ago, he had written, posing as his own uncle. "Does he take his whipping as something he has earned? Is he sorry after it?" He flipped over a page, turned to another letter at random, and the shameful words leapt out at him. "Unless he strips, the birch is quite ineffective. . . ."

"For God's sake, Lawrence!" Across from him, Churchill exploded, his fist pounding on the desk. Despite the cigar, his mouth twisted in pain and disgust. "How could you do it, man? *Why* did you do it?"

He could feel it coming, that horrible hooting laugh. In Damascus, it had earned him a slap across the mouth from a British officer who saw only a bloody-minded, hysterical wog. He forced himself to breathe deeply, to try to control himself.

"The English vice, they call it," Churchill commented. "The results of public school."

Easy enough for a Duke's cousin, educated at Harrow, raised at Blenheim Palace, to say. Easy enough for him to shrug it off. But not for Lawrence. For Ned Lawrence and his queer brothers, a day school had been good enough; the closest they got to Blenheim—assuming they had saved the ready to buy sweets—was on Public Days. The P.M. could afford this aristocratic disgust.

Lawrence looked up. Churchill's contempt would be his punishment. But the man's disgust was for the folder of letters, which Lawrence laid carefully aside. "If I had known, we could have helped you. You see what Dr. Jones is able to do—"

"No one can help me," he said.

"Think yourself some sort of Knight Templar, do you, Lawrence? I'm telling you: you *will* go to North Africa, or so help *me*, I'll publish those letters."

Lawrence choked down the laughter rising in his throat again and knew it for the onset of madness. *The line is 'publish and be damned,' I believe*, he thought. But could he force it out? What would those letters do to his eldest brother, a queer fish of a missionary, totally in his mother's control? What about his mother, who'd lost two sons already and lived like an anchoress, to conceal her sin with the man who was not, had never been her husband? His youngest brother might understand. But what would it do to his family?

Lawrence sighed. "Tell me what you need me to do," he said.

"Thank you, Lawrence. And please believe me. I am truly sorry. After your job is done, you shall have those . . . letters back. Please burn them. Then we will see what else can be done for you."

"There is one thing that I want," said Lawrence. "Shall I have it?"

"Name it."

"To be left alone!"

"Agreed," said Churchill with such despatch that Lawrence could not believe him. "I will have you briefed. You leave for Cairo as soon as we can assemble a convoy."

"Wait," said Lawrence. A debt remained outstanding: the little matter of his pride as he had entered Number 10 and people had whispered his name. "I would like to thank Aaronsohn."

That would be a fitting punishment.

"Jones said you'd probably say something like that. He and Weizmann are here," said the P.M. He rang for his secretary. Colvin appeared, impervious and unspotted. Pray God *he* never violated his soul—or had to strip it bare—as Lawrence had done. But there was no way of passing that lesson on.

"Show Colonel Lawrence into the Cabinet Room, and ask Dr. Weizmann and Mr. Aaronsohn to join him."

Lawrence rose, saluted as if he were still in the R.A.F., and marched out of the room, aware of Churchill's eyes on his back. Outside waited at least two secretaries, one carrying a dispatch box, the other burdened with books and documents. Both leaned against the wall, looking more tired than the Prime Minister, who was at least forty years their senior.

"That bastard," he heard Churchill mutter in that bulldog rasp of his, all the throatier for the late hour and the many cigars. "That poor, damned bastard."

One hand on the polished conference table, Lawrence waited as if for an attack. His hand was trembling, he saw, and stifled a curse. Of all the times for his malaria to recur!

Aaronsohn had saved his life, but nevertheless, he had enough pride left to want to face the man without fighting the sweats, the chills, and the shakes.

Despite his dreams of unifying the races in Palestine, under the technical leadership of what he was awed enough to call the eternal miracle of Jewry, Lawrence had to admit that he had trouble with Jews. With Zionists, most of all. How *did* Churchill put up with the stiffnecked bastards? For example, there was the time when some great, redheaded farmer, seeing Lawrence in his robes and imagining him to be some poor, sullen Arab not quick enough to step out of his way, knocked him down. And then, there was the time that Weizmann met with Lawrence, Sykes himself, Balfour, and his dead prince Faisal—and argued them to a standstill.

Aaronshon, though, was a different breed. If Weizmann were a scientist with a cause, as much a catalyst as one of his own chemical reactions, Aaronsohn was, pure and simple, a zealot, and the leader of zealots. Their very name confirmed it, taken as it was from the lines of Samuel, condemning Saul for not having destroyed the Amalekites. *Netzach Yisroel lo yishaker*. The strength of Israel will not lie. Nor, for that matter, repent. Nor would Aaronsohn.

Yet he had saved Lawrence, who wiped the sweat from his forehead and wished for quinine tablets. The door swung wide, and Weizmann entered first, Aaronsohn limping after him. He was still stocky, still reddened, unable even after a lifetime spent in Palestine to brown rather than to redden. He looked almost as Irish as Lawrence himself. Weizmann, bearing the dark complexion and intensity of his Russian blood, seemed far more recognizably Jewish.

"It's been a long time, Colonel." For a moment, Weizmann hesitated.

Lawrence moved forward. "They fixed me up," he said. Reluctantly, he extended his hand. "Nothing will fall off."

Neither of the Zionists laughed, but eyed him with the intensity that he remembered. They stood until standing became awkward, and Lawrence remembered, belatedly, to gesture them to chairs. The silence grew, became demanding.

"I have to thank you," Lawrence said. "The Prime Minister says that you helped pull me out of that crash."

Weizmann was shaking his head. "Better let Aaron explain that."

The veteran leaned forward. "We had you followed, Lawrence," he said. "Just as well, too. That was no crash, but a very well set up assassination attempt by the Germans. We've gotten used to such things in *Eretz Yisroel*."

Aaronsohn's use of the Hebrew name that the Zionists used for their dreamed-of homeland was, of course, deliberate provocation. Lawrence let it pass. He remembered now; even as he slipped from consciousness, expecting never to wake, he had heard German.

"A bullet or two drove them off, and I sent one of my people to fetch the police. Good thing we were on the spot; if the Germans hadn't set you up, the way you rode that cycle of yours might have been the death of you."

Lawrence looked down. He had always pushed his luck with his cycles, had raced them against cars and planes, had usually won until this last time when he saw two boys on bicycles and made the deliberate decision to swerve abruptly, knowing that at his speed and with the van coming at him, this was one crash he could never walk away from. *Did I truly want to die?* Jones had croaked about that a good deal in the five painful years of reconstruction.

"Germans," he mused.

"Apparently, Colonel," Weizmann said, laying gentle stress on the title, "they believed that you meant what you said about being out of the picture, just as much as Churchill does—or as we do. So they planned to make sure of your death.

"I take it," Weizmann continued as Lawrence sat quietly, sure that he should not divulge Churchill's plans, "that he's sending you to North Africa. No doubt, you've been following Rommel's victories there."

Lawrence shook his head gently. "Only a little. My reading has been . . . carefully supervised."

"You're needed. If there's anyone who can hunt the Desert Fox, it's you."

"You're needed for other things," Aaronsohn said, lips twisting as if the words were sour. "Show him the pictures, Chaim."

So you need me, too? What for, I wonder.

Weizmann reached into his briefcase, pulled out an envelope, and laid it gently on the table before Lawrence. "You said your reading was supervised. Then you don't know what's been going on. Look at these pictures!" The Russian chemist's voice grew husky. "For God's sake, look. They are killing us!"

Lawrence unwound the cord that closed the envelope and slid its contents out. Yellowing copies of major papers from around the world, some dated as early as November 1938.

"I was," he said, "quite out of the picture when these were published. In one hospital or another. But Churchill says—"

"Churchill doesn't *know*!" both men interrupted.

"Pogroms," Weizmann said. "Like my family fled in Russia. Only this one in Germany—they call it *Kristallnacht*—spanned an entire nation and was administered with German efficiency." His voice grated on the last, sarcastic words.

"They want Germany *Judenrein*," Aaronsohn broke in. "Free of Jews. Only no one will take them in. No other nation. Roosevelt said point-blank that he wouldn't increase the United States quota on Jews; we have no place of our own to go to. So they've found their own solutions to getting rid of the Jews. In Germany and every other country they've entered: France, Poland, Russia, if they win there. Our people smuggled out photos of those solutions. Deutschland'll be *Judenrein*, all right, once all its Jews are dead. And then, what of the rest of us?"

The malaria definitely had its claws in Lawrence. That had to be the only reason that his hands shook so and sweat began to drip down his sides. Here was a photo of children packed into trucks; here a flaming synagogue; here, piled high, like cord . . .

"I can't believe we could be so wrong. Not after what he tried to do before the White Paper. But he doesn't care," Aaronsohn whispered loudly to Weizmann. "Look at him sitting there. If they were his precious Arabs—!"

Hastily, Lawrence laid the last photo face down on the table. The pictures showed atrocity, slashed across the face of Europe. It was Tafas after the slaughter; it was the Horns of Hattin; it was Golgotha.

"Jesus wept," he whispered. He would have to believe that even his mother's vengeful god, in whose name she had beaten him, trying to break his spirit, would weep at the final solution that the Germans had found. "Jesus wept." He was shaking now, but not just from the fever and chills.

"Your God hasn't got a monopoly on tears, Lawrence," said Aaronsohn. "I hate to admit it, but we need your help."

"You couldn't have known this in '35," Lawrence mused. "We knew *something*."

Against his will, he turned over the ghastly file of pictures and headlines, forced himself to study them. He could have the flesh lashed from his bones (though he flushed with shame to think that Churchill knew of that), could spend his life in penance, could live like an anchorite in Sinai; and nothing would make a difference in the face of such universal suffering.

"In a civilized age!" he protested in a whisper and heard Aaronsohn laugh painfully. He wanted to believe that these documents were forged, that civilized people—even Germans—could not wreak such horrors on their fellow men; he wanted to deny that he had ever seen them. But he could not.

"Stop Rommel, and you break the back of Germany's power in North Africa," Aaronsohn said, offering him the solace of direct action.

Only he felt the shakes spread out from his center, to take possession of his whole body. He sagged against the table, sweating forehead pressed on the cool wood near the scattered photos and clippings. "The man's sick," Weizmann said. "I'll ring—"

"It's malaria," Aaronsohn said. "You don't spend the time he's spent in the East without getting it. Here, Lawrence. Forget your quinine along with your guts?"

The familiar bitterness of quinine filled his mouth. He took the glass that Weizmann filled, holding it carefully in both hands.

"Churchill wants you to stop Rommel," Weizmann said. "You're not likely to meet him, army to army—"

"That's not how desert wars are fought," Lawrence muttered.

Aaronsohn broke in, his violent enthusiasms making him seem much younger than his age, which was close to the Prime Minister's. "It would be better to *turn* him. He's like you, Lawrence. Enslaved to an idea, in this case the idea of a thousand-year Reich. Does he know what his masters are doing? *Show* him, and he'll know what his choices are. He'll have to."

"Like me? You overestimate us both, I'm afraid."

"That's not what my sister said."

For the second time that night, Lawrence fought to stifle a hoot of laughter that would have gotten him punched in the face. Sarah Aaronsohn, Aaron's younger sister, who had taken command of his people while he was agitating in Europe. He had met her once or twice . . . in Cairo and Jerusalem; met her and been struck not just by her zeal, which matched her brother's for fervor, or her brains (which were far better), but by the power, the special charisma that she possessed. Blue-eyed, blonde, an Artemis or a Deborah of a woman, she had fascinated all who had come into contact with her.

Only the Turks had resisted her. They had beaten her and her sixty-five-year-old father savagely. Afterward, she had stolen a pistol and shot herself. She was twenty-seven, the whole of life before her; and it had taken her four days to die, and weeks for the news to reach her brother and the rest of the western world. Years later, after Deraa, Lawrence had remembered her. *She* had not feared to sacrifice her life; all he had managed was to retch and beg for mercy. Yes, and steal corrosive sublimate to use if he were recaptured.

Aaronsohn stared narrowly at Lawrence. *Were they true, those rumors?* Again, Lawrence fought not to giggle. He had proposed marriage once in his life, and the woman had laughed at him, had become engaged to his brother Will, also dead now in the War. He was not a man for women, not that way. Lawrence shook his head. *Would you want your sister to marry one?* The question became a terrible irony.

"I didn't think so," Aaronsohn muttered. "Too much in love with pain, or—"

Weizmann laid a hand on his arm, cautioning him. Aaronsohn shook it off. "Bygones are bygones, Chaim. We need him, poor devil that he is."

A particularly strong explosion rattled the windows and the glasses in the conference room. All three men glanced at the ceiling, as if expecting it to collapse.

"That was a close one," Aaronsohn said. "If the Germans' aim gets any better, we may none of us survive the night."

Weizmann opened his gold watch. "It's almost morning.

We can expect the bombardment to stop soon. Then it will be time to go."

"Will you help us?" Aaronsohn asked, the hostility gone from his voice.

"I will fight," said Lawrence. "For all of us."

"We would welcome your help," Weizmann said, diffident now. "And your voice, when the war is over."

Will I be alive after the war is over? Will I even want to be? Lawrence wondered. Time to discuss that later.

"The P.M. said I should be briefed. With your pardon, gentlemen, I'll find his secretary and get started." He gathered up the pictures that neither Weizmann or Aaronsohn seemed willing to touch. "By your leave, I will keep these. Study them. *Remember.*" Again, he was struck at how easy it was to be Colonel Lawrence, ending a staff meeting. "I shall do my best for you. You have my word on it."

Weizmann and Aaronsohn were at the door when Aaronsohn turned. "Lawrence?" he called.

Lawrence paused on his way to the windows. No, he had better not lift the blackout yet. And what good was dawn now, in a world gone wild? If dawn were rosy-fingered, as every schoolboy learned when he studied Homer, it was from dabbling in blood. He had seen blood on the sand, dawn over a battlefield; somehow this carnage in a city where the dying gasped their last words in his own language turned dawn into sacrilege.

"What is it?"

Aaronsohn shook his head, almost shy as he seemed to struggle to find words. "Only an old saying I wanted to tell you: next year in Jerusalem."

The door closed behind him.

The big Liberator Commando labored over the Mediterranean, struggling toward Cairo. Its cramped cabin stank of oil and human fear, and the oxygen mask made Lawrence's head ache and red lights go off behind his eyes.

He had been two days in flight for a trip that ordinarily took six days, making short hops between Takoradi, Kano, Fort Lamy, El Obeid, and so on until Cairo.

But "there is no time for safety!" Churchill had declared, and so the Commando, its bomb racks stripped to let its passengers sleep, blanket-wrapped like frozen mummies, on metal shelves, had flown out of Lyneham to Gibraltar. It flew eastward in the afternoon across Vichy as dusk fell. At Gibraltar it acquired its escort of Spitfires. Then it proceeded across the Mediterranean, flying to intercept the Nile at about Asyût. There it would fly north to the Cairo landing grounds northwest of the pyramids.

The plane was freezing, and Lawrence abandoned his comfortless shelf for the observer's seat in the cockpit. The Commando had reached the point of no return, when just enough fuel had been burned to make retreat impossible, even if it had been allowed, when the Luftwaffe arrived. They had expected it. Immediately the Liberator and its guardian Spitfires climbed steeply, above fifteen thousand feet . . . sixteen thousand . . . seventeen—to where the fighters' engines strained to function.

And there the Spitfires turned to dive on the Messerschmitts, while the bomber continued to climb to twenty-five thousand feet. A shot to one suicidal Messerschmitt blew away part of the tail assembly; the German plane exploded (like a Turkish train in smears of orange and black) and the converted bomber bounced in the shock waves. And still climbed. Lawrence had not known that it was possible to be so cold, or to feel so helpless as three of his escorts exploded into crimson horror or spiraled and smoked down into the water with the German planes they had destroyed instants before.

Those deaths are on your soul, he told himself, and ached to lose his guilt in action. Instead, he must sit, wrapped in blankets and strapped like a senile millionaire into his seat and his parachute, breathing cold oxygen through the painful constrictions of a mask, while the plane strained in the thin air toward safety. For moments at a time, he felt no fear; then panic—to die, strapped in, flaming down to crash like Phaëthon into a cruel sea—clutched him, and he despised himself. After all, he owed England and Germany both a death; did it matter if it occurred in 1935 (as the papers said) or now, in the winter of 1941?

I haven't risen from the dead, he wanted to tell the sweating, muttering men who had tended him throughout the trip with a mixture of worship and worry. They were young men, dying at an old man's orders so a middle-aged man (no man at all, if the truth be known) could be landed safely in North Africa to confront another middle-aged man who built his war on the lives of his young men. It galled him that they regarded him as a hero. If they saw those letters that Churchill had extracted from that wretched Bruce, the respect, the awe, even, of those junior officers, would change to contempt.

Best not chance that, not when so much depended on his actually *being* the garish Lawrence that American journalists had created. But he found their solicitude—kindness and concern for the old, sick man—more taxing than his malaria. Which had, in any case, abated, till the next time, leaving a curious lassitude and an even more curious clarity of mind, which the brief, sharp terror of the dogfight had only made more keen.

His mind ranged ahead of the wind that whistled over the injured aircraft, singing descant to the panting engines. After awhile, he turned from watching imperfectly understood instruments to reviewing what he had been told.

With fingers stiff in their fur-lined gloves, he checked to make certain that he still had the precious oilskin envelope of photographs that he would take with him into the desert. Topmost was the picture of his quarry. He fumbled the packet out and drew forth the photo: Erwin Rommel, general that was and field marshall hereafter; Rommel with his fox's grin, his ferocity, and the chivalry that seemed so odd and so familiar. They were much alike, in some ways: both middle-aged, both of less-than-average stature; both with a gift for sensing the presence of the enemy and using the desert itself as a weapon; both quite capable of marshaling and moving heaven and earth to compel men to their goals.

And, in the end, it was their names, as much as any army, that won them their victories. A stocky man, a punctilious man with his careful hats and uniforms, his blue *Pour le Mérite* at the throat. A family man, this Rommel, with a wife he rarely saw. Now that was unlike Lawrence. Rommel had a son, too, and professed himself never to be happier than when he was guiding young people. How did Rommel feel, Lawrence wondered, about sending the young men of the crack Afrika Korps out to die?

Well, Lawrence could show him other young people who would have been glad of his protection: the dead of

Europe, the lifeless, accusing faces that grinned sightlessly and forever at the camera. *If you can kill him, do so,* Churchill had ordered. *Dead is safe.* But Churchill, as Lawrence had known for years, was a man who well understood the value of inspiration.

What if Rommel could be *turned,* a knife snatched from a killer and used upon him instead? What if, indeed? Perhaps the cold, the exhaustion, and the thin air had spawned this fancy, Lawrence thought. At such times of stress, intellect and instinct fused, and his mind ranged apart from his waking self in a condition akin to prophecy or perhaps madness. If he could shatter Rommel's faith . . . it might even be that Germany would take care of his death. And Lawrence had had a bellyful of causing death.

Rommel, in "Mammut," the armored command truck that was a prize from the British, roved where he would, over the sand, to menace Cairo with his Panzers and turn the waste between the British command and his own into a mine field. What if Lawrence joined the Berbers, traveling lighter and faster, anticipating Rommel's every move until, finally, they could come face to face? It was either inspired strategy, or the ravings of a lunatic; but reason had meant very little in the War thus far.

"Colonel?" came a voice that managed to be deferential and well-bred even through the tinniness of the oxygen. *Oxford,* Lawrence thought, and probably one of the posher colleges. Trinity, perhaps, or The House.

He laid a hand over the photo, almost guarding it from sight. Rommel was *his* designated prey, a relationship and task too intimate to be shared by this young lieutenant with the unshaven face, the red-veined eyes, and the keenness of a man for whom such things were but temporary.

"Yes, Lieutenant?"

"We'll be descending soon. And, see, it's dawn, sir."

His eyes closed in relief.

Dawn flashed on the wings of the Liberator Commando and the surviving Spitfires as they descended. Lawrence blinked hard at the violence of the light. The wings burned silver as the water flowing through black earth toward the Delta and Alexandria—which, even now, Lawrence had heard, Mussolini dreamed of entering in triumph. If Lawrence had anything to say about it, Alexander's city should not fall to such as he.

Cairo. Because of Lawrence's travels in the East and his work in Carchemish, he had spent two years in Intelligence there. There was little there for him, now: not among the Gallicized aristocrats whose daughters collected gold for their dowries along with Paris gowns; certainly not among the English enclave that politely thronged Shepheards, concerned with tea, tennis, and tonic. *For we were strangers in the land of Egypt.* He wondered if that had been his thought, or thrust into his brain by his talk with Weizmann and that zealot Aaronsohn.

Help for the East, or, for that matter, for the world, if it came from Cairo at all, might come from the unknown *fellahin* by the Nile, from whom some advocate might rise as religions rose from the desert itself. For Lawrence, Cairo was a staging point. This war's incarnation of his old service would brief him, equip him, and send him out into the desert.

His hands clenched and his palms were sweating.

To his horror, he realized how eager he was.

The winter rain poured down as Lawrence rode past the border wire into Libya. For the thousandth time, he thought what a dirty war it was into which he had been thrust. Blackmailed—if a man as guilty as he had a right to use the term—blackmailed and sentenced to a war full of whispers. In Cairo, spies of all the powers rubbed shoulders in safety, greeted each other with circumspect nods before retiring to their mutterings.

Lawrence himself was one such whisper. The rank and file might mutter that he hadn't really died in that cycle crash in May of 1935; they were entitled to hope. But it was another thing for him to confront narrow-eyed MI officers, present the P.M.'s authorizations, and watch them nod. "Churchill must be desperate," one man had remarked. Yet even he had stared at Lawrence as at a welcome ghost.

How do you hunt a desert fox? You use a myth, if you can first tame it.

In the end, Lawrence left Cairo almost unnoticed. Weighted against General Auchinleck's preparations of the Eighth Army to defend Tobruk against Rommel, even the appearance of a shadow from the last War was no more than a simple ruse: welcome, if it succeeded, but not expected to accomplish much. Auchinleck, in fact, had snorted and chuffed that the P.M. was pulling rabbits out of a hat again—damned mummery!—but he was welcome to try. He, however, was preparing for what had been named, rather grandiosely, Operation Crusader; Lawrence hoped that it had somewhat better luck than the Crusaders he had chronicled long ago in school.

Unlikely Crusaders, to resent an ally. But that had been the way of it in what Lawrence thought of as "his" war too: professional soldiers might envy his results, but did not trust him. Allenby, he remembered, had handled him with the care that he had used for explosives. Still, he had ridden with Allenby into Jerusalem. Now there was a Crusade!

Once again, he had the sense that knowledge that he needed was being withheld. It infuriated him. For God's sake, what did he care for their games of powers and principalities? His honor, if he could claim to possess any, lay in the safety of the men with him and, perhaps, in any chance he might have to expiate some of the fresh guilt that had gnawed his liver since he had seen the pictures that he carried as a talisman. In the last war he had carried a battered volume of Malory.

Here he was, in the desert he had longed for, yet it was a sea of mud, not the red sand and glowing *ghibli* of the North, nor the vast austerities of Arabia. Nor did he wear the white robes of a sharif of Mecca, but drab and coarse garments, heavier—but not heavy enough to keep out the rain. They clung, leechlike, to numbing skin, draining the endurance from him.

All the stillness that he remembered had vanished. North Africa was full of noises: the sputter of overused engines, polyglot curses, and overwhelming all, the steady rainfall. It seemed impossible that these sounds should ever change or fade.

But one of Lawrence's guards (were they set to spy on him as well as guard him?) stiffened and drew closer. That *had* been a new sound, not the ringing in his ears. He reached for his pistol and slid off the safety.

He had been told to be prepared to encounter friendlies: here, apparently, they were. He was trying to remember the properties of greeting Berbers, as opposed to the many Arab tribes with which he had dealt, when the newcomers' leader rode up to him.

Berbers were fined down by their life; this man's sodden clothing outlined a stockier frame. As he neared, Lawrence saw that under the mud, the exhaustion, and the deep weathering, the man's skin was pale and his eyes light.

"Colonel Lawrence, sir?" said this "Berber," carefully coming to not-quite-attention before saluting in the native style. The intensity of his gaze was almost an assault.

Lawrence nodded.

"Thank God, sir! I'm John Haseldon." His eyes gleamed and he all but peered into Lawrence's own, standing too close for English tastes, let alone his own, as Semites always did. Lawrence groaned inwardly.

"What news, sir?" Haseldon asked. "Where *is* Rommel now?" he asked. Cairo headquarters had told Lawrence that he had been in Rome for his birthday, November 15.

"Wouldn't you have more recent news than I?" Lawrence asked.

"He landed safely in Africa, more's the pity. Anwar here," Haseldon gestured at a man indistinguishable from the other riders, "says that he and his brothers have seen him at Beda Littoria."

"We're headed there?"

Haseldon nodded, chewed things over, then spoke again.

"Sir, you've been at Headquarters. Any chance," he asked in a rush, "that Rommel will bypass Tobruk?"

Lawrence shook his head. "None at all."

The Italian General Bastico had argued for it, and Rommel had flown off to Rome to confer with Mussolini. The Eighth Army had men and tanks enough to hurl against the Afrika Korps, but the Afrika Korps had Rommel, man and myth.

Another man might have relished this contest. Lawrence rode with water dripping in miserable rivulets down his *kuffiyeh* and wished that the newcomer wasn't quite so energetic. "It's good you've come, sir," said Haseldon. "Glad to have you here; we can show you quite a nice bit of action."

"Like the whole Eighth Army?" Lawrence asked.

"A little livelier than a major action," said this Haseldon, who wore his native dress with as much ease as once Lawrence had done. "Mad" English, as brave as he was crazy; and with the colossal bad fortune to have come to manhood after the singularly unfortunate event of Lawrence's involuntary celebrity. Haseldon, apparently, lived as a native among natives . . . and behind enemy lines. *God help the bloody fool*, thought Lawrence.

"What have you planned, then?" Lawrence asked, and beckoned Haseldon to ride at his side. The indigs with him nodded, one chief acknowledging a second. Gravely, Lawrence turned to them, saluting in the Arab fashion because Berber courtesies had quite flown from his memory.

"First we ride."

"And then?" If this downpour got any worse, they might as well ride into the sea.

"Cozy little raid on headquarters at Beda Littoria, sir," said Haseldon. "I've been living outside of Rommel's HQ there for quite some time now."

"Is that where we're headed?"

Haseldon shook his head. "First, we head out toward Cyrene to pick up a few commandos that'll be dropped off by sub."

I knew nothing of this! Lawrence thought. For a moment, *The P.M. will learn of this!* thundered in his mind. Then, he fought against the disastrous laughter that could turn too easily into hysterics. *Would I believe someone who claimed to be me, either?*

He fell silent and Haseldon, respecting his moods, was silent until they camped. He and his men crouched too closely together, showing Lawrence their maps. *Here* was the grain silo, followed by a row of bungalows. *Soldiers there*, Lawrence pointed, and Haseldon nodded, before indicating a larger mark on the map.

"That building, the 'Prefettura,' set back in a grove of cypress . . . that's where he lives. It's dark, isolated."

Lawrence nodded. "So, now what?"

"Now, we wait."

"For the sub?" Lawrence asked. Haseldon ducked his head, and Lawrence waited, testing. Had the man been warned not to confide totally in Lawrence? Who had warned him of that, in any case? In Wellington's words, this was an infamous army, each officer keeping secrets, and no trust anywhere.

The night dragged on as they waited for the rhythmic splashes, camouflaged in the persistent rain, of the commandos' arrival. From time to time, Haseldon stared at Lawrence, then at his maps.

"Was it like this?" he finally blurted, "when you took Aqaba?"

"Much drier," Lawrence observed, and a grin spread across the younger man's taut face. "We had the desert to cross, and we knew that the guns were fixed to face seaward. That much could put our minds at rest. . . ." And curiously, that much was true. "What may have made it easier, though, was that all we faced were some Turks and nameless Germans. Not Rommel."

The younger man gave a quick, relieved sigh. "Waiting's the hardest part," he admitted.

"Waiting for the trains to come was always the worst. You always wanted to push the plunger and explode the track long before it was safe to. Sometimes we did. Usually, we lost those—"

A sharp hiss brought both men around, their hands snatching for sidearms. Three men waded out of the water, and Haseldon started forward. Lawrence found himself tensing, ready to leap forward should there prove to be yet another betrayal . . . but it was all right; they were shaking hands. In the dampness, Lawrence heard names: Keyes, a major, and the men under his command, Campbell and Terry. Haseldon guided them toward what soggy hospitality he could offer, and Lawrence faded imperceptibly among the Berbers.

At midnight, Major Keyes and his team headed for the Prefettura. Haseldon started out of hiding but "Get back!" Keyes gestured. Then he strode forward and pounded on the front door, demanding admission in German, pushing past the sentry.

Two shots were fired, and the house in the cypress grove went dark.

Lawrence reached Haseldon's side just as a burst of fire exploded, filling one room with light as if it were a stage on which a man, mortally wounded, fell, and another staggered. Just in time, Lawrence caught Haseldon's arm.

"Ours?" Haseldon whispered hoarsely.

"Either way, you can't help them," Lawrence warned him. Haseldon was younger, stronger than Lawrence; if he wanted to break free, he was going to, unless . . . surreptitiously, Lawrence drew his sidearm.

"The man who fell. He wasn't wearing a German uniform. They may be dead, dying—"

"Just you hope that they are," Lawrence told him, holding his eyes, which were white and staring in the dark. *Not so heroic now, is it, watching men die for your schemes?* If the man wanted to play desert hero, that was one lesson he'd better learn tonight. "That was the worst part. We didn't want to leave our wounded for the Turks, but sometimes— Shh! Who's coming?"

A dark blotch wavered toward them, and Lawrence snapped the safety off his weapon and readied it—until Haseldon forced the barrel of his pistol down.

"*Wie geht's?*" he called.

"Terry!" The commando's voice shook. "The major's dead. Campbell's down . . . the bastards had guards there . . . but not Rommel . . . he never stays here, I heard."

It was exhaustion, not judgment, in the fugitive's eyes, but Haseldon flinched.

"They say Rommel's near Gambut at Ain Gazala."

Haseldon pounded his fist into his palm. "God, I could kill myself! We've got to get the bastard!"

"He can't stay here," Lawrence muttered, careful to keep his voice down so Terry couldn't hear him. Memories of old retreats came to his aid. "Get him away from here. They had to have some plans for getting the team out. What were they?"

"Right," Haseldon nodded sharply. "Hitler's got standing orders to shoot commandos on sight." He gestured, detaching five Berbers who surrounded Terry and, despite his protests, bore him away. "Take him back to Cyrene, and keep him safe till pickup," he ordered.

Haseldon sank onto the ground, and Lawrence divided his attention between him and the Prefettura. He had played decoy before. What if an old, weary native straggled by to gain information? Given that a raid on the place had just occurred, he'd be lucky if he weren't shot, that's what, he told himself acerbically. For the first time in his campaigns in a Muslim world, he wished for a flask of brandy; Haseldon looked as if he could use it.

"We should leave, too," he hinted, but the man sat, all but unstrung. His courage was all of the quick, gallant kind; eager to act, but equally swift to despair. Rommel was said to be of that sort, too.

Haseldon nodded, and they rose. Seconds later, though, the renewed downpour forced them to huddle into what shelter they could contrive. "The roads will be washed out," Haseldon muttered through chattering teeth. "The *wadis* will be flooded."

"Maybe he'll drown," Lawrence soothed him.

"We've got to do something!"

"We will." Fraud that he was, he knew how to fill his voice—even in a whisper—with conviction. He would inspire, would use this man too to bring him to Rommel. And then what?

He knew now what his own role must be. Somehow he must reach Rommel; must get close enough—no, he did not think that the P.M. meant to turn him into an assassin. This attempt might draw the German out of his lair just long enough for Lawrence to catch his attention. That would be the moment of supreme risk: catch the general's attention, avoid being shot, and then, somehow, convince him . . . of what?

God only knew; and these days, God wasn't speaking to one Thomas Edward Lawrence. *Let it go for now,* came the voice of instinct within him that he had learned years ago to trust. *Wait with the trees, the bodies, the Germans.*

The rain poured down like the Nile from its mountain cataracts, and Lawrence hunched over, trying hard not to think.

Dawn came, then night, which they spent huddling in Haseldon's mean shelter well away from Beda Littoria, then another dawn. Carefully chosen men crept back and forth. The last one came at a run, nearly tripping over himself, almost incoherent with his news. Rommel was sending his own chaplain to conduct the services for three Germans and the dead English major.

"Rommel won't come," Haseldon mourned. "He's got a war to fight."

"So do we, man," said Lawrence. "And the first thing is to live to fight it. That chaplain won't come all by himself. Let's move!"

To the West lay only the shore. Safety lay in Egypt; but between them and Egypt were Tobruk and Operation Crusader. Time after time, they dodged the trucks and tanks that crawled like rats up and down the escarpments, crept past smoking rubble, lay flat as aircraft, English or German, flew overhead. Their supplies ran out, but—"Stealing from the dead . . . " protested Haseldon.

"Would you rather starve with your work undone?" demanded Lawrence, and forced himself to open the first pack he found.

Lawrence had been hunted before; had lived with a price on his head. But never before had he fully understood what it was like to flee too lightly equipped and armed to do anything but cower as the armies raged by. Their retreat stretched out, seemed endless, compared with what now seemed the effortless progresses by truck or beast. Haseldon's grimy face had long since fined down; his blue eyes looked like sky piercing through a skull's eyesockets. He was being remade in this retreat, forged into a man stronger and madder than anyone would wish for him. Knowing what it felt like, Lawrence would stand godfather to that second birth. He doubted that it—or he—would live much longer, unless more luck than he deserved rode with them.

Their luck held all the way to Sidi Omar, on the Egyptian border.

"Down!" The ground shook. Overhead, shells burst, staining the afternoon sky with flame and smoke.

"Look!" Haseldon pointed at a lean-to, set up behind an army truck. Painted on the truck's side was a red cross. "That's one of ours," he whispered. "Our truck; our field hospital. Thank God." He let his head fall into his hands.

In whose hands? Lawrence refused to ask. He glanced at the armored vehicles. "Do we go in?"

"Let's investigate."

Crouching low to the ground, Lawrence dodged around the smoking carcass of a tank. Old scars and surgeries screamed pain at him, but he ignored them.

A blow thrust him to the ground. He writhed around to grapple with his attacker. It was Haseldon, his face and body twisting as a bullet hit him. Swearing hopelessly in Arabic, Lawrence wadded up his headcloth and thrust it against the wounded man's side, where it turned red and sodden far too rapidly. Now it did not matter who controlled that field hospital.

"Bear up, lad," Lawrence whispered. Before he could remember that he was old, sick, and half-crazed, and that he hated to be touched, he swung Haseldon's arm over his shoulder and started across the field toward the wretched hospital. The bursts of light, the shaking of the ground as each shell exploded—all faded from his consciousness; his horizons narrowed to the next step, the step after that.

The command to stop came in German and was reinforced with a warning shot and men in his path, barring his way to the surgery. Speaking or looking up might be fatal. He eased Haseldon to the ground.

"That one's done for." The soldiers spoke over his head. Lawrence turned Haseldon's face away, afraid that its pallor would betray them both.

"Just as well. Those Berbers are treacherous little beasts."

"Still, if the English are wasting supplies, we should . . ."

"You can't disturb the surgeons now. They're operating on Colonel Stephan of the Fifth Panzer."

There was a murmur of dismay. "When was he brought in?"

"Around noon. He's got a bad chest wound. Shrapnel. The General wanted the English surgeon, this Major Aird, to put a pressure dressing on it, so Colonel Stephan could be flown out. But the doctor insisted on operating, said Stephan would die if he didn't."

Someone shouted an order in harsh German from the lean-to.

"They want the armored cars to pull back?" the soldier standing nearby demanded. "So the noise won't disrupt the surgery? Maybe we could put up little curtains to make the operating room more *gemütlich*, too."

"*Schweig;* they're operating on one of ours. Tender-hearted, those English."

"What about the natives there?"

"Let them wait. They're worthless."

The roar of engines as the armored cars withdrew made Lawrence shudder. He had hoped that playing the role of fugitive, aiding a wounded tribesman, might win him help from the English surgeons. But clearly the Germans were not going to let him get near the surgery. They were just going to let Haseldon die here, weren't they? And why? Because he wasn't one of theirs. Lawrence thought of the photos he carried, then of Tafas. "The best of you brings me the most Turkish dead," he had said then. Atrocious: the stiffened bodies in the desert; the bled-out bodies in the grave pits; the sight of a man who had admired him dying in his arms. *As flies to wanton boys are we to the gods,* the line ran through his head. *They kill us for their sport.*

Fingers struggled toward his, and he grasped Haseldon's hand as firmly as he might. "Sorry," came a faint whisper.

"No one could have done better," Lawrence replied, "and I'll remember." He heard Haseldon struggle for breath, and drew him closer, holding the dying man's head up until it lolled back, and Lawrence knew that he was dead.

The ground had stopped shaking. Now only the tramp of booted feet, not bombshells, made Lawrence tense. A crowd of Panzer officers was leaving the tent.

"We'll return again tomorrow on our way back into Egypt," one of them told the bloodstained man who accompanied them out of the operating room.

Last of all, as if in defiance of protocol, was a general, not too tall, somewhat stocky, wearing an Iron Star and a blue order, *Pour le Mérite,* at his throat.

Lawrence knew that face from his pictures, from the waking nightmare that his life had long been. He waited until all the others had passed. Then, in an undertone, he called, "Herr General Rommel!"

Unsnapping the catch of his holster, Rommel strode toward him. Lawrence took a deep breath and raised his head, and Rommel halted. His hand went up, and his mouth opened and closed on Lawrence's name.

"So, do ghosts now fight alongside the quick and the dead?" Rommel asked, elaborately sarcastic, in his heavily accented Swabian German. "A fraud, of course."

"I am quite what I seem to be," Lawrence stated in the carefully cultivated German of the Oxford scholar he had once been.

Rommel gestured with distaste at Haseldon's body, half-sprawled over Lawrence's knees. "So I see."

Lawrence grimaced and straightened Haseldon's body on the ground. Any moment now, Rommel would shout for guards to take him away, if he didn't just draw his Luger and kill Lawrence himself. "Apparently, your assassins had never heard of German efficiency. I survived."

Rommel stared down at Haseldon, and Lawrence followed his glance, saw the glazed stare of filming blue eyes, and shut them with a convulsive motion of one bloodstained hand. He had a sudden impulse to pour dirt over the dead man's face. "He was under my command," Lawrence said. "I'd be grateful if he had a decent burial."

Rommel snapped his fingers for the guards to take the body away. "And you, too?"

"Before or after I give you Prime Minister Churchill's message? I'd appreciate a safe-conduct out of here."

"You have my word on it. I would have been disappointed if the English had sunk to using the notorious Lawrence as an assassin or a spy." He glanced around, as if he could see an English regiment about to attack and rescue Lawrence.

"I'm quite alone, I promise you."

"You're dead! Men don't disappear for five years, have funeral sermons preached over them, then appear in the middle of a war—"

Lawrence laughed softly. "Herr General, you are not the only soldier known for being unpredictable. Would you not use your death—or a lie about it—to help your country?"

"What assurances do I have that *you* are not a lie?" Already, Rommel was beckoning Lawrence toward "Mammut," as if he preferred to debrief a spy in private. A junior officer hurried up, waving a message.

"This is war the way the ancient Teutons used to fight it. I don't even know at this moment whether the Afrika Korps is on the attack or not!" Rommel cursed.

His mood had shifted from the ironic whimsicality of a moment ago. Lawrence knew there was not much time. Operation Crusader was keeping Rommel on the run with its very unpredictability.

"Well?" he snapped at Lawrence.

Moving slowly, keeping his hands in view at all times,

Lawrence took off his weapons belt. "My word of honor," he said.

Rommel raised an eyebrow, and part of Lawrence agreed with him.

"The word," he went on, hating the theatricality of his words, "of a man who rode with Allenby into Jerusalem at the head of the first Christian army to take it since the Crusades."

Rommel laughed, a sound resembling the bark of a fox. "Crusade! Not precisely my favorite word," he said.

Lawrence shrugged. "Soldiers can only do what they can. We too must follow our orders, no matter how they tie our hands or short us on supplies."

"The Russian front! God only knows how sick I am of the damned Russian front! They want Cairo, Alexandria . . . I could give them all Egypt, but not one man, not one penny for Africa, but that it's begrudged—"

"And sent to Russia?" Lawrence asked. "Germany has some magnificent strategic minds; but Russia? Napoleon foundered there. Do you think that your Führer can succeed where Napoleon failed?"

"Is this what your Churchill sent you to do?" Rommel snapped. "To test my loyalty to the Führer? My oath holds."

"You sound like one of Charlemagne's paladins, off to fight the Moors."

Rommel bowed slightly, in pleased acknowledgment.

"I do not think that this is the same kind of war, do you?" Lawrence continued. "Or even the type of war we fought in '17."

"The war is the war. I follow orders."

But Rommel's answer sounded automatic. If he lost interest now, it could cost Lawrence his life. And if Rommel chose to reveal who had visited him, it could cost Churchill—and England—even more.

"You do more than follow orders," Lawrence said. "You serve your country. We are two of a kind, you know. I was silenced for more than five years, until England had a use for me once more. You . . . you are kept short of men and equipment, praised, but not truly given the honors due you—"

"Let me tell you, Colonel, if this is an attempt to subvert me, it is a very crude one—"

"I didn't cross a battlefield to try anything that stupid," Lawrence snapped.

"What did you come to do?"

"To ask you questions. You say you took an oath to Hitler. Well enough. Oaths should not be broken. What about your oath to Germany?

"Look at this war. Look at how you've been treated. In the name of God, look at the man you call the Führer and the people he's surrounded himself with. These are the men who are going to build your new Empire, your thousand-year Reich. Do you think they can do it? Can you honestly say of Hitler, 'This is the man who will rule like a Charlemagne or Barbarossa'?"

"Clearly, you want me to say, 'No, I can't.' You may proceed. But make it quick. I'm getting bored."

"I gave you my weapon," Lawrence said. "But I did come armed with something else." Moving slowly, praying that his hands would not tremble with the sudden, dreadful fear that chilled him, Lawrence reached into his clothing and withdrew the photos he had carried for so long. "Look at these," he said, and laid them down near Rommel's hand. He was glad to step back; he had not realized that his life still held such value for him.

The general opened the oilskin-wrapped packet and glanced at the pictures, one by one. He was a cool one, Lawrence would give him that, if he could look at those pictures and betray no reaction.

"They could be frauds, you know," said Rommel. "Since when did you become such a Zionist?"

Lawrence drew himself up. "It has never been said of me that I have been a good friend to the Jews," he said carefully. Aaronsohn, he thought, would certainly testify to that. "The pictures are not important because they depict Jews," he said. "It would be the same if they showed Hottentots or Red Indians. What those pictures show is *your* Germany, *your* country to which you swore an oath, committing acts that will make its Reich last a thousand years only in infamy. A criminal Empire! Is that what you want?"

Rommel snatched his Luger from his holster, but Lawrence grabbed his wrist. "It's easy enough to kill me," he hissed at Rommel. "After all, I'm 'dead' already. But it won't kill the questions I've raised. And you wouldn't be ready to shoot me if they hadn't been questions you've already asked yourself. *Do* you approve of the way this war is being fought, or what else is going on? *Can* you honestly say that Hitler is a man of sanity and honor who is fit to rule the world?"

"He holds my oath!" Rommel repeated.

"I remind you. You gave your oath to Germany first. As I did to England."

"And you do this for England?" Rommel asked with heavy sarcasm.

Lawrence nodded. "So I can make peace with myself, as I have not done since the Great War ended. Then it seemed that betrayal was everywhere; and so I left service until now, when I have been offered a chance, perhaps, to even the score."

Abruptly, weariness replaced Lawrence's fear. At this very moment, Haseldon was being shoveled into a grave among his enemies, and Lawrence almost envied him. But he could not rest, not when he had more barbs to place.

"I came in here with as fine a man as ever served with me," he said. "Dead now. Look at your Afrika Korps, General. They fight like tigers. And look at your Italian soldiers. But what about the officers who command them?"

"Shits they are and shits they have always been," Rommel declared.

"And is Mussolini any better? Or the drug addict Hitler has appointed as Air Marshal, who daily kills innocent English children? But you, you are a man of honor, a patriot, serving with such people. Do you truly think that, when this is all ended, they will reward you? They are likelier by far to turn on you for the very thing that makes you different."

"If I were *not* a man of honor, I could almost be a rat," Rommel mused. "As it is, I know I'm going to regret talking with you or telling you that you can have your life, if you get out of here now."

"I'll *have* my life, General," Lawrence said. "But you, you're going to die here. Unless you do what Napoleon did, and Vespasian before him: use Egypt as your bastion, and move north!"

"I said get out!"

"You, though. We could talk with you. If you headed the Reich, you and the Allies might be able to come to some agreement, push Germany's borders out to their old limits or beyond a bit. And we'd have an end to this killing, this stupidity! Remember that, Rommel. England could deal with you. But with Hitler? We'll fight to the last man."

"I follow my orders," Rommel said once again.

"You've violated orders time and time again. Commandos are to be shot; you've let them live. Good God, you're going to let me live. You've already broken your oath to honor a greater one. Honor that oath, by all means! Think about what it means, and what, to honor it as it deserves, you may have to do. Just think; that's all I—all the world—ask."

Tentatively, Lawrence reached for his weapon—*and* the pictures. The gesture was a risk. But he could not cross Egypt unarmed, and he would not leave the photos among Germans.

"I'm going now," he said.

"What will you tell your Prime Minister?" Again, the heavy sarcasm, mixed with exhaustion like Lawrence felt and something that he recognized as indecision.

"I? Nothing. I have obeyed my orders and spoken with you. He promised me that when I had done so, I should go free. You will not hear of me again."

Rommel nodded. "So that is why you want the weapon. Sometimes that is the only way out . . . for such as we." He started to hold out his hand, then withdrew it.

"Wise of you, General," Lawrence said. "Your men will simply think that you have heard your pet spy and sent him about his business. You and I will know differently, though. And, depending on how you act, so will history."

"You have your life," Rommel said. "I will see you out of here. There are armed cars . . . short as we are, we can say that you stole one, unless your *honor*"—heavy irony on the word—"forbids that."

Rommel shouted for a signals officer and a mechanic. "Get me Berlin!" he demanded. "And you, fuel up my Heinkel!"

"But the battle, Herr General—"

"Am I to be obeyed, or not?" demanded Rommel. "Get moving!"

"This much," Rommel murmured, "I can do. I can ask, and I can see."

He saw Lawrence still standing there, a small man in filthy, bloodstained robes, and started perceptibly.

Lawrence almost smiled at him. Now that his work was

finished, he felt curiously light, like a cartridge when its charge is spent. At Rommel's gesture, Lawrence gathered the filthy folds of his native robes about him and stepped down from Mammut.

"That way," Rommel said. "There's the car. Get moving."

Lawrence could almost feel the explosion of a bullet between his shoulderblades as he walked to the car. Behind him, he heard a shout of warning, a command to stop, then a shot—but no pain.

As he started the car, he dared to steal a glance back at Rommel, who had knocked aside the barrel of a Walther P-38 from a soldier's hand.

"I told you not to fire! I gave that man my word of honor that he would have safeconduct out of here," Rommel raged.

The car started with a roar. If it had a full tank of petrol and luck was with him, it would be hours before he ran out of fuel. And then what? Then, somehow, he would join up with the sons of the men he had known long ago, men who would help him cross the desert, and take those damnable pictures to a place where, finally, he might lose and forget them forever. Whether or not Rommel played Faust to his Mephistopheles and turned on Hitler, whether the war had been shortened might matter to the rest of the world, but not to him. He would have begun the penance that would occupy him for the rest of his life.

Aaronsohn's ironic "Next year in Jerusalem" had become an obsession for him. The man had wanted Jerusalem for his people; in death, *these* at least would rest there. That seemed like the least he could do, if he were sentenced to go on living. Rommel had been right to stop him from being shot. Life was a more cruel sentence by far . . . perhaps for both of them.

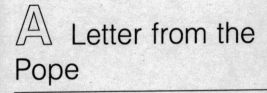

A Letter from the Pope

HARRY HARRISON AND TOM SHIPPEY

Introduction

In the year 865, according to the Anglo-Saxon Chronicle, a "great army" of the Vikings landed in England, led in legend and probably in fact by the sons of Ragnar Hairy-Breeks. In the following years this army wiped out the rival dynasties of Northumbria, killed Edmund, king of East Anglia, and drove Burgred, king of Mercia overseas, replacing him with a puppet ruler. By 878 all the kingdoms of the English had been conquered—except for Wessex. In Wessex Alfred, the last of five brothers, continued to fight.

But then the Vikings turned their full effort on him. At Twelfth Night 878, when all Christians were still getting over Christmas and when campaigning was normally out of the question, they made a surprise attack on Wessex, establishing a base at Chippenham, and according to the Chronicle again driving many Englishmen overseas and compelling others to submit. Alfred was forced to go into hiding and conduct a guerilla campaign "with a small force, through the woods and the fastnesses of the fens." It was at this time that—so the story goes—he was reduced to sheltering in a peasant's hut, where immersed in his problems he burnt the goodwife's cakes and was violently rebuked for it.

Yet Alfred managed somehow to stay alive, keep on fighting, and arrange for the army of Wessex to be gathered under the Vikings' noses. He then, quite against the odds, defeated the "great army" decisively, and finally made a master stroke of statesmanship. He treated the Viking king Guthrum with great forbearance, converted him to Christianity, and became his godfather. This set up a reasonable relationship between English and Vikings, gave Wessex security, and became the basis for the later reconquest of all England by Alfred's son, grandson and later descendants (of whom Queen Elizabeth II is one).

Many historians have noted that if Alfred had not held

on in the winter of early 878, England would have become a Viking state, and the international language of the world would presumably now be a form of Danish. Yet there is another possibility.

By 878 Alfred and Wessex stood for Christianity, and the Vikings for paganism. The later reconquest of England was for Christ as well as for the Wessex kings, and monastic chroniclers were liable to see Alfred as an early crusader. But we know, from his own words, that Alfred was already by 878 deeply dissatisfied with the ineptitude of his churchmen. We also know that about the same time Ethelred, archbishop of Canterbury, had written to the pope to protest about Alfred's extortions—which were very likely only a demand for further contributions to resist the pagan assaults. Pope John VIII responded by sending Alfred a letter of severe reproof—at exactly the moment when Alfred was "journeying in difficulties through the woods and fens." This letter never arrived. No doubt the letter carrier could not find the king, or thought the whole situation far too dangerous even to try.

But what would have happened if the letter had been received? Would it have been the last straw for a king already isolated, almost without support even from his own subjects and his own Church? A king also with clear precedent for simply retiring to safety? Or would Alfred (as he so often did in reality) have thought of another bold, imaginative and unprecedented step to take?

This story explores that last possibility.

Alfred, Guthrum, Ethelnoth, Odda, Ubbi, Bishop Ceolred, the archbishop of Canterbury, as well as the pope, are all historical characters. The pope's letter is based on examples of his known correspondence.

A dark figure moved under the trees ahead, barely visible through the heavy mist, and King Alfred raised his sword. Behind him the last army of England—all eighteen of them—stirred with unease, weapons ready as well.

"Easy," Alfred said, lowering his sword and leaning on it wearily. "It is one of the peasants from the village." He looked down at the man who was now kneeling before him, gaping up at the gold torque and bracelets that marked the king.

"How many are there?"

"Tw—twelve, lord King," the peasant stammered.

"In the church?"

"Yes, lord King."

The Vikings were conquerors, not raiders. Guthrum's men always quartered themselves in the timber churches, leaving the peasants' huts and the larger thanes' dwellings undamaged—as long as there was no resistance. They meant to take the country over, not destroy it. The mist was rising and the lightless village was visible below.

"What are they doing now?"

As if in reply the church door swung open, a square of red light against the blackness, and struggling figures passed across it before it slammed shut again. A female shriek hung in the air, then was drowned out by a roar of welcome.

Edbert, the king's chaplain, stirred with anger. He was lean, just string and bones, all the fat squeezed out by the passion of his faith. His voice loud and resonant, had been formed by that same faith. "They are devils, heathen devils! Even in God's own house they practice their beastly lusts. Surely He shall strike them in the middle of their sin, and they shall be carried to the houses of lamentation where the worm—"

"Enough, Edbert."

Alfred knew that his chaplain was vehement against the heathens, striking out strongly enough with his heavy mace, for all his leanness and apparent reluctance to shed blood against the canons of the Church. But talk of miracles could only anger men who had wished for divine assistance many times—so far without reward. He turned back to the peasant. "You're sure there are twelve?"

"Yes, lord King."

The odds were not good. He needed a two-to-one advantage to guarantee victory. And Godrich was still coughing, near dead with cold. He was one of the eleven king's companions who had right of precedence in every battle. But not this time. A sound reason must be concocted for leaving him behind.

"I have a most important duty for you, Godrich. If the attack should fail we will need the horses. Take them all down the track. Guard them with your life. Take Edi to help you. All others follow me."

Alfred put his hand on the kneeling peasant's shoulder.
"How will we know the door is unbarred?"

"My wife, lord King . . ."

"She is in there with the Vikings?"

"Aye, lord King."

"You have a knife in your belt? Follow, then. I grant you
the throats of the wounded, to cut."

The men surged forward across the meadow, grimly
eager now to end the waiting, to strike at least one nest of
their enemies from the board.

This nighttime raid was a pale shadow of past encoun-
ters. Nine times now Alfred had led whole armies, real
armies, thousands of men, against the drawn-up line of the
enemy. With the war horns bellowing, the men drumming
their spears against the hollow shields, the champions in the
front rank throwing up their gold-hilted swords and catching
them as they called on their ancestors to witness their deeds.
And always, always the Viking line had stood watching them,
unafraid. The horses' heads on poles grinning over their
array, the terrible Raven banner of the sons of Ragnar spreading its wings in triumph.

How bold the attack; how bad the defeat. Only once, at
Ashdown, had Alfred made the enemy fall back.

So there would be no triumph in this night encounter,
no glory. But when this band of plunderers vanished, the rest
of the invaders would know there was one Saxon king still left
in England.

As they pushed through the gap in the thorn hedge and
strode into the miserable cluster of wattle-and-daub huts,
Alfred jerked his shield down so he could seize the handgrip,
and cleared the sax knife in its sheath. In pitched battle he
carried long sword and iron-mounted spear, but for these
scrimmages among the houses the men of Wessex had gone
back to the weapons of their ancestors, the Saxons. The men
of the sax: short, pointed, single-edged cleavers. He strode
quickly so that the hurrying companions could not squeeze
past him. Where was the Viking sentry? When they had
reached the last patch of shadow before the churchyard the
men stopped at his signal and pushed forward the peasant
guide. Alfred looked at him once, and nodded.

"Call now to your woman."

The peasant drew in his breath, shivering with fear,

then ran forward five paces into the little open square before the church. He halted and at the top of his voice uttered the long, wailing ululation of the wolf, the wild wolf of the English forests.

Instantly a harsh voice roared out from the church's tiny belfry, little more than a platform above the roof. A javelin streaked down at the howling man, but he had already leapt aside. There was a scrape of metal as the Saxons drew their weapons. The door swung suddenly outwards; Alfred held his shield in front of him and charged for the center of the door.

Figures pushed furiously in front of him, Tobba on the left, Wighard, captain of the king's guard, on the right. As he burst into the room men were already down, bare-skinned bearded figures rolling in blood. A naked, screeching woman ran across his path, and behind her he saw a Viking jumping for the ax that leaned against the wall. Alfred hurled himself forward and as the Viking turned back he drove the sax in under his chin. When he spun round, shield raised in automatic defence, he realized the skirmish was already over. The English had fanned out in one furious sweep and driven from wall to wall, cutting every Viking down, stabbing savagely at the fallen; no veteran of the Athelney winter thought for an instant of honor, or display. A Viking with his back turned was all they wanted to see.

Even as relief flooded into him Alfred remembered that there was one task left undone. Where was that Viking sentry? He had been on the belfry, awake and armed. He had had no time to come down and fall in the slaughter. Behind the altar there was a staircase leading up, little more than a ladder. Alfred called out in warning to the milling Englishmen and sprang towards it with his shield high. He was too late. Elfstan, his old companion, stared at his king without comprehension, threw up his arms, and fell forward. The javelin was bedded deep in his spine.

Slowly, deliberately, an armed Viking stepped down the ladder. He was the biggest man Alfred had ever seen, taller even than himself. His biceps swelled above gleaming bracelets, the rivets of his mail shirt straining to contain the bulk inside. Round his neck and waist shone the loot of a plundered continent. Without haste the Viking threw aside his shield and tossed a great poleax from one hand to the other.

His eyes met the king's. He nodded, and pointed the spiked head of the ax at the planked floor.

"Kom. Thou. *Konungrinn*. De king."

The fight's already won, thought Alfred. *Lose my life now? Insane. But can I turn aside from a challenge? I should have the churls with their bows to shoot him down. That is all that any pirate deserves from England.*

The Viking was already halfway down the stair, moving as fast as a cat, not stopping to whirl up the ax but stabbing straight forward with the point. Reflex hurled Alfred's shield up to push the blow aside. But behind it came two hundred and eighty pounds of driving weight. The attacker fought for a neck-break hold, snatching at the sax in Alfred's hand. For a moment all the king could do was struggle to get free. Then he was hurled aside. As he hit the wall there was a clang of metal, a moan. He saw Wighard falling back, his useless right arm trying to cover the rent in his armor.

Tobba stepped forward, his fist a short flashing arc which ended at the Viking's temple. As the giant staggered back towards him Alfred stepped forward and drove his sax with all his strength deep into the enemy's back, twisted furiously, withdrew as the man fell.

Tobba grinned at him and displayed his right fist. Five metal rings encircled the thumb and fingers.

"I 'ad the metalsmith mek it for me," he said.

Alfred stared round the room, trying to take stock. Already the place was crowded, the men of the village pushing in, calling to each other—and to their women, now struggling into their clothes. They gaped down at the gashed and bloody corpses while a furtive figure was already rummaging beneath discarded armor for the loot all plunderers carried with them. Wulfhun saw this and knocked the man aside. Wighard was down, obviously on the point of death. The Viking's ax had almost severed his arm and driven far too deep between neck and shoulder. Edbert, again priest not warrior, was bent over him, fussing with a phial, frowning at the mortally wounded man's words. As Alfred watched, the dying man fixed his eyes on his king, spoke haltingly to the chaplain, and then fell back, choking.

The pirate at his feet was moving too, saying something. Alfred's lifted hand stayed the eager peasant who rushed forward with his knife raised.

"What?" he said.

The pirate spoke again, in the kind of pidgin used by the invaders' captive women and slaves.

"Good stroke were that. I fought in front for fifteen years. Never saw stroke like him."

He fumbled for something round his neck, a charm pendant beneath the massive golden neck ring, concern coming into his eyes till his hand closed over it. He sighed, raised himself.

"But now I go!" he called. "I go. To Thruthvangar!"

Alfred nodded, and the peasant sprang forward.

Three days later the king sat on the camp stool which was all that Athelney could offer for a throne, waiting for the conucillors to come to the meeting he had called, still tossing the Viking's mysterious pendant meditatively from hand to hand.

There was no doubt what it was. When he had first pulled it out and shown it to the others, Edbert had said straight away, with a gasp of horror: "It is the *pudendum hominis*! It is a sign of the beastly lusts of the devil's children, abandoned to original sin! It is the pillar which the heathen worship, so boldly destroyed by our countryman the worthy Boniface in Detmar! It is—"

"It's a prick," said Tobba, putting the matter more simply.

It was a token, the king thought now, closing his fist angrily on it. A token for all the difficulties he continued to face.

He had had two dozen companions when they all set out from Athelney. But as they made their long, circuitous ride across Somerset, first one man had dropped out with horse trouble and then another. In darkness they simply faded away into the dusk; they had had their fill of the endless, losing battles. Noblemen, king's companions, men whose fathers and grandfathers had fought for Christ and Wessex. They would go home quietly to their estates, sit and watch, perhaps send discreet emissaries to the Viking king at Chippenham. Sooner or later one of them would betray the secret of the camp at Athelney, and then Alfred too would wake one night, as he had woken so many Viking stragglers, with shrieks around him and a knife already in his throat.

It would be sooner if they heard he had begun to refuse battle with the heathen. Small as the action had been, that night raid had been important. Eighteen men could still make a difference. But why had those eighteen stayed with him? The companions, no doubt, because they still felt it their duty. The churls, maybe, because they thought the heathens had come to take their land. But how long would either motivation last against continuous defeat and fear of death? Deep in his bones Alfred knew that there was only one man in his army, only one man in Athelney, who genuinely and without pretence had no fear of any Viking who ever breathed, and that was the grim and silent churl Tobba. No one knew where he came from. He had simply appeared in the camp one dawn, with a Viking ax in his hand and two mail shirts over his gigantic shoulder, saying nothing about where he had gotten them, or how he had slipped through the sentries round the marsh. He was just there. To kill the invaders. If only the king could find a thousand subjects like him.

Alfred opened his fist and the golden token swung before his eyes, a shining symbol of all that troubled him. First and foremost, he simply could not beat the Vikings in the open field. During the battle-winter eight years before, he and his brother King Ethelred had led the men of Wessex to fight the Vikings' Great Army nine times. Eight times they had been beaten.

The ninth time was at Ashdown. . . . Well, he had gained great credit there, and still had some of it left. While his brother had dallied at the prebattle mass, Alfred had seen that the Vikings were beginning to move down the hill. When Ethelred refused to curtail the mass and leave early, Alfred had stridden forward on his own, and had led the men of Wessex up the hill himself, charging in the front like a wild boar, or so the poets said. Just that one time his fury and frustration had inspired the men so that in the end the Vikings had yielded, retreated to leave a field full of dead, two heathen kings and five jarls among them. They had been back again two weeks later, as ready to fight as ever.

In some ways that day's battle had resembled the little skirmish so recently fought. Total surprise, with the fight as good as won even as it began. But though the skirmish had been won, there had still been one Viking left, ready to fight on. He had cost Alfred two good men, and had come within a hair of ending the campaign forever by killing the last of all the English kings still prepared to resist.

He had died well too. Better than his victim Wighard, Alfred was forced to admit. Very, very reluctantly Edbert had been compelled to reveal what the last words of the king's captain were. He had died saying: "God should have spared me this." How many years in purgatory that would cost him, Edbert had lamented, how little the faith of these degenerate times. . . . Well, the dying Viking had had faith. Faith in something. Maybe that was what made them fight so with such resolution.

It was the English who were not fighting well. That was Alfred's second problem, and he knew exactly what caused it. They expected to lose. Soon after every battle began the first of the wounded would be begging their friends not to leave them on the field to be dispatched when the English withdrew—as everyone knew they would. And their friends were only too ready to help them back to their ponies. Sometimes those who assisted returned to the front, sometimes they didn't. It was surprising in a way that so many men were still prepared to obey their king's call, to turn out and fight for their lands and their right not to obey foreigners.

But the thanes were beginning to hope that when the end finally came they could make a deal with the invaders, keep their lands, maybe pay higher taxes, bow to foreign kings. They could do what the men of the north, and of the Mark, had done. Five years before Burgred, king of the Mark, had given up, collected his treasury and the crown jewels, and slipped away to Rome. The pony-loads of gold and silver he had taken with him would buy him a handsome estate in the sun for the rest of his life. Alfred knew that some of his followers were already wondering whether it would not be a good plan to depose their king, the last stubborn atheling of the house of Cerdic, and replace him with someone more biddable. There was little chance for him to forget Burgred's treachery. Far too often Alfred's wife Ealhswith reminded him of her kinsman, the former king of the Mark.

She had a son and daughter to think of. But he had a kingdom—reason enough for him to battle on. As for the rest of the English, if they fought badly it was not due to any lack of skill or want of courage. It was because they had plenty to lose and almost nothing to gain. Nor had he anything to offer the loyal. No land. It had been twenty years since his pious father had given a whole tenth of all his land in all the kingdom to the Church. Land that ordinarily would have gone to supporting warriors, pensioning off the injured, making the old companions ready and eager to breed sons and send them into service in their turn. Alfred had none now to give.

He hadn't been able to beat the Vikings when he had an army—and now it was impossible to raise one. The Vikings had all but caught him in bed three months before, when every Christian in Wessex was sleeping off the Christmas festivities. He had barely escaped them, fleeing like a thief into the night. Now the Viking king sat in Chippenham and sent his messengers along the high roads. The true king must skulk in the marsh and hope that in the end news of his continued resistance would somehow seep out.

And that took him to the third of his problems. He couldn't beat the Vikings because his men would not support him. He couldn't get his men to support him because their rewards had gone to the Church. And the Church . . .

The sound of challenges from outside told him that his councillors had arrived and were about to be shown in. Swiftly Alfred gave the pendant—prick, pudendum or holy sign, whatever it was—one last look and then stuffed it into his belt-bag and forgot about it. He touched the cross that hung from a silver chain about his neck. The cross of the true Christ. Might His power still be with him. The canvas screen of his shelter was pulled aside.

He looked glumly at the seven men who came in, as they slowly and with inappropriate courtesy found places among the motley assortment of seats he could provide. Only one councillor had an unquestioned right to be there. At least two of the others he could much better have spared. But they were all he had to work with.

"I will say who is present, for those who have not met before," he began. "First, all should know Alderman Ethelnoth." The rest nodded politely to the red-faced heavy man who sat nearest to the king: the only shire-leader still to be in the field, still fighting from a bivouac like Alfred's own.

"Next, we have a spokesman from Alderman Odda."

Odda was the shire-leader of Devon. "Wihtbord, what know you of the enemy?"

The young, scarred man spoke briefly and without shyness. "I have heard that Ubbi is in Bristol fitting out a fleet. He has the Raven banner with him. My master, Odda, has called out the shire levy, a thousand men at a time. He is watching the coast."

This was news—and bad news. Ubbi was one of the dreaded sons of Ragnar. Two of the others were gone. Halfdan had retired to the north, Sigurd Snake-eye was thought to be ravaging in Ireland. And—thank God—no one had heard of Ivar the Boneless for some time. Bad news. Alfred had hoped that he would only have to deal with the relatively weaker King Guthrum. But with Ubbi outfitting a fleet, the Ragnarssons still presented a great danger.

"Representing both Dorset and Hampshire we have Osbert."

Glum silence greeted this remark. The presence of Osbert reminded them that the true aldermen of these two shires could not or would not come. Everyone knew that the alderman of Hampshire had fled overseas, while the alderman of Dorset had cravenly submitted to the Viking Guthrum, so could not be trusted with knowledge of his king's whereabouts.

Almost with relief Alfred turned to the three churchmen present.

"Bishop Daniel is here in his own right, to speak for the Church—"

"And also for my lord the archbishop of Canterbury."

"—and I have further invited Bishop Ceolred to join us, for his wisdom and his experience."

Eyes turned curiously to the old man, evidently in very poor health, who sat nearest the door. He was in fact the bishop of Leicester, far beyond the borders of Wessex. But Leicester was now a Viking town, and the bishop had fled to what he thought was safety with the king of Wessex. Perhaps he regretted it now. Still, Alfred thought, he might at least get some sense through to this overbearing idiot Daniel, and his lord of Canterbury.

"Finally Edbert my chaplain is here to make note of all decisions reached. And Wulfsige is present as captain of my guard."

Alfred looked around at his handful of followers and kept

a stern face so his black depression would not show. "Nobles, I have to tell you this. There will be a battle. I am calling the muster of Wessex for Ascension Day. It will be at Edgebright's Stone, east of Selwood. Every man of Wessex must be there or forfeit all land-right and kin-right forever."

There were slow nods. Every Christian knew when Easter was, if he knew nothing else. It had been ten days ago. In thirty more days it would be Ascension. Everyone knew Edgebright's Stone. And it was far enough away from the Viking center at Chippenham to make a muster possible.

"Bishop Daniel, I rely on you to pass this message to every priest in your diocese and in the archdiocese of your lord, so that they can tell every Christian in every parish."

"How am I to do that, my lord? I have no hundreds of horsemen."

"Write, then. Make a hundred writs. Send riders on circuits."

Edbert coughed apologetically. "Lord king, not all priests may be able to read. True they are pious men, worthy men, but—"

"They read and write quick enough when it comes to snatching land by charter!" Wulfsige's snarl was echoed by all the laymen.

Alfred silenced them with a sharp motion. "Send the messages, Bishop Daniel. Another day we will take up the question of whether priests who cannot read should be priests or not. The day of the muster is fixed, and I will be there, even if none of the rest of Wessex follows me. But I trust my subjects' loyalty. We will have an army to fight the heathens. What I need to know is, how can I be sure of victory—this time?"

There was a long silence, while most of the men present stared at the floor. Alderman Ethelnoth slowly shook his head from side to side. No one could doubt his courage, but he had been at a lot of lost battles too. Only Daniel the bishop kept his head firmly erect. Finally, and with an impatient frown, he spoke.

"It is not for a servant of the Lord to give advice on secular matters—while laymen sit silent. But is it not clear that the issue of all battles is in the hands of God? If we do our part, he will do his, and will succor us as he did Moses and the Israelites from Pharoah, or the people of Bethulia

rear, their horses useless on that steep and broken ground, the enemy all but ignored; they fell on the train itself, their howls drowning out even the shrieks of women and the death-cries of horses and cattle.

The Bretons frayed at the edges. Hands reached for pommels, men braced to spring astride their horses. Roland's voice lashed them back, away from the stumbling, hindering, helpless beasts, into a formation they all knew. Then, fiercely, forward.

They drove like a lance into the column. And for a little while, no one resisted them. Oliver grinned in his helmet. There was a use after all for the Roman foot-drill that the king had inflicted on them—a game, he said; an idea he had, that Roland, always apt for mischief, was willing to try. Now it served them in this most impossible of places, drove them into the enemy, mowed the attackers down and swept them aside under the hoofs of panicked beasts.

But there were too many of them; and the cavalry shield was little use in building the Roman shieldwall. Frayed already by startlement and rage and the Franks' inborn resistance to marching in step, they tore apart as the enemy rallied. Men were down. Oliver could not count, could not reckon. He had his own life to look after, and his brother's.

Roland was always calm enough when a battle began, well able to array his troops and judge their moment. But let his sword taste blood, and he was lost.

Someone was on Roland's other side, sword-side to Oliver's shield-side. Turpin, again. He had the bull of Mithras on his shield. It seemed to dance among the fallen, its white hide speckled with blood.

Oliver's foot slipped. He spared a glance for it: blood, entrails, a hand that cracked like bunched twigs under his boot. His eye caught a flash; his spear swung round, swift, swift, but almost too late. Fool's recompense, for casting eye on aught but the enemy. The good ash shaft jarred on steel and shattered. He thrust it in a howling face, let it fall, snatched out his sword. Roland's was out already, his named-blade, Durandal, running with blood.

Most often a battle runs like the sea: in ebbs and flows, in eddies and swirls and moments of stillness. But that is where armies are matched, and one side cannot count twenty men for every man of the other. Here, there were no respites. Only battle, and battle, and more battle. Death on every side, no time even for despair. They three had fought their way clear to the front of the battle and backed against the wall of the pass, as high up as the fallen stones would allow. Through the press of the fight they could see the downward way: a roil of ants in the nest, no head raised that did not wear a turban, and everywhere the sight and stench of slaughter.

Oliver, turning a bitter blow, was numb to the marrow. So soon? he wondered. So soon, they are all fallen?

So soon, in their heavy armor that was never made for fighting on foot; dragged down and slaughtered by the sheer mass of their enemies. His arm was leaden. He flailed at a stroke he barely saw, and never saw the one that glanced off his helmet. He staggered, head ringing, and fell to one knee. Lightning smote the man who stooped to the kill.

Durandal, and Roland's face behind it, white in the helmet, burning-eyed. He had dropped his shield, or lost it. His olifant was in his hand.

Oliver cursed him, though he had no breath to spare for it. "What use now? It will never bring the king. He's too far ahead."

Roland gave a yelling savage a second, blood-fountained mouth, and sent him reeling back among his fellows. For an impossible moment, none came forward in his place. There were easier pickings elsewhere; a whole baggage train to plunder. Roland set the horn to his lips.

Oliver, who knew what he would hear, clapped hands to his ears. Even that was barely enough to blunt the edge of it. The great horn roared like the aurochs from which it was won; shrieked up to heaven; sang a long plaint of wrath and valor and treachery. Roland's face was scarlet. A thin trail of blood trickled down from his ear.

The horn dropped, swung on its baldric. Roland half-fell against Oliver. Turpin caught him; they clung to one another. The enemy had frozen in their places. Many had fallen, smitten down by the power of the horn.

They rose like grass when the wind has faded. They turned their faces toward the three of all their prey who yet lived. They reckoned anew their numbers, and the number that opposed them. They laughed, and fell upon them.

Oliver could not reckon the moment when he knew that

one of his wounds was mortal. It was not when he took the wound, he was reasonably sure of that. He had others in plenty, and they were in his way, shedding blood to weaken his arm and foul his footing. But this one was weakening him too quickly. He found himself on the ground, propped against the rock, trying to lift his sword. A foot held him down. It was Roland's; that came to him when he tried to hack at it and the voice over his head cursed him in his brother's voice. "Sorry," he tried to say. "Can't see. Can't—"

"Be quiet," said Roland fiercely. Oliver was too tired to object. Except that he wanted to say something. He could not remember what. Something about horns. And kings. And turbans, with faces under them. Faces that should be—should be—

"Oliver."

Somebody was crying. It sounded like Roland. Roland did not often cry. Oliver wondered why he was doing it now. Had something happened? Was the king hurt? Dead? No, Oliver could not conceive of that. The king would never die. The king would live forever.

Oliver blinked. There was Roland's face, hanging over him. Another by it: Turpin's. They looked like corpses. "Am I dead?" Oliver asked, or tried to. "Is this Hades? Or the Muslims' Paradise? Or—"

"You talk too much," Roland growled.

They were alive. But it was very quiet. Too quiet. No shrilling of enemy voices. Unless that were they, faint and far away and fading slowly, like wind in empty places.

"They're gone," the priest said, as if he could understand what Oliver was thinking. Maybe he could. Priests were unchancy folk. But good: very good, in a fight. "They took what they came for."

"Did they?"

They both heard that. Roland glared. "Wasn't the king's whole baggage train enough?"

"You," Oliver said. "You live. Still."

Roland burst into tears again. But he looked worse than furious. He looked deadly dangerous.

The dark was closing in. "Brother," Oliver said through it, shouting in full voice against the failing of his body.

"Brother, look. The enemy. Turbans—turbans wrong. Not Saracen. Can you understand? *Not Saracen.*"

Maybe Oliver dreamed it. Maybe he only needed to hear it. But it was there, on the other side of the night. "I understand."

"I understand," Roland said. The weight in his arms was no greater and no less. But suddenly it was the weight of a world.

He knew the heft of death in his arms. Not Oliver, not now: not those wide blue eyes, emptying of life as they had, moments since, emptied of light.

He flung his head back and keened.

"My lord." Dry voice, with calm behind it. Turpin was weary: he had lain down beside Oliver, maybe with some vanishing hope of keeping him warm.

Or himself. Not all the blood on him was the enemy's. Some of it was bright with newness, glistening as it welled from a deep spring.

Dying, all of them. Roland, too. The enemy had seen to that before they left. He had not intended to tell either of his companions about the blade that stabbed from below, or the reason why he held himself so carefully when he rose. When he had finished doing what he must do, he would let go. It would not be a slow death, or an easy one, but it was certain. A good death for a fool, when all was considered.

He spoke lightly; he was proud of that lightness. "I'm going to see if I can find our fellows," he said to the one who could hear him and the one who was past it: "give them a word of passage; cast earth on the ones who'll need it."

Turpin nodded. He did not offer to rise. But there was, Roland judged, a little life in him yet. Enough to mount guard over Oliver, and keep the crows from his eyes. They were feasting already and long since, and the vultures with them: racing against the fall of the dark.

He walked the field in the gathering twilight, dim-lit by the glow of the sky above him. The birds of battle were as thick as flies; but where they were thickest, there he knew he would find his men. Two here, three there, five fallen together in the remnant of a shieldring. The king's seneschal; the count of his palace, the *palatium* that was not a thing of walls and stone but of the household that went with the king wherever he journeyed. Lost, here, gone down the long road with men in knotted turbans.

But not all of those who had come to seize, it had left the field. Many of their dead, they had taken, but they had left many, pressed by the fall of the dark and the need to escape with their booty before the King of the Franks swept down in the full force of his wrath. There at Roland's feet, locked in embrace like lovers, lay a camp follower who had lost her man at Pamplona, and a brigand; but there was a knife in his heart and a look of great surprise on his face. Roland could not tell if she smiled. There was too little left of her.

The man, sheltered by her body, was barely touched by the crows. Roland grasped him by the foot and dragged him into what light there was. The turban fell from a matted and filthy head. Roland bent to peer. The face—anonymous dead face. But odd. Ruthlessly he rent the tunic away from neck and breast and belly. The trousers, he need hardly tear at. He saw beneath them all that he needed to see.

His breath left him in a long sigh. With care, holding his middle lest his entrails spill upon the ground, he made his way among the enemy's dead. All; all alike.

Not far from the place where Oliver had died, he found the last thing, the thing that drained the strength from his legs, the life from his body. But he smiled. He took what he needed, and the body with it, crawling now. The night, which seemed to have waited for him, fell at last.

Turpin was stiff and still. Oliver lay untouched beside him, familiar bulk gone unfamiliar in death. Roland kissed him, and with every last vestige of his strength, staggered upright. The stars stared down. "Allah!" he called out. His voice rang in the gorge. "Allah! Will you take us all, if I speak for us? Will you, then? He'd like your Paradise, my brother. All the lovely maidens. Will you take him if I ask?"

The stars were silent. Roland laughed and flung up Durandal. He had, somehow, remembered to scour the blade of blood: prudence worn to habit. A pity for a good sword to die, though its master must. "Take my sword, Allah. Take my soul and my oath; if only you take my brother with it. You'll find him waiting hereabout. Come, do you hear him whispering? He'd say it with me if he could. Listen! *There is no god but God, and Muhammad is the Prophet of God.*"

The echoes throbbed into silence. Roland sank down in them. His heart was light. In a little while he was going to convulse in agony, but for this moment, he knew no pain. Only a white, mad joy. To have chosen, and chosen so. To have taken the purest revenge of all, on Ganelon who had betrayed him.

Oliver was waiting. Roland laid Durandal on the broad breast, and his head beside it, and sighed. Then at last, with all the courage that was left in him, he let go.

III

Charles the king stood once more on the sweet soil of Gaul, the horrors of the pass behind him, the army finding new vigor in the sight of their own country spread below. But he was not easy in his mind. Word from the rear was unvarying. No sign of the baggage. A scout or two, sent out, did not return.

As the sun sank low, he called a halt. Without the baggage they could not raise a proper camp, but every man had his store of food and drink, and many had women who marched with them and carried the necessities of living. They settled willingly enough.

The king left his servants to make what shift they could with what they had, and rode back a little, up toward the pass. One or two men rode with him. The empress's ambassador; the caliph's man, not to be outflanked; Ganelon. Beyond the fringe of the army, the king paused.

"Do you hear a horn?" he asked.

They glanced at one another. "A horn?" Ganelon inquired. "No, sire. I hear nothing but the wind."

"Yes," said Charles. "The wind. That's what it must be. But I could have sworn . . ."

"My lord's ears are excellent," the Arab said. No; Charles should be precise, even in his mind. The man was a Persian. The Persian, then, and a smoothly smiling fellow he was, oily as a Greek, and yet, for all of that, a man worth liking. "Perhaps he hears the rearguard as it comes through the pass."

"Perhaps," said Ganelon. The Greek, for a marvel, said nothing at all.

They sat their tired horses, waiting, because the king waited. He could not bring himself to turn away. He had not liked the pass as he scaled it, and he had not liked the failure of his scouts to come back. Still less did he like his folly in letting the rearguard fall so far behind. He had been in haste to abandon the pass, to see his own lands again. He had let himself be persuaded to press on. The one man he sent back to find the rearguard, had not found him again.

In the falling dark, in silence barely troubled by the presence of an army, he saw what he had willed not to see. He saw it with brutal clarity; he knew it for what it was. There was no pain, yet. Later, there would be; a whole world of it. But now, only numbness that was not blessed. Oh, no. Not blessed at all. "They are dead," he said, "my Bretons. There was an ambush in the pass."

"My lord," said Ganelon, "you cannot know that. They will have been sensible: seen that night was falling, and stopped, and made camp. In time their messenger will come. Only wait, and rest. You can hardly ride back now. Night will catch you before you mount the pass."

"Yes," said Charles. "It will, won't it?"

His voice must have betrayed more than he knew. Ganelon stiffened; his mouth set. His eyes darted. Charles noticed where they fell first. The Byzantine refused them, gazing expressionless where Charles's mind and heart were.

With great care, the king unknotted his fists. He had no proof. He had nothing but the feeling in his bones, and the absence of his rearguard. His valiant, reluctant, pitifully inadequate rearguard.

He was, first of all, king. He turned his back on the pass of Roncesvalles, and went to see to his army.

The king did not sleep that night. When he drowsed, his mind deluded him: gave him the far cry of a horn, a great olifant, blown with the desperation of a dying man. Roland was dead. He knew it. Dead in battle; dead by treachery.

He rose before dawn. His army slept; he silenced the trumpeter who would have roused them. "Let them sleep," he said. "We go nowhere until the baggage comes."

When his horse came, others came with it. The Greek and the Persian, again and perpetually; Ganelon; a company of his guardsmen. He greeted them with a nod. They were all, like the king, armed as if to fight. It was odd to see the Byzantine in mail, carrying a sword. Charles had not known that he owned either.

Morning rose with them, surmounted the pass, sped above them while they went down. They picked their way with care, finding no trace of the baggage, and nothing ahead of them but fading darkness.

A wall of tumbled stones where none had been before, woke in the king no surprise, not even anger. Wordlessly he dismounted, handed his horse to the man nearest, and set himself to scale the barrier. It was not high, if much confused. At the top of it he paused.

He had expected nothing less than what he saw. He had seen sights like it ever since he could remember. But it was never an easy thing to see; even when the dead were all the enemy's.

Someone had seen to the dead of Gaul. Each was consecrated in his own fashion: a cross drawn in blood on the brow of the Christian, a scattering of earth for him who held to Julian's creed, a simple laying out in dignity for the follower of Mithras or of the old faith. But hope, having swelled, died swiftly. No living man walked that field.

Beyond them, as if they had made a last stand, lay three together. Turpin the priest of Mithras with his bones given to the birds of the air, and Roland and Oliver in one another's arms as they had been since they shared their milkmother's breast. They had died well, if never easily.

The king was aware, distantly but very clearly, of the men nearest him: Greek, Persian, Frankish counselor. None ventured to touch the dead. He knelt beside them, and gently, as if the boy could feel it still, took Roland in his arms.

Roland clasped something to his breast, even in death. His olifant. Which Charles had heard; he was certain of it now. Heard, and never come. The king steadied it as it slipped. It was heavier than it should be, unwieldy. It eluded the king's hand and fell, spilling brightness on the grass.

Byzantine gold. And mingled with it, the rougher coin of Gaul, and Charles's face on every one.

He did not glance, even yet, at his companions. There was a message here; he was meant to read it. At the brothers' feet lay one of the enemy's dead, whom Charles had had no eyes to see. But there was no other close by, and this one looked to have been brought here.

Charles laid Roland again in Oliver's arms, and examined the body. He was perfectly, icily calm. Intent on his own dead, he had not seen more than that the enemy wore turbans over dark faces. This one's turban had fallen beside him; his tunic was rent and torn, baring white skin, skin too white for the face. And between them, a ragged line, the stain rubbed on in haste with no expectation of need for greater concealment. And, below, what Charles did not need the Persian to say for him.

"This man is not a Muslim. He is not circumcised."

"So," said Charles, "I notice."

Even dying, Roland had kept his wits about him. Gold of Byzantium, gold and silver of Gaul. An infidel in Muslim guise. Trap, and battle, and the deaths of great lords of the Franks.

Here was treachery writ large.

He read it, writ subtle, in Ganelon's face. He could never have thought to be so betrayed, and so simply. And by his brainless braggart of a stepson.

They had all drawn back from him. He seemed just now to realize it. He was white under his elegant beard, struggling to maintain his expression of innocence. Ganelon, who had never made a secret of his hatred for Roland; whose very openness had been deceit. Who would have expected that he would turn traitor? Open attack, surely, daggers drawn in hall, a challenge to a duel; but this, no one had looked for. Least of all, and most damnably of all, the king.

"It would have been better for you," Charles said, "if you had killed him before my face. Clean murder bears a clean penalty. For this, you will pay in your heart's blood."

"Pay, sire?" Ganelon struggled even yet to seem baffled. "Surely, sire, you do not think—"

"I know," said Charles. His eyes burned. They were wide, he knew, and pale, and terrible. When they fell on the Greek, the man blanched.

"I am not," he said, "a part of this. I counseled against it. I foresaw this very outcome."

"You sanctioned it with your empress' gold," said the king.

"For what an agent does with his wages, I bear no responsibility."

Charles laughed. His guards had drawn in, shoulder to shoulder. If the traitor had any thought of escape, he quelled it. He regarded his quondam ally with no surprise, if with nothing approaching pleasure.

"You shall be tried," the king said to him, "where the law commands, before my tribunal in Gaul. I expect that you will receive the extremest penalty. I devoutly pray that you may suffer every pang of guilt and grief and rage to which even a creature of your ilk should be subject."

Ganelon stiffened infinitesimally, but not with dismay. Was that the beginning of a smile? "You have no certain proof," he said.

"God will provide," said Charles.

"God? Or Allah?"

Bold, that one, looking death in the face. If death it was that he saw. It was a long way to Gaul, and his tongue was serpent-supple. Had not Charles himself been taken in by it?

Charles met his eyes and made them fall. "Yes," he said, answering the man's question. "There you have it. God, or Allah? The Christians' God, or all the gods of my faith who in the end are one, or the God of the Prophet? Would you have me choose now? Julian is dead, his teachings forgotten everywhere but in my court. The Christ lives; the sons of the Prophet rule in Baghdad, and offer alliance. I know what I am in this world. Byzantium dares to hope in me, to hold back the armies of Islam. Islam knows that without me it can never rule in the north of the world. How does it twist in you, betrayer of kin, to know that I am the fulcrum on which the balance rests?"

"Islam," said Ganelon without a tremor, "offers you the place of a vassal king. Byzantium would make you its emperor."

"So it would. And such a marriage it would be, I ruling here in Gaul, and she on the Golden Horn. Or would I be expected to settle in Constantinople? Who then would rule my people? You, kinslayer? Is that the prize you played for?"

"Better I than a wild boy who could never see a battle without flinging himself into the heart of it."

The king's fist lashed out. Ganelon dropped. "Speak no ill of the dead," Charles said.

The others were silent. They did not press him; and yet it was there, the necessity, the making of choices. If he would take vengeance for this slaughter, he must move now.

He began to smile. It was not, he could well sense, pleasant to see. "Yes," he said. "Revenge. It's fortunate for my sister-son, is it not, that I'm pagan, and no Christian, to have perforce to forgive. You plotted well, kinslayer. You thought to turn me against Islam and cast me into the empress' arms. Would there be a dagger for me there? Or, more properly Greek, poison in my cup?"

"Sire," said Ganelon, and that was desperation, now, at last. "Sire, do not judge the empire by the follies of a single servant."

"I would never do that," Charles said. "But proof of long conviction will do well enough. I will never set my people under the Byzantine heel. Even with the promise of a throne. Thrones can pass, like any other glory of this world; and swiftly, if those who offer them are so minded."

"Still, my lord, you cannot choose Islam. Would you betray all that the Divine Julian fought for? Would you turn against Rome herself?"

If the Greek had said it, Charles would have responded altogether differently. But it was Ganelon who spoke, and Ganelon who felt the pain of it.

"I am," said Charles, "already, in the caliph's eyes, his emir over Spain. I am not able for the moment to press the claim. Gaul needs me, and Gaul is mine first. If Baghdad will grant the justice in that, then yes," he said, "I choose Islam."

No thunder roared in the sky; no shaking rent the earth. There were only a handful of men in a narrow pass, and the dead, and the sun too low still to cast its light on them. Spain was behind them; the mountain before, and beyond it, Gaul. What its king chose, it also would choose. He knew his power there.

He bent and took up Roland's horn. It rang softly, bearing still a weight of imperial gold. With it in his hands, he said the words which he must say. If his conviction was not yet as pure as it might be, then surely he would be forgiven. He was doing it for Gaul, and for the empire that would be.

But before even that, for Roland who was his sister's son, who had died for Byzantine gold.

Charles was, when it came to it, a simple man. The choice had not been simple, until Ganelon made it so. A better traitor than he knew, that one. Traitor even to his own cause.

"*There is no god but God*," said the king of the Franks and the Lombards, "*and Muhammad is the Prophet of God*."

His Powder'd Wig, His Crown of Thornes

MARC LAIDLAW

Grant Innes first saw the icon in the Indian ghettos of London, but thought nothing of it. There were so many gewgaws of native "art" being thrust in his face by faddishly war-painted Cherokees that this was just another nuisance to avoid, like the huge radios blaring obnoxious "Choctawk" percussions and the high-pitched warbling of Tommy Hawkes and the effeminate Turquoise Boys; like the young Mohawk ruddies practicing skateboard stunts for sluttish cockney girls whose kohled black eyes and slack blue lips betrayed more interest in the dregs of the bottles those boys carried than in the boys themselves. Of course, it was not pleasure or curiosity that brought him into the squalid district, among the baggy green canvas street-teepees and graffitoed storefronts. Business alone could bring him here. He had paid a fair sum for the name and number of a Mr. Cloud, dealer in Navaho jewelry, whose samples had proved of excellent quality and would fetch the highest prices, not only in Europe but in the Colonies as well. Astute dealers knew that the rage for turquoise had nearly run its course, thank God; following the popularity of the lurid blue stone, the simplicity of black-patterned silver would be a welcome relief indeed. Grant had hardly been able to tolerate the sight of so much garish rock as he'd been forced to stock in order to suit his customers; he was looking forward to this next trend. He'd already laid the ground for several showcase presentations in Paris; five major glossies were bidding for rights to photograph his collector's pieces, antique sand-cast *najas* and squash-blossom necklaces, for a special fashion portfolio.

Here in the slums, dodging extruded plastic kachina dolls and machine-woven blankets, his fine-tuned eye was offended by virtually everything he saw. It was trash for tourists. Oh, it had its spurts of cheap popularity, like the war bonnets which all the cyclists had worn last summer, but such moments were as fleeting as pop hits, thank God. Only true quality could ever transcend the dizzying gyres of public favor. Fine art, precious stones, pure metal: These were investments that would never lose their value.

So much garbage ultimately had the effect of blinding him to his environment; avoidance became a mental as well as a physical trick. He was dreaming of silver crescents gleaming against ivory skin when he realized that he must have passed the street he sought. He stopped in his tracks, suddenly aware of the hawkers' cries, the pulse of hide-drums and synthesizers. He spun about searching for a number on any of the shops.

"Lost, guv?" said a tall young brave with gold teeth, his bare chest ritually scarified. He carried a tall pole strung with a dozen gruesome rubber scalps, along with several barristers' wigs. They gave the brave the appearance of a costume merchant, except for one morbid detail: Each of the white wigs was spattered with blood . . . red dye, rather, liberally dripped among the coarse white strands.

"You *look* lost."

"Looking for a shop," he muttered, fumbling Mr. Cloud's card from his pocket.

"No, I mean really lost. Out of balance. *Koyaanisqatsi*, guv. Like the whole world."

"I'm looking for a shop," Grant repeated firmly.

"That all, then? A shop? What about the things you really lost? Things we've all lost, I'm talking about. Here."

He patted his bony hip, which was wrapped in a black leather loincloth. Something dangled from his belt, a doll-like object on a string, a charm of some sort. Grant looked over the brave's head and saw the number he sought, just above a doorway. The damn ruddy was in his way. As he tried to slip past, avoiding contact with the rubbery scalps and bloodied wigs, the brave unclipped the charm from his belt and thrust it into his face.

Grant recoiled, nearly stumbling backward in the street. It was an awful little mannequin, face pinched and soft, its agonized expression carved from a withered apple.

"Here—here's where we lost it," the brave said, thrusting the doll up to his cheek, as if he would have it kiss or nip him with its rice-grain teeth. Its limbs were made of jerked beef, spread-eagled on wooden crossbars, hands and feet fixed in place with four tiny nails. It was a savage Christ—an obscenity.

"He gave His life for you," the brave said. "Not just for one people, but for everyone. Eternal freedom, that was His promise."

"I'm late for my appointment," Grant said, unable to hide his disgust.

"Late and lost," the brave said. "But you'll never catch up—the time slipped past. And you'll never find your way unless you follow Him."

"Just get out of my way!"

He shoved the brave aside, knocking the hideous little idol out of the Indian's grasp. Fearing reprisal, he forced an apologetic expression as he turned back from the hard-won doorway. But the brave wasn't watching him. He crouched over the filthy street, retrieving his little martyr. Lifting it to his lips, he kissed it gently.

"I'm sorry," Grant said.

The brave glanced up at Grant and grinned fiercely, baring his gold teeth; then he bit deep into the dried brown torso of the Christ and tore away a ragged strip of jerky.

Nauseous, Grant hammered on the door behind him. It opened abruptly and he almost fell into the arms of Mr. Cloud.

He next saw the image the following summer, in the District of Cornwallis. Despite the fact that Grant specialized in provincial art, most of his visits to the colonies had been for business purposes, and had exposed him to no more glorious surroundings than the interiors of banks and mercantile offices, with an occasional jaunt into the Six Nations to meet with the creators of the fine pieces that were his trade. Sales were brisk, his artisans had been convinced to ply their craft with gold as well as silver, supplanting turquoise and onyx with diamonds and other precious stones; the trend toward high-fashion American jewelry had already surpassed his highest expectations. Before the inevitable decline and a panicked search for the next sure thing, he decided to accept the offer of an old colonial acquaintance who had long extended an open invitation to a tour of great American monuments in the capital city.

Arnoldsburg, D.C., was sweltering in a humid haze, worsened by exhaust fumes from the taxis that seemed the the city's main occupants. Eyes burning, lungs fighting against collapse, he and his guide crawled from taxi after taxi and plunged into cool marble corridors reeking of urine and crowded with black youths selling or buying opiates. It was hard not to mock the great figures of American history, thus surrounded and entrapped by the ironic fruits of their victories. The huge seated figure of Burgoyne looked mildly bemused by the addicts sleeping between his feet; the bronze brothers Richard and William Howe stood back to back embattled in a waist-high mob, as though taking their last stand against colonial Lillilputians.

His host, David Mickelson, was a transplanted Irishman. He had first visited America as a physician with the Irish Royal Army, and after his term expired had signed on for a stint in the Royal American Army. He had since opened a successful dermatological practice in Arnoldsburg. He was a collector of native American art, which practice had led him to deal with Grant Innes. Mickelson had excellent taste in metalwork, but Grant chided him for his love of "these marble monstrosities."

"But these are heroes, Grant. Imagine where England would be without these men. An island with few resources and limited room for expansion? How could we have kept up the sort of healthy growth we've had since the Industrial Revolution? It's impossible. And without these men to secure this realm for us, how could we have held onto it? America is so vast—really, you have no concept of it. These warriors laid the way for peace and proper management, steering a narrow course between Spain and France. Without such fine ambassadors to put down the early rebellion and ease the cosettling of the Six Nations, America might still be at war. Instead its resources belong to the crown. This is our treasure house, Grant, and these are the keepers of that treasure."

"Treasure," Grant repeated, with an idle nudge at the body of an old squaw who lay unconscious on the steps of the Howe Monument.

"Come with me, then," Mickelson said. "One more sight, and then we'll go wherever you like."

They boarded another taxi which progressed by stops

and starts through the iron river of traffic. A broad, enormous dome appeared above the cars.

"Ah," said Grant. "I know what that is."

They disembarked at the edge of a huge circular plaza. The dome that capped the plaza was supported by a hundred white columns. They went into the lidded shadow, into darkness, and for a moment Grant was blinded.

"Watch out, old boy," Mickelson said. "Here's the rail. Grab on. Wouldn't want to stumble in here."

His hands closed on polished metal. When he felt steady again, he opened his eyes and found himself staring into a deep pit. The walls of the shaft were perfectly smooth, round as a bullet hole drilled deep into the earth. He felt a cold wind coming out of it, and then the grip of vertigo.

"The depths of valor, the inexhaustible well of the human spirit," Mickelson was saying. "Makes you dizzy with pride, doesn't it?"

"I'm . . . feeling . . . sick. . . ." Grant turned and hurried toward daylight.

Out in the sunshine again, his sweat gone cold, he leaned against a marble podium and gradually caught his breath. When his mind had cleared somewhat, he looked up and saw that the podium was engraved with the name of the hero whose accomplishments the shaft commemorated. His noble bust surmounted the slab.

BENEDICT ARNOLD
First American President-General, appointed such
by King George III as reward for his valiant role in
suppressing the provincial revolt of 1776–79.

David Mickelson caught up with him.

"Feeling all right, Grant?"

"Better. I—I think I'd like to get back to my rooms. It's this heat."

"Surely. I'll hail a cab, you just hold on here for a minute."

As Grant watched Mickelson hurry away, his eyes strayed over the circular plaza where the usual hawkers had laid out the usual souvenirs. Habit, more than curiosity, drove him out among the ragged blankets, his eyes swiftly picking through the merchandise and discarding it all as garbage.

Well, most of it. This might turn out to be another fortunate venture after all. His eyes had been caught by a display of absolutely brilliant designs done in copper and brass. He had never seen anything quite like them. Serpents, eagles, patterns of stars. The metal was all wrong, but the artist had undoubtedly chosen them by virtue of their cheapness and could be easily convinced to work in gold. He looked up at the proprietor of these wares and saw a young Indian woman, bent on her knees, threading colored beads on a string.

"Who made these?" he said, softening the excitement he felt into a semblance of mild curiosity.

She gazed up at him. "My husband."

"Really? I like them very much. Does he have a distributor?"

She didn't seem to know what he meant.

"That is . . . does anyone else sell these pieces?"

She shook her head. "This is all he makes, right here. When he makes more, I sell those."

In the distance, he heard Mickelson shouting his name. The dermatologist came running over the marble plaza. "Grant, I've got a cab!"

Grant gestured as if to brush him away. "I'll meet you later, David, all right? Something's come up."

"What have you found?" Mickelson tried to look past him at the blanket, but Grant spun him around in the direction of the taxis—perhaps a bit too roughly. Mickelson stopped for a moment, readjusted his clothes, then stalked away peevishly toward the cars. So be it.

Smiling, Grant turned back to the woman. His words died on his tongue when he saw what she was doing with beads she'd been stringing.

She had formed them into a noose, a bright rainbow noose, and slipped this over the head of a tiny brown doll.

He knew that doll, knew its tough leathered flesh and pierced limbs, the apple cheeks and teeth of rice. The cross from which she'd taken it lay discarded on the blanket, next to the jewelry that suddenly seemed of secondary importance.

While he stood there unspeaking, unmoving, she lifted the dangling doll to her lips and daintily, baring crooked teeth, tore off a piece of the leg.

"What . . . what . . ."

He found himself unable to ask what he wished to ask. Instead, fixed by her gaze, he stammered, "What do you want for all of these?"

She finished chewing before answering. "All?"

"Yes, I . . . I'd like to buy all of them. In fact, I'd like to buy more than this. I'd like to commission a piece, if I might."

The squaw swallowed.

"My husband creates what is within the soul. He makes dreams into metal. He would have to see your dreams."

"My dreams? Well, yes, I'll tell him exactly what I want. Could I meet him to discuss this?"

The squaw shrugged. She patiently unlooped the noose from the shrivelled image, spread it back onto its cross and pinned the three remaining limbs into place, then tucked it away in a bag at her belt. Finally, rising, she rolled up the blanket with all the bangles and bracelets inside it, and tucked the parcel under her arm.

"Come with me," she said.

He followed her without another word, feeling as though he were moving down an incline, losing his balance with every step, barely managing to throw himself in her direction. She was his guide through the steaming city, through the crowds of ragged cloth, skins ruddy and dark. He pulled off his customary jacket, loosened his tie, and struggled after her. She seemed to dwindle in the distance; he was losing her, losing himself, stretching into a thin strand of beads, beads of sweat, sweat that dripped through the gutters of Arnoldsburg and offered only brine to the thirsty. . . .

But when she once looked back and saw him faltering, she put out her hand and he was standing right beside her, near a metal door. She put her hand upon it and opened the way.

It was cool inside, and dark except for the tremulous light of candles that lined a descending stairway. He followed, thinking of catacombs, the massed and desiccated ranks of the dead he had seen beneath old missions in Spanish Florida. There was a dusty smell, and far off the sound of hammering. She opened another door and the sound was suddenly close at hand.

They had entered a workshop. A man sat at a metal table

cluttered with coils of wire, metal snips, hand torches. The woman stepped out and closed the door on them.

"Good afternoon," Grant said. "I . . . I'm a great admirer of your work."

The man turned slowly, the metal stool creaking under his weight, although he was not a big man. His skin was very dark, like his close-cropped hair. His face was soft, as though made of chamois pouches; but his eyes were hard. He beckoned.

"Come here," he said. "You like my stuff? What is it that you like?"

Grant approached the workbench with a feeling of awe. Samples of the man's work lay scattered about, but these were not done in copper or brass. They were silver, most of them, and gleamed like moonlight.

"The style," he said. "The . . . substance."

"How about this?" The Indian fingered a large eagle with spreading wings.

"It's beautiful—almost alive."

"It's a sign of freedom." He laid it down. "What about this one?"

He handed Grant a small rectangular plaque inscribed with an unusual but somehow familiar design. A number of horizontal stripes, with a square inset in the lower right corner, and in that square a wreath of thirteen stars.

"Beautiful," Grant said. "You do superior work."

"That's not what I mean. Do you know the symbol?"

"I . . . I think I've seen it somewhere before. An old Indian design, isn't it?"

The Indian grinned. Gold teeth again, bridging the distance between London and Arnoldsburg, reminding him of the jerked beef martyr, the savage Christ.

"Not an Indian sign," he said. "A sign for all people."

"Really? Well, I'd like to *bring* it to all people. I'm a dealer in fine jewelry. I could get a very large audience for these pieces. I could make you a very rich man."

"Rich?" The Indian set the plaque aside. "Plenty of Indians are rich. The tribes have all the land and factories they want—as much as you have. But we lack what you also lack: freedom. What is wealth when we have no freedom?"

"Freedom?"

"It's a dim concept to you, isn't it? But not to me." He

put his hand over his heart. "I hold it here, safe with the memory of how we lost it. A precious thing, a cup of holy water that must never be spilled until it can be swallowed in a single draft. I carry the cup carefully, but there's enough for all. If you wish to drink, it can be arranged."

"I don't think you understand," Grant said, recovering some part of himself that had begun to drift off through the mystical fog in which the Indians always veiled themselves. He must do something concrete to counteract so much vagueness. "I'm speaking of a business venture. A partnership."

"I hear your words. But I see something deeper in you. Something that sleeps in all men. They come here seeking what is lost, looking for freedom and a cause. But all they find are the things that went wrong. Why are you so out of balance, eh? You stumble and crawl, but you always end up here with that same empty look in your eyes. I've seen you before. A dozen just like you."

"I'm an art dealer," Grant said. "Not a—a pilgrim. If you can show me more work like this, I'd be grateful. Otherwise, I'm sorry for wasting your time, and I'll be on my way."

Suddenly he was anxious to get away, and this seemed a reasonable excuse. But the jeweler now seemed ready to accommodate him.

"Art, then," he said. "All right. I will show you the thing that speaks to you, and perhaps then you will understand. Art is also a way to the soul."

He slipped down from the stool and moved toward the door, obviously intending Grant to follow.

"I'll show you more than this," the Indian said. "I'll show you inspiration."

After another dizzying walk, they entered a derelict museum in a district that stank of danger. Grant felt safe only because of his companion; he was obviously a stranger here, in these oppressive alleys. Even inside the place, which seemed less a museum than a warehouse, he sensed that he was being watched. It was crowded by silent mobs, many of them children, almost all of them Negro or Indian. Some sat in circles on the cement floors, talking quietly among themselves, as though taking instruction. Pawnee, Chickasaw, Blackfoot, Cheyenne, Comanche . . . Arnoldsburg was a popular site for tourists, but these didn't have the look of the ruddy middle-class traveler; these were lower-class ruddies, as tattered as the people in the street. Some had apparently crossed the continent on foot to come here. He felt as if he had entered a church.

"Now you shall see," said the jeweler. "This is the art of the patriots. The forefathers. The hidden ones."

He stopped near a huge canvas that leaned against a steel beam; the painting was caked with grease, darkened by time, but even through the grime he could see that it was the work of genius. An imitation of da Vinci's *Last Supper,* but strangely altered . . .

The guests at Christ's table wore not Biblical attire, but that of the eighteenth century. It was no windowed building that sheltered them, but a tent whose walls gave the impression of a strong wind beating against them from without. The thirteen were at table, men in military outfits, and in their midst a figure of mild yet radiant demeanor, humble in a powdered wig, a mere crust of bread on his plate. Grant did not recognize him, this figure in Christ's place, but the man in Judas's place was recognizable enough from the numerous busts and portraits in Arnoldsburg. That was Benedict Arnold.

The Indian pointed at several of the figures, giving them names: "Henry Knox, Nathaniel Greene, Light-Horse Harry Lee, Lafayette, General Rochambeau—"

"Who painted this?"

"It was the work of Benjamin Franklin," said his guide. "Painted not long after the betrayal at West Point, but secretly, in sadness, when the full extent of our tragedy became all too apparent. After West Point, the patriots continued to fight. But this man, this one man, was the glue that held the soldiers together. After His death, the army had many commanders, but none could win the trust of all men. The revolution collapsed and our chance for freedom slipped away. Franklin died without finishing it, his heart broken."

"But that man in the middle?"

The Indian led him to another painting. This was much more recent, judging from the lack of accumulated soot and grease. Several children stood gazing at it, accompanied by a darkie woman who was trying to get them to analyze the meaning of what was essentially a simple image.

"What is this?" she asked.

Several hands went up. "The cherry tree!" chimed a few voices.

"That's right, the cherry tree. Who can tell us the story of the cherry tree?"

One little girl pushed forward. "He chopped it down and when He saw what He had done, He said, 'I cannot let it die.' So He planted the piece He cut off and it grew into a new tree, and the trunk of the old tree grew too, because it was magic."

"Very good. Now that's a fable, of course. Do you know what it really means? What the cherry tree represents?"

Grant felt like one of her charges, waiting for some explanation, innocent.

"It's an English cherry," the teacher hinted.

Hands went up. "The tree!" "I know!" "It's England."

"That's right. And the piece He transplanted?"

"America!"

"Very good. And do you remember what happened next? It isn't shown in this painting, but it was very sad. Tinsha?"

"When His father saw what He had done, he was very scared. He was afraid his son was a devil or something, so he tore up the little tree by the roots. He tore up America."

"And you know who the father really was, don't you?"

"The . . . king?" said Tinsha.

Grant and his guide went on to another painting, this one showing a man in a powdered wig and a ragged uniform walking across a river in midwinter—not stepping on the floes, but moving carefully between them, on the breast of the frigid water. With him came a band of barefoot men, lightly touching hands, the first of them resting his fingers on the cape of their leader. The men stared at the water as if they could not believe their eyes, but there was only confidence in the face of their commander—that and a serene humility.

"This is the work of Sully, a great underground artist," said the jeweler.

"These . . . these are priceless."

The Indian shrugged. "If they were lost tomorrow, we would still carry them with us. It is the feelings they draw from our hearts that are truly beyond price. He came for all men, you see. If you accept Him, if you open your heart to Him, then His death will not have been in vain."

"Washington," Grant said, the name finally coming to him. An insignificant figure of the American Wars, an archtraitor whose name was a mere footnote in the histories he'd read. Arnold had defeated him, hadn't he? Was that what had happened at West Point? The memories were vague and unreal, textbook memories.

The jeweler nodded. "George Washington," he repeated. "He was leading us to freedom, but He was betrayed and held out as an example. In Philadelphia He was publicly tortured to dispirit the rebels, then hung by His neck after his death, and His corpse toured through the colonies. And that is our sin, the penance which we must pay until every soul had been brought back into balance."

"Your sin?"

The Indian nodded, drawing from the pouch at his waist another of the shriveled icons, Christ—no, Washington—on the cross.

"We aided the British in that war. Cherokee and Iroquois, others of the Six Nations. We thought the British would save us from the colonists; we didn't know that they had different ways of enslavement. My ancestors were master torturers. When Washington was captured, it fell to them—to us—to do the bloodiest work."

His hands tightened on the figure of flesh; the splintered wood dug into his palm.

"We nailed Him to the bars of a cross, borrowing an idea that pleased us greatly from your own religion."

The brown hand shook. The image rose to the golden mouth.

"First, we scalped Him. The powdered hair was slung from a warrior's belt. His flesh was pierced with thorns and knives. And then we flayed Him alive."

"Flayed . . ."

Grant winced as golden teeth nipped a shred of jerky and tore it away.

"Alive . . . ?"

"He died bravely. He was more than a man. He was our deliverer, savior of all men, white, red, and black. And we murdered Him. We pushed the world off balance."

"What is this place?" Grant asked. "It's more than a museum, isn't it? It's also a school."

"It is a holy place. His spirit lives here, in the heart of

the city named for the man who betrayed Him. He died to the world two hundred years ago, but He still lives in us. He is champion of the downtrodden, liberator of the enslaved." The jeweler's voice was cool despite the fervor of his theme. "You see . . . I have looked beyond the walls of fire that surround this world. I have looked into the world that should have been, that would have been if He had lived. I saw a land of the free, a land of life, liberty, and happiness, where the red men lived in harmony with the white. Our plains bore fruit instead of factories. And the holy cause, that of the republic, spread from the hands of the Great Man. The king was dethroned and England too made free. The bell of liberty woke the world; the four winds carried the cause." The jeweler bowed his head. "That is how it would have been. This I have seen in dreams."

Grant looked around him at the paintings, covered with grime but carefully attended; the people, also grimy but with an air of reverence. It was a shame to waste them here, on these people. He imagined the paintings hanging in a well-lit gallery, the patina of ages carefully washed away; he saw crowds of people in fine clothes, decked in his gold jewelry, each willing to pay a small fortune for admission. With the proper sponsorship, a world tour could be brought off. He would be a wealthy man, not merely a survivor, at the end of such a tour.

The Indian watched him, nodding. "I know what you're thinking. You think it would be good to tell the world of these things, to spread the cause. You think you can carry the message to all humanity, instead of letting it die here in the dark. But I tell you . . . it thrives here. Those who are oppressed, those who are broken and weary of spirit, they are the caretakers of liberty."

Grant smiled inwardly; there was a bitter taste in his mouth.

"I think you underestimate the worth of all this," he said. "You do it a disservice to hide it from the eyes of the world. I think everyone can gain something from it."

"Yes?" The Indian looked thoughtful. He led Grant toward a table where several old books lay open, their pages swollen with humidity, spines cracking, paper flaking away.

"Perhaps you are right," he said, turning the pages of one book entitled *The Undying Patriot*, edited by a Parson Weems. "It may be as Doctor Franklin says. . . ."

Grant bent over the page, and read:

Let no man forget His death. Let not the memory of our great Chief and Commander fade from the thoughts of the common people, who stand to gain the most from its faithful preservation. For once these dreams have fad'd, there is no promise that they may again return. In this age and the next, strive to hold true to the honor'd principals for which He fought, for which he was nail'd to the rude crucifix and his flesh stript away. Forget not His sacrifice, His powder'd wig and crown of thornes. Forget not that a promise broken can never be repair'd.

"I think you are right," said the jeweler. "How can we take it upon ourselves to hide this glory away? It belongs to the world, and the world shall have it."

He turned to Grant and clasped his hands. His eyes were afire with a patriotic light. "He brought you to me, I see that now. This is a great moment. I thank you, brother, for what you will do."

"It's only my duty," Grant said.

Yes. Duty.

And now he stood in the sweltering shadows outside the warehouse, the secret museum, watching the loading of several large vans. The paintings were wrapped in canvas so that none could see them. He stifled an urge to rush up to the loading men and tear away the cloth, to look once more on that noble face. But the police were thick around the entrance.

"Careful," said David Mickelson at his elbow.

News of the find had spread through the city and a crowd had gathered, in which Grant was just one more curious observer. He supposed it was best this way, though he would rather it was his own people moving the paintings. The police were unwontedly rough with the works, but there was nothing he could do about that.

Things had gotten a little out of hand.

"Hard to believe it's been sitting under our noses all this time," said Mickelson. "You say you actually got a good look at it?"

Grant nodded abstractedly. "Fairly good. Of course, it was dark in there."

"Even so . . . what a catch, eh? There have been rumors of this stuff for years, and you stumble right into it. Amazing idea you had, though, organizing a tour. As if anyone would pay to see that stuff aside from ruddies and radicals. Even if it weren't completely restricted."

"What . . . what do you think they'll do with it?" Grant asked.

"Same as they do with other contraband, I'd imagine. Burn it."

"Burn it," Grant repeated numbly.

Grant felt a restriction of the easy flow of traffic; suddenly the crowd, mainly black and Indian, threatened to change into something considerably more passionate than a group of disinterested onlookers. The police loosened their riot gear as the mob began to shout insults.

"Fall back, Grant," Mickelson said.

Grant started to move away through the crowd, but a familiar face caught his attention. It was the Indian, the jeweler; he hung near a corner of the museum, his pouchy face unreadable. Somehow, through all the confusion, among the hundred or so faces now mounting in number, his eyes locked onto Grant's.

Grant stiffened. The last of the vans shut its doors and rushed away. The police did not loiter in the area. He had good reason to feel vulnerable.

The jeweler stared at him. Stared without moving. Then he brought up a withered brown object and set it to his lips. Grant could see him bite, tear, and chew.

"What is it, Grant? We should be going now, don't you think? There's still time to take in a real museum, or perhaps the American Palace."

Grant didn't move. Watching the Indian, he put his thumb to his mouth and caught a bit of cuticle between his teeth. He felt as if he were dreaming. Slowly, he tore off a thin strip of skin, ripping it back almost down to the knuckle. The pain was excruciating, but it didn't seem to wake him. He chewed it, swallowed.

"Grant? Is anything wrong?"

He tore off another.

Departures

HARRY TURTLEDOVE

The monks at Ir-Ruhaiyeh did not talk casually among themselves. They were not hermits; those who wanted to be pillar-sitters like the two Saints Symeon went off into the Syrian desert by themselves and did not join monastic communities. Still, the Rule of St. Basil enjoined silence through much of the day.

Despite the Cappadocian Father's Rule, though, a whispered word ran through the monastery regardless of the canonical hour: "The Persians. The Persians are marching toward Ir-Ruhaiyeh."

The abbot, Isaac, heard the whispers, though monks had to shout when they spoke to him. Isaac was past seventy, with a white beard that nearly reached his waist. But he had been abbot here for more than twenty years, and a simple monk for thirty years before that. He knew what his charges thought almost before they thought it.

Isaac turned to the man he hoped would one day succeed him. "It will be very bad this time, John. I feel it."

The prior shrugged. "It will be as God wills, father abbot." He was half the abbot's age, round-faced and always smiling. What would from many men have had the ring of a prophecy of doom came from his lips as a prediction of good fortune.

Isaac was not cheered, not this time. "I wonder if God does not mean this to be the end for us Christians."

"The Persians have come to Ir-Ruhaiyeh before," John said stoutly. "They raided, they moved on. When their campaigns were through, they went back to their homeland once more, and life resumed."

"I was here," Isaac agreed. "They came in the younger Justin's reign, and Tiberius's, and Maurice's. As you say, they left again soon enough, or were driven off. But since this beast of a Phokas murdered his way to the throne of the Roman Empire—"

"Shh." John looked around. Only one monk was nearby, on his hands and knees in the herb garden. "One never knows who may be listening."

"I am too old to fear spies overmuch, John," the abbot said, chuckling. At that moment, the monk in the herb garden sat back on his haunches so he could wipe sweat from his strong, swarthy face with the sleeve of his robe. Isaac chuckled again. "And can you seriously imagine *him* betraying us?"

John laughed too. "That one? No, you have me there. Ever since he came to us, he's thought of nothing but his hymns."

"Nor can I blame him, for they are a gift from God," Isaac said. "Truly he must be inspired, to sing the Lord's praises so sweetly when he knew not a word of Greek before he fled his horrid paganism to become a Christian and a monk. Romanos the Melodist was a convert too, they say— born a Jew."

"Some of our brother's hymns are a match for his, I think," John said. "Perhaps they love Christ the more for first discovering Him with the full faculties of grown men."

"It could be so," Isaac said thoughtfully. Then, as the monk in the garden resumed his work, the abbot came back to his worries. "When I was younger, we always knew the Persians were harriers, not conquerors. Sooner or later, our soldiers would drive them back. This time I think they are come to stay."

John's sunny face was not well adapted to showing concern, but it did now. "You may be right, father abbot. Since the general Narses rebelled against Phokas, since Germanos attacked Narses, since the Persians beat Germanos and Leontios—"

"Since Phokas broke his own brother's pledge of safe-conduct for Narses and burned him alive, since Germanos was forced to become a monk for losing to the Persians—" Isaac took up the melancholy tale of Roman troubles. "Our armies now are a rabble, those that have not fled. Who will, who can, make king Khosroes's soldiers leave the Empire now?"

John looked this way and that again, lowered his voice so that Isaac had to lean close to hear him at all. "Perhaps it would be as well if they did stay. I wonder," he went on wistfully, "if the young man with them truly is Maurice's son

Theodosios. Even with Persian backing, he would be better than Phokas."

"No, John." The abbot shook his head in grim certainty. "I am sure Theodosios is dead; he was with his father when Phokas overthrew them. And while the new Emperor has many failings, no one can doubt his talent as a butcher."

"True enough," John sighed. "Well, then, father abbot, why *not* welcome the Persians as liberators from the tyrant?"

"Because of what I heard from a traveler out of the east who took shelter with us last night. He was from a village near Daras, where the Persians have had a couple of years now to decide how they will govern the lands they have taken from the Empire. He told me they were beginning to make the Christians thereabouts become Nestorians."

"I had not heard that, father abbot," John said, adding a moment later, "Filthy heresy!"

"Not to the Persians. They exalt Nestorians above all other Christians, trusting their loyalty because we who hold to the right belief have persecuted them so they may no longer live within the Empire." Isaac sadly shook his head. "All too often, that trust has proven justified."

"What shall we do, then?" John asked. "I will not abandon the true faith, but in truth I would sooner serve the Lord as a living monk than as a martyr, though His will be done, of course." He crossed himself.

So did Isaac. His eyes twinkled. "I do not blame you, my son. I have lived most of my life, so I am ready to see God and His Son face to face whenever He desires, but I understand how younger men might hesitate. Some, to save their lives, might even bow to heresy and forfeit their souls. I think, therefore, that we should abandon Ir-Ruhaiyeh, so no one will have to face this bitter choice."

John whistled softly. "As bad as that?" His glance slid to the monk in the garden, who had looked up at the musical tone but went back to his weeding when the prior's eye fell on him.

"As bad as that," Isaac echoed. "I need you to begin drawing up plans for our withdrawal. I want us to leave no later than a week from today."

"So soon, father abbot? As you wish, of course; you know you have my obedience. Shall I arrange for our travel west to Antioch or south to Damascus? I presume you will want us safe behind a city's walls."

"Yes, but neither of those," the abbot said. John stared at him in surprise. Isaac went on, "I doubt Damascus is strong enough to stand against the storm that is rising. And Antioch—Antioch is all in commotion since the Jews rose and murdered the patriarch, may God smile upon him. Besides, the Persians are sure to make for it, and it can fall. I was a tiny boy the last time it did; the sack, I have heard, was ghastly. I would not want us caught up in another such."

"What then, father abbot?" John asked, puzzled now.

"Ready us to travel to Constantinople, John. If Constantinople falls to the Persians, surely it could only portend the coming of the Antichrist and the last days of the world. Even that may come. I find it an evil time to be old."

"Constantinople. The city." John's voice held awe and longing. From the Pillars of Herakles to Mesopotamia, from the Danube to Nubia, all through the Roman Empire, Constantinople was *the* city. Every man dreamed of seeing it before he died. The prior ran fingers through his beard. His eyes went distant as he began to think of what the monks would need to do to get there. He never noticed Isaac walking away.

What did call him back to his surroundings was the monk leaving the herb garden a few minutes later. Had the fellow simply passed by, John would have paid him no mind. But he was humming as he walked, which disturbed the prior's thoughts.

"Silence, brother," John said reprovingly.

The monk dipped his head in apology. Before he had gone a dozen paces, he was humming again. John rolled his eyes in rueful despair. Taking the music from that one was the next thing to impossible, for it came upon him so strongly that it possessed him without his even realizing it.

Had he not produced such lovely hymns, the prior thought, people might have used the word *possessed* in a different sense. But no demon, surely, could bring forth glowing praise of the Trinity and the Archangel Gabriel.

John dismissed the monk from his mind. He had many more important things to worry about.

"A *nomisma* for that donkey, that piece of crowbait?" The monk clapped a hand to his tonsured pate in theatrical disbelief. "A goldpiece? You bandit, may Satan lash you with sheets of fire and molten brass for your effrontery! Better you should ask for thirty pieces of silver. That would only be six more, and would show you for the Judas you are!"

After fierce haggling, the monk ended up buying the donkey for ten silver pieces, less than half the first asking price. As the trader put the jingling miliaresia into his pouch, he nodded respectfully to his recent opponent. "Holy sir, you are the finest bargainer I ever met at a monastery."

"I thank you." Suddenly the monk was shy, not the fierce dickerer he had seemed a moment before. Looking down to the ground, he went on, "I was a merchant once myself, years ago, before I found the truth of Christ."

The trader laughed. "I might have known." He gave the monk a shrewd once-over. "From out of the south, I'd guess, by your accent."

"Just so." The monk's eyes were distant, remembering. "I was making my first run up to Damascus. I heard a monk preaching in the marketplace. I was not even a Christian at the time, but it seemed to me that I heard within me the voice of the Archangel Gabriel, saying, 'Follow!' And follow I did, and follow I have, all these years since. My caravan went back without me."

"A strong call to the faith indeed, holy sir," the trader said, crossing himself. "But if you ever wish to return to the world, seek me out. For a reasonable share of the profits I know you will bring in, I would be happy to stake you as a merchant once again."

The monk smiled, teeth white against tanned, dark skin and gray-streaked black beard. "Thank you, but I am content and more than content with my life as it is. *Inshallah—*" He laughed at himself. "Here I've been working all these years to use only Greek, and recalling what I once was makes me forget myself so easily. *Theou thelontos,* I should have said— God willing—I would have spent all my days here at Ir-Ruhaiyeh. But that is not to be."

"No." The trader looked east. No smoke darkened the horizon there, not yet, but both men could see it in their minds' eyes. "I may find a new home for myself as well."

"God grant you good fortune," the monk said.

"And you, holy sir. If I have more beasts to sell, be sure I shall look for a time when you are busy elsewhere."

"Spoken like a true thief," the monk said. They both

laughed. The monk led the donkey away toward the stables. They were more crowded now than at any other time he could recall, with horses, camels, and donkeys. Some the monks would ride, others would carry supplies and the monastery's books and other holy gear.

Words and music filled the monk's mind as he walked toward the refectory. By now the words came more often in Greek than his native tongue, but this time, perhaps because his haggle with the merchant had cast memory back to the distant pagan days he did not often think of anymore, the idea washed over him in the full guttural splendor of his birthspeech.

Sometimes he crafted a hymn line by line, word by word, fighting against stubborn ink and papyrus until the song had the shape he wanted. He was proud of the songs he shaped that way. They were truly his.

Sometimes, though, it was as if he saw the entire shape of a hymn complete at once. Then the praises to the Lord seemed almost to write themselves, his pen racing over the page as an instrument not of his own intelligence but rather a channel through which God spoke for himself. Those hymns were the ones for which the monk had gained a reputation that reached beyond Syria. He often wondered if he had earned it. God deserved more credit than he did. But then, he would remind himself, that was true in all things.

This idea he had now was of the second sort, a flash of inspiration so blinding that he staggered and almost fell, unable to bear up under its impact. For a moment, he did not even know—or care—where he was. The words, the glorious words reverberating in his mind, were all that mattered.

And yet, because the inspiration came to him in his native language, his intelligence was also engaged. How could he put his thoughts into words his fellows here and folk all through the Empire would understand? He knew he had to; God would never forgive him, nor he forgive himself, if he failed here.

The refectory was dark but, filled with summer air and sweating monks, not cool. The monk took a loaf and a cup of wine. He ate without tasting what he had eaten. His comrades spoke to him; he did not answer. His gaze was inward, fixed on something he alone could see.

Suddenly he rose and burst out, "There is no God but the Lord, and Christ is His Son!" That said what he wanted to say, and said it in good Greek, though without the almost hypnotic intensity the phrase had in his native tongue. Still, he saw, it served his purpose: several monks glanced his way, and a couple, having heard only the bare beginning of the song, made the sacred sign of the cross.

He noticed the others in the refectory only peripherally. Only later would he realize he had heard John say in awe to the abbot Isaac, "The holy fit has taken him again."

For the prior was right. The fit had taken him, and more strongly than ever before. Words poured from somewhere deep within him: "He is the Kindly, the Merciful, Who gave His only begotten Son that man might live. The Lord will abide forever in glory, Father, Son, and Holy Spirit. Which of the Lord's blessings would you deny?"

On and on he sang. The tiny part of him not engaged in singing thanked God for granting him what almost amounted to the gift of tongues. His spoken Greek, especially when dealing with things of the world, was sometimes halting. Yet again and again now, he found the words he needed. That had happened before, but never like this.

"There is no God but the Lord, and Christ is His Son!" Ending as he had begun, the monk paused, looking around for a moment as he slowly came back to himself. His knees failed him; he sank back to his bench. He felt drained but triumphant. The only comparison he knew was most unmonastic: he felt as he had just after a woman.

He rarely thought, these days, of the wife he had left with all else when he gave over the world for the monastery. He wondered if she still lived; she was a good deal older than he. With very human vanity, he wondered if she ever thought of him. With his own characteristic honesty, he doubted it. The marriage had been arranged. It was not her first. Likely it would not have been her last, either.

The touch of the prior's hand on his arm brought him fully back to the confines he had chosen as his own. "That was most marvelous," John said. "I count myself fortunate to have heard it."

The monk dipped his head in humility. "You are too kind, reverend sir."

"I do not think so." John hesitated, went on anxiously, "I

trust—I pray—you will be able to write down your words, so those not lucky enough to have been here on this day will yet be able to hear the truth and grandeur of which you sang."

The monk laughed—again, he thought, as he might have at any small thing after going in unto his wife. "Have no fear there, reverend sir. The words I recited are inscribed upon my heart. They shall not flee me."

"May it be as you have said," the prior told him.

John did not, however, sound as though he thought it was. To set his mind at ease, the monk sang the new hymn again, this time not in the hot flush of creation but as one who brings out an old and long-familiar song. "You see, reverend sir," he said when he was done. "What the Lord, the Most Bountiful One, has granted me shall not be lost."

"Now I have been present at two miracles," John said, crossing himself: "hearing your song the first time and then, a moment later, again with not one single change, not a different word, that I noticed."

With his mind, the monk felt of the texture of his creation, comparing his first and second renditions of the hymn. "There were none," he said confidently. "I would take oath to it before Christ the Judge of all."

"No need on my account. I believe you," John said. "Still, even miracles, I suppose, may be stretched too far. Therefore I charge you, go at once to the writing chamber, and do not leave it until you have written out three copies of your hymn. Keep one yourself, give me one, and give the third to any other one of the brethren you choose."

For the first time in his life, the monk dared protest his prior's command. "But, reverend sir, I should not waste so much time away from the work of preparing for our journey to the city."

"One monk's absence will not matter so much there," John said firmly. "Do as I tell you, and we will bring to Constantinople not only our humble selves, but also a treasure for all time in your words of wisdom and prayer. That is why I bade you write out three copies: if the worst befall and the Persians overrun us, which God prevent, then one might still reach the city. And one must, I think. These words are too important to be lost."

The monk yielded. "It shall be as you say, then. I had not thought on why you wanted me to write out the hymn three times—I thought it was only for the sake of Father, Son, and Holy Spirit."

To his amazement, John bowed to him. "You are most saintly, thinking only of the world of the spirit. As prior, though, I have also to reckon with this world's concerns."

"You give me too much credit," the monk protested. Under his swarthy skin he felt himself grow hot, remembering how moments ago he had been thinking, not of the world to come, but of his wife.

"Your modesty becomes you," was all John said to that. The prior bowed again, discomfiting the monk even more. "Now I hope you will excuse me, for I have my work to see to. Three fair copies, mind, I expect from you. In that matter I will accept no excuses."

The monk made one last try. "Please, reverend sir, let me labor too and write later, when our safety is assured. Surely I will earn the hatred of my brethren for being idle while they put all their strength into readying us to go."

"You are not idle," John said sternly. "You are in the service of the Lord, as are they. You are acting under my orders, as are they. Only vicious fools could resent that, and vicious fools will have to deal with *me*." The prior set his jaw.

"They will do as you say, reverend sir," the monk said—who could dare disobey John? "But they will do it from obedience alone, not from conviction, if you take my meaning."

"I know what you mean," the prior said, chuckling. "How could I be who I am and not know it? Here, though, you are wrong. Not a man who was in the refectory and heard your hymn will bear you any but the kindest of wills. All will be as eager as I am to have it preserved."

"I hope you're right," the monk said.

John laughed again. "How could I be wrong? After all, I am the prior." He thumped the monk on the back. "Now go on, and prove it for yourself."

With more than a little trepidation, the monk did as he had been ordered. He was surprised to find John right. Though he sat alone in the writing chamber, from time to time monks bustling past paused a moment to lean their burdens against the wall, stick their heads in the doorway, and encourage him to get his song down on papyrus.

The words flowed effortlessly from his pen—as he'd told the prior, they truly were inscribed upon his heart. He took

that to be another sign of God's speaking directly throug
him with this hymn. He sometimes found writing a barrie
the words that sang in his mind seemed much less fine whe
written out. And other times his pen could not find the rig
words at all, and what came from it was not the fine thing h
had conceived, but only a clumsy makeshift.

Not today. When he finished the first copy, the cruci
one, he compared it to what he had sung. It was as if he ha
seen the words of the hymn before him as he wrote. Her
they were again, as pure and perfect as when the Lord ha
given them to him. He bent his head in thanksgiving.

He took more papyrus and began the second and thir
copies. Usually when he was copying, his eyes went back
the original every few words. Now he hardly glanced at
He had no need, not today.

He was no fine calligrapher, but his hand was cle
enough. After so long at Ir-Ruhaiyeh, writing from left
right had even begun to seem natural to him.

The bell rang for evening prayer. The monk noticed
startled, that the light streaming in through the window w
ruddy with sunset. Had his task taken any longer, he woul
have had to light a lamp to finish it. He rubbed his eyes, fe
for the first time how tired they were. Maybe he should hav
lit a lamp. He did not worry about it. Even if the light of th
world was failing, the light of the Holy Spirit had sustaine
him while he wrote.

He took the three copies of the hymn with him as h
headed for the chapel. John, he knew, would be pleased tha
he had finished writing in a single afternoon. So much sti
remained to be done before the monks left Ir-Ruhaiyeh.

Donkeys brayed. Horses snorted. Camels groaned, as
in torment. Isaac knew they would have done the same ha
their loads been a single straw rather than the bails an
panniers lashed to their backs. The abbot stood outside th
monastery gates, watching monks and beasts of burden fi
past.

The leavetaking made him feel the full weight of hi
years. He rarely did, but Ir-Ruhaiyeh had been his home a
his adult life. One does not abandon half a century and mor
of roots without second thoughts.

Isaac turned to John, who stood, as he so often did, at the abbot's right hand. "May it come to pass one day," Isaac said, "that the Persians be driven back to their homeland so our brethren may return here in peace."

"And may you lead that return, father abbot, singing songs of rejoicing in the Lord," John said. The prior's eyes never wandered from the gateway. As each animal and man came by, he made another check mark on the long roll of papyrus he held.

Isaac shook his head. "I am too old a tree to transplant. All other soil will seem alien to me; I shall not flourish elsewhere."

"Foolishness," John said. For all his effort, though, his voice lacked conviction. Not only was he uneasy about reproving the abbot in any way; he also feared Isaac knew whereof he spoke. He prayed both he and his superior were wrong.

"As you will." The abbot sounded reassuring—deliberately so, John thought. Isaac knew John had enough to worry about right now.

The procession continued. At last it came to an end: almost three hundred monks, trudging west in hope and fear. "Is everyone safely gone?" Isaac asked.

John consulted his list, now black with checks. He frowned. "Have I missed someone?" He shouted to the nearest monk in the column. The monk shook his head. The question ran quickly up the line, and was met everywhere with the same negative response.

John glowered down at the unchecked name, muttered under his breath. "He's off somewhere devising another hymn," the prior growled to Isaac. "Well and good—on any day but this. By your leave—" He started back into the now abandoned (or rather, all but abandoned) monastery.

"Yes, go fetch him," Isaac said. "Be kind, John. When the divine gift takes him, he forgets all else."

"I've seen." John nodded. "But even for that we have no time today, not if we hope to stay in this world so God may visit us with His gifts."

Entering Ir-Ruhaiyeh after the monks had gone out of it was like seeing the corpse of a friend—no, John thought, like the corpse of his mother, for the monastery had nurtured and sheltered him as much as his fleshly parents. Hearing only the wind whistle through the courtyard, seeing doors flung carelessly open and left so forever, made John want to weep.

His head came up. The wind was not quite all he heard. Somewhere among the deserted buildings, a monk was singing quietly to himself, as if trying the flavor of words on his tongue.

John found him just outside the empty stables. His back was turned, so even as the prior drew near he caught only snatches of the new hymn. He was not sure he was sorry. This song seemed to be the complement of the one the monk had created in the refectory; instead of praise for the Lord, it told of the pangs of hell in terms so graphic that ice walked John's back.

"For the unbelievers, for the misbelievers, the scourge. Their hearts shall leap up and choke them. Demons shall seize them by feet and forelocks. Seething water shall be theirs to drink, and—" The monk broke off abruptly, jumping in surprise as John's hand fell on his shoulder.

"Come, Mouamet," the prior said gently. "Not even for your songs will the Persians delay. Everyone else has gone now; we wait only on you."

For a moment, he did not think the monk saw him. Something that was almost fear prickled in him. Could the church itself handle a man with a gift the size of Mouamet's, especially if he came to its heart at Constantinople? Then, slowly, John's worry eased. The church was six centuries old, and bigger even than the Empire. No one man could twist it out of shape. Had the monk stayed among his wild cousins in Arabia, now, with no weighty tradition to restrain him . . .

At last Mouamet's face cleared. "Thank you, reverend sir," he said. "With the Lord giving me this hymn, I'd forgotten the hour." The abstracted expression that raised awe in John briefly returned. "I think I shall be able to recover the thread."

"Good," the prior said, and meant it. "But now—"

"—I'll come with you," Mouamet finished for him. Sandals scuffling in the dust, they walked together out of the monastery and set out on the long road to Constantinople.

Instability

RUDY RUCKER AND PAUL DI FILIPPO

Jack and Neal, loose and blasted, sitting on the steps of the ramshackle porch of Bill Burroughs's Texas shack. Burroughs is out in the yard, catatonic in his orgone box, a copy of the Mayan codices in his lap. He's already fixed M twice today. Neal is cleaning the seeds out of a shoebox full of Mary Jane. Time is thick and slow as honey. In the distance the rendering company's noon whistle blows long, shrill and insistent. The rendering company is a factory where they cut up the cow's that're too diseased to ship to Chicago. Shoot and cut and cook to tallow and canned cancer consommé.

Burroughs rises to his feet like a figure in a well-greased Swiss clock. "There is scrabbling," goes Bill. "There is scrabbling behind the dimensions. Bastards made a hole somewhere. You ever read Lovecraft's 'Colour Out of Space,' Jack?"

"I read it in jail," says Neal, secretly proud. "Dig, Bill, your mention of that document ties in so exactly with my most recent thought mode that old Jung would hop a hard-on."

"*Mhwee-heee-heee,*" says Jack. "The Shadow knows."

"I'm talking about this bomb foolishness," harrumphs Burroughs, stalking stiff-legged over to stand on the steps. "The paper on the floor in the roadhouse john last night said there's a giant atom-bomb test taking place tomorrow at White Sands. They're testing out the fucking 'trigger bomb' to use on that god-awful new *hydrogen* bomb Edward Teller wants against the Rooshians. Pandora's box, boys, and we're not talking cooze. That bomb's going off in New Mexico tomorrow, and right here and now the shithead meat-flayers' noon whistle is getting us all ready for World War Three, and if we're all ready for that, then we're by Gawd ready to be a great civilian army, yes, soldiers for Joe McCarthy and Harry J. Anslinger, poised to stomp out the Reds 'n' queers 'n' dope fiends. Science brings us this. I wipe my queer junkie ass

with science, boys. The Mayans had it aaall figured out a
loooong time ago. Now take this von Neumann fella. . . ."

"You mean Django Reinhardt?" goes Jack, stoned and
rude. "Man, this is your life, their life, my life, a dog's life,
God's life, the life of Riley. The army's genius von Neumann
of the desert, Bill, it was in the Sunday paper Neal and I
were rolling sticks on in Tuscaloosa, I just got an eidetic
memory flash of it, you gone wigged cat, it was right before
Neal nailed that cute Dairy Queen waitress with the Joan
Crawford nose."

Neal goes: "Joan Crawford, Joan Crawfish, Joan Fish-
hook, Joan Rawshanks in the fog. *McVoutie!*" He's toking a
hydrant roach, and his jay-wrapping fingers are laying rapid
cable. Half the damn box is already twisted up.

Jack warps a brutal moodswing. There's no wine. *Ti Jack
could use a widdly sup pour bon peek, like please, you ill
cats, get me off this Earth. . . .* Is he saying this *aloud*, in
front of Neal and Burroughs?

"And fuck the chicken giblets," chortles Neal obscurely,
joyously, in there, and then suggests, by actions as much as by
words, *Is he really talking, Jack?* "That we get back to what's
really important, such as rolling up this here, ahem, um, urp,
Mexican see-gar, yes!"

Jack crab-cakes slideways on fingertips and heels to Neal's
elbow, and they begin to lovingly craft and fashion and croon
upon—and even it would not be too much to say give birth
to—a beautiful McDeVoutieful hair-seeded twat of a reefer,
the roach of which will be larger than any two normal sticks.

They get off good.

Meanwhile, Bill Burroughs is slacked back in his rocker,
refixed and not quite on the nod because he's persistently
irritated, both by the thought of the hydrogen bomb and,
more acutely, by the fly-buzz derry Times Square jive of the
jabbering teaheads. Time passes, so very slowly for Sal and
Dean, so very fast for William Lee.

So Doctor Miracle and Little Richard are barreling along
the Arizona highway, heading east on Route 40 out of Vegas,
their pockets full of silver cartwheels from the grinds they've
thimblerigged, and also wallets bulging with the hi-denom
bills they demanded when cashing in their chips after beating

the bank at the roulette wheels of six different casinos with their unpatented probabilistic scams that are based on the vectors of neutrons through six inches of lead as transferred by spacetime Feynman diagrams to the workings of those rickety-clickety simple-ass macroscopic systems of balls and slots.

Doctor Miracle speaks. He attempts precision, to compensate for the Hungarian accent and for the alcohol-induced spread in bandwidth.

"Ve must remember to zend Stan Ulam a postcard from Los Alamos, reporting za zuccess of his Monte Carlo modeling method."

"It woulda worked even better over in Europe," goes Little Richard. "They got no double-zero slots on their wheels."

Doctor Miracle nods sagely. He's a plump guy in his fifties: thinning hair, cozy chin, faraway eyes. He's dressed in a double-breasted suit, with a bright hula-girl necktie that's wide as a pound of bacon.

Little Richard is younger, skinnier, and more Jewish, and he has a thick pompadour. He's wearing baggy khakis and a white T-shirt with a pack of Luckys rolled up in the left sleeve.

It is not immediately apparent that these two men are ATOMIC WIZARDS, QUANTUM SHAMANS, PLUTONIUM PROPHETS, and BE-BOPPIN' A-BOMB PEE AITCH DEES!

Doctor Miracle, meet Richard Lernmore. Little Richard, say hello to Johnny von Neumann!

There is a case of champagne sitting on the rear seat in between them. Each of the A-scientists has an open bottle from which he swigs, while their car, a brand-new 1950 big-finned land-boat of a two-toned populuxe pink-'n'-green Caddy, speeds along the highway.

There is no one driving. The front seat is empty.

Von Neumann, First Annointed Master of Automata, has rigged up the world's premier autopilot, you dig. He never could drive very well, and now he doesn't have to. Fact is, no one has to! The Caddy has front- and side-mounted radar that feeds into a monster contraption in the trunk, baby cousin to Weiner and Ulams's Los Alamos MANIAC machine, a thing all vacuum tubes and cams, all cogs and Hollerith sorting rods, a mechanical brain that transmits cybernetic impulses directly to the steering, gas, and brake mechanisms.

The Trilateral Commission has rules that the brain in the Cad's trunk is too cool for Joe Blow, much too cool, and a self-driving car isn't going to make it to the assembly line ever. The country needs only a few of those supercars, and this one has been set aside for the use and utmost ease of the two genius-type riders who wish to discuss high quantum-physical, metamathematical, and cybernetic topics without the burden of paying attention to the road. Johnny and Dickie's periodic Alamos-to-Vegas jaunts soak up a lot of the extra nervous tension these important bomb builders suffer from.

"So whadda ya think of my new method for scoring showgirls?" asks Lernmore.

"Dickie, although za initial trials vere encouraging, ve must have more points on the graph before ve can extrapolate," replies von Neumann. He looks sad. "You may haff scored, you zelfish little prick, but I—I did not achieve satisfactory sexual release. Far from it."

"Waa'll," drawls Lernmore, "I got a fave nightclub in El Paso where the girls are hotter'n gamma rays and pretty as parity conservation. You'll get what you need for sure, Johnny. We could go right instead of left at Albuquerque and be there before daylight. Everyone at Los Alamos'll be busy with the White Sands test anyway. Security won't look for us till Monday, and by then we'll be back, minus several milliliters of semen."

"El Paso," mutters von Neumann, taking a gadget out of his inner jacket pocket. It's—THE FIRST POCKET CALCULATOR! Things the size of a volume of the *Britannica,* with Bakelite buttons, and what makes it truly hot is that it's got all the road distances from the *Rand McNally Road Atlas* data-based onto the spools of a small wire-recorder inside. Von Neumann's exceedingly proud of it, and although he could run the algorithm faster in his head, he plugs their present speed and location into the device; calls up the locations of Las Vegas, Albuquerque, El Paso, and Los Alamos; and proceeds to massage the data.

"You're quite right, Dickie," he announces presently, still counting the flashes of the calculator's lights. "Ve can do as you say and indeed eefen return to za barracks before Monday zunrise. Venn is za test scheduled, may I ask?"

"Eight A.M. Sunday."

Von Neumann's mouth broadens in a liver-lipped grin.

"How zynchronistic. Ve'll be passing White Sands just zen. I haff not vitnessed a bomb test since Trinity. And zis is za biggest one yet; zis bomb is, as you know, Dickie, za Ulam cascade initiator for za new hydrogen bomb. I'm for it! Let me reprogram za brain!"

Lernmore crawls over the front seat while the car continues its mad careening down the dizzy interstate, passing crawling tourist Buicks and mom-'n'-dad Studebakers. He lugs the case of champagne into the front seat with him. Von Neumann removes the upright cushion in the backseat and pries off the panel, exposing the brain in the trunk. Consulting his calculator from time to time, von Neumann begins reprogramming the big brain by yanking switchboard-type wires and reinserting them.

"I'm tired of plugging chust metal sockets, Richard. Viz za next girl, I go first."

Now it's night, and the stoned beats are drunk and high on bennies, too. Neal, his face all crooked, slopes through Burroughs's shack and picks Bill's car keys off the dresser in the dinette where Joan is listening to the radio and scribbling on a piece of paper. Crossing the porch, thievishly heading for the Buick, Neal thinks Bill doesn't see, but Bill does.

Burroughs the beat morphinist, whose weary disdain has shaded catastrophically with the Benzedrine and alcohol into fried impatience, draws the skeletized sawed-off shotgun from the tube of hidden gutterpipe that this same Texafied Burroughs has suspended beneath a large hole drilled in the eaten wood of his porch floor. He fires a twelve-gauge shotgun blast past Neal and into Neal's cleaned and twisted box of Mary Jane, barely missing Jack.

"*Whew, no doubt,*" goes Neal, tossing Burroughs the keys.

"Have ye hard drink, mine host?" goes Jack, trying to decide if the gun really went off or not. "Perhaps a pint of whiskey in the writing desk, old top? A spot of sherry?"

"To continue my afternoon fit of thought," says Burroughs, pocketing his keys, "I was talking about thermonuclear destruction and about the future of all humanity, which species has just about been squashed to spermaceti in the rictal mandrake spasms of Billy Sunday's pimpled ass-cheeks."

He pumps another shell into the shotgun's chamber. His eyes are crazed goofball pinpoints. "I am sorry I ever let you egregious dope-suckin' latahs crash here. I mean you especially, jailbird con man Cassady."

Neal sighs and hunkers down to wail on the bomber Jack's lit off a smoldering scrap of shotgun wadding. Before long he and Jack are far into a rap, possibly sincere, possibly jive, a new rap wrapped around the concept that the three hipsters assembled here on the splintery porch 'neath the gibbous prairie moon have formed or did or will form or, to be quite accurate, *were forming and still are forming right then and there*, an analogue of those Holy B-Movie Goofs, THE THREE STOOGES!

"Yes," goes Jack, "those Doomed Saints of Chaos, loosed on the work-a-daddy world to scramble the Charles Dickens cark and swink of BLOOEY YER FIRED, those Stooge Swine are the anarchosyndicalist truly wigged sub-Marxists, Neal man, *bikkhu* Stooges goosing ripeassmelons and eating fried chicken for supper. *We* are the Three Stooges."

"Bill is Moe," says Neal, hot on the beam, batting his eyes at Bill, who wonders if it's time to shed his character-armor. "Mister Serious Administerer of Fundament Punishments and Shotgun Blasts, and me with a Lederhosen ass!"

"Ah you, Neal," goes Jack, "you're Curly, angelic madman saint of the uncaught mote-beam fly-buzz fly!"

"And Kerouac is Larry," rheums Burroughs, weary with the knowledge. "*Mopple-lipped, lisped, muxed, and completely flunk* is the phrase, eh, Jack?"

"Born to die," goes Jack. "We're all born to die, and I hope it do be cool, Big Bill, if we goam take yo cah. Vootie-oh-oh." He holds out his hand for the keys.

"Fuck it," says Bill. "Who needs this noise." He hands Jack the keys, and before you know it, Neal's at the wheel of the two-ton black Buick, gunning that straight-eight mill and burping the clutch. Jack's at his side, and they're on the road with a long honk good-bye.

In the night there's reefer and plush seats and the radio, and Neal is past spaced, off in his private land that few but Jack and Alan can see. He whips the destination on Jack.

"This car is a front-row seat to the A-blast."

"What."

"We'll ball this jack to White Sands, New Mexico, dear

Jack, right on time for the bomb test Sunday 8 A.M. I stole some of Bill's M, man, we'll light up *on* it."

In Houston they stop and get gas and wine and benny and Bull Durham cigarette papers and keep flying west.

Sometime in the night, Jack starts to fade in and out of horror dreams. There's a lot of overtime detox dream-work that he's logged off of too long. One time he's dreaming he's driving to an atom-bomb test in a stolen car, which is of course true, and then after that he's dreaming he's the dead mythic character in black and white that he's always planned to be. Not to mention the dreams of graves and Memere and the endless blood sausages pulled out of Jack's gullet by some boffable blonde's sinister boyfriend . . .

". . . been oh rock and roll gospeled in on the *bomb foolishness* . . ." Neal is going when Jack screams and falls off the backseat he's stretched out on. There's hard wood and metal on the floor. ". . . and Jack, you do understand, buckaroo, that I have hornswoggled you into yet another new and unprecedentedly harebrained swing across the dairy fat of her jane's spreadness?"

"Go," goes Jack feebly, feeling around on the backseat floor. Short metal barrel, lightly oiled. Big flat disk of a magazine. Fuckin' crazy Burroughs. It's a Thompson submachine gun Jack's lying on.

"And, ah Jack, man, I knew you'd know past the suicidal norm, Norm, that it was . . . *DeVoutie!*" Neal fishes a Bakelite ocarina out of his shirt pocket and tootles a thin, horrible note. "Goof on this, Jack, I just shot M, and now I'm so high I can drive with my eyes closed."

Giggling Leda Atomica tugs at the shoulders of her low-cut peasant blouse with the darling petit-point floral embroidery, trying to conceal the vertiginous depths of her cleavage, down which Doctor Miracle is attempting to pour flat champagne. What a ride this juicy brunette is having!

Leda had been toking roadside Albuquerque monoxide till 11:55 this Saturday night, thumb outstretched and skirt hiked up to midthigh, one high-heel foot perched on a little baby blue hand case with nylons and bra straps trailing from its crack. Earlier that day she'd parted ways with her employer, an Oakie named Oather. Leda'd been working at Oather's juke joint as a waitress and as a performer. Oather had put her in this like act wherein she strutted on the bar in high heels while a trained swan untied the strings of her atom-girl costume, a cute leatherette two-piece with conical silver lamé tit cups and black shorts patterned in intersecting friendly-atom ellipses. Sometimes the swan bit Leda, which really pissed her off. Saturday afternoon the swan had escaped from his pen, wandered out onto the road, and been mashed by a semi full of hogs.

"That was the only bird like that in Arizona," yelled Oather. "Why dintcha latch the pen?"

"Maybe people would start payin' to watch you lick my butt," said Leda evenly. "It's about all you're good for, limp-dick."

Et cetera.

Afternoon and early evening traffic was sparse. The drivers that did pass were all upstanding family men in sensible Plymouths, honest salesmen too tame for the tasty trouble Leda's bod suggested.

Standing there at the roadside, Leda almost gave up hope. But then, just before midnight, the gloom parted and here came some kind of barrel-assing Necco-Wafer-colored Caddy!

When the radars hit Leda's boobs and returned their echoes to the control mechanism, the cybernetic brain nearly had an aneurysm. Not trusting Lernmore's promises, von Neumann had hard-wired the radars for just such a tramp-girl eventuality, coding hitchhiking Jane Russell T&A parameters into the electronic brain's very circuits. The Caddy's headlights started blinking like a *fellah* in a sandstorm, concealed sirens went off, and Roman candles mounted on the rear bumper discharged, shooting rainbow fountains of glory into the night.

"SKIRT ALERT!" whooped Doctor Miracle and Little Richard.

Before Leda knew what was happening, the cybernetic Caddy had braked at her exact spot. The rear door opened, Leda and her case were snatched on in, and the car roared off, the wind of its passage scattering the tumbleweeds.

Leda knew she was hooked up with some queer fellas as soon as she noticed the empty driver's seat.

She wasn't reassured by their habit of reciting backward all the signs they passed.

"Pots!"

"Egrem!"

"Sag!"

But soon Leda takes a shine to Doctor Miracle and Little Richard. Their personalities grow on her in direct proportion to the amount of bubbly she downs. By the time they hit Truth or Consequences, N.M., they're scattin' to the cool sounds of Wagner's *Nibelungenlied* on the long-distance radio, and Johnny is trying to baptize her tits.

"Dleiy!" croons Doctor Miracle.

"Daeha thgil ciffart!" goes Lernmore, all weaseled in on Leda's other side.

"Kcuf em won syob!" says Leda, who's gone seven dry weeks without the straight-on loving these scientists are so clearly ready to provide.

So they pull into the next tourist cabins and get naked and find out what factorial three really means. I mean . . . do they get it on or *what*? Those stag-film stars Candy Barr and Smart Alec have got nothing on Leda, Dickie, and Doctor Miracle! Oh baby!

And then it's near dawn and they have breakfast at a greasy spoon, and then they're on Route 85 south. Johnny's got the brain programmed to drive them right to the 7:57 A.M. White Sands space-time coordinate; he's got the program tweaked down to the point where the Cad will actually cruise past ground zero and nestle itself behind the observation bunker, leaving them ample time to run inside and join the other top bomb boys.

Right before the turnoff to the White Sands road, von Neumann decides that things are getting dull.

"Dickie, activate the jacks!"

"Yowsah!"

Lernmore leans over the front seat and flips a switch that's breadboarded into the dash. The car starts to buck and rear like a wild bronco, its front and tail alternately rising and plunging. It's another goof of the wondercaddy—von Neumann has built B-52 landing gear in over the car's axles.

As the Caddy porpoises down the highway, its three occupants are laughing and falling all over each other, playing grab-ass, champagne spilling from an open bottle.

Suddenly, without warning, an *ooga-ooga* Klaxon starts to blare.

"Collision imminent," shouts von Neumann.

"Hold onto your tush!" advises Lernmore.

"Be careful," screams Leda and wriggles to the floor.

Lernmore manages to get a swift glimpse of a night black Buick driving down the two-lane road's exact center, heading straight toward them. No one is visible in the car.

Then the road disappears, leaving only blue sky to fill the windshield. There is a tremendous screech and roar of ripping metal, and the Caddy shudders slowly to a stop.

When Lernmore and von Neumann peer out of their rear window, they see the Buick stopped back there. It is missing its entire roof, which lies crumpled in the road behind it.

For all Neal's bragging, M's not something he's totally used to. He has to stop and puke a couple of times in El Paso, early early with the sky going white. There's no sympathy from Jack, 'cause Jack picked up yet another bottle of sweet wine outside San Antone, and now he's definitely passed. Neal has the machine gun up in the front seat with him; he knows he ought to put it in the trunk in case the cops ever pull them over, but the *dapperness* of the weapon is more than Neal can resist. He's hoping to get out in the desert with it and blow away some cacti.

North of Las Cruces the sun is almost up, and Neal is getting a bad disconnected feeling; he figures it's the morphine wearing off and decides to fix again. He gets a Syrette out of the Buick's glove compartment and skin-pops it. Five more miles and the rosy flush is on him; he feels better than he's felt all night. The flat empty dawn highway is a gray triangle that's driving the car. Neal gets the idea he's a speck of paint on a perspective painting; he decides it would be cool to drive lying down. He lies down sideways on the driver's seat, and when he sees that it works, he grins and closes his eyes.

The crash tears open the dreams of Jack and Neal like some horrible fat man's can opener attacking oily smoked sardines. They wake up in a world that's horribly different. Jack's sluggish and stays in the car, but Neal is out on the road doing dance incantation trying to avoid death that he feels so thick in the air. The Thompson submachine gun is in his hand, and he is, solely for the rhythm, you understand, firing it and raking the landscape, especially his own betraying Buick, though making sure the fatal lead is only in the lower parts, e.g. tires as opposed to sleepy Jack backseat or gas tank, and, more than that, he's trying to keep himself from laying a steel-jacketed; flat horizontal line of lead across the hapless marshmallow white faces of the rich boys in the Cadillac. They have a low number government license plate. Neal feels like Cagney in *White Heat*, possessed by total crazed rage against authority, ready for a mad-dog last-stand showdown that can culminate only in a fireball of glorious fuck-you-copper destruction. But there's only two of them here to kill. Not enough to go to the chair for. Not yet, no matter how bad the M comedown feels. Neal shoots lead arches over them until the gun goes to empty clicks.

Slowly, black Jack opens the holey Buick door, feeling God it's so horrible to be alive. He blows chunks on the meaningless asphalt. The two strange men in the Cadillac give off the scent of antilife evil, a taint buried deep in the bone marrow, like strontium 90 in mother's milk. Bent down wiping his mouth and stealing an outlaw look at them, Jack flashes that these new guys have picked up their heavy death-aura from association with the very earth-frying, retina-blasting all-bomb that he and Neal are being ineluctably drawn to by cosmic forces that Jack can *see*, as a matter of fact, ziggy lines sketched out against the sky as clear as any peyote mandala.

"Everyone hates me but Jesus," says Neal, walking over to the Cadillac, spinning the empty Thompson around his callused thumb. "Everyone is Jesus but me."

"Hi," says Lernmore, "I'm sorry we wrecked your car."

Leda rises up from the floor between von Neumann's legs, a fact not lost on Neal.

"We're on our way to the bomb test," croaks Jack, lurching over.

"Ve helped invent the bomb," says von Neumann. "Ve're rich and important men. Of course ve vill pay reparations and additionally offer you a ride to the test, *ezpecially* since you didn't kill us."

The Cadillac is obediently idling in park, it's robot-brain having retracted the jacks and gone into standby mode after the oil-pan-scraping collision. Neal mimes a wide-mouthed blow job of the hot tip of the Thompson, flashes Leda an easy smile, slings the gun out into the desert, and then he and shuddery Jack clamber into the Cad's front seat. Leda, with her trademark practicality, climbs into the front seat with them and gives them a bottle of champagne. She's got the feeling these two brawny drifters can take her faster farther than science can.

Von Neumann flicks the RESET cyberswitch in the rear seat control panel, and the Cad rockets forward, pressing them all back into the deep cushioned seats. Neal fiddles with the steering wheel, fishtailing the Cad this way and that, then observes, "Seems like this tough short's got a mind of its own."

"Zis car's brobably as smart as you are," von Neumann can't help observing. Neal lets it slide: 7:49.

The Cad makes a hard squealing right turn onto the White Sands access road. There's a checkpoint farther on; but the soldiers recognize von Neumann's wheels and wave them right on through.

Neal fires up a last reefer and begins beating out a rhythm on the dash with his hands, grooving to the pulse of the planet, his planet awaiting its savior. Smoke trickles out of his mouth; he shotguns Leda, breathing the smoke into her mouth, wearing the glazed eyes of a mundane gnostic messiah, hip to a revelation of the righteous road to salvation. Jack's plugged in, too, sucking his last champagne, telepathy-rapping with Neal. It's almost time, and Doctor Miracle and Little Richard are too confused to stop it.

A tower rears on the horizon off to the left, and all at once the smart Cad veers off the empty two lane road and rams its way through a chain-link fence. Nerve-shattering scraping and lumbering thumps.

"Blease step on za gas a bit," says von Neumann, unsurprised. He programmed this shortcut in. "I still vant to go under za tower, but is only three minutes remaining. Za program is undercompensating for our unfortunate lost time." It is indeed 7:57.

Neal drapes himself over the wheel now, stone committed to this last holy folly. Feeling a wave of serene, yet exultant resignation, Jack says, "Go." It's almost all over now, he thinks, the endless roving and raging, brawling and fucking, the mad flights back and forth across and up and down the continent, the urge to get it all down on paper, every last feeling and vision in master-sketch detail, because we're all gonna die one day, man, all of us—

The Caddy, its sides raked of paint by the torn fence, hurtles on like God's own thunderbolt messenger, over pebbles and weeds, across the desert and the sloping glass craters of past tests. The tower is ahead: 7:58.

"Get ready, Uncle Sam," whispers Neal. "We're coming to cut your balls off. Hold the boys down, Jack."

Jack body-rolls over the seat back into the laps of Lernmore and von Neumann. Can't have those mad scientists fiddle with the controls while Neal's pulling his cool automotive move!

Leda still thinks she's on a joyride and cozies up to Neal's biceps, and for a second it's just the way it's supposed to be, handsome hard-rapping Neal at the wheel of big old bomb with a luscious brunette squeezed up against him like gum.

And now, before the guys in back can do much of anything, Neal's clipped through the tower's southern leg. As the tower starts to collapse, Neal, flying utterly on extrasensory instincts, slows just enough to pick up the bomb, which has been jarred prematurely off its release hook.

No Fat Boy, this gadget represents the ultimate to date in miniaturization: it's only about as big as a fifty-gallon oil drum, and about as weighty. It crunches down onto the Caddy's roof, bulging bent metal in just far enough to brush the heads of the riders.

And no, it doesn't go off. Not yet: 7:59.

Neal aims the mighty Cad at the squat concrete bunker half a mile off. This is an important test, the last step before the H-bomb, and all the key assholes are in there, every atomic brain in the free world, not to mention dignitaries and politicians aplenty, all come to witness this proof of American military superiority, all those shit-nasty fuckheads ready to kill the future.

King Neal floors it and does a cowboy yodel, Jack is laughing and elbowing the scientists, Leda's screaming luridly, Dickie is talking too fast to understand, and Johnny is—8:00.

They impact the bunker at eighty mph, folding up

accordian-style, but not feeling it, as the mushroom blooms, and the atoms of them and the assembled bigwigs commingle in the quantum instability of the reaction event. Time forks.

Somewhere, somewhen, there now exists an Earth where there are no nuclear arsenals, where nations do not waste their substance on missiles and bombs, where no one wakes up thinking each morning might be the world's last—an Earth where two high, gone wigged cats wailed and grooved and ate up the road and Holy Goofed the world off its course.

For you and me.

No Spot
of Ground

WALTER JON WILLIAMS

The dead girl came as a shock to him. He had limped into the Starker house from the firelit military camp outside, from a cacophony of wagons rattling, men driving tent pegs, provost marshals setting up the perimeter, a battalion of Ewell's Napoleon guns rolling past, their wheels lifting dust from the old farm road, dust that drifted over the camp, turning the firelight red and the scene into a pictured outpost of Hell. . . .

And here, to his surprise, was a dead girl in the parlor. She was perhaps sixteen, with dark hair, translucent skin, and cheeks with high spots of phthisis red. Her slim form was dressed in white. She lay in her coffin with candles at her head and feet, and her long-faced relatives sat in a semicircle of chairs under portraits of ancestors and Jefferson Davis.

A gangly man, probably the dead girl's father, rose awkwardly to welcome the surprised stranger, who had wandered into the parlor in hopes of asking for a glass of lemonade.

The intruder straightened in surprise. He took off his soft white hat and held it over his heart. The little gold knots on the ends of the hat cord rattled on the brim like muffled mourning drums.

"I am sorry to intrude on your grief," he said.

The father halted in what he was going to say, nodded, and dropped back into his chair. His wife, a heavy woman in dark silk, reached blindly toward him, and took his hand.

The intruder stood for a long moment out of respect, his eyes fixed on the corpse, before he turned and put on his hat and limped out of the house. Once he had thought this sight the saddest of all; once he had written poems about it.

What surprised him now was that it still happened, that people still died this way.

He had forgotten, amid all this unnatural slaughter, that a natural death was possible.

*   *   *

That morning he had brought his four brigades north into Richmond, marching from the Petersburg and Weldon depot south of the James break-step across the long bridge to the Virginia Central depot in the capital. Until two days ago he'd commanded only a single brigade in the defense of Petersburg; but poor George Pickett had suffered a collapse after days of nerve-wrenching warfare in his attempt to keep the city safe from Beast Butler's Army of the James; and Pickett's senior brigadier was, perforce, promoted to command of the whole division.

The new commander was fifty-five years old, and even if he was only a division commander till Pickett came back, he was still the oldest in the army.

At school he had been an athlete. Once he swam six miles down the James River, fighting against the tide the whole way, in order to outdo Byron's swim across the Hellespont. Now he was too tired and ill to ride a horse except in an emergency, so he moved through the streets of Richmond in a two-wheel buggy driven by Sextus Pompeiius, his personal darky.

He was dressed elegantly, a spotless gray uniform with the wreathed stars of a brigadier on his collar and bright gold braid on the arms, English riding boots, black doeskin gloves. His new white wide-brimmed hat, a replacement for the one shot off his head at Port Walthall Junction twenty days ago, was tilted back atop his high forehead. Even when he was young and couldn't afford anything but old and mended clothes, he had always dressed well, with the taste and style of a gentleman. Sextus had trimmed his grizzled mustache that morning, back in camp along the Petersburg and Weldon, and snipped at the long gray curls that hung over the back of his collar. A fine white-socked thoroughbred gelding, the one he was too ill to ride, followed the buggy on a lead. When he had gone south in 1861 he had come with twelve hundred dollars in gold and silver, and with that and his army pay he had managed to keep himself in modest style for the last three years.

As he rode past the neat brick houses he remembered when it was otherwise. Memories still burned in his mind: the sneers of Virginia planters' sons when they learned of his background, of his parents in the theater and stepfather in commerce; his mounting debts when his stepfather Mr. Allan had twice sent him to college, first to the University of Virginia and then to West Point, and then not given him the means to remain; the moment Allan had permitted the household slaves to insult him to his face; and those countless times he wandered the Richmond streets in black despondent reverie, when he couldn't help gazing with suspicion upon the young people he met, never knowing how many of them might be living insults to his stepmother, another of Mr. Allan's plentiful get of bastards. . . .

The brigadier looked up as the buggy rattled over rusting iron tracks, and there it was: Ellis & Allan, General Merchants, the new warehouse of bright red brick lying along a Virginia Central siding, its loading dock choked with barrels of army pork. The war that had so devastated the Confederate nation had been kind only to two classes: carrion crows and merchants. The prosperous Ellis & Allan was run by his stepbrothers now, he presumed, possibly in partnership with an assortment of Mr. Allan's bastards—in *that* family, who could say? The brute Allan, penny-pinching as a Jew with the morals of a nigger, might well have given part of the business to his illegitimate spawn, if for no other reason than to spite his foster son. Such was the behavior of the commercial classes that infected this city.

Richmond, he thought violently. Why in the name of heaven are we defending the place? Let the Yanks have it, and let them serve it as Rome served Carthage, burned to the foundations and the scorched plain sown with salt. There are other parts of the South better worth dying for.

Sextus Pompeiius pulled the mare to a halt, and the general limped out of the buggy and leaned on his stick. The Virginia Central yards were filled with trains, the cars shabby, the engines worn. Sad as they were, they would serve to get the division to where it was going, another fifteen miles up the line to the North Anna River, and save shoe leather while doing it.

The detestable Walter Whitman, the general remembered suddenly, wrote of steam engines in his poems. Whitman surely had not been thinking of engines like these, worn and ancient, leaking steam and oil as they dragged from front to front the soldiers as worn and tattered as the engines. Not trains, but ghosts of trains, carrying a ghost division, itself raised more than once from the dead.

The lead formation, the general's old Virginia brigade, was marching up behind the buggy, their colors and band to the front. The bandsmen were playing "Bonnie Blue Flag." The general winced—brass and percussion made his taut nerves shriek, and he could really tolerate only the soft song of stringed instruments. Pain crackled through his temples.

Among the stands of brigade and regimental colors was another stand, or rather a perch, with a pair of black birds sitting quizzically atop: Hugin and Munin, named after the ravens of Wotan. The brigade called themselves the Ravens, a compliment to their commander.

The general stood on the siding and watched the brigade as it came to a halt and broke ranks. A few smiling bandsmen helped the general load his horses and buggy on a flatcar, then jumped with their instruments aboard their assigned transport. The ravens were taken from their perch and put in cages in the back of the general's carriage.

A lance of pain drove through the general's thigh as he swung himself aboard. He found himself a seat among the divisional staff. Sextus Pompeiius put the general's bags in the rack over his head, then went rearward to sit in his proper place behind the car, in the open between the carriages.

A steam whistle cried like a woman in pain. The tired old train began to move.

Poe's Division, formerly Pickett's, began its journey north to fight the Yanks somewhere on the North Anna River. When, the general thought, would these young men see Richmond again?

One of the ravens croaked as it had been taught: "Nevermore!"

Men laughed. They thought it a good omen.

General Poe stepped out of the mourning Starker house, the pale dead girl still touching his mind. When had he changed? he wondered. When had his heart stopped throbbing in sad, harmonic sympathy at the thought of dead young girls? When had he last wept?

He knew when. He knew precisely when his heart had broken for the last time, when he had ceased at last to mourn

Virginia Clemm, when the last ounce of poetry had poured from him like a river of dark veinous blood. . . .

When the Ravens had gone for that cemetery, the tombstones hidden in dust and smoke.

When General Edgar A. Poe, CSA, had watched them go, that brilliant summer day, while the bands played "Bonnie Blue Flag" under the trees and the tombstones waited, marking the factories of a billion happy worms . . .

Poe stood before the Starker house and watched the dark form of his fourth and last brigade, the new North Carolina outfit that had shown their mettle at Port Walthall Junction, now come rising up from the old farm road like an insubstantial battalion of mournful shades. Riding at the head came its commander, Thomas Clingman. Clingman saw Poe standing on Starker's front porch, halted his column, rode toward the house, and saluted.

"Where in hell do I put my men, General? One of your provost guards said up this way, but—"

Poe shook his head. Annoyance snapped like lightning in his mind. No one had given him any orders at all. "You're on the right of General Corse, out there." Poe waved in the general direction of Hanover Junction, the little town whose lights shone clearly just a quarter mile to the east. "You should have gone straight up the Richmond and Fredericksburg tracks from the Junction, not the Virginia Central."

Clingman's veinous face reddened. "They told me wrong, then. Ain't anybody been over the ground, Edgar?"

"No one from *this* division. Ewell pulled out soon's he heard we were coming, but that was just after dark and when we came up, we had no idea what to do. There was just some staff creature with some written orders, and he galloped away before I could ask him what they meant."

No proper instruction, Poe thought. His division was part of Anderson's corps, but he hadn't heard from Anderson and didn't know where the command post was. If he was supposed to report to Lee, he didn't know where Lee was either. He was entirely in the dark.

Contempt and anger snarled in him. Poe had been ignored again. No one had thought to consult him; no one had remembered him; but if he failed, everyone would blame him. Just like the Seven Days'.

Clingman snorted through his bushy mustache. "Confound it anyway."

Poe banged his stick into the ground in annoyance. "Turn your men around, Thomas. It's only another half mile or so. Find an empty line of entrenchments and put your people in. We'll sort everyone out come first light."

"Lord above, Edgar."

"Fitz Lee's supposed to be on your right. Don't let's have any of your people shooting at him by mistake."

Clingman spat in annoyance, then saluted and started the process of getting his brigade turned around. Poe stared after him and bit back his own anger. Orders would come. Surely his division hadn't been forgotten.

"Massa Poe?"

Poe gave a start. With all the noise of marching feet and shouted orders, he hadn't heard Sextus Pompeiius creeping up toward him. He looked at his servant and grinned.

"You gave me a scare, Sextus. Strike me if you ain't invisible in the dark."

Sextus chuckled at his master's wit. "I found that cider, Massa Poe."

Poe scowled. If his soft cider hadn't got lost, he wouldn't have had to interrupt the Starkers' wake in search of lemonade. He began limping toward his headquarters tent, his cane sinking in the soft ground.

"Where'd you find it?" he demanded.

"That cider, it was packed in the green trunk, the one that came up with the divisional train."

"I instructed you to pack it in the brown trunk."

"I know that, Massa Poe. That fact must have slipped my mind, somehow."

Poe's hand clenched the ivory handle of his came. Renewed anger poured like fire through his veins. "Worthless nigger baboon!" he snapped.

"Yes, Massa Poe," Sextus said, nodding, "I is. I *must* be, the way you keep saying I is."

Poe sighed. One really couldn't expect any more from an African. Changing his name from Sam to Sextus hadn't given the black any more brains than God had given him in the first place.

"Well, Sextus," he said. "*Fortuna favet fatuis,* you know." He laughed.

"Massa always has his jokes in Latin. He always does."

Sextus's tone was sulky. Poe laughed and tried to jolly the slave out of his mood.

"We must improve your knowledge of the classics. Your *litterae humaniores,* you understand."

The slave was annoyed. "Enough human litter around here as it is."

Poe restrained a laugh. "True enough, Sextus." He smiled indulgently. "You are excused from your lessons."

His spirits raised by the banter with his darky, Poe limped to his headquarters tent, marked by the division flags and the two ravens on their perch, and let Sextus serve him his evening meal. The ravens gobbled to each other while Poe ate sparingly, and drank two glasses of the soft cider. Poe hadn't touched spirits in fifteen years, even though whiskey was a lot easier to find in this army than water.

Not since that last sick, unholy carouse in Baltimore.

Where were his orders? he wondered. He'd just been ordered to occupy Ewell's trenches. Where was the rest of the army? Where was Lee? No one had told him anything.

After the meal, he'd send couriers to find Lee. Somebody had to know something.

It was impossible they'd forgotten him.

Eureka, he called it. His prose poem had defined the universe, explained it all, a consummate theory of matter, energy, gravity, art, mathematics, the mind of God. The universe was expanding, he wrote, had exploded from a single particle in a spray of evolving atoms that moved outward at the speed of divine thought. The universe was still expanding, the forms of its matter growing ever more complex; but the expansion would slow, reverse; matter would coalesce, return to its primordial simplicity; the Divine Soul that resided in every atom would reunite in perfect self-knowledge.

It was the duty of art, he thought, to reunite human thought with that of the Divine, particled with unparticled matter. In his poetry he had striven for an aesthetic purity of thought and sentiment, a detachment from political, moral, and temporal affairs. . . . Nothing of Earth shone in his verse, nothing contaminated by matter—he desired harmonies, essences, a striving for Platonic perfection, for the dialogue of one abstract with another. Beyond the fact that he wrote in English, nothing connected the poems with America, the nineteenth century, its life, its movements. He disdained even standard versification—he wrote with unusual scansions, strange metrics—the harmonies of octameter catalectic, being more rarified, seemed to rise to the lofty ear of God more than could humble iambic pentameter, that endless trudge, trudge, trudge across the surface of the terrestrial globe. He wanted nothing to stand between himself and supernal beauty, nothing to prevent the connection of his own mind with that of God.

He had poured everything into *Eureka*, all his soul, his hope, his grief over Virginia, his energy. In the end there was the book, but nothing left of the man. He lectured across America, the audiences polite and appreciative, their minds perhaps touched by his own vision of the Divine—but all his own divinity had gone into the book, and in the end Earth reached up to claim him. Entire weeks were spend in delirium, reeling drunk from town to town, audience to audience, woman to woman. . . .

Ending at last in some Baltimore street, lying across a gutter, his body a dam for a river of half-frozen October sleet.

After the meal Poe stepped outside for a pipe of tobacco. He could see the soft glow of candlelight from the Starker parlor, and he thought of the girl in her coffin, laid out in her dress of virgin white. How much sadder it would have been had she lived, had she been compelled to grow old in this new, changing world, this sad and deformed Iron Age dedicated to steam and slaughter . . . better she was dead, her spirit purged of particled matter and risen to contemplation of the self-knowing eternal.

His thoughts were interrupted by the arrival of a man on horseback. Poe recognized Colonel Moxley Sorrel, a handsome Georgian, still in his twenties, who was Longstreet's chief of staff. He had been promoted recently as a result of leading a flank assault in the Wilderness that had crushed an entire Union corps, though, as always, the triumph had come too late in the day for the attack to be decisive.

"General." Sorrel saluted. "I had a devil of a time finding you. Ewell had his command post at Hackett's place, over yonder." He pointed at the lights of a plantation house just north of Hanover Junction. "I reckoned you'd be there."

"I had no notion of where Ewell was. No one's told me a thing. This place seemed as likely as any." Poe looked off toward the lights of Hanover Junction. "At least there's a good view."

Sorrel frowned. He swung out of the saddle, and Sextus came to take the reins from his hand. "Staff work has gone up entirely," Sorrel said. "There's been too much chaos at the top for everything to get quite sorted out."

"Yes." Poe looked at him. "And how is General Longstreet?"

The Georgian's eyes were serious. "He will recover, praise God. But it will be many months before he can return to duty."

Poe looked up at the ravens, half expecting one of them to croak out "Nevermore." But they'd stuck their heads under their wings and gone to sleep.

He will recover, Poe thought. That's what they'd said of Stonewall; and then the crazed Presbyterian had died suddenly.

Just like old Stonewall to do the unexpected.

The army had been hit hard the last few weeks. First Longstreet wounded in the Wilderness, then Jeb Stuart killed at Yellow Tavern, just a few days ago. They were the two best corps commanders left to Lee, in Poe's opinion. Longstreet had been replaced by Richard Anderson; but Lee had yet to appoint a new cavalry commander—both, in Poe's mind, bad decisions. Anderson was too mentally lazy to command a corps—he was barely fit to command his old division—and the cavalry needed a firm hand now, with their guiding genius gone.

"Will you come inside, Colonel?" Poe gestured toward the tent flap with his stick.

"Thank you, sir."

"Share some cider with me? That and some biscuits are all the *rafraîchissements* I can manage."

"You're very kind." Sorrell looked at the uncleared table. "I've brought your orders from General Anderson."

Poe pushed aside his gold-rimmed dinner plate and moved a lantern onto the table. Sorrel pulled a folded map out of his coat and spread it on the pale blue tablecloth. Poe reached for his spectacles and put them on his nose. The map gave him, for the first time, an accurate look at his position.

This part of the Southern line stretched roughly northwest to southeast, a chord on an arc of the North Anna. The line was more or less straight, though it was cut in half by a swampy tributary of the North Anna, with steep banks on either side, and at that point Poe's entrenchments bent back a bit. The division occupied the part of the line south of the tributary. In front of him was dense hardwood forest, not very useful for maneuver or attack.

"We're going on the offensive tomorrow," Sorrel said, "thank the lord." He gave a thin smile. "Grant's got himself on the horns of a dilemma, sir, and General Lee intends to see he's gored."

Poe's temper crackled. "No one's going to get gored if division commanders don't get their instructions!" he snapped.

Sorrel gave him a wary smile. "That's why I'm here, sir."

Poe glared at him, then deliberately reined in his anger. "So you are." He took a breath. "Pardon my . . . display."

"Staff work, as I say, sir, has been a mite precarious of late. General Lee is ill, and so is General Hill."

Poe's anxiety rose again. "Lee?" he demanded. "Ill?"

"An intestinal complaint. We would have made this attack yesterday had the general been feeling better."

Poe felt his nervousness increase. He was not a member of the Cult of Lee, but he did not trust an army without a capable hand at the top. Too many high-ranking officers were out of action or incompetent. Stuart was dead, Longstreet was wounded, Lee was sick—great heavens, he'd already had a heart attack—Ewell hadn't been the same since he lost his leg, Powell Hill was ill half the time. . . . And the young ones, the healthy ones, were as always dying of bullets and shells.

"Your task, general," Sorrel said, "is simply to hold. Perhaps to demonstrate against the Yanks, if you feel it possible."

"How am I to know if it's possible?" He was still angry. "I don't know the ground. I don't know where the enemy is."

Sorrel cocked an eyebrow at him, said, "Ewell didn't show you anything?" But he didn't wait for an answer before beginning his exposition.

The Army of Northern Virginia, he explained, had been

continually engaged with Grant's army for three weeks—first in the Wilderness, then at Spotsylvania, now on the North Anna; there hadn't been a single day without fighting. Every time one of Grant's offensives bogged down, he'd slide his whole army to his left and try again. Two days before, on May 24, Grant had gone to the offensive again, crossing the North Anna both upstream and down of Lee's position.

Grant had obviously intended to overlap Lee on both flanks and crush him between his two wings; but Lee had anticipated his enemy by drawing his army back into a V shape, with the center on the river, and entrenching heavily. When the Yanks saw the entrenchments they'd come to a stumbling halt, their offensive stopped in its tracks without more than a skirmish on either flank.

"You're facing a Hancock's Second Corps, here on our far right flank," Sorrel said. His manicured finger jabbed at the map. Hancock appeared to be entirely north of the swampy tributary. "Warren and Wright are on our left, facing Powell Hill. Burnside's Ninth Corps is in the center—he tried to get across Ox Ford on the twenty-fourth, but General Anderson's guns overlook the ford and Old Burn called off the fight before it got properly started. Too bad—" Grinning. "Could've been another Fredericksburg."

"We can't hope for more than one Fredericksburg, alas," Poe said. "Not even from Burnside." He looked at the map. "Looks as if the Federals have broken their army into pieces for us."

"Yes, sir. We can attack either wing, and Grant can't reinforce one wing without moving his people across the North Anna twice."

General Lee had planned to take advantage of that with an offensive against half Grant's army. He intended to pull Ewell's corps off the far right, most of Anderson's out of the center, and combine them with Hill's for a strike at Warren and Wright. The attack would have been made the day before if Lee hadn't fallen ill. In the end he'd postponed the assault by one day.

The delay, Poe thought, had given the Yanks another twenty-four hours to prepare. Confederates aren't the only ones who know how to entrench.

Plans already laid, he thought. Nothing he could do about it.

He looked at the map. Now that Ewell and most of Anderson's people had pulled out, he was holding half the Confederate line with his single division.

"It'll probably work to the good," Sorrel said. "Your division came up to hold the right for us, and that will allow us to put more soldiers into the attack. With your division and Bushrod Johnson's, which came up a few days ago, we've managed to replace all the men we've lost in this campaign so far."

Had the Yankees? Poe wondered.

"When you hear the battle start," Sorrel said, "you might consider making a demonstration against Hancock. Keep him interested in what's happening on his front."

Poe looked up sharply. "One division," he said, "against the Yankee Second Corps? Didn't we have enough of that at Gettysburg?"

"A demonstration, general, not a battle." Politely. "General Anderson has also put under your command the two brigades that are holding the center, should you require them."

"Whose?"

"Gregg's Brigade, and Law's Alabamans."

Poe's mind worked through this. "Are Gregg and Law aware they are under my orders?"

"I presume so."

"Presume," Poe echoed. There was too much *presuming* in this war. He took off his spectacles and put them in his pocket. "Colonel Sorrel," he said, "would you do me the inestimable favor of riding to Gregg and Law tonight and telling them of this? I fear the staff work may not have caught up with General Anderson's good intent."

Sorrel paused, then gave a resigned shrug. "Very well, General. If you desire it."

"Thank you, Colonel." His small triumph made Poe genial. "I believe I have been remiss. I remember promising you cider."

"Yes. A glass would be delightful, thank you."

They sat at the folding table, and Poe called for Sextus to serve. He opened a tin box and offered it to Sorrel. "I have some of Dr. Graham's dietary biscuits, if you desire."

"Thank you, sir. If I may put some in my pockets for later. . . ?"

"Make free of them, sir."

Sorrel, possessing by now an old soldier's reflexes, loaded his pockets with biscuits and then took a hearty swallow of the cider. Sextus refilled his glass.

"General Pickett's campaign south of the James," Sorrel said, "has been much appreciated here."

"The form of appreciation preferable to us would have been reinforcements from General Lee."

"We were, ah, tangled up with Grant at the time, sir."

"Still, for several days we had two brigades against two entire corps. Two *corps*, sir!" Indignation flared in Poe. His fists knotted in his lap.

"The glory of your victory was all the greater." The Georgian's tone was cautious, his eyes alert.

Condescending, Poe thought. A black anger settled on him like a shroud. These southern gentlemen were always condescending. Poe knew what Sorrell was thinking. It's just Poe, hysterical Code-breaker Poe. *Poe* always thinks he's fighting the whole Yankee army by himself. *Poe* is always sending off messages screaming for help and telling other people what to do. What? Another message from Poe? It's just the fellow's nerves again. Ignore it.

"I've always been proved right!" Poe snapped. "I was *right* during the Seven Days' when I said Porter was dug in behind Boatswain Swamp! I was *right* about the Yankee signal codes, I was right about the charge at Gettysburg, and I was right again when I said Butler had come ashore at Bermuda Hundred with two whole Yankee corps! If my superiors would give me a little credit—"

"Your advice has always been appreciated," said Sorrel.

"My God!" Poe said. "Poor General Pickett is broken down because of this! It may be months before his nerves recover! Pickett—if he could stand what Lee did to the Division at Gettysburg, one might think he could stand anything! But *this*—*this* broke him! Great heavens, if Butler had committed more than a fraction of the forces available to him, he would have lost Petersburg, and with Petersburg, Richmond!"

"I do not think this is the place—" Sorrel began.

Too late. Poe's mind filled with the memory of the Yankees coming at the Ravens at Port Walthall Junction, four brigades against Pickett's two, and those four only the advance of Butler's entire army. He remembered the horror of it, the regimental flags of the Federals breaking out of the cover of the trees, brass and bayonets shining in the wind; shellfire bursting like obscene overripe blossoms; the whistling noise made by the tumbling bullet that had carried away Poe's hat; the sight of George Pickett with his face streaked by powder smoke, his long hair wild in the wind, as he realized his flanks were caving in and he was facing another military disaster . . .

"Screaming for reinforcements!" Poe shouted. "We were *screaming* for reinforcements! And what does Richmond send? *Harvey Hill!* Hah! Major General interfering Harvey Hill!"

Sorrel looked at him stonily. The old fight between Poe and Hill was ancient history.

"Hill is a madman, sir!" Poe knew he was talking too much, gushing like a chain pump, but he couldn't stop himself. Let at least one person know what he thought. "He is a fighter, I will grant him that, but he is quarrelsome, tempestuous—impossible to reason with. He is not a rational man, Colonel. He hasn't an ounce of rationality or system in him. No more brains than a nigger."

Sorrel finished his cider, and raised a hand to let Sextus know not to pour him more. "We may thank God that the movement was made by Butler," he said.

Poe looked at him. "The Yankees will not forever give their armies to men like Butler," he said.

Sorrel gazed resentfully at the lantern for a long moment. "Grant is no Butler, that is certain. But we will do a Chancellorsville on him nonetheless."

"We may hope so," said Poe. He had no confidence in this offensive. Lee no longer had the subordinates to carry things out properly, could no longer do anything in the attack but throw his men headlong at Federal entrenchments.

The young colonel rose. "Thank you for the cider, General. I will visit Generals Law and Gregg on my return journey."

Poe rose with him, memory still surging through his mind like the endless waves of Yankee regiments at Port Walthall Junction. He knew he had not made a good impression, that he had confirmed in Sorrel's mind, and through him the minds of the corps staff, the stories of his instability, his hysteria, and his egotism.

Harvey Hill, he thought, seething. Send Harvey Hill to tell *me* what to do.

Sextus brought Colonel Sorrel his horse and helped the young man mount. "Thank you for speaking to Gregg and Law," Poe said.

"Use their forces as you see fit," Sorrel said.

"This division has had hard fighting," Poe said. "I will be sparing in my use of them."

"We've all had hard fighting, sir," Sorrel said. A gentle reproach. "But with God's help we will save Richmond again this next day."

Poe gave a swift, reflexive glance to the ravens, anticipating another "Nevermore," but saw they were still asleep. No more omens tonight

Sorrel saluted, Poe returned it, and the Georgian trotted off into the night.

Poe looked out at the Yankee campfires burning low off on his left. How many times, he wondered, would this army have to save Richmond? McDowell had come for Richmond, and McClellan, and Pope, Burnside, Hooker, Meade, and Butler. Now there was Grant, who had seized hold of Lee's army in the Wilderness and declined to let it go, even though he'd probably lost more men than the others put together.

Maybe Lee would turn tomorrow into another Chancellorsville.

But even if he did, Poe knew, one day this or another Yank general would come, and Richmond would not be saved. Even Lee could only fight history for so long.

The politicians were counting on the Northern elections to save them, but Poe had no more confidence in George McClellan as a candidate than as a general—Lincoln could outmaneuver him at the polls as handily as Lee had in the Seven Days' Battle.

No, the South was doomed, its Cause lost. That was obvious to anyone with any ratiocinative faculty whatever. But there was nothing else to do but fight on, and hope the North kept giving armies to the likes of Ben Butler.

"Massa Poe?" Sextus was at his elbow. "Will we be sleeping outside tonight?"

Poe cocked an eye at the sky. There was a heavy dew on the ground, but the few clouds in sight were high and moving fast. There should be no rain.

"Yes," Poe said. "Set up the beds."

"Whatever you say, massa."

Sextus was used to it, poor fellow. Poe hadn't been able to sleep alone since Virginia died, and he had always disliked confined spaces. Sleeping out of doors, under a heavy buffalo cloak, with Sextus wrapped in another robe nearby, was the ideal solution. Poe loved to look up at the sweep of brilliant stars, each an eye of God, to feel his soul rising beyond the atmosphere, through the luminiferous ether to merge with the Eternal, the Sublime. . . .

How he came to the gutter in Baltimore he would never know. He had apparently given a lecture there a few nights before, but he couldn't remember it. Perhaps he would have died there, had not a passing widow recognized him, drunk and incapable, and brought him into her carriage. She had talked with him after his lecture, she told him, and found his conversation brilliant. He couldn't remember her either.

Her name was Mrs. Forster. Her late husband had been addicted to alcohol, and she had cured him; she would apply her cure as well to Mr. Poe.

Her plantation, within a half day's journey of Baltimore, was called Shepherd's Rest; she owned close to two thousand slaves and the better part of a county. She loved poetry and philosophy, read French and German, and had a passing knowledge of Latin.

She had a daughter named Evania, a green-eyed girl of fourteen. When Poe first saw her, sitting in the east parlor with the French wallpaper only a shade darker than her eyes, Evania was playing the guitar, her long fingers caressing the strings as if they were a lover's hair. Her long tresses, falling down her neck, seemed to possess the mutable spectrum of a summer sunrise.

Once before Poe, at the end of his wits and with the black hand of self-slaughter clutching at his throat, had been rescued by a widow with a daughter. In Mrs. Forster Poe could almost see Mrs. Clemm—but Mrs. Clemm idealized, perfected, somehow rarified, her poverty replaced by abundance, her sadness by energy, inspiration, and hope. How could he help but see Virginia in her sparkling daughter? How could he help but give her his love, his troth, his ring—He was not being faithless to Virginia, he thought; his second marriage was a fulfillment of the first. Did Evania and

Virginia not possess, through some miracle of transubstantia-
tion, the same soul, the same perfection of spirit? Were they
not earthly shades of the same pure, angelic lady, differing
only in color, one dark, one bright?

Were they not blessings bestowed by Providence, a just
compensation for poor Poe, who had been driven nearly mad
by soaring, like Icarus, too near the divine spark?

For a moment, after Poe opened his eyes, he saw her
floating above him—a woman, dark-tressed, pale-featured,
crowned with stars. He could hear her voice, though distantly; he could not make sense of her speech, hearing only a
murmur of long vowel sounds. . . .

And then she was gone, faded away, and Poe felt a knife
of sorrow enter his heart. He realized he was weeping. He
threw off his buffalo robe and rolled upright.

The Starker house loomed above him, black against the
Milky Way. The candles' glow still softly illuminated the
parlor window.

Poe bent over, touching his forehead to his knees until he
could master himself. He had seen the woman often in his
dreams, sometimes in waking moments. He remembered her
vividly, the female form rising over the streets of Richmond,
during some barely-sane moments after Virginia's death, the
prelude to that last spree in Baltimore. Always he had felt
comforted by her presence, confirmed in his dreams, his
visions. When she appeared it was to confer a blessing.

He did not remember seeing her since his war service
started. But then, his war service was not blessed.

Poe straightened, and looked at the soft candlelight in
the Starker windows. He looked at the foot of his cot, and
saw Sextus wrapped in blankets, asleep and oblivious to his
master's movements. Sometimes Poe thought he would give
half his worth for a single night of sleep as deep and dream-
less as that of his body-servant.

He put his stockinged feet in the carpet slippers that
waited where Sextus had put them, then rose and stepped
out into the camp in his dressing gown. The slippers were
wet with dew inside and out. Poe didn't care. A gentle, warm
wind was flitting up from the south. With this heavy dew,

Poe thought, the wind would raise a mist before dawn. Maybe it would postpone Lee's offensive.

He remembered hiking in New York with Virginia, spending days wandering down hilly lanes, spending their nights in country inns or, when the weather was fine and Virginia's health permitted, wrapped in blankets beneath the open sky. His friends had thought his interest in nature morbid. Buried in the life of the city and the life of the mind, they could not understand how his soul was drawn skyward by the experience of the outdoors, how close he felt to the Creator when he and Virginia shared a soft bank of moist timothy and kissed and caressed one another beneath the infinite range of fiery stars. . . .

Poe realized he was weeping again. He looked about and saw he had wandered far from his tent, amid his soldiers' dying campfires.

Nothing like this had happened to him in years. The sight of that dead girl had brought back things he thought he'd forgotten.

He mastered himself once more and walked on. The rising southern wind stirred the gray ashes of campfires, brought little sparks winking across his path. He followed them, heading north.

Eventually he struck his entrenchments, a deep line of the kind of prepared works this army could now throw up in a few hours, complete with head log, communications trenches, firing step, and parapet. Soldiers huddled like potato sacks in the trenches, or on the grass just behind the line. An officer's mare dozed over its picket. Beyond, Poe could hear the footsteps of the sentries patrolling.

Once, just after the war had first started, Robert Lee had tried to get this army to dig trenches—and the soldiers had mocked him, called him "The King of Spades," and refused to do the work. Digging was no fit work for a white man, they insisted, and besides, only a coward would fight from entrenchments.

Now the army entrenched at every halt. Three years' killing had made them lose their stupid pride.

Poe stepped onto the firing step, and peered out beneath the head log as he tried to scan his front. Beyond the vague impression of gentle rolling hills beyond, he could see little. Then he lifted his head as he heard the challenging scream of a stallion. The sound came from away north, well past the entrenchments.

The mare picketed behind the entrenchments raised its head at the sound. The stallion challenged again. Then another horse screamed, off to the right, and another. The mare flicked its ears and gave an answer.

The mare was in heat, Poe realized. And she was flirting with Yankee horses. None of his men could be out that far.

The wind had carried the mare's scent north, to the nose of one northern stallion. Other stallions that hadn't scented the mare nevertheless answered the first horse's challenge.

Poe's head moved left to right as one horse after another screamed into the night. Sorrel's map hadn't shown the Yankee line stretching that far, well south of the tributary, beyond Clingman's brigade to where Fitz Lee's cavalry was supposed to be, out on his right flank.

He listened as the horses called to one another like bugles before a battle, and he thought: *The Yankees are moving, and they're moving along my front.*

Suddenly the warm south wind turned chill.

How many? he thought.

Sobbing in the mist like men in the extremes of agony, the crying horses offered no answer.

He became a child again, living with Evania in her perfect kingdom, that winding blue river valley west of Baltimore. Never before had he known rest; but there he found it, a cease from the despairing, agonized wanderings that had driven him, like a leaf before a black autumn storm, from Richmond to Boston and every city between.

At last he knew what it was to be a gentleman. He had *thought* he had achieved that title before, through education and natural dignity and inclination—but now he knew that before he had only aspired to the name. Mr. Allan fancied himself a gentleman; but his money was tainted with trade, with commerce and usury. Now Poe understood that the highest type of gentleman was produced only through ease and leisure—not laziness, but rather the freedom from material cares that allowed a man to cultivate himself endlessly, to refine his thought and intellect through study and application of the highest forms of human aspiration.

He was not lazy. He occupied himself in many ways. He moved Mrs. Clemm to Baltimore, bought her a house, arranged for her an annuity. He added to the mansion, creating a new façade of Italian marble that reflected the colors of the westering sun; he employed the servants to move tons of earth in order to create a landscape garden of fully forty acres that featured, in the midst of a wide artificial lake, an arabesque castle, a lacy wedding-cake gift to his bride.

He had always thought landscape gardening fully an equal of poetry in its ability to invoke the sublime and reveal the face of the deity. In this he was a disciple of de Carbonnieres, Piranesi, and Shenstone: The garden was nature perfected, as it had been in the mind of God, a human attempt to restore the divine, Edenic sublimity. He crafted his effects carefully—the long, winding streams through which one approached Poe's demiparadise in swan-shaped boats, the low banks crowded with moss imported from Japan, natural-seeming outcroppings of uniquely colored and textured rock. At the end was a deep, black chasm through which the water rushed alarmingly, as if to Hades—but then the boat was swept into the dazzling wide lake, the sun sparkling on the white sand banks, the blue waters—and then, as the visitor's eyes adjusted from blackness to brightness, one perceived in the midst of a blue-green island the white castle with its lofty, eyelike windows, the symbol of purest Mind in the midst of Nature.

Nothing was suffered to spoil the effects that had taken a full six years to create. Not a stray leaf, not a twig, not a cattail was permitted to sully the ground or taint the water—fully thirty Africans were constantly employed to make certain that Poe's domain was swept clean.

It cost money—but money Poe had, and if not there was always more to be obtained at three and one half percent. His days of penny-counting were over, and he spent with a lavish hand.

He fulfilled another ambition: he started a literary magazine, the *Southern Gentleman*, with its offices in Baltimore. For it he wrote essays, criticism, occasional stories, once or twice a poem.

Only once or twice.

Somehow, he discovered, the poetry had fled his soul.

And he began to feel, to his growing horror, that his loss

of poetry was nothing but a just punishment. True poetry, he knew, could not reside in the breast of a man as faithless as he.

The Starker house on its small eminence stood hard-edged and black against a background of shifting mist, like an isolated tor rising above the clouds. It was a little after four. The sun had not yet risen, but already the eastern horizon was beginning to turn gray. The ravens, coming awake, crackled and muttered to one another as they shook dew from their feathers.

Poe leaned on his stick before a half-circle of his brigadiers and their mingled staffs. Hugin and Munin sat on their perch behind him. Poe was in his uniform of somber gray, a new paper collar, a black cravat, the black doeskin gloves. Over his shoulders he wore a red-lined black cloak with a high collar, an old gift from Jeb Stuart who had said it made him look like a proper raven.

Most of his life Poe had dressed all in black. The uniform was a concession to his new profession, but for sake of consistency with his earlier mode of dress he had chosen the darkest possible gray fabric, so dark it was almost blue.

There was the sound of galloping; riders rose out of the mist. Poe recognized the man in the lead: Fitzhugh Lee, Robert Lee's nephew and the commander of the cavalry division on his right. He was a short man, about Poe's height, a bandy-legged cavalryman with a huge spade-shaped beard and bright, twinkling eyes. Poe was surprised to see him—he had asked only that Lee send him a staff officer.

He and Poe exchanged salutes. "Decided to come myself, General." He dropped from his horse. "Your messenger made it seem mighty important."

"I thank you, sir." Fitz Lee, Poe realized, outranked him. He could take command here if he so desired.

He would not *dare*, Poe thought. A cold anger burned through him for a moment before he recollected that Fitz Lee had as yet done nothing to make him angry.

Still, Poe was uneasy. He could be superceded so easily.

"I think the Yankees are moving across my front," he said. He straightened his stiff leg, felt a twinge of pain. "I think Grant is moving to his left again."

The cavalryman considered this. "If he wants Richmond," he said, "he'll go to his right. The distance is shorter."

"I would like to submit, *apropos*, that Grant may not want Richmond so much as to defeat us in the field."

Fitz Lee puzzled his way through this. "He's been fighting us nonstop, that's the truth. Hasn't broken off so much as a day."

"Nevermore," said one of the ravens. Fitz Lee looked startled. Poe's men, used to it, shared grins. Poe's train of thought continued uninterrupted.

"Moreover, if Grant takes Hanover Junction, he will be astride both the Virginia Central and the Richmond and Fredericksburg. That will cut us off from the capital and our sources of supply. We'll have to either attack him there or fall back on Richmond."

"Mebbe that's so."

"All that, of course, is speculation—a mere exercise of the intuition, if you like. Nevertheless, whatever his intent, it is still an *observed* fact that Grant is moving across my front. *Quod erat demonstrandum.*"

Lee's eyes twinkled. "*Quod libet*, I think, rather." Not quite convinced.

"I have heard their horses. They are well south of where they are supposed to be."

Lee smiled through his big beard and dug a heel into the turf. "If he's moving past you, he'll run into my two brigades. I'm planted right in his path."

There was a saying in the army, *Who ever saw a dead cavalryman?* Poe thought of it as he looked at Lee. "Can you hold him?" he asked.

"Nevermore," said a raven.

Lee's smile turned to steel. "With all respect to your pets, General, I held Grant at Spotsylvania."

Gravely, Poe gave the cavalryman an elaborate, complimentary bow, and Lee returned it. Poe straightened and hobbled to face his brigade commanders.

Perhaps he had Fitz Lee convinced, perhaps not. But he knew—and the knowledge grated on his bones—that Robert Lee would not be convinced. Not with Poe's reputation for hysteria, for seeing Yankees everywhere he looked. The army commander would just assume his high-strung imagination crested illusory armies behind every swirl of mist. As much as Poe hated it, he had to acknowledge this.

"General Lee has made his plans for today," he said. "He will attack to the west, where he conceives General Grant to be. He may not choose to believe any message from his other wing that the Yanks are moving."

Poe waited for a moment for a reply from the cavalryman. Fitz Lee was the commanding general's nephew; perhaps he could trade on the family connection somehow. But the bearded man remained silent.

"They are going to strike us, that is obvious," Poe said. "Grant has his back to the bend of the river, and he'll have to fight his way into the clear. But his men will have to struggle through the woods, and get across that swamp and the little creek, and they're doing it at night, with a heavy mist. They will not be in position to attack at first light. I suggest, therefore, that we attack him as soon as the mist clears, if not before. It may throw him off balance and provide the evidence we need to convince the high command that Mr. Grant has stolen a march upon us."

"Nevermore," said the ravens. "Nevermore."

Poe looked at Sextus, who was standing respectfully behind the half-circle of officers. "Feed the birds," he said. "It may keep them quiet."

"Yes, massa."

"General Poe." Fitz Lee was speaking. "There are two bridges across that creek—small, but they'll take the Yankees across. The water won't hold up the Yanks as long as you might think."

Poe looked at him. "The bridges were not burned after Hancock crossed the North Anna?"

Lee was uneasy. "General Ewell may have done it without my knowledge."

"If the bridges exist, that's all the more reason to attack as soon as we can."

"General." Clingman raised a hand. "Our brigades marched up in the dark. We ain't aligned, and we'll need to sort out our men before we can go forward."

"First light, General," said Poe. "Arrange your men, then go forward. We'll be going through forest, so give each man about two feet of front. Send out one combined company per regiment to act as skirmishers—we'll want to overwhelm their pickets and get a look at what lies in there before your main body strikes them."

Another brigadier piped up. "What do we align on, sir?"

"The rightmost brigade of the division—that's Barton's?" Heads nodded. Poe continued, gesturing into the mist with his stick, sketching out alignments. "Barton will align on the creek, and everyone will guide on him. When Barton moves forward, the others will move with him." He turned to Gregg and Law, both of whom were looking dubious. "I cannot suggest to Generals Gregg and Law how to order their forces. I have not been over the ground."

Law folded his arms. "General. You're asking us to attack a Yankee corps that's had two days to entrench."

"And not just any corps," Gregg added. "This is *Hancock*."

"We'll be outnumbered eight to one," Law said. "And we don't have any woods to approach through, the way y'all do. We'll have to cross a good quarter mile of open ground before we can reach them."

Poe looked at him blackly. Frustration keened in his heart. He took a long breath and fought down his growing rage.

Winfield Scott Hancock, he thought, known to the Yanks as Hancock the Superb. The finest of the Yankee commanders. He thought about the Ravens going up that little green slope toward the cemetery, with Hancock and his corps waiting on top, and nodded.

"Do as best as you can, gentlemen," he said. "I leave it entirely to you. I wish only that you show some activity. Drive in his pickets. Let him see some regimental flags, think he is going to be attacked."

Law and Gregg looked at one another. "Very well, sir," Law said.

Anger stabbed Poe again. They'd do nothing. He knew it; and if he ordered them into a fight they'd just appeal over his head to Anderson.

Nothing he could do about it. Keep calm.

Poe turned toward Fitz Lee. "I hope I may have your support."

The small man nodded. "I'll move some people forward." He gave a smile. "My men won't like being in the woods. They're used to clear country."

"Any additional questions?"

There were none. Poe sent his generals back to their commands and thanked Fitzhugh Lee for his cooperation.

"This may be the Wilderness all over again," Lee said. "Woods so heavy no one could see a thing. Just one big ambush with a hundred thousand men flailing around in the thickets."

"Perhaps the Yankees will not see our true numbers, and take us for a greater force," Poe said.

"We may hope, sir." Lee saluted, mounted, and spurred away.

Poe found himself staring at the black Starker house, that one softly lit eye of a window. Thinking of the dead girl inside, doomed to be buried on a battlefield.

Virginia Poe had been beautiful, so beautiful that sometimes Poe's heart would break just to look at her. Her skin was translucent as bone china, her long hair fine and black as midnight, her violet eyes unnaturally large, like those of a bird of Faerie. Her voice was delicate, as fragile and evanescent as the tunes she plucked from her harp. Virginia's aspect was unearthly, refined, ethereal, like an angel descended from some Mussulman paradise, and as soon as Poe saw his cousin he knew he could never rest unless he had that beauty by him always.

When he married her she was not quite fourteen. When she died, after five years of advancing consumption, she was not yet twenty-five. Poe was a pauper. After Virginia's death came *Eureka*, dissipation, madness. He had thought he could not live without her, had no real intention of doing so.

But now he knew he had found Virginia again, this time in Evania. With Evania, as with Virginia, he could throw off his melancholy and become playful, gentle, joyful. With her he could sit in the parlor with its French wallpaper, play duets on the guitar, and sing until he could see the glow of his happiness reflected in Evania's eyes.

But in time a shadow seemed to fall between them. When Poe looked at his young bride, he seemed to feel an oppression on his heart, a catch in the melody of his love. Virginia had not asked for anything in life but to love her cousin. Evania was proud; she was willful; she grew in body and intellect. She developed tastes, and these tastes were not those of Poe. Virginia had been shy, otherworldly, a presence so ethereal it seemed as if the matter had been refined from her, leaving only the essence of perfected beauty and melancholy; Evania was a forthright presence, bold, a tigress in human form. She was a material presence; her delights were entirely those of Earth.

Poe found himself withdrawing before Evania's growing clarity. He moved their sleeping chamber to the topmost floor of the mansion, beneath a roof of glass skylights. The glass ceiling was swathed in heavy Oriental draperies to keep out the heat of the day; the windows were likewise covered. Persian rugs four deep covered the floor. Chinese bronzes were arranged to pour gentle incense into the room from the heads of dragons and lions.

With the draperies blocking all sources of the light, in the near-absolute, graveyard darkness, Poe found he could approach his wife. The fantastic decor, seen only by such light as slipped in under the door or through cracks in the draperies, heightened Poe's imagination to a soaring intensity. He could imagine that the hair he caressed was dark as a raven's wing; that the cheek he softly kissed with porcelain-pale; he could fancy, under the influence of the incense, that the earthy scent of Evania had been transformed to a scent far more heavenly; and he could almost perceive, as ecstasy flooded him, that the eyes that looked up into his were the large, luminous, angelic eyes of his lost love, the lady Virginia.

Poe sat in his tent and tried to eat an omelette made of eggs scavenged from Starker chickens. Fried ham sat untouched on the plate. Around him, the reserve divisional artillery creaked and rattled as the guns were set up on the Starkers' slight eminence. The ravens gobbled and cawed.

Poe put down his fork. He was too agitated to eat.

A drink, he thought. A soothing glass of sherry. The Starkers must have some; it would be easy to obtain.

He took a gulp of boiled coffee, took his stick, and hobbled out of the tent. The sky had lightened, and the mist had receded from the Starker plantation; Poe could see parts of his own line, a flag here and there, the crowns of trees. His men were moving forward out of their trenches, forming up on the far side of the abatis beyond. Officers' shouts carried faintly to his ear. The alignment was proceeding with difficulty. The battalions had become too confused as they marched to their places in the dark.

He remembered the Ravens in the cemetery, shrouded by gray gunsmoke as they were now hidden by gray mist.

Sherry, he thought again. The thought seemed to fill his mind with a fine, clear light. He could almost feel the welcome fire burning along his veins. A drink would steady him.

A color sergeant came running up from the Ravens, saluted, and took the two birds away to march with their brigade. Limbers rattled as horses pulled them out of harm's way down the reverse slope of the hill. Artillerymen lounged by their Napoleons and Whitworths, waiting for a target.

My god, Poe thought, why am I doing this? Suddenly it seemed the most pointless thing in the world. An offensive would only make things worse.

A horse trotted toward him from the Starker driveway. Poe recognized Moses, another of Anderson's aides, an eagle-nosed miniature sheeny that Longstreet had unaccountably raised to the rank of major. One of Longstreet's little lapses in taste, Poe thought; but unfortunately, as someone with pretensions to the title himself, he was honor-bound to treat the Hebrew as if his claim to the title of gentleman were genuine.

Sextus took Major Moses's horse, and Moses and Poe exchanged salutes. There weren't many men shorter than Poe, but Moses was one of them—he was almost tiny, with hands and feet smaller than a woman's. "General Anderson's compliments, sir," Moses said. "He wants to emphasize his desire for a diversionary attack."

"Look about you, Major," Poe said. "What do you see?"

Moses looked at the grayback soldiers rolling out of their entrenchments and shuffling into line, the artillerists waiting on the hilltop for a target, officers calling up and down the ranks.

"I see that General Anderson has been anticipated, sir," Moses said. "My mission has obviously been in vain."

"I would be obliged if you'd wait for a moment, Major," Poe said. "I may have a message for General Anderson by and by."

"With permission, sir, I should withdraw. The general may need me." Moses smiled. Dew dripped from his shoulder-length hair onto his blue riding cape. "Today promises to be busy, sir."

"I need you *here*, sir!" Poe snapped. "I want you to witness something."

Moses seemed startled. He recovered, a sly look entering his eyes, then he nodded. "Very well, sir."

In a motionless instant of perfect clarity, Poe understood the conspiracy of this calculating Jew. Moses would hang back, wait for confirmation of Poe's madness, Poe's error, then ride back to Anderson to try to have Poe removed from command. Moxley Sorrel might already have filled the staff tent with tales of Poe's nerves about to crack. Perhaps, Poe thought furiously, the sheeny intended to replace Poe *himself!*

Cold triumph rolled through Poe. Conspire though Moses might, Poe would be too crafty for him.

"When will the attack begin, Major?" Poe asked.

"It has already begun, sir. The mist cleared early to the west of us. The men were moving out just as I left General Anderson's headquarters."

Poe cocked his head. "I hear no guns, Major Moses."

"Perhaps there has been a delay. Perhaps—" Moses shrugged. "Perhaps the wet ground is absorbing the sound. Or there is a trick of the wind—"

"Nevertheless," Poe said, "I hear no guns."

"Yes, sir." Moses cleared his throat. "It is not unknown, sir."

"Still, Major Moses," said Poe. "I hear no guns."

Moses fell silent at this self-evident fact. Poe whirled around, his black cape flying out behind him, and stalked toward his tent. He could hear Moses's soft footsteps following behind.

Men on horseback came, reporting one brigade after another ready to move forward. Poe told them to wait here for the word to advance, then return to their commanders. Soon he had heard from every brigade but those of Gregg and Law—a messenger even came from Fitz Lee, reporting the cavalryman's readiness to move forward at Poe's signal. After ten minutes of agitated waiting, while the sky grew ever paler and the mist retreated to lurk among the trees, Poe sent an aide to inquire.

Poe gave an irritated look at his division waiting in their ranks for the signal. If the enemy had scouts out this way, they'd see the Confederates ready for the attack and warn the enemy.

Go forward with the four brigades he had? he wondered. Yes. No.

He decided to wait till his aide came back. He looked at his watch, then cast a glance over his shoulder at Major Moses.

"I hear no guns, Major," he said.

"You are correct, sir." Moses smiled thinly. "I take it you intend to enlighten me as to the significance of this?"

Poe nodded benignly. "In time, Major."

Moses swept off his hat in an elaborate bow. "You are known as the master of suspense, sir. I take my hat off sir, I positively do."

Poe smiled. The Jew was amusing. He tipped his own hat. "Thank you, Major."

Moses put on his hat. "I am an enthusiast of your work, sir. I have a first edition of the *Complete Tales*. Had I know I would encounter you, I would have had my wife send it to me and begged you to inscribe it."

"I should be glad to sign it," Poe said, surprised. The *Complete and Corrected Tales and Poems of Edgar A. Poe* had been published at his own expense six years ago and had sold precisely two hundred and forty-nine copies throughout the United States—he knew precisely, because the rest of the ten-thousand-copy edition was sitting in a lumber room back home at Shepherd's Rest.

"Before the war," Moses said, "I used to read your work aloud to my wife. The poems were particularly lovely, I thought—so delicate. And there was nothing that would bring a blush to her lovely cheek—I *particularly* appreciate that, sir." Moses grew indignant. "There are too many passages from poets that one cannot in decency read to a lady, sir. Even in Shakespeare—" Moses shook his head.

"Fortunately," said Poe, "one has Bowdler."

"I thank that gentleman from my heart," said Moses. "As I thank Tennyson, and Mr. Dickens, and Keats."

"Keats." Poe's heart warmed at the mention of the name. "One scarcely could anticipate encountering his name here, on a battlefield."

"True, sir. He is the most rarified and sublime of poets—along, I may say, with yourself, sir."

Poe was surprised. "You flatter me, Major."

"I regret only that you are not more appreciated, sir." His tiny hands gestured whitely in the air. "Some of my correspondents have informed me, however, that you are better known in Europe."

"Yes," Poe said. A dark memory touched him. "A London publisher has brought out an edition of the *Complete Tales*. Unauthorized, of course. It has achieved some success, but I never received so much as a farthing from it."

"I am surprised that such a thing can happen, sir."

Poe gave a bitter laugh. "It isn't the money—it is the brazen provocation of it that offended me. I hired a London solicitor and had the publisher prosecuted."

"I hope he was thrown in jail, sir."

Poe gave a smile. "Not quite. But there will be no more editions of my work in London, one hopes."

"I trust there won't be."

"Or in France, either. I was being translated there by some overheated poet named Charles Baudelaire—no money from that source, either, by the way—and the fellow had the effrontery to write me that many of my subjects, indeed entire texts, were exactly the same as those he had himself composed—except mine, of course, had been written earlier."

"Curious." Moses seemed unclear as to what he should make of this.

"This *gueux* wrote that he considered himself my *alter ego*." A smile twisted across Poe's face at the thought of his triumph. "I wrote that what *he* considered miraculous, *I* considered plagiarism, and demanded that he cease any association with my works on penalty of prosecution. He persisted in writing to me, so I had a French lawyer send him a stiff letter, and have not heard from him since."

"Very proper." Moses nodded stoutly. "I have always been dismayed at the thought of so many of these disreputable people in the literary world. Their antics can only distract the public from the true artists."

Poe gazed in benevolent surprise at Major Moses. Perhaps he had misjudged the man.

A horseman was riding toward him. Poe recognized the spreading mustachios of the aide he'd sent to Gregg and Law. The young man rode up and saluted breathlessly.

"I spoke to General Law, sir," he said. "His men were still eating breakfast. He and General Gregg have done *nothing*, sir, *nothing!*"

Poe stiffened in electric fury. "You will order Generals Gregg and Law to attack *at once!*" He barked.

The aide smiled. "Sir!" he barked, saluted, and turned his horse. Dirt clods flew from the horse's hooves as he pelted back down the line.

Poe hobbled toward the four messengers his brigadiers had sent to him. Anger smoked through his veins. "General Barton will advance at once," he said. "The other brigades will advance as soon as they perceive his movement has begun. Tell your commanders that I desire any prisoners to be sent to me at once." He pointed at Fitzhugh Lee's aide with his stick. "Ride to General Lee. Give him my compliments, inform him that we are advancing, and request his support."

Men scattered at his words, like shrapnel from his explosion of temper. He watched them with cold satisfaction.

"There is nothing more beautiful, sir," said Major Moses in his ear, "than the sight of this army on the attack."

Poe looked with surprise at Moses; in his burst of temper he had forgotten the man was here. He turned to gaze at the formed men a few hundred yards below him on the gentle slope. They had been in garrison for almost a year, and their uniforms and equipment were in better condition than most of this scarecrow army. They were not beautiful in any sense that Poe knew of the word, but he understood what the major meant. There was a beauty in warfare that existed in a realm entirely distinct from the killing.

"I know you served in Greece, sir," Moses said. "Did the Greek fighters for liberty compare in spirit with our own?"

Poe's heart gave a lurch, and he wondered in alarm if his ears were burning. "They were—indifferent," he said. "Variable." He cleared his throat. "Mercenary, if the truth be told."

"Ah." Moses nodded. "Byron found that also."

"I believe he did." Poe stared at the ground and wondered how to extricate himself. His Greek service was a lie he had encouraged to be published about himself. He had never fought in Greece when young, or served, as he had also claimed, in the Russian army. Instead—penniless, an outcast, thrown on his own resources by his Shylock of a stepfather—he had enlisted in the American army out of desperation, and served three years as a volunteer.

It had been his dread, these years he'd served the Confederacy, that he would encounter some old soldier who remembered serving alongside the eighteen-year-old Private Edgar A. Perry. His fears had never been realized, fortunately, but he had read everything he could on Byron and the Greek War of Independence in hopes he would not be tripped up by the curious.

"Ah," Poe said. He pointed with his stick. "The men are moving."

"A brilliant sight, sir." Moses's eyes shone.

Calls were rolling up the line, one after another, from Barton on the left to the Ravens next in line, then to Corse— all Virginia brigades—and then to Clingman's North Carolinians on the right. Poe could hear the voices distinctly.

"Attention, battalion of direction! Forward, guide centerrrr—*march!*"

The regiments moved forward, left to right, clumps of skirmishers spreading out ahead. Flags hung listlessly in the damp. Once the order to advance had been given, the soldiers moved in utter silence, in perfect parade-ground formation.

Just as they had gone for that cemetery, Poe thought. He remembered his great swell of pride at the way the whole division had done a left oblique under enemy fire that day, taking little half-steps to swing the entire line forty-five degrees, and then paused to dress the line before marching onward.

Sweeping through tendrils of mist that clung to the soldiers' legs, the division crossed the few hundred yards of ground between the entrenchments and the forest, and disappeared into the darkness and mist.

Poe wondered desperately if he was doing the right thing.

"Did you know Byron, sir?" Moses again.

Poe realized he'd been holding his breath, anticipating the sound of disaster as soon as his men began their attack. He let his breath go, felt relief spreading outward, like rot, from his chest.

"Byron died," he said, "some years before I went abroad."

Byron had been feeding worms for forty years, Poe thought, but there were Byrons still, hundreds of them, in this army. Once he had been a Byron himself—an American Childe Harold dressed in dramatic black, ready with the power of his mind and talent to defeat the cosmos. Byron had intended to conquer the Mussulman; Poe would do him better, with *Eureka*, by conquering God.

Byron had died at Missolonghi, bled to death by his personal physician as endless gray rain fell outside his tent and drowned his little army in the Peloponnesian mud. And nothing had come of Byron in the end, nothing but an example that inspired thousands of other young fools to die in similar pointless ways throughout the world.

For Poe the war had come at a welcome moment. His literary career had come to a standstill, with nine thousand seven hundred fifty-one copies of the *Complete Tales* sitting in his lumber room; his mother-in-law had bestirred herself to suggest, in kind but firm fashion, that his literary and landscaping projects were running up too fantastic a debt; and his relations with Evania—on Poe's part at least—were at best tentative.

When Virginia seceded and Maryland seemed poised to follow, Poe headed south with Sextus, a pair of fine horses, equipage, a curved Wilkinson light cavalry sword, Hardee's *Tactics*, a brace of massive nine-shot Le Mat revolvers, and of course the twelve hundred in gold. He kissed Evania and his beloved Mrs. Forster farewell—within a few months he would return with an army and liberate Shepherd's Rest and the rest of Maryland. He, as well as Byron, could be martial when the cause of liberty required it. He rode away with a singing heart.

Before him, as he woke in his bed his first night in Richmond, he saw his vision, the benevolent madonna giving him her benediction. In going south he was being, he thought, faithful to Virginia; and he hoped to find the spirit, as well as the name, of his lost love embodied in the state to which he swore allegiance.

Jefferson Davis was pleased to give a colonel's commission to a veteran of the wars of Greek liberation, not to mention a fellow West Pointer—the West Point story, at least, being true, though Poe did not remind the President that, because the horrid Allan refused to support him, Poe had got himself expelled from the academy after six months.

There was no regiment available for the new colonel, so Poe began his military career on the staff of General Joseph E. Johnston, commanding in the Shenandoah Valley. He occupied himself by creating a cypher for army communications which, so far as he knew, had survived three years unbroken.

Johnston's army moved east on the railroad to unite with Beauregard's at First Manassas, and there Poe saw war for the first time. He had expected violence and death, and steeled himself against it. It gave him no trouble, but what shocked him was the *noise*. The continual roll of musketry, buzzing bullets, shouted orders, the blast of cannon, and the shriek of shells—all were calculated to unstring the nerves of a man who couldn't abide even a loud orchestra. Fortunately he was called upon mainly to rally broken troops—it had shocked him that Southern men could run like that—but in the end, after he'd got used to the racket, he had ridden, bullets singing over his head, in the final screaming, exhilarating charge that swept the Yankee army from the field, and he could picture himself riding that way forever, the fulfillment of the Byronic ideal, sunset glowing red on the sword in his hand as he galloped north to Maryland and the liberation of his home. . . .

Maryland never managed to secede, somehow, and Poe's Byronic liberation of his home state had to be postponed. Via blockade-runner, Poe exchanged passionate letters with his wife while remaining, in his heart, faithful to Virginia.

At the horrible, bungled battle of Seven Pines the next year, Major General Daniel Harvey Hill made a properly Byronic, if unsupported, attack against McClellan's left and lost half his men, as well as one of his brigadiers. Poe was promoted and given the shattered brigade. Joe Johnston, during the same battle, had been severely wounded, and the Army of Northern Virginia now had a new commander, one Robert E. Lee.

It did not take Poe long to discover that the ferocious, dyspeptic Harvey Hill was both an ignoramus and a lunatic. Before more than a few days had passed, neither spoke to the other: they communicated only in writing. Poe broke the Yanks' wigwag signal code, which didn't mean much at the time but was of help later, at Second Manassas.

But by then Poe was not with the army. Only a few days after taking command, Lee went on the offensive, and Poe, supported by exemplary reasoning and logic, refused point-blank Harvey Hill's order to take his brigade into Boatswain Swamp.

Now, after three years of war, almost all the American Byrons were dying or had been shot to pieces. Jeb Stuart, Jackson, Albert Sidney Johnston, Dick Garnett, Ewell, Hood, now Longstreet—all dead or maimed.

And Edgar A. Poe, leaning on his stick, a sick ache throbbing in his thigh, knew in his heart that Byron's death had been more merciful than anyone had known.

He had written the eulogy himself, never knowing it at the time: *But he grew old— /This knight so bold— /And o'er his heart a shadow /Fell as he found /No spot of ground/That looked like Eldorado.*

Byron's eulogy. Poe's, too. Stuart's, everyone's.

"Forty years dead," he said. "We have other poets now."

"Yourself, of course," said Major Moses, "and Tennyson."

"Walter Whitman," said Poe. The name left a savage, evil taste in his mouth.

"Obscene." Moses shivered. "Filth."

"I agree."

"You have denounced him yourself."

"Repeatedly."

Poe stared at the dark trees that had swallowed up his entire division. How many, he wondered, would come out of those woods nevermore? Sickness welled up inside him. In another minute he might weep. He turned and shouted for Sextus to bring him a chair.

The first edition of *Leaves of Grass* had happily escaped his notice. The second edition, with the preface by Emerson, had been sent to him for review at the *Southern Gentleman*. He had denounced it. Whitman and Emerson replied; Poe printed their replies and returned fire, and the fight went on for years, a war that prefigured the more deadly one begun in 1861.

A showdown, he had thought triumphantly. He had long distrusted the New England clique and feared their grip on the *North American Review*—the fact that they regarded the pedestrian and bourgeoise Longfellow as a genius was reason enough for distrust. But now the south had its own literary magazine; Poe was no longer dependent on the approval of New England literary society for employment and regard.

Whitman, he wrote, knew nothing of versification. Whitman thought prostitutes and steam engines and common laborers fit subject for verse. Whitman knew nothing of the higher truths, of the sublime. Whitman filled his verses with the commonplace, with references so mundane and contemporary that in a hundred years no one would know what he was talking about. Whitman did not even *look* like a literary man. In the ambrotype used as a frontispiece, Whitman was dressed only in his shirt, looking like a farmer just come in from the fields, not an elevated, rarified, idealized creature—a poet—who spoke the language of the gods.

And Whitman was obscene. Grossly so. Clearly he was a degenerate of the worst description. Poe preferred not to imagine what Whitman did with those young men he wrote about in such evocative terms. Emerson might have used every rhetorical trick he knew to disguise the filth, or talk around it, but he never denied it—and this from someone who affected to worship the transcendental, meaning the refined and pure. It was then that Poe knew how bankrupt the North was, how desperate, as compared with his refined, elegant southland.

"Whitman is the perfect Yankee poet," Poe said. He drove his stick into the soil as if the earth hid Walter Whitman's heart. "No sublimity, no beauty, just stacks of prose disguised as poetry—sometimes not even prose, only lists. Lists of ordinary things. Produced so much stanzas an hour, like yards of cloth in a shoddyworks." He drove the stick again. "Like Yankee soldiers. Not inspired, just numerous."

Moses gave a laugh. "I must remember that, sir. For when General Longstreet returns. It will amuse him."

Poe stared at the woods, grinding his teeth. He hadn't meant to be witty; he was trying to make a point.

There was sudden musketry from the hardwoods, a succession of popping sounds turned hollow by multiple echoes. Then there was silence. Poe listened intently for a moment.

"Pickets," Moses said.

How many Yankees? Poe wondered. He turned back in the direction of his tent. Sextus was nowhere to be seen.

"Bring a chair, you blasted orangutan!" he shouted. He had no idea whether or not Sextus heard him.

More popping sounds came from the woods—individual shots this time. From a different part of the line, Poe thought.

"Byrons can only die," he said. Moses looked at him in surprise. "We real poets, we're all too in love with death. Whitman writes about life, even the obscene parts of it, and that's why he will win. Why," he took a breath, trying to make himself clearer, "why the North will win."

Moses seemed to be struggling to understand this. "Sir," he said. "Sir, I don't understand."

More crackling from the woods. Poe's head moved left and right, trying to find where it was coming from. A savage exultation beat a long tattoo in his heart. He was right, he was right, he was right *again*. He stepped up to Moses, stared into his eyes at a few inches' range.

"Do you hear guns from the east, Major?" he demanded. "Do you hear anything at all from Lee's offensive?"

"Why—" Major Moses stopped dead, licked his lips. There was pure bewilderment in his eyes. "Why are you doing this? Why are you fighting for the Cause?"

"I *hate* Whitman!" Poe shrieked. "I hate him, and I hate steam engines, I hate ironclad ships and repeating rifles and rifled artillery!"

"Your chair, Massa Poe," said Sextus.

A cacophony of sound was coming from the woods now, regular platoon volleys, one after another. The sound battered Poe's ears.

"I fight for the South because we are *right*, Major Moses!" Poe shouted. "I believe it—I have proved it rationally—we are *superior*, sir! The South fights for the right of one man to be superior to another, because he *is* superior, because he *knows* he is superior."

"Here's your chair, Massa Poe," said Sextus.

"Superior in mind, superior in cognitive faculty, superior in erudition! Superior in knowledge, in training, in sagacity! In appreciation of beauty, of form, of moral sense!" Poe pointed his stick at the woods. "Those Yankees—they are democracy, sir! Dragging even *poetry* into the muck! Walter Whitman addresses his verses to *women of the street*—that is democracy for you! Those Yankee soldiers, they are Whitmans with bayonets! I fight them because I must, because *someone* must fight for what is noble and eternal, even if only to die, like Byron, in some pointless—pointless—"

Pain seized his heart and he doubled over, coughing. He swung toward where Sextus stood with his camp chair, the cane still outstretched, and though he didn't mean to strike the African he did anyway, a whiplike crack on the upper arm. Sextus dropped the chair and stepped back, surprise on his face. Anger crackled in Poe, fury at the African's stupidity and inability to get out of the way.

"Take that, damn you, worthless nigger!" Poe spat. He spun and fell heavily into his chair.

The battle in the woods had progressed. Now Poe heard only what Great Frederick called *bataillenfeuer*, battle fire, no longer volleys but simply a continuous din of musketry as the platoon sergeants lost tactical control of their men and the battle dissolved into hundreds of little skirmishes fought simultaneously. Poe heard no guns—no way to get artillery through those woods.

Moses was looking at Poe with wide, staring eyes. He reached into a pocket and mopped Poe's spittle from his face. Poe gave him an evil look.

"Where is Lee's offensive, sir?" he demanded. "Where is the sound of *his* fight?"

Moses seemed confused. "I should get back to General Anderson, sir," he said. "I—"

"Stay by me, Major," Poe said. His voice was calm. An absolute lucidity had descended upon him; perhaps he was the only man within fifty miles who knew precisely what was happening here. "I have not yet shown you what I wish to show you."

He listened to the fight roll on. Sometimes it nearly died away, but then there would be another outburst, a furious racket. Lines of gunsmoke rose above the trees. It would be pointless for Poe to venture into the woods himself—he could not control an entire division if he could not see twenty feet beyond his own position.

A horseman galloped up. "General Gregg's compliments, sir. He and General Law are ready to advance."

Poe felt perfectly sunny. "My compliments to General Gregg. Tell him that Poe's division is a little ahead of him. I would be obliged if he'd catch up."

The man rode away. People were leaking back out of the

woods now: wounded men, some crawling; skulkers, stragglers; bandsmen carrying people on stretchers. Here and there were officers running, bearing messages, guards marching back with blue prisoners.

"Lots of Yankees, sir!" The first messenger, a staff lieutenant of perhaps nineteen, was winded and staggering with the effort it had taken him to run here. "We've hit them in flank. They were in column of march, sir. Colonel Terry wishes you to know he's driving them, but he expects they'll stiffen."

"Good job, boy." Terry was the man who commanded the Ravens in Poe's absence. "Give Colonel Terry my thanks."

"Sir!" Another messenger. "General Clingman's compliments. We've driven them in and captured a battery of guns."

Guns, Poe thought. Useless in the woods. We can't get them away, and the Yankees'll have them back in another few minutes.

The sound of musketry staggered higher, doubled and tripled in fury. The messengers looked at each other, breathing hard, appalled at the noise. The Yanks, Poe concluded, had rallied and were starting to fight back.

"Tell Colonel Terry and General Clingman to press them as hard as possible. Try to hold them in the woods. When the Yanks press too hard, retire to the trenches."

"Yes, sir."

"Prisoners, sir." Another voice. "General Barton sends them as requested."

Stunned-looking Yanks in dew-drenched caped overcoats, all captured in the first rush. None of them looked over twenty. Poe rose from his chair and hobbled toward them. He snatched the cap from the first prisoner and swung toward Major Moses.

"Major Moses," he said in triumph, "do you know the motto of the Yankee Second Corps?"

Moses blinked at him. "No, sir."

" 'Clubs are Trumps!' " Poe told him. "Do you know why, sir?"

Moses shook his head.

"Because Hancock's Corps wears a trefoil badge on their forage caps, like a club on a playing card." He threw the prisoner's cap down before Moses's feet. "What do you see on *that* forage cap, sir?" he asked.

"A cross," said Moses.

"A *saltire*, sir!" Poe laughed.

He had to be thorough. The upper echelons were never easily convinced. Two years before, during the Seven Days', he had demonstrated, with complete and irrefutable logic, that it was suicidal for Harvey Hill's division to plunge forward into Boatswain Swamp in hopes of contacting Yankees on the other side. When the ignorant madman Hill repeated his order, Poe had stood on his logic and refused—and been removed from command and placed under arrest. He had not been comforted when he had been proven right. His cherished new brigade, along with the rest of D.H. Hill's division, had been shattered by three lines of Union infantry dug into a hill just behind the swamp, with artillery lined hub-to-hub on the crest. And when, red-faced with anger, he had challenged Hill to a duel, the lunatic had only laughed at him to his face.

"Specifically," Poe said pedantically, pointing at the Yankee forage cap, "a *white* saltire on a blue background! That means these men come from the Second Division of the Sixth Corps—*Wright's* Corps, major, not Hancock's! The same Sixth Corps that Lee was supposed to attack this morning, on the other end of the line! *I am facing at least two Yankee corps with one division, and Lee is marching into empty air! Grant has moved his army left again while we slept!*"

Moses's eyes widened. "My God," he said.

"Take that cap to General Anderson with my compliments! Tell him I will need his support!"

Moses picked up the cap. "Yes, sir."

Poe lunged among the prisoners, snatching off caps, throwing them to his aides. "Take *that* to General Lee! And *that* to Ewell! And *that* to A.P. Hill! Say I must have their support! Say that *Wright* is here!"

As Moses and Poe's aides galloped away, the firing died down to almost nothing. One side or another had given way.

Poe returned to his seat and waited to see which side it had been.

It was Poe's division had pressed back in the woods, but not by much. Messengers panting back from his brigades reported that they'd pushed the Yanks as far as possible, then fallen back when they could push no more. The various units were trying to reestablish contact with one another in the woods and form a line. They knew the Yankee assault was coming.

Pull them back? Poe wondered. He'd made his case to his superiors—maybe he'd better get his men back into their trenches before the Yanks got organized and smashed them.

Action, he thought, and reaction. The two fundamental principles of the operating Universe, as he had demonstrated in *Eureka*. His attack had been an action; the Yankee reaction had yet to come.

He tapped gloved fingers on the arm of his chair while he made careful calculations. The Yankees had been struck in the right flank as they were marching south along narrow forest roads. Due to surprise and their tactical disadvantage, they had been driven in, then, as the rebel attack dissipated its force, turned and fought. This reaction, then, had been instinctive—they had not fought as units, which must have been shattered, but as uncoordinated masses of individuals. The heavy forest had broken up the rebel formation in much the same manner, contributing to their loss of momentum.

The Yankees would react, but in order to do so in any coordinated way they would have to reassemble their units, get them in line of battle, and push them forward through trees that would tend to disperse their cohesion. Wright had three divisions; normally it would take a division about an hour, maybe more, to deploy to the right from column of march. The woods would delay any action. The bluecoats' own confusion would worsen things even more. Say two hours, then.

Any attack made before then would be uncoordinated, just local commanders pushing people forward to the point of contact. Poe's men could handle that. But in two hours a coordinated attack would come, and Poe's division would be swamped by odds of at least three to one, probably more.

Poe looked at his watch. He would keep his men in the woods another ninety minutes, then draw them back. Their presence in the woods might serve to make the Yanks cautious, when what Grant really wanted to do was drive straight forward with everything he had.

His thoughts were interrupted by a message from Evander

Law on his left flank. He and Gregg had about completed their preparations to advance, the messenger reported, when they discovered that Hancock's men across the woods were leaving their trenches and preparing to attack *them*. Gregg and Law had therefore returned to their trenches to ready themselves for the attack.

Poe bit back on his temper. It *might* be true. He would have to see in person. He told one of his aides to remain there and direct any messages to the left of the line, then told Sextus to ready his buggy.

Sextus looked at him in a sullen, provoking way. He was cradling the arm Poe had struck with his cane. "You'll have to drive yourself, massa," he said. "You broke my arm with that stick."

Annoyance warmed Poe's nerves. "Don't be ridiculous! I did not hit you with sufficient force. Any schoolboy—"

"I'm sorry, massa. It's broke. I broke an arm before, I know what it's like."

Poe was tempted to hit Sextus again and break the arm for certain; but instead he lurched for his buggy, hopped inside, and took the reins. He didn't have the time to reason with the darky now. Sextus heaved himself up into the seat beside Poe, and Poe snapped the reins. His staff, on horseback, followed.

The battle broke on the left as he drove, a searing, ripping sound bounding up from the damp, dead ground. Poe seized the whip and labored his horse; the light buggy bounded over the turf, threatened to turn over, righted itself.

The first attack was over by the time Poe's buggy rolled behind Law's entrenchments, and the wall of sound had died down to the lively crackle of sharpshooters' rifles and the continual boom of smoothbore artillery. It took Poe a while to find Law—he was in the first line of works—and by the time Poe found him, the second Yankee attack was beginning, a constant hammering roar spreading across the field.

Law stood in the trench, gnawing his lip, his field glasses in his hand. There was a streak of powder residue across his forehead and great patches of sweat under the arms of his fine gray jacket. Law jumped up on the firing step, jostling his riflemen who were constantly popping up with newly loaded muskets, and pointed. "Gibbon's men, sir! The Black Hats! Look!"

Poe swung himself up behind the brigadier, peered out beneath the head log, and saw, through rolling walls of gunsmoke and the tangle of abatis, lines of blue figures rolling toward him. He heard the low moaning sound made by Northern men in attack, like a choir of advancing bears. . . . The ones coming for him were wearing black felt hats instead of their usual forage caps, which marked them as the Iron Brigade of Gibbon's division, the most hard-hitting unit of the hardest-hitting corps in the Yankee army. *We've got two brigades here*, Poe thought frantically, *and we've got an entire corps coming at us.*

A Yankee Minié whacked solidly into the head log above him. Poe jerked his head back and turned to Law. The smell of powder was sharp in his nostrils. The air filled with the whistling sound of cannon firing canister at close range.

"You must hold, sir! No going back!"

Law grinned. "Do you think the Yankees'll *let* us go back?"

"Hold to the last! I will bring up support!"

Law only looked at him as if he were mad. And then the Yankees were there, their presence at first marked by a swarm of soldiers surging back from the firing step, almost knocking Poe from his feet as he was carried to the muddy back of the trench, the soldiers pointing their muskets upward, groping in their belts for bayonets . . .

Poe reached automatically for one of his Le Mat revolvers and then realized he'd left them in his headquarters tent—they were just too heavy to carry all the time. His only weapon was his stick. He stiffened and took a firmer grip on the ivory handle. His mind reeled at the suddenness of it all.

The sky darkened as bluecoats swarmed up on the head log, rifles trained on the packed Confederates. The Stars and Stripes, heavy with battle honors, rose above the parapet, waved by an energetic sergeant with a bushy red beard and a tattered black hat. Musketry crackled along the trench as men fired into one another's faces. "Look at 'em all!" Law screamed. "Look at 'em all!" He shoved a big Joslyn revolver toward the Yankees and pulled the trigger repeatedly. People were falling all over. Screams and roars of defiance and outrage echoed in Poe's ears

He stood, the sound battering at his nerves. All he could

do here, he thought bitterly, was get shot. He was amazed at his own perfect objectivity and calm.

And then the Union standard-bearer was alone, and grayback infantry were pointing their rifles at him. "Come to the side of the Lord!" Evander Law shouted; and the red beard looked around him in some surprise, then shrugged, jumped into the ditch, and handed over the flag of the Twenty-fourth Michigan.

The soldiers declined to shoot him, Poe thought, as a compliment to his bravery. *Never let it be said we are not gallant.*

Poe jumped for the firing step, and saw the blue lines in retreat. Dead men were sprawled over the abatis, their black hats tumbled on the ground. The ground was carpeted with wounded Yanks trying to find little defilades where they would be sheltered from the bullets that whimpered above their heads. They looked like blue maggots fallen from the torn belly of something dead, Poe thought, and then shuddered. Where was the poetry in this? Here even death was unhallowed.

Soldiers jostled Poe off the firing step and chased off the bluecoats with Minié balls. Confederate officers were using swords and knives to cut up the Yankee flag for souvenirs. Poe stepped up to Law.

"They'll be back," Law said, mumbling around a silver powder flask in his teeth. He was working the lever of his Joslyn revolver, tamping a bullet down on top of the black powder charge.

"I will bring men to your relief."

"Bring them soon, sir."

"I will find them somewhere."

Law rotated the cylinder and poured another measured round of fine black powder. "Soon, sir. I beg you."

Poe turned to one of his aides. "Find General Gregg on the left. Give him my compliments, and tell him what I have told General Law. He must hold till relieved. After that, ride to General Anderson and persuade him to release the rest of Field's division to come to the aide of their comrades."

Wounded men groaned in the trenches and on the firing step, cursing, trying to stop their bleeding. Yankee blood dripped down the clay trench wall. Cannon still thundered, flailing at the bluecoats. Southern sharpshooters banged away with Armstrong rifles equipped with telescopic sights almost as long as the gun, aiming at any officers. Poe found himself astounded that he could have an intelligible conversation in this raucous, unending hell.

He limped away down a communications trench and found Sextus in the rear, holding his buggy amid a group of waiting artillery limbers. Poe got into the buggy without a word and whipped up the horses.

Behind him, as he rode, the thunder of war rose in volume as Hancock pitched into another attack. This time the sound didn't die down.

On the way back to his tent Poe encountered a courier from Fitz Lee. His men had moved forward dismounted, run into some startled bluecoats from Burnside's Ninth Corps, and after a short scrap had pulled back into their entrenchments.

Burnside. That meant three Yankee corps were facing two southern divisions, one of them cavalry.

Burnside was supposed to be slow, and everyone knew he was not the most intelligent of Yankees—anyone who conducted a battle like Fredericksburg had to be criminally stupid. Poe could only hope he would be stupid today.

Back at his tent, he discovered Walter Taylor, one of Robert Lee's aides, a young, arrogant man Poe had never liked. Poe found himself growing angry just looking at him.

"Burnside, sir!" he snapped, pulling the buggy to a halt. "Burnside, Wright, *and* Hancock, and they're all on my front!"

Taylor knit his brows. "Are you certain about Burnside, sir?" he asked.

"Fitzhugh Lee confirms it! That's three fourths of Grant's army!"

Taylor managed to absorb this with perfect composure. "General Lee would like to know if you have any indication of the location of Warren's Fifth Corps."

Poe's vitals burned with anger. "I don't!" he roared. "But I have no doubt they'll soon be heading this way!"

Poe lurched out of his buggy and headed for his tent and the Le Mat revolvers waiting in his trunk. Judging by the sound, Gregg and Law were putting up a furious fight behind him. There was more fighting going on, though much less intense, on his own front.

Poe flung open the green trunk, found the revolvers,

and buckled on the holsters. He hesitated for a moment when he saw the saber, then decided against it and dropped the trunk lid. Chances were he'd just trip on the thing. Lord knew the revolvers were heavy enough.

Taylor waited outside the tent, bent over to brush road dirt from his fine gray trousers. He straightened as Poe hobbled out. "I will inform General Lee you are engaged," he said.

Poe opened his mouth to scream at the imbecile, but took a breath instead, tried to calm his rage. With the high command, he thought, always patience. "My left needs help," Poe said. "Hancock's attacking two brigades with his entire corps. I'm facing Wright on my front with four brigades, and Fitz Lee's facing Burnside with two on the right."

"I will inform General Lee."

"Tell him we are in direst extremity. Tell him that we cannot hold onto Hanover Junction unless substantially reinforced. Tell him my exact words."

"I will, sir." Taylor nodded, saluted, mounted his horse, rode away. Poe stared after him and wondered if the message was going to get through it all, of if the legend of Poe's alarmism and hysteria were going to filter it—alter it—make it as nothing.

More fighting burst out to his front. Poe cupped his ears and swiveled his head, trying to discover direction. The war on his left seemed to have died away. Poe returned to his chair and sat heavily. His pistols were already weighing him down.

Through messengers he discovered what had happened. On his third attack, Hancock had succeeded in getting a lodgement in the Confederate trenches between Gregg and Law. They had been ejected only by the hardest, by an attack at bayonet point. Evander Law had been killed in the fighting; his place had been taken by Colonel Bowles of the 4th Alabama. Bowles requested orders. Poe had no hope to give him.

"Tell Colonel Bowles he must hold until relieved."

There was still firing to his front. His brigadiers in the woods were being pressed, but the Yankees as yet had made no concerted assault. Poe told them to hold on for the present. It would be another forty-five minutes, he calculated, before the Yanks could launch a coordinated assault.

Comparative silence fell on the battlefield. Poe felt his nerves gnawing at him, the suspense spreading through him like poison. After forty-five minutes, he gave his brigades in the woods permission to fall back to their entrenchments.

As he saw clumps of men in scarecrow gray emerging from the woods, he knew he could not tell them what he feared, that Robert Lee was going to destroy their division. Again.

After the Seven Days' Battle, Lee had chosen to lose the paperwork of Poe's impending court-martial. Poe, his brigade lost, his duel unfought, was assigned to help construct the military defenses of Wilmington.

Later, Poe would be proven right about Harvey Hill. Lee eventually shuffled him west to Bragg's army, but Bragg couldn't get along with him either and soon Hill found himself unemployed.

Poe took small comfort in Hill's peregrinations as he languished on the Carolina coast while Lee's army thrashed one Yankee commander after another. He wrote long letters to any officials likely to get him meaningful employment, and short, petulant articles for Confederate newspapers: Why wasn't the South building submarine rams? Why did they not take advantage, like the North, of observation from balloons? Why not unite the forces of Bragg and Johnston, make a dash for the Ohio, and reclaim Kentucky?

There were also, in Wilmington, women. Widows, many of them, or wives whose men were at war. Their very existence unstrung his nerves, made him frantic; he wrote them tempestuous letters and demanded their love in terms alternately peremptory and desperate. Sometimes, possibly because it seemed to mean so much to him, they surrendered. None of them seemed to mind that he snuffed all the candles, drew all the drapes. He told them he was concerned for their reputation, but he wanted darkness for his own purposes.

He was remaining faithful to Virginia.

Perhaps the letter-writing campaign did some good; perhaps it was just the constant attrition of experienced officers that mandated his reemployment. His hopes, at any rate, were justified. A brigade was free under George Pickett, and furthermore it was a lucky brigade, one that all three Confederate corps commanders had led at one time or another. Perhaps, Poe thought, that was an omen.

Poe was exultant. Lee was going north after whipping Hooker at Chancellorsville. Poe thought again of liberating Maryland, of riding on his thoroughbred charger to Shepherd's Rest, galloping to the heart of the place, to the white arabesque castle that gazed in perfect isolate splendor over the fabulous creation of his soul, his own water paradise. Once he fought for it, Shepherd's Rest would be *his;* he could dispossess the restless spirits that had made him so uneasy the last few years.

Determination entered his soul. He would be the perfect soldier. He would never complain, he would moderate his temper, he would offer his advice with diffidence. He had a reputation to disprove. The army, to his relief, welcomed him with open arms. Hugin and Munin appeared, delivered by grinning staff men who wore black feathers in their hats and chanted "Nevermore." His immediate superior, the perfumed cavalier George Pickett, was not a genius; but unlike many such he knew it, and happily accepted counsel from wiser heads. Longstreet, Poe's corps commander, was absolutely solid, completely reliable, the most un-Byronic officer imaginable but one that excited Poe's admiration. Poe enjoyed the society of his fellow brigadiers, white-haired Lo Armistead and melancholy Dick Garnett. The Southern officer corps was young, bright, and very well educated—riding north they traded Latin epigrams, quotations from *Lady of the Lake* or *The Corsair,* and made new rhymes based on those of their own literary celebrity, whose works had been read to many in childhood. *Of the rapture that runs,* quoth Lo Armistead, *To the banging and the clanging of the guns, guns, guns. Of the guns, guns, guns, guns, guns, guns, guns—To the roaring and the soaring of the guns!*

It was perfect. During the long summer marches into the heart of the North, Poe daydreamed of battle, of the wise gray father Lee hurling his stalwarts against the Yankees, breaking them forever, routing them from Washington, Baltimore, Shepherd's Rest. Lee was inspired, and so was his army. Invincible.

Poe could feel History looking over his shoulder. The world was holding its breath. This could be the last fight of the war. If he could participate in this, he thought, all the frustrating months in North Carolina, all the battles missed, would be as nothing.

Pickett's division, the army's rear guard, missed the first two days of the battle centered around the small crossroads town in Pennsylvania. Arriving that night, they made camp behind a sheltering ridge and were told that they would attack the next day in the assault that would shatter the Yankees for good and all. Pickett, who had been assigned elsewhere during Lee's last two victories, was delighted. At last he would have his opportunity for glory.

The next morning the officers of Pickett's division and the other two divisions that would make the attack were taken forward over the sheltering ridge to see the enemy positions. The attack would go *there*, said Lee, pointing with a gloved hand. Aiming for those umbrella-shaped trees on the enemy-held ridge, beneath which there was said to be a cemetery.

Standing in the stirrups of his white-socked thoroughbred, craning at the enemy ridge, Poe felt a darkness touching his heart. Across a half-mile of open ground, he thought, in plain sight of the enemy, an enemy who has had two days in which to dig in . . .

Was Lee serious? he thought. Was Lee mad?

No. It was not to be thought of. Lee hadn't lost a major battle in his entire career, Sharpsburg, of course, being a draw. There was method in this, he thought, and he could discern it through ratiocination. Perhaps the Yanks were weary, perhaps they were ready to give way. In any case, he had resolved not to complain.

Pickett left the ridge whistling, riding toward the Yanks to scout out the ground. Poe and the other brigadiers followed.

Longstreet remained behind. Poe discovered later that he had seen the same things that Poe had seen, and wanted a last chance to change Lee's mind. When time came to order the advance, Longstreet could not give the order. He just nodded, and then turned his head away.

Later that day Poe brought his men forward, marching with drawn sword at the head of the Ravens, Hugin and Munin crackling and fluffing their feathers on their perch just behind. He remembered with vivid intensity the wildflowers in the long grass, the hum of bees, the chaff rising from the marching feet, the absolute, uncharacteristic silence of the soldiers, seeing for the first time what was expected of them.

And then came the guns. There were two hundred cannon in the Northern lines, or so the Yankee papers boasted afterward, and there was not a one of them without an unobstructed target. In the last year Poe had forgotten what shell-fire was like, the nerve-shattering shriek like the fabric of the universe being torn apart, the way the shells seemed to hover in air forever, as if deliberately picking their targets, before plunging into the Confederate ranks to blossom yellow and black amid the sounds of buzzing steel and crying men.

The sound was staggering, the banging and the clanging of the guns, guns, guns, but fortunately Poe had nothing to do but keep his feet moving forward, one after another. The officers had been ordered to stay dismounted, and all had obeyed but one: Dick Garnett, commanding the brigade on Poe's left, was too ill to walk all that way, and had received special permission to ride.

Garnett, Poe knew, would die. The only mounted man in a group of twelve thousand, he was doomed and knew it.

Somehow there was an air of beauty about Garnett's sacrifice, something fragile and lovely. Like something in a poem.

The cemetery, their target, was way off on the division's left, and Pickett ordered a left oblique, the entire line of five thousand swinging like a gate toward the target. As the Ravens performed the operation, Poe felt a slowly mounting horror. To his amazement he saw that his brigade was on the absolute right of the army, nothing beyond him, and he realized that the oblique exposed his flank entirely to the Union batteries planted on a little rocky hill on the Yankee left.

Plans floated through his mind. Take the endmost regiment and face it toward Yankees? But that would take it out of the attack. Probably it was impossible anyway. But who could guard his flank?

In the meantime Pickett wanted everyone to hit at once, in a compact mass, and so he had the entire division dress its ranks. Five thousand men marked time in the long grass, each with his hand on the shoulder of the man next to him, a maneuver that normally took only a few seconds but that now seemed to take forever. The guns on the rocky hill were plowing their shot right along the length of the rebel line, each shell knocking down men like tenpins. Poe watched, his nerves wailing, as his men dropped by the score. The men couldn't finish dressing their ranks, Poe thought, because they were taking so many casualties they could never close the ranks fast enough, all from the roaring and the soaring of the guns, guns, guns. . . . He wanted to scream in protest. *Forward! Guide center!* But the evolution went on, men groping to their left and closing up as the shells knocked them down faster than they could close ranks.

Finally Pickett had enough and ordered the division onward. Poe nearly shrieked in relief. At least now the Yankees had a moving target.

But now they were closer, and the men on the Yankee ridge opened on Poe's flank with muskets. Poe felt his nerve cry at every volley. Men seemed to drop by the platoon. How many had already gone? Did he even have half the brigade left?

The target was directly ahead, the little stand of trees on the gentle ridge, and between them was a little white Pennsylvania farmhouse, picture-book pretty. Somewhere around the house Poe and his men seemed to lose their sense of direction. They were still heading for the cemetery, but somehow Garnett had gotten in front of them. Poe could see Garnett's lonely figure, erect and defiant on his horse, still riding, floating really, like a poem above the battle.

The cemetery was closer, though, and he could see men crouched behind a stone wall, men in black hats. The Iron Brigade of Hancock's Corps, their muskets leveled on the stone wall, waiting for Garnett to approach . . .

And then suddenly the battle went silent, absolutely silent, and Poe was sitting upright on the ground and wondering how he got there. Some of his aides were mouthing at him, but he snatched off his hat and waved it, peremptory, pointing at the cemetery, ordering everyone forward. As he looked up he saw in that instant the Federal front blossom with smoke, and Dick Garnett pitch off his horse with perhaps a dozen bullets in him; and it struck Poe like a blow to the heart that there was no poetry in this, none whatever. . . .

His men were plowing on, following Garnett's. Poe tried to stand, but a bolt of pain flashed through him, and all he could do was follow the silent combat from his seated position. A shell had burst just over his head, deafening him and shattering his right thigh with a piece of shrapnel that hadn't even broken his skin.

Another line of men rushed past Poe, Armistead's, bayonets leveled. Poe could see Armistead in the lead, his black hat raised on saber-tip as a guide for his men, his mouth open in a silent cheer, his white mane flying. . . . And then the last of Pickett's division was past, into the smoke and dust that covered the ridge, charging for the enemy trees and the cemetery that claimed them, leaving Poe nothing to do but sit in the soft blossoming clover and watch the bees travel in silence from one flower to another. . . .

The first sound he heard, even over the tear of battle, was a voice saying "Nevermore." Hugin and Munin were croaking from the clover behind him, their standard-bearer having been killed by the same shell that had dropped Poe.

The sounds of battle gradually worked their way back into his head. Some of his men came back, and a few of them picked him up and carried him rearward, carried him along with the ravens back to the shelter of the ridge that marked the Confederate line. Poe insisted on facing the Yanks the entire way, so that if he died his wounds would be in the front. A pointless gesture, but it took away some of the pain. The agony from the shattered bone was only a foretaste of the soul-sickness that was to come during the long, bouncing, agonizing ambulance ride to the South as the army deserted Pennsylvania and the North and the hope of victory that had died forever there with Armistead, he had died on Cemetery Ridge, shot dead carrying his plumed hat aloft on the tip of his sword, his other hand placed triumphantly on the barrel of a Yankee gun.

"Law is dead, General Gregg is wounded," Poe reported. "Their men have given way entirely. Colonel Bowles reports he's lost half his men, half at least, and the remainder will not fight. They have also lost some guns, perhaps a dozen."

Robert Lee looked a hundred years dead. His intestinal complaint having struck him again, Lee was seated in the back of a closed ambulance that had been parked by the Starker house. He wore only a dressing gown, and his white hair fell over his forehead. Pain had drawn claws down his face, gouging deep tracks in his flesh.

"I have recalled the army," Lee said. "Rodes's division will soon be up." He gave a look to the man who had drawn his horse up beside the wagon. "Is that not correct, General Ewell?"

"I have told them to come quickly, General." Ewell was a bald man with pop eyes. He was strapped in the saddle, having lost a leg at Second Manassas—during a fight with those damned Black Hats. Now that Poe thought about it, perhaps the Black Hats were becoming a *leitmotiv* in all this shambles. Ewell's horse was enormous, a huge shambling creature, and the sight of it loping along with Ewell bobbing atop was considered by the soldiers to be a sight of pure high comedy.

Poe thought it pathetic. All that stands between Grant and Richmond, he thought, is a bunch of sick old men who cannot properly sit a horse. The thought made him angry.

"We must assemble," Lee said. His voice was faint. "We must assemble and strike those people."

Perhaps, Poe thought, Lee was a great man. Poe could not bring himself, any longer, to believe it. The others here had memories of Lee's greatness. Poe could only remember George Pickett, tears streaming down his face, screaming at Lee when the old man asked him to rally his command: *"General Lee, I have no division!"*

Poe looked from Ewell to Lee. "Gentlemen," he said, "I would suggest that Rodes be sent north to contain Hancock."

Lee nodded.

"The next division needs to be sent to Hanover Junction. If we lose the railroad, we will have to fall back to Richmond or attack Grant where he stands."

Lee nodded again. "Let it be so." A spasm passed across his face. His hands clutched at his abdomen and he bent over.

We may lose the war, Poe thought, because our commander has lost control of his bowels. And a case of the sniffles killed Byron, because his physician was a cretin.

The world will always destroy you, he thought. *And the world will make you ridiculous while it does so.*

General Lee's spasms passed. He looked up, his face hollow. Beads of sweat dotted his nose. "I will send an urgent message to General W.H.F. Lee," he said. "His cavalry division can reinforce that of General Fitzhugh Lee."

Bitter amusement passed through Poe at Lee's careful correctness. He would not call his son "Rooney," the way everyone else did; he referred to him formally, so there would be no hint of favoritism. Flattened by dysentery the man might be, and the Yankees might have stolen a day's march on him; but he would not drop his Southern courtesy.

Another spasm struck Lee. He bent over double. "Pardon me, gentlemen," he gasped. "I must retire for a moment."

His aides carefully drew the little rear doors of the ambulance to allow the commander-in-chief a little privacy. Ewell turned his head and spat.

Poe hobbled a few paces away and looked down at his own lines. Gregg and Law's brigades had given way an hour ago, on the fourth assault, but of the Yanks in the woods there had been no sign except for a few scouts peering at the Confederate trenches from the cover of the trees. Poe knew that the longer the Yankees took to prepare their attack, the harder it would be.

A four-wheel open carriage came up, drawn by a limping plow horse, probably the only horse the armies had spared the soberly dressed civilians who rode inside.

They were going to the funeral of the Starker girl. Battle or no, the funeral would go on. There was humor in this, somewhere; Poe wondered if the funeral was mocking the battle or the other way around.

He tipped his new hat to the ladies dismounting from the carriage and turned to study the woods with his field glasses.

Hancock had broken through to the north of the swampy stream, but hadn't moved much since then—victory had disorganized his formations as much as defeat had disorganized the losers. Hancock, when he moved, could either plunge straight ahead into the rear of Anderson's corps or pivot his whole command, like a barn door, to his left and into Poe's rear. In the latter case Poe would worry about him, but not till then. If Hancock chose to make that lumbering turn, a path which would take him through dense woods that would make the turn difficult to execute in any case, Poe would have plenty of warning from the remnants of Gregg and Law's wrecked brigades.

The immediate danger was to his front. What were Burnside and Wright waiting for? Perhaps they had got so badly confused by Poe's attack that they were taking forever to sort themselves out.

Perhaps they were just being thorough.

Poe limped to where his camp chair waited and was surprised that the short walk had taken his breath away. The Le Mats were just too heavy. He unbuckled his holsters, sat, and waited.

To the west, Rodes's division was a long cloud of dust. To the south, Rooney Lee's cavalry division was another.

Another long hour went by. A train moved tiredly east on the Virginia Central. Rooney Lee's men arrived and went into position on the right. Amid the clatter of reserve artillery battalions galloping up were more people arriving for the funeral: old men, women, children. The young men were either in the army or hiding from conscription. Soon Poe heard the singing of hymns.

Then the Yankees were there, quite suddenly and without preamble, the trees full of blue and silver, coming to the old Presbyterian melody rising from the Starker house. The bluecoats made no more noise on the approach than Pickett's men had on the march to Cemetery Ridge. Poe blinked in amazement. Where had they all come from?

Then suddenly the world was battle, filled with the tearing noise of musketry from the trenches, the boom of Napoleon guns, the eerie banshee wail of the hexagonal-shaped shells from the Whitworth rifled artillery fired over the heads of Poe's men into the enemy struggling through the abatis, then finally the scream and moan and animal sounds of men fighting hand to hand. . . .

Poe watched through his field glasses, mouth dry, nerves leaping with every cannon shot. There was nothing he could do, no reserves he could lead into the fight like a Walter Scott cavalier on horseback, no orders he could give that his own people in the trenches wouldn't know to give on their own. He was useless.

He watched flags stagger forward and back, the bluecoats breaking into his trenches at several points, being flung again into the abatis. He felt a presence over his shoulder and turned to see Lee, hobbling forward in his dressing gown and slippers, an expression of helplessness on his face. Even army commanders were useless in these situations.

The fighting died down after Wright's first assault failed, and for the first time Poe could hear another fight off on his right, where the Lee cousins were holding off Burnside. The battle sounded sharp over there. Poe received reports from his commanders. Three of his colonels were wounded, one was dead, and Clingman had been trampled by both sides during a squabble over a trench but rose from the mud full of fight.

The Yankees came on again, still with that grim do-or-die silence, and this time they gained a lodgement between the Ravens and Corse, and the Confederates tried to fling them out but failed. "Tell them they must try again," Poe told his messengers. He had to shout over the sound of Whitworths firing point-blank into the Yankee salient. He looked at the sad figure of Lee standing there, motionless in his carpet slippers, his soft brown eyes gazing over the battlefield. "Tell the men," Poe said, "the eyes of General Lee are upon them."

Maybe it was Lee's name that did it. Poe could no longer believe in great men but the men of this army believed at least in Lee. The second counterattack drove the shattered Yankees from the works.

The Yankees paused again, but there was no lack of sound. The Confederate artillery kept firing blind into the trees, hoping to smash as many of the reassembling formations as they could.

What did a man mean in all this? Poe wondered. Goethe and Schiller and Shelley and Byron thought a man was all, that inspiration was everything, that divine intuition should overthrow dull reason—but what was inspiration against a Whitworth shell? The Whitworth shell would blow to shreds any inspiration it came up against.

Poe looked at Lee again.

A messenger came from Fitz Lee to tell the commanding general that the cavalry, being hard pressed, had been obliged by the enemy to retire. A fancy way, Poe assumed, for saying they were riding like hell for the rear. Now both Poe's flanks were gone.

Lee gave a series of quiet orders to his aides. Poe couldn't hear them. And then Lee bent over as another spasm took him, and his young men carried him away to his ambulance.

There was no more fighting for another hour. Eventually the rebel artillery fell silent as they ran short of ammunition. Reserve ammunition was brought up. Messages came to Poe: Hancock was moving, and Burnside was beginning a turning movement, rolling up onto Poe's right flank. Poe ordered his right flank bent back, Clingman's men moving into Hanover Junction itself, making a fort of every house. His division now held a U-shaped front.

What did a man mean in all this? Poe wondered again. Nothing. Byron and Shelley were ego-struck madmen. All a man could do in this was die, die along with everything that gave his life meaning. And it was high time he did.

Poe rose from the chair, strapped on his pistols, and began to walk the quarter mile to his trenches. He'd give Walter Whitman a run for his money.

The fight exploded before Poe could quite walk half the distance. Wright's men poured out of the woods; Burnside, moving fast for once in his life, struck at Hanover Junction on the right; and unknown to anyone Hancock had hidden a few brigades in the swampy tributary of the North Anna, and these came screaming up out of the defile onto Poe's under-manned left flank.

The battle exploded. Poe began limping faster.

The battle ended before Poe could reach it. His men gave way everywhere, the Yankees firing massed volleys into their backs, then going after them with bayonets. Poe wanted to scream in rage. The world would not let him make even a futile gesture.

The shattered graybacks carried him back almost bodily, back to the Starker house where civilians were solemnly loading a coffin into a wagon, and there Poe collapsed on the lovely green lawn while the batteries opened up, trying to slow down the advance of Wright's triumphant men. Limbers were coming up, ready to drag the guns away. Lee's ambulance was already gone.

Poe found himself looking at the coffin. A dead girl was a poem, he thought as his head rang with gunfire, but no one had asked the girl if she wanted to be a poem. She would probably have chosen to live and become prose, healthy bouncing American prose, like his Evania. That was why he couldn't love her, he thought sadly; he couldn't love prose. And the world was becoming prose, and he couldn't love that either.

The artillery began pulling out. Poe could hear Yankee cheers. Poe's staff had vanished, lost in the whirlwind of the retreat, but there was Sextus, standing by the buggy, looking at the advancing Yankee line with a strange, intent expression. Poe dragged himself upright and walked toward the buggy.

"Come along, Sextus," he said. "We must go."

Sextus gave him a look. There was wildness in it.

Poe scowled. This was no time for the African to take fright. Bullets fluttered overhead. "Take the reins, Sextus. I'm too tired. We must leave this *champ du Mars*."

At the sound of the French, Poe saw a strange comprehension in Sextus's eyes. Then Sextus was running, clutching his supposedly injured arm, running down the gentle hill as fast as his legs could carry him, toward the advancing Northern army. Poe looked after him in amazement.

"Sextus!" he called. "You fool! That's the wrong way!" The fighting had obviously turned the darky's wits.

Sextus gave no indication he had heard. "The wrong way! We're running *away* from the Yankees, not *toward* them!" Poe limped after him. "*Madman!*" he shrieked. "*Baboon! Animal!*" His nerves turned to blazing fire, and he clawed for one of his Le Mat revolvers. Holding the heavy thing two-handed, Poe drew the hammer back and sighted carefully. A few Yankee bullets whistled over his head.

Sextus kept running. The dark masses of Union men were just beyond him. The pistol's front sight wavered in Poe's vision.

Stupid, Poe thought.

He cocked his arm back and threw the revolver spinning after Sextus. There was a bang as the Le Mat went off on impact, but Poe didn't bother to look. He turned to the buggy and stepped into it; he whipped up the mare and followed the guns and the funeral procession through a cornfield toward the Confederate rear. Behind him he heard Yankee cheers as they swarmed up onto the deserted Starker lawn.

The corn was just sprouting. The buggy bounded over furrows. The field was covered with wounded Confederates staggering out of the way of the retreating guns. There was a cloud of dust on the border of the field.

On, no, Poe thought.

Men moved out of the dust, became two divisions of A.P. Hill's corps, moving in perfect battle formation. Marching to the rescue, like something out of Walter Scott.

Poe halted, examined the advancing Confederates through his field glasses, and then whipped up again once he found the man he wanted to see.

Little Powell Hill was riding in another buggy—another officer too sick to ride—but he was wearing the red flannel he called his "battle shirt," and his heavy beard, a contrasting shade of red, was veritably bristling with eagerness for battle.

Poe passed through Hill's lines, turned his buggy in a wide circle, and brought it on a parallel course to Hill. He and Hill exchanged salutes.

"I hope you've left some Yankees for us, General." Hill's voice was cheerful.

Poe looked at him. "Plenty of Yankees, sir," he said. "None of *my* men left, but plenty of Yankees."

Powell Hill grinned. "I'll reduce 'em for you."

"I hope you will."

"You should rally your men. I need your support."

Where were you when I needed your *support!* Poe wanted to say it, but he couldn't. Instead he just saluted, and brought the buggy to a halt.

His broken men gathered around him. Hill's marched on, into the swelling battle.

The battle died down at sunset. The blows and counterblows weren't clear to Poe, but Hanover Junction, after having changed hands several times, ended up back with the Confederacy, and Grant's army was safely penned in the bend of the North Anna. The burning Starker house was a bright glow on the horizon, a pillar of fire. Someone's shellfire had set it alight.

Among all the other dead was Hugin, shot by a Yankee bullet. The raven lay wrapped in a handkerchief at the foot of his tall perch. Munin moved from side to side on the perch, his head bobbing, mourning the loss of his mate.

Poe stood under the perch in the light of a campfire,

listening to reports from his subordinates. Torn and dying men were lying around him in neat rows. The living, some distance off, were cooking meat; Poe could smell salt pork in the air. From the reports he gathered that he had lost about sixty percent of his men, killed, wounded, or missing. He had lost eighty percent of his officers the rank of captain or above. The figures were almost as bad as the attack at Gettysburg, last July.

A buggy moved carefully through the darkness and came to a halt. Walter Taylor helped Robert Lee out. Lee had apparently recovered somewhat; he was dressed carefully in a well-brushed uniform. Poe hobbled to him and saluted.

"General Lee."

Lee nodded. "This army owes you its thanks," he said. "You have saved Richmond."

"I have lost my division."

Lee was silent a moment. "That is hard," he said. "But you must tell your men how well they fought, how they have saved the capital. Perhaps it will make their sorrows easier to bear."

Poe nodded. "I will tell them." He looked at Lee. "What will I tell George Pickett? They were his men, not mine."

"You will tell him what you must."

Is this, Poe wondered, how Lee had got such a reputation for wisdom? Repeating these simple things with such utter sincerity?

Lee stepped forward, took Poe's arm. "Come. I would like to speak with you apart."

Poe allowed himself to be led off into the darkness. "Grant will move again," Lee said, "as soon as he gets his wounded to the rear and his cavalry comes back from the Yellow Tavern raid. There will be another battle, perhaps more than one. But sooner or later there will be a pause."

"Yes, sir."

"I would take advantage of that pause, General Poe. I would like to send a division to the Valley on this railroad you have saved us, to defeat the invaders there and strike at Washington. I would like to say, sir, that I am considering you for the command."

An independent Shenandoah Valley command, thought Poe. A chance for glory. The same command had been the making of Stonewall.

"My division is destroyed," Poe said. "I can't commit them to battle."

"Your division," gently, "is General Pickett's. When he recovers his health, he will return to command it. I refer to a new division, assembled with an eye to the Valley adventure."

"I see." Poe walked in silence for a moment, and stopped suddenly as his boots thudded against a wooden surface. He looked at it and realized it was the Starker girl's coffin, lying alone in the rutted cornfield. Apparently it had been thrown out of the wagon during the retreat.

Glory, he thought.

The Cause was lost. He couldn't believe in it anymore. That afternoon he'd told Moses one should fight for something noble, even if its time was gone. Now he no longer believed it. None of this was worth it.

He should have died, he thought savagely. He should have died on that last spree in Baltimore. It would have spared him all this. And perhaps spared his men, too.

If he hadn't anticipated Grant's maneuver, all this savagery might have been avoided. And the war would be over all that much sooner. The one chance he had to change things, to become the great man, and all he'd done was prolong the nation's agony. Put more good men in their graves.

He thought of the lines of wounded and dying men, lying in the cornfield waiting for the morning, and he felt his heart crack. One fought for them, or nothing.

He straightened, took a breath. "I must decline the command, sir," he said. "My health and spirits are too poor."

Lee looked at him somberly. "You may wish to reconsider, General. It's been a hard day."

"I want to stay with my men, sir," Poe said.

Lee was silent for a long time. "I will speak to you again on this matter, General Poe," he said. He began walking back toward the raven standard. Poe followed.

"Your men shall be spared further fighting," Lee said. "Your men will be assigned to bury the dead."

For some reason this made Poe want to laugh. "Yes, sir," he said.

"I thank you for your part today."

Poe saluted. "Sir."

Walter Taylor snapped the reins, and Lee's buggy trotted away into the darkness.

He has left me in command of the dead, Poe thought. Sexton-general in charge of dead hopes, dead causes, dead ravens, dead verse, dead girls.

He looked at his officers, gathered under the standard for his instructions. Poe stepped to the perch and picked up Hugin's body.

"About fifty yards out there," he said, pointing, "there's a dead girl in a coffin. Find some men, find a wagon, and deliver her to the graveyard in New Market." He held out the dead raven. "Bury this poor bird with her," he said.

"Yes, sir."

He pulled his black cloak around him. He could hear the moans and muttering of the wounded. They were his responsibility when alive; now they were his, too, when they were in the grave.

In a quiet voice, he gave his instructions.

Above him the raven mourned, and said nothing.

About the Editors

Gregory Benford is the author of several acclaimed novels, including *Tides of Light, Great Sky River, Heart of the Comet* (with David Brin), *In the Ocean of Night, Across the Sea of Suns,* and *Timescape,* which won the Nebula Award, the British Science Fiction Award, the John W. Campbell Memorial Award, and the Australian Ditmar Award. Dr. Benford, a Woodrow Wilson Fellow, is a professor of physics at the University of California, Irvine. He and his wife live in Laguna Beach.

Martin H. Greenberg is the editor or author of over 300 books, the majority of them anthologies in the science fiction, fantasy, horror, mystery, and western fields. He has collaborated editorially with such authors as Isaac Asimov, Robert Silverberg, Gregory Benford, and Frederik Pohl. A professor of political science at the University of Wisconsin, he lives with his wife and baby daughter in Green Bay.

The groundbreaking novels of

GREGORY BENFORD